'I loved this story of a group of wonderful "others" fighting to find their place and purpose in a glittering, but unforgiving, Victorian England' Marika Cobbold

'The very best kind of gothic, full of mystery and suspense, and oh so compelling' Lianne Dillsworth

'Atmospheric, gripping and ultimately uplifting, it's a tale of cruelty and depravity, but also love, friendship and acceptance' Karen Coles

'Rich, dark and heady … a glorious gothic carnival … a tale that – at its warm, wonderful heart – is about family, acceptance and love' Kate Griffin

'Richly detailed, beautifully written and, dare I say it, an altogether fascinating read!' Michael J. Malone

'Full of delights and horrors, this is a masterful book by one of my faves … a real treat. You too will be spellbound' Louise Swanson

'A classic gothic story, and is very well told' John Jackson

'A kaleidoscopic, twisting, devilish novel guaranteed to dazzle and delight. I was utterly beguiled' Dan, Waterstones bookseller

'A tale of abject cruelty overcome by love and compassion … It fascinates, it thrills, it scares and it is immensely moving … I adored it' Live & Deadly

'Filled with colourful and enthralling characters and underpinned with dark deeds and fetishistic desires' Jen Med's Book Reviews

'A wonderful exploration of human character and acceptance' Lynda's Book Reviews

'Beautifully written and takes the reader to the heart of Victorian England. This book had me hooked' Sally Boocock

THE FASCINATION

ABOUT THE AUTHOR

Essie Fox was born and raised in rural Herefordshire, which inspires much of her writing. After studying English Literature at Sheffield University, she moved to London where she worked for the *Telegraph Sunday Magazine*, then the book publishers George Allen & Unwin – before becoming self-employed in the world of art and design. Always an avid reader, Essie now spends her time writing historical gothic novels. Her debut, *The Somnambulist,* was shortlisted for the National Book Awards, and featured on Channel 4's *TV Book Club*. *The Last Days of Leda Grey,* set in the early years of silent film, was selected as *The Times* Historical Book of the Month. Her latest novel, *The Fascination,* is based in Victorian country fairgrounds, the glamour of the London theatres, and an Oxford Street museum full of morbid curiosities. Essie is also the creator of the popular blog: *The Virtual Victorian*. She has lectured on this era at the V&A, and the National Gallery in London.

Follow Essie on her website, www.essiefox.com.

THE FASCINATION

ESSIE FOX

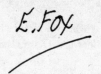

E.Fox

**ORENDA
BOOKS**

Orenda Books
16 Carson Road
West Dulwich
London SE21 8HU
www.orendabooks.co.uk

First published in the United Kingdom by Orenda Books 2023
Copyright © Essie Fox 2023

A catalogue record for this book is available from the British Library.

Hardback ISBN 978-1-914585-52-4
B-format paperback ISBN 978-1-914585-53-1
eISBN 978-1-914585-54-8

Typeset in Garamond by typesetter.org.uk

Printed and bound by CPI Group (UK) Ltd, Croydon CR0 4YY

For sales and distribution, please contact *info@orendabooks.co.uk*
or visit *www.orendabooks.co.uk*.

To Millie Anna Prelogar
You are an inspiration

'Whoever fights monsters should see to it that in the process he does not become a monster ... if you gaze long enough into the abyss, the abyss will gaze back into you.'

—Friedrich Nietzsche

PART ONE

Suffer the Little Children

ONE
An Introduction to
THE MONSTERS

Grandfather snatches at his arm and drags him through the study door. The boy has never been inside, because the room is always locked, though he has often stood on tiptoe with one eye pressed to the keyhole – only to see a soup of shadows. But there are smells, and smells seep out. The ones that puddle round this door are wood and leather and vanilla from the pipe Grandfather smokes. Is that what stains his teeth so brown, even the tips of his moustache and the tufts of bristled white that are sprouting from his ears?

His grandfather looks like an owl, and his nest is very dark, although some buttered rods of light are creeping in around the shutters closed across the big bay windows. They form a ladder on the floor leading towards the painted globe set on a stand beside the hearth. How the boy would like to spin it, to look at all the greens and blues, the lands and oceans of the world. But to do so he would need to navigate the tiger skin lying on the boards before it. The tiger's head is still attached. The tiger's eyes reflect the flames blazing red in the grate. They seem alive, and dangerous.

Less threatening are the deer heads mounted high upon the walls. Their softer, melancholy gaze falls across the rows of tables laid with trays containing beetles, butterflies – or are they moths? – of almost every size and colour he could possibly imagine. Inside glass domes are birds and fish, and other animals the like of which he's never seen before. At least not when he's been exploring in the gardens or the fields that spread for miles around the house.

These specimens – the old man calls them, letting go of the boy's arm as he gruffly points them out – are macabre, but beautiful. Some are embossed with silver pins that fix them down on squares of velvet. Some hang on wires, invisible between the palest pinks of corals, pearly shells, or stems of leaves, all being artfully arranged to form the backdrops of displays that represent the distant places where these creatures had once lived. Lived, before they died.

Did his grandfather go travelling to find and then to kill them, to bring them back to Dorney Hall? Sadly, it is too easy to imagine such a thing. And while continuing to stare the child is all but overwhelmed by a sense of loss and sorrow. *This*, he often thinks when he is older, looking back, is the moment when he first becomes aware that in some vague and unknown future everything that ever lived is doomed to die; although the notion slips away with a blast of onion breath, when his grandfather demands, 'What sort of age are you these days? I'll be damned if I can tell. Such a stumpy little imp. But I believe you must have had another birthday recently.'

'Yes, my birthday was last week, and now I'm seven years of age,' the boy replies, feeling confused, because birthdays are not events Grandfather likes to celebrate. But Cook, and all the maids, and his governess, Miss Miller, they gathered round the kitchen table. They had him standing on a chair while everyone sang *Happy Birthday ... Happy Birthday, dearest Theo!* How they'd cheered and clapped and laughed, and said that he must make a wish as he was blowing out the candles on his favourite kind of cake. The sort with strawberries and cream.

'Seven? Is that so?' Grandfather sounds surprised. His heavy brow is concertinaed into furrows of concern. There is a pause. A mucus crackle in his throat, and then a cough, 'Well, that's a rather special number. I must set affairs in motion. You should be off to school by now or you'll end up a pampered fool, being fussed and molly-coddled by the women in this house.'

Why is the number seven special? Theo thinks about the stories from the Bible he has heard on Sunday mornings when Miss Miller takes him to the village church, and being eager to impress this man he barely ever sees – to prove that he is not a fool – his voice is piping in excitement: 'God made the world in seven days. Adam and Eve. The sun and stars. When it rained, there was an ark. A great big ship made out of wood. A man called Noah built it, and then he filled it up with every kind of animal on earth. They came in marching, two by two.'

'The past crushed up as sugared pills and swallowed down by simpletons!' Another weary sigh precedes the damning interruption. 'You must think deeper. Dig for truths. What if there were other species? What if the beasts we now imagine as being nothing more than myth may once have actually existed? May *still* exist today, in far-off corners of the world.'

'Do you mean the dragons? The ...' *What is the word?* The boy forgets and, glancing back towards the globe, he recollects a recent lesson when Miss Miller told a story all about some giant bones being discovered by a girl not much older than himself. She'd been walking on some cliffs in quite another part of England. The place, it had a funny name. Something like limes? Or ... was it lemons?

'Dinosaurs,' Grandfather says. 'There are displays in London. The British Museum. Perhaps one day you'll get to see them. But, for now, I'd say it's time for you to view my own collection.'

'Your collection?' *Dinosaurs?* This is a thrill beyond all measure. How can it be? *Where* could they be? But then this house is very big. So many places you could hide things. In the cellars, or the stables, or the barns, or mausoleum underneath the private chapel.

'No,' Grandfather snaps, before his lips curl in a smile through which his yellowed teeth protrude, 'But, as it happens, I do have some unusual exhibits.'

Another door is opened. A door you'd never guess was there,

made to look like shelves of books. A fusty smell is seeping out. And something sharp and sour too. Is it vinegar, or bleach? The things Cook uses when she's on a cleaning spree down in the kitchens?

His grandfather is swallowed in a curdling of gloom, although his voice remains quite clear. 'I'll light the gas. There are no windows. The darkness helps to stabilise the preservation fluids, whereas the objects that are stuffed...' There is a grunt of disapproval. 'Must get my butler to come in and lay more poison down. The wretched vermin in this house!'

Grandfather's mutterings have stopped, and now the boy can hear the rasping of a lucifer on tinder. There is a swimming green and gold, and the hissing sound of gas as flames illuminate the darkness. It is the eeriest illusion, almost like being underwater. Suddenly, he cannot breathe and even fears he might be drowning. Can he turn and run away, back through the hall, and up the stairs?

But the doorway to the hall is entirely lost from view when, for the second time that day, Grandfather reaches for his arm and almost lifts him off his feet, 'For pity's sake! Stop whimpering. There's nothing here to be afraid of. At least' – a phlegmy chuckle precedes the cryptic inference – 'not in their present forms.'

Like Alice falling through the glass, the boy's whole world turns upside down. Now he is on the other side of what appears to be a cupboard, little bigger than the store in which Cook keeps her jams and pickles. His head is spinning. He feels sick as he inhales metallic fumes. His eyes are drawn towards the dirty-looking leather of a glove left on a stand beside the entrance. But, oh, the horror of the thing when Grandfather picks it up and says it's not a glove at all, but a hand that has been severed from a man accused of murder, who met his death upon the gallows, over three hundred years ago.

'It's called a Hand of Glory.' Grandfather holds the ghastly thing underneath a burning jet, and now the boy can clearly see the stringy tendons that protrude through the mummified grey flesh, the horny ridging of the nails. 'People had them dipped in wax, threaded the fingers through with wicks ... lit them up like candelabras!'

The hand is thrust towards him. The boy cries out and stumbles back against the wall with a thud. His shoulder is hurting, but there's no sympathy to follow. Only the bark, 'Where is your backbone? Lily-livered little urchin! My wife was just the same. Not that long before she died, she found me here ... and what a scene. Ran through the house screaming blue murder.'

The boy would like to scream. The sweat is breaking on his brow. The flutter of his heart could almost be a frightened bird; wings beating hard against the trap of the ribs that curve around it. His breaths are coming much too loud, almost like thunder in his ears when, behind a wall of glass he sees a head without a body. The marbled blue of shocked round eyes could be his own reflected back. But from this other child's brow protrudes a gnarled and curving horn, like the tusk of the rhinoceros he'd looked at yesterday in Miss Miller's illustrated *Animals of Africa*.

He turns away with a shudder, only to see a larger head. This face is covered in dark hair. The sawdust spilling through one nostril looks like a lump of crusted snot. Two dark-brown eyes stare blankly out through a pair of swollen lids. A snout has lips curling back to show the sharpness of the teeth poised in the moment of a snarl. Underneath, fixed to the plinth on which this horror has been mounted is a tarnished metal plate. Silently he mouths the syllables engraved in the brass: 'Ly...can...thrope.'

What does it mean?

Feet shuffle on. His nose is pressed against another wall of glass, mouth dropping open as he wonders, *Can this be a real mermaid?* He thinks it is a she, but ugly like a chimpanzee. A face as wrinkled as a prune below a scalp entirely bald. The tail extending from the waist is the dull brown of flaking rust. Several scales have fallen off and are scattered like confetti across the base of the container.

What's left is blighted by black mould, like rotting carrots left forgotten in the bottom of Cook's basket.

A narrow ray of sunlight shafts through the door and draws his eye towards a jar that, till that moment, had been concealed in veils of shadow. The skin of what it holds is white and luminous, like pearls, while underneath there is a pale-purple tracery of veins. The tiny hands are splayed like starfish. The shell-like ears are pixie-pointed. A rosebud mouth appears to smile, as do a pair of milky eyes that are occasionally hidden by some wisps of fine fair hair that slowly waver as they float in a cloudy amber liquid.

He feels the queerest of sensations, as sweet as honey in his belly when he notices the place where the shoulder blades should be, and where...

Is that a pair of wings? But, if they're wings, is this is a fairy? A real-life fairy, in a bottle?

The fascination has begun.

TWO

IT IS RESPECTFULLY ANNOUNCED THAT THE
PUBLIC EXHIBITION OF THIS

REMARKABLE
PHENOMENON

WILL BE REVEALED THIS PRESENT SATURDAY, JUNE 22ND, 1889
AT THE EGYPTIAN HALL IN LONDON.

Miss 'Tilly' Lovell, widely renowned for her
Drury Lane appearance
as 'THE FAIRY QUEEN MATILDA',
is of symmetrical proportions,
and free from all deformity.
It is impossible to offer a just conception
of her most exquisite beauty and diminutiveness
without observing her in person.

Some freaks are born, and some are made. But when it came to Tilly
Lovell, it was no natural quirk of fate the way that I kept sprouting
up to reach a normal adult height, whereas she stopped at three foot
six. Who would believe that we were twins, and identical at that?
As like as peas in the one pod on the day that we were born, when
– according to our pa, Alfred Nehemiah Lovell – he could cup his
mewling daughters in the palms of both his hands. One on the left.
One on the right. Like a pair of kitchen scales.

A miracle that we survived. The child that followed us did not. We should have had a baby brother, but Pa said he wasn't right. Unlike ourselves, he'd been too big. Ma wasn't strong, and as she'd lain there on the bed and breathed her last, our ill-fated little sibling also gave a feeble gasp. He left this world held in her arms. They lie together in one coffin.

Such a tragedy it was, and what a thorn of bitter gall it left in Alfred Lovell's heart. Not that his heart was ever sweet. To tell the truth he wasn't fit to play the part of any father – which is exactly what I'd say if the man should have the cheek to show his face to us again. Though I occasionally wonder, would I know him if he did after so many years of absence? Would his hair have turned to grey or still be gleaming, black as coal? Would his whiskers still be tweezed to two waxed tips below a nose swollen and grogged with boozy veins? I have no doubt I'd recognise him by his one remaining eye, always the mirror of our own. Very dark and slightly slanting, loaning a hint of the exotic – which is because we have the blood of the Gyptians in our veins. And that's a heritage I'm proud of, although I'm somewhat less inclined to boast of an affiliation with the mercenary man who thought so little of his daughters that he gambled them away one summer dawn on Windsor Brocas. For all he knew he could have flung us both into the fires of Hell. Instead of which, my sister Tilly, she went soaring like the brightest of the stars in London's skies ... in which the Fairy Queen Matilda bedazzled all who came to see her.

❖

When did Tilly stop her growing? We were five, or thereabouts. Our ma had died, and Alfred Lovell was too rarely in the house to offer comfort when we cried ourselves to sleep most every night. Our attic room had beams so low we only had to raise our arms to touch the cobwebs spun between them, where the moonlight often shafted through the latticed window glass.

Beyond those drifts of silvered gauze, me and Tilly would pretend that we could see the spirit features of our mother smiling down. Her dark-brown eyes were filled with sparkle. Her cold white fingers stroked our hair as it lay loose across the pillow she'd once slept upon herself. For many months after she'd gone we could still smell her body's fragrance seeping through its cotton cover. Rose and amber and patchouli. But little else of her was left. What Pa had done with all her clothes, her silky scarfs and coloured beads, we didn't know. Not at the time. But we had watched him strip the linen from their bed, then lug the mattress to the bottom of the garden. The lot was doused in paraffin and set ablaze in a great pyre.

It was still smouldering next morning when me and Tilly poked some twigs around the glowing ruby embers. All we could see were gritty ashes stirred by a sudden draught of wind to rise and float towards the cottage, almost as if our mother's soul was creeping back through all the cracks around the rotting window frames. Or was she hiding in the thatching, among the nests of birds and vermin, from where her fingernails would scratch and tap above us in the night? And what about the layers of grime that, in her absence, settled thick on every surface in the house? It was a wonder that our pa had not been buried in that shroud, for if he wasn't in the pub, he'd be slumped across a chair, his open mouth drooling black spittle from the baccy he'd been chewing.

As he festered grim and silent, we went unwashed, wore filthy clothes and lived on crusts of mouldy bread, or else the rancid nibs of cheese that, before, our ma would use to bait the traps for any vermin. Meanwhile, we fretted over how to tell our father of our plight, for with the man so rarely sober we were more likely to receive a spiteful lashing from his tongue than any words of consolation.

Still, desperation made us brave, particularly Tilly. Always the twin to take the lead, there came the night when she advanced across the parlour's creaking boards so as to tug upon Pa's sleeve.

When that garnered no response more than a heavy grunting snort, her fingers stroked across his brow and traced the netting of the scars that puckered close to his blind eye. Meanwhile she turned to me and whispered, 'Keziah, Pa feels hot. You don't suppose he might be...'

Sick? About to die? Is what we thought, for if our ma could pass so unexpectedly, then why not Pa as well?

'Give his hair a good old pull. Do it hard, and like you mean it,' was my suggestion at the time, which Tilly did, while calling out, 'Pa, please ... you must wake up! We can't find anything to eat.'

As quick as lightning he revived from his intoxicated trance, but with a terrible result. Barely before his good eye opened, one of his hands grabbed for the poker that was lying in the hearth. As he lashed out, the iron tip whacked against poor Tilly's temple. She stumbled back and hit her head upon the floor with such a crack I feared her skull had split in two.

All Hell broke out in that one moment. Between my screaming, Pa rose up, jabbing his weapon left and right as if he thought he was a knight intent on slaughtering a dragon. A dragon no one else could see. Quite petrified, I wasn't sure if I should find somewhere to hide, or face his wrath and rescue Tilly. But, in the end there was no need. It was as if the mist of rage melted from his cyclops eye. Now, standing still, but for the swaying back and forwards on his feet, his voice was slurred and thick with guilt. 'I thought your sister an intruder. Mayhap the bailiffs, come to take whatever valuables are left. There's rent still owing on this house for which the farmer grows impatient. And then the funeral expenses. That bastard of an undertaker! I should 'ave burned your mother's body with the bed, or carried it up to the woods, to dig a hole...'

I pressed my hands against my ears to try and stop the awful words. I couldn't bear to think of Ma shut up inside her wooden box in the graveyard of the church. And what if Tilly went there too?

For then, my sister's eyes were open, staring blankly up at mine, before they rolled back in her head. With just the whites of them remaining it was the most alarming sight, as was the way her sightless body twitched and shuffled on the boards.

'Pa, you *have* to do something!' I all but screamed in my distress.

He merely muttered with resentment, 'Suppose this means more money spending. We must hope it's just the doctor. Not another bloody coffin.'

His hands delved into trouser pockets. There was a satisfying chink, but when he drew the money out, he only scowled and shook his head before he stormed from the house, slamming the door so hard behind him that any objects not nailed down and hammered into place rattled and thrummed like tambourines.

With my own nerves in tattered shreds, I climbed the stairs to fetch Ma's pillow, coming back to gently rest my sister's head upon its feathers. After that, I settled down on the floor at Tilly's side and spooned my body into hers – which was what I always did when we were sleeping in our bed. Above the flutter of her breaths, I heard the twitter of the birds in the trees outside the window. I saw the shadows of the leaves dancing like fairies on the plaster of the walls between the beams as daylight dimmed and turned to dusk. When there was nothing but the gleaming of the moon on Tilly's face to show a spreading purple bruise, she suddenly let out a moan, and then complained of being thirsty.

Off I went to fill a cup with water from the garden pump, which Tilly drank in one long gulp before she drifted back to sleep. Much relieved and oh-so grateful to think my sister would recover, I also dozed, but fitfully, until the dawn when she awoke a second time and grabbed my hand...

'Keziah,' Tilly said, 'my head is aching something awful, and the room is spinning round. I think I'm going to be sick.'

What to do? I didn't know. Could I soothe her with a story? Perhaps the one our ma had read to us so often we were able to recite the words by heart – just as we'd done beside her grave after the funeral was done, when our pa and his clan of bosky drinkers disappeared to continue with their mourning at the local village tavern.

As we'd settled on the grass, legs dangling down into the void in which Ma's coffin had been laid, we'd found more comfort in the words from her old book of fairy tales than anything the vicar read from his Bible in the church. To us, Ma's book was just as sacred, with its covers of green leather worn as soft and smooth as velvet, in which the pages were so thin they seemed no more than wisps of air. But they contained such wondrous tales that lived and bloomed inside our heads, such as *Snow-White and Rose-Red*, which our ma had always said was like a mirror of our lives –

THERE WAS ONCE A POOR WOMAN who lived in a lonely cottage. She had two children who were twins. One was called Snow-White, and the other was Rose-Red, named for the rose trees grown in pots beside their cottage door.

The girls were always happy, and loved each other dearly, so much so that if Snow-White should chance to say: 'How I hope we are never forced to part,' Rose-Red would reply: 'Never so long as we're both living.'

In summertime, the girls would often gather berries in the forest, where the deer would stand and watch them and the birds would perch on branches of the trees and sweetly sing. Even if they lost their way or lingered late into the night, they would simply rest their heads on mounds of moss and then awake to carry home the wild flowers to place upon their mother's pillow.

During the winter months, the sisters stayed at home keeping warm beside the fire. One cold, dark night when it was snowing, and so thickly that the forest was a wonderland of white, they heard the sound of distant howling, after which their mother shivered and then said, 'Snow-White, get up. Go and bolt the cottage door. We must be sure to keep it locked against the hungry wild creatures that might try to come and eat us.'

Another evening they were sitting by the fire when they heard the loudest knocking at the door. This time, their mother said, 'Quick! Rose-Red, undo the bolts, for it may be a traveller lost in the woods and seeking shelter.'

Rose-Red did as she was told, but instead of any man or woman standing in the porch she saw a big black bear, which pushed its head in through the door, and...

How strange to think that while my sister and myself had been immersed in the reciting of that tale we'd never dreamed that, in due course, a bear would enter our own lives.

Ah! Your ears are pricking up. But on that day the only sound to prick our ears had been the singing of the birds among the trees as we got up to pick some flowers to decorate Ma's coffin lid – just as the sisters in the tale placed flowers on their mother's pillow. The sole adornment from our father had been the handful of dry soil scattered down into the grave during the saying of the prayers. Now, me and Tilly found some daisies growing by the churchyard gates. Yellow chrysanthemums as well from a fancy iron urn. And, yes, we knew it was a sin to steal from another grave, but there was no one there to see us...

If a sin has not been witnessed, does it count as being real? Would our ma have been ashamed and disappointed in her daughters? If only she'd been there to ask, and again a few weeks later when my sister lay there senseless on the floor with rays of dawn gilding her bruised and swollen face. The morning light, it also flickered on the darkness of the mole that could be seen on her left cheek. The only difference between us, it looked exactly like a heart, and how I'd hankered for the same. However, Tilly didn't like it, one day picking till it bled, after which it was to form a sore and crusty-looking scab.

That would have been about the time when Ma was swelling with our brother, and come one warm spring afternoon when she'd gone upstairs to rest, Pa said he'd take us on a stroll to offer her an hour of peace.

In an uncommon cheery mood, he led us on a detour through the trees that formed a dingle at the outskirts of the village, on the other side of which was the home of Betsy Jones. We didn't like that gloomy cottage where every window we could see was laden up with old clay pots. So many plants with funny smells, while above them were the corpses of frogs, or mice and moles strung up on metal wires, looking like strips of shrivelled leather.

Betsy herself looked somewhat feral, with brindle hair and amber eyes. She was what people in those parts would label as a cunning woman, somewhat in the witchy mould; what with the writing of her charms to help to heal a person's woes, which she would often do for free. But, for the potions brewed from herbs, or else ingredients you wouldn't want to think about at all, then Betsy always wanted money, and if the coin was not supplied her medicines would never work. Well, that's what Betsy said.

On that day, our pa gave Betsy Jones a shining silver sixpence, the reason being – so *he* said – that our ma had grown concerned about the state of Tilly's mole, and if Betsy had a charm that could spirit it away, or simply stop the girl from picking, he would be immensely grateful.

Was it true that Ma had sent him? It may have been. I don't remember. But there we stood in Betsy's house, watching mutely as she led our pa behind the old sack curtain that led on into her kitchen; supposedly to go and make themselves a brew of tea – though who would guess that such a task could prove to be so arduous? What heavy sighs and gasping groans were punctuated by a deal of rhythmic knocking and loud crashes. We had to wonder, were they throwing all the china from the shelves?

Eventually, the noise subsided and we could hear Pa telling Betsy, in a breathless sort of voice, 'I fear the child may have been cursed ... that the devil's left his fingerprint to mark her as his own. Isn't that what people say?'

As our hearts began to pound, Tilly's hand reached out for mine, and Betsy Jones let out the most disturbing cackle of a laugh. 'Alfred Lovell, I would say your head's more addled than I thought. That is nought but superstition. But if you wish...'

More mumbled words, too subdued for us to hear, and then the curtain was flung back and there was Pa, and there was Betsy, and pincered in the woman's fingers was a common garden snail.

'Come over here now, Tilly dear.' Betsy beckoned with a smile as she swayed across the parlour and settled on a chair drawn up close beside her fire. Smoke was rising. Flames were dancing. Logs of wood were crackling with small explosions of red embers – almost as if to warn my sister not to venture any nearer. But, to my open-mouthed amazement, Tilly obliged and bravely walked straight into Betsy's ham-hock arms, where she was lifted from the ground as if she weighed no more than air. My sister didn't even gasp when Betsy Jones then proceeded to hold the snail against her cheek. But, oh, to see that sluggy body extending from its shell to leave a trail of silver glue across the scab of Tilly's mole! Truly, I thought that I should faint.

At least the job was swiftly done. Betsy set Tilly down again, and then told Pa, 'I'll put the snail in a box. You take it home. Make sure to bury it in soil directly underneath the window of the room where Tilly sleeps. As the creature dies and shrivels in its shell, so Tilly's mark will also fade and disappear.'

Well, if that wasn't superstition, I don't know what Betsy called it – and it didn't even work. By the summer following, when Tilly lay there near to senseless on our own hard parlour floor, the mole was very far from shrivelled. If anything, I thought it larger, tracing a finger round its contours, before I stood and made my way towards the window to the lane.

Peering morosely through the curtains, between the overgrowth of roses and the ivy that was clambering across our cottage front, I strained to see a little further through the tunnelled green of trees where morning birds were symphonising. A breeze was playing through the leaves, and as they fluttered up and soughed, I heard the whisper in my mind: *Where are you, Pa? Why have you left us?*

Not expecting any answer, I took myself into the kitchen, where I stared in bleak dismay at the copper that once heated the water for our baths. How long could it have been since Ma last soaped our dirty hair, while me and Tilly sat and giggled in the scummy froths of bubbles? Although in truth, the final time, Ma had been so big with child she couldn't bend and had to leave us to our own splashing devices. But she'd still smiled; that lovely smile, in which she had a certain way of almost pursing up her mouth, as if inviting you to kiss it. Who wouldn't want to kiss those lips, or stroke a finger through the lustrous hair that shone as dark as jet? Who wouldn't want to gaze at eyes always so bright and luminous, with a magnetic sort of glamour? Why, even Pa, on one occasion, in a fit of reminiscing, told us those eyes had been the thing about our ma that won his heart, that just one flutter of her lashes and his darling could have lured all of the birds down from the trees.

That last day we'd spent with Ma, when we'd been soaking in the tub, her eyes were puffed and red, ringed with the shadows of exhaustion. Her hair was limp and thick with grease, much of it falling from the scarf she'd used to hold it from her face. When she sank down into her chair her feet were raised upon another, hoping that way to ease the swelling of the flesh around her ankles. Her hands were just as bad, blown up as fat as sausages. The night before, Pa was so worried he'd gone off to visit Betsy, only returning hours later, looking flushed about the face and holding phials containing tinctures made from dandelion flowers mixed with the boiled leaves of nettles – for all the good that potion did.

Ma's wedding ring became so tight the skin around it turned to black. She'd had to rub it with the soap from our bath to grease it free, and then she'd dropped the flimsy band onto the table at her side. After that she'd closed her eyes and touched a chain around her neck, on which another ring was looped. In the glisten of the candle that was burning on the table I saw the glint of coloured stones and excitedly enquired, 'Where did you get such treasure, Ma?'

'Long ago, this belonged to my great-great-grandmother. She was a legend in our tribe. Bohemia was her name, and bohemian her nature. Ah, what tales she would recount about the lovers in her life ... even the time when she once had two husbands living in her vardo.'

'Both of them at once?'

Ma didn't seem to hear my question, her tale already moving on, 'Then she took up with the admirer who'd gifted her this ring ... whose veins ran blue with royal blood.'

'Who was it, Ma? The king of England?' Now Tilly's interest had been piqued.

'Bohemia would never say. But I don't doubt she told the truth. She'd been a beauty in her time, but she was also sharp as nails, knowing her letters and her numbers, which in turn she taught to me. Now I have passed them on to you. My clever girls!' Ma smiled indulgently before she carried on...

'Bohemia had a gift for the prophesying arts. She used her deck of tarot cards, and a crystal ball for scrying. So accurate were her readings, rumours spread to say she must have had some dealings with the devil. Perhaps there was a darker side.' Here, Ma sighed and left a pause as if considering her thoughts. 'I never did approve of curses, but I know to my own cost that Bohemia possessed a power mightier than most. When I was but a girl of ten and she much nearer to a hundred, she predicted my own future.'

'Did she read...' I started off, while Tilly finished with, '...your palm?'

We were like chicks inside a nest, cheeping as one, mouths opened wide as Ma continued to explain, 'We used her cards. I cut the deck and laid them out, and...' Ma's dark eyes went oddly vacant, making me fear that her mind had wandered back into the past and left her body in the kitchen. 'What resulted from that reading was the warning that the man I chose to wed would first betray me, then lead me to an early grave, in which...' She placed a hand on the great doming of her belly '...I would not lie alone.'

'Did Bohemia mean Pa? Did she mean Pa would try and hurt you?' My voice was breathless with the dread.

'Well, I have had no other husband, and from the moment we first met, I must confess that I was lost, quite bedazzled by his charm.'

Here, Ma began to sing:

A blacksmith courted me nine months, and he fairly won my heart.
His cheeks were red as roses, his hat was decked with marigolds.
He looked so handsome and so clever with his hammer in his hand,
I thought, if he could be my love, I...'

Ma broke off for a good while before she spoke to us again. 'I didn't know. How could I know?'

Know what? What could we say to fill the silence she'd left hanging? But, on the other hand, though we were not much more than babes, Tilly and me had seen enough to understand that there were often ugly demons that possessed our father's body, and his mind. Mostly those times when he'd been drinking.

It wasn't something good to think of. The air felt ominous and heavy. Such a relief when Ma's dour frown melted back into a smile. 'I'm glad I didn't listen to the warnings I was given, for if I'd never wed your pa I wouldn't have my darling girls, and you do bring my heart such joy. Will you both remember that, even when I am no longer sitting here to tell you so? And in time, when you are older, promise me you'll get away ... as far from Pa as possible.'

She raised the chain that held Bohemia's old ring above her head, setting it down upon the table where its glamour put to shame the battered wedding band from Pa. She slowly stroked the coloured stones, and said, 'When it's time for you to go, then with my blessings you may sell this. Share the value equally. But, for now, I'll keep it hidden. Just in case...'

She must have meant in case of Pa rooting through her valuables, taking away the better objects to pawn, or else barter, though what he did with any money, it was a mystery. And when it came to buying food...

Oh, how I hungered that morning, when my sister still lay senseless in the room across the hall – when I stood there in the kitchen and dreamed of mornings when we'd wake to hear the kettle's breakfast whistle, leaving our attic bed to make our yawning way downstairs, seeing the table newly scrubbed and laid with plates of still-warm bread smeared with butter, sweet red jams, or golden honey from the jars now empty on the dresser shelves.

While I was staring at those jars, I heard the distant, hollow chiming of the church bell in the village. Holding my breath, I concentrated as I counted: *One, two, three, four, five, six, seven...*

Could it really be that hour and still no sign of Pa come home? Where had he gone, to be so long? The doctor's house was not that far. Had he been set upon by thieves, or maybe stumbled on the way and hit his head, the same as Tilly?

With my own noggin filled with panic, the awful gnawing in my belly drew my eye towards a tin that still contained stale biscuit crumbs. Spitting on a finger, I rubbed the tip around inside, and as I licked the grains of sweetness I scanned the dresser shelves once more – to see a jar containing oats, though much too high for me to reach. But, if I dragged a chair up close and stood on that, then stretched my arms...

I heard the slow but steady thud of footsteps coming up the lane, and then the whining of the gate, before the rattle of the latch. Somebody at the cottage door?

'Pa?' I called his name, heard no reply, so called again, but in a voice far less assured, because my mind was all a spiral: *A stranger in the house*? *One of those men our pa had mentioned coming here for money owing?*

A desperate trembling overwhelmed me, and my balance, which had been precarious to say the least, was now entirely lost. At the same time my fingers brushed against a decorated vase that held dried stems of lavender. Flying to the floor, I only suffered a sharp jolt to my arse and my left elbow. But the vase, it fared much worse. My legs were splayed among what looked to be a hundred shards of china, and scattered through the debris were the beads of purple flowers that had fallen from their stems. There were other things as well. Pennies, tuppences and crowns, and – could that be a sovereign? I also saw the plain gold ring that had been pinching at Ma's finger. And then the one with coloured stones, both of them spinning rapidly on a trajectory that led them straight towards the pair of dusty boots planted in the kitchen doorway.

Raising my eyes, I couldn't help but see how rumpled Pa was looking, even worse than usual. Mud was smeared across his trousers. Long stems of grass and curls of ivy were tangled through his hair. Had he been sleeping in a ditch?

While thinking this, I struggled up and stood among the broken china. Rubbing a hand at my sore elbow, I asked, 'Pa, where is the doctor?'

His reply was but a grunt, his good eye focused on the rings that now lay still beside his feet: 'Where is your sister?'

'She's still sleeping. Where you left her.' I took a step towards him, meaning to try and steer his body round to face the parlour door. But as I pulled, he jerked away, his voice so low I barely heard it. 'All these coins. Your mother's rings. Where did you find them, girl?'

'In the vase. I'm sorry Pa. I didn't mean to break it. I knocked it off the shelf when I was looking for—'

His laughter drowned me out. 'Well I'll be damned. The wily

bitch, hiding all of this away from me, when I was shamed to have to beg to save her from a pauper's grave.'

'Pa, please...' How to distract him? 'I'll fetch a brush. I'll clean the mess. But, what are we to do with Tilly?'

'Don't nag! Bad as your mother,' he snapped aggressively. 'You can pick up all these coins, and no filching while you're at it, for I shall know, and you'll be punished!'

Before my task had even started, he'd snatched the rings from the floor and stuffed them deep into the pockets where coins had jangled hours before. Meanwhile, I forced myself to ask about the doctor yet again.

'Wasn't home.' Pa growled his answer. 'Visiting another patient. But, as it chanced, my luck was in. I stopped by The Angel Inn, and...'

'Oh Pa!' As I was setting all the coins upon the table, the disappointment I felt was too apparent in my voice. Had he been drinking through the night? I couldn't help but think of times when Ma despaired of his behaviour, of how she'd cried when he'd eventually come home to her again. I felt inclined to do the same, but was afraid of his reaction, especially when he drew nearer, hot blasts of breath and sprays of spittle falling on my upturned face: 'Shut the pester of thy mouth! That doctor's nothing but a leech, bloated and fat with what he sucks from ailing folk he claims to save. Now, Betsy...'

'Betsy Jones?' I couldn't breathe. In my mind's eye I saw again the squirming snail, the gluey slime on Tilly's cheek.

'The very one.' Pa took a pause and started counting through the coins, which he then placed in separate piles arranged according to their value. 'We shared a bevvy, me and Betsy, and she suggested just the thing to help revive your sister's spirits. I would have brought it back the sooner, but...' His one eye glinted as a hand dipped in his pocket for a bottle. 'This 'ere is Betsy's potion. Only two pennies, and she swears that it will perk our Tilly up. Worth a punt, wouldn't you say?'

I thought, but didn't say that Betsy's snail hadn't worked, so why should this be any different? I watched him turn towards the hall, feet crunching over broken china as I followed in the wake of booze and sweat the man exuded. And something else I didn't know. Something yeasty, sweet and musty. It made me feel a little sick, having to swallow back the bile as my eyes were firmly fixed on the bottle in Pa's hand. It held a liquid, dark and viscous, clinging like glue to the glass sides. Same as the words inside my mouth, too thick to speak, but still the thought: *What if it is poison? Did Betsy's potions kill our ma?*

There came a sudden popping as the bottle was uncorked. I saw Pa lift it to his mouth and take a swig of what it held. So, perhaps it wasn't poison. But it did reek of something fierce, and under that ... was it molasses? What Ma laced through her Christmas biscuits? I must admit, like miracles said to occur during that season, the medicine did seem to hold the magic spell to cure Pa's ills, for he sighed with satisfaction, smacked his lips, then made his way into the room where Tilly lay.

Following behind, I stood and watched and held my breath as he knelt down upon the boards. I saw him lift my sister's head and pour the potion in her mouth. I heard her gasp, and then a cough before she struggled to sit up and rub her knuckles at her eyes, after which it did appear some vibrant flame was set alight. Something that filled my sister's blood and stirred her up like rising batter. First, she looked in my direction, then at Pa as she enquired, 'What happened? Did I sleep here in the parlour all last night? I can't remember anything, only a hurting in my head. But now I'm better, and I'm hungry. Is there anything to eat?'

Pa laughed and cupped her face between his rough spade hands. He kissed her button nose, and then the spreading purple bruise. What a sweet and tender vision. It left me feeling quite neglected, until I found that I was bathed in his benevolence as well. A thing so rare that when it happened you couldn't help but feel beguiled. You quite forgot about the moody, moaning monster he had been only a moment earlier. When you saw this other Pa, you understood why Ma had fallen for his handsome, roguish charms. It was as if a golden light was somehow shining through the mud. It made you want to smile. It made you feel as if you'd trust him to the moon and back again – that you'd do anything he said.

So, there I was, his willing slavey when he spoke in a voice as dark and syrupy as what he'd just poured into Tilly's mouth: 'My darling girl, Keziah, won't you take yourself a shilling from the table and then walk across the fields to Kenton's farm. Ask for butter, eggs and milk. A loaf of bread if they should have it. And leave the change towards what's owing. When you're back, we three shall have ourselves a proper slap-up breakfast, before your pa goes off to make another visit with his Betsy ... for it do seem,' he tapped the pocket that now held our mother's rings, 'I have the means and the ambition to invest in a new venture. An enterprise that cannot fail.'

THREE
DINNER WITH MISS MILLER

Theo's top hat, his black-tailed coat and white cravat are on the floor. As the waistcoat also drops, he settles on the bedroom chair. He holds his head cupped in his hands, rests his elbows on his knees, and wonders to himself: *Which of my prisons is the worse?*

Is it Dorney Hall, where he's returned to spend the summer, or Eton College, where he boards, which is so near that he could walk all the way there and back again between his breakfast and his lunch? At least he has a private dorm, and although it may be spartan, almost anything is better than the prep school he was sent to at the age of seven years. A real 'do the boys', where the luxuries of down and quilted silk were replaced by cold damp mattresses and sheets, with pupils crammed into the beds like sardines inside a can. Theo, who'd known no siblings, who had no friends of his own age, was tortured by the clamour of all the laughing, snoring, farting, or the sobs from other boys who mourned the absence of their mothers.

Theo misses his mother, even though he's never known her. But this room at Dorney Hall had been her nursery as a child, and though it may be fanciful there are times when he believes he can hear her girlish laughter, as if an echo on the air. He likes to wake in the same bed. He likes to touch the dark oak bedposts carved with winding leaves and flowers, or the drapes of blue damask, the colour of a summer's sky. The walls beyond, a pale-green silk.

Today with all the casements to the garden being opened, the air is hazed with specks of gold. Sprays of coloured rainbows flash from his waistcoat's silver buttons and also dazzle on the mirrors set into the wardrobe doors. If he squints into the glass he can still see the little boy who'd loved to ride the rocking horse in the window's curving bay – who used to hold his arms out wide and make believe that he was flying over the garden and the trees, into the clouds, towards the stars. The stars on which he'd wished to grow to be a man as tall, or taller, than his grandfather, Lord Seabrook.

These days the bully's stance is somewhat less intimidating. Lord Seabrook's shoulders slope. His once-thick hair is little more than a straggling grey fringe around a freckled, monkish dome. As for the tusks of his moustache, it is impossible to see him without thinking of a walrus – "'O Oysters, come and walk with us!" The Walrus did beseech. A pleasant walk, a pleasant talk..."'

Lord Seabrook has no pleasant talk. And when it comes to walking...

Theo was only five when his grandfather decided that his legs were much too short and not as straight as they should be. One day, a specialist arrived, taking measurements with pincers. A week later, he returned to fix some callipers in place. A leather strap was buckled tightly under each of Theo's knees, and from these a metal rod – to be adjusted every month – ran down each outer calf; almost like a pair of stirrups fitting underneath his boots. He'd had to wear them every day, no matter how they chaffed and blistered. And they did. They made him limp. They were so heavy he'd been forced to drag his feet when he was walking. Running was impossible. It was his governess, Miss Miller, who'd finally insisted that the boy be left to live as Nature had designed him, and that the tortuous contraptions were never buckled on again.

What sort of warped sadistic mind would think to do that to a child? Theo ponders as he strokes the fuzz of golden stubble newly bristled on his chin. What grows around his sex is now much wirier to touch. Unconsciously, his hand is lowered, beneath his shirt, across the tautness of the muscles of his belly, further down as he drifts into another fantasy about the doe-eyed Persian boy who once came into his dorm to ask advice about some essay, or was it maths? Theo forgets. But he remembers soft brown skin, and parted lips, and …

And from lower in the house the dinner gong is sounding, which stirs another thought even more urgent and demanding: *Must get dressed for dinner. Must not be late and risk incurring the wrath of the old man.*

When the gig arrived to fetch him home that afternoon, the driver handed him a note in which his grandfather requested Theo join him for dinner. How oddly formal that had seemed. Will Miss Miller be there too? His ageing governess's sweetness always dilutes the air of tension between Lord Seabrook and himself. Even though he has no need of her tutoring these days, her constant presence in the house provides the comfort and affection most other boys would find in mothers – which is why Theo experienced a pang of disappointment not to see her on the steps when all the other household staff came out to greet him earlier.

Has something happened? Has she left? Surely someone would have said?

With a sense of dark foreboding, hurriedly, a little clumsily, he stands and steps across the clothes discarded earlier. Opening the wardrobe doors, he stretches up and removes his favourite linen jacket. But what had fitted well last summer has already grown too tight. The seams are straining, fit to burst; horizontally at least. The torment of the swimming and the rowing he's endured these past few years at Eton College have honed and sculpted his physique, though he's not sure about his mind. Grandfather's barking inquisitions almost always leave him tongue-tied.

The gong resounds a second time. He thrusts his feet into his boots, still warm and damp from earlier. Hobbling at first, his pace increases by the time he's reached the old oak staircase. Treads groan and squeak as he descends. Somewhat more mutely he's observed by the glazed and dusty eyes of all the Seabrook ancestors who stare from frames hung on the walls. And above the final stair there is the portrait of his mother.

Theo lingers as he contemplates the face of Theodora, who died when he was born. Not that he needs to look that hard. It is engrained upon his mind, this romantic Millais vision of a beautiful young woman sitting on the large carved chest still in the drawing room today. As are the yellow drapes that form the background of the portrait. Forever seventeen – the same age that he is now – her arms are bare, as is her neck, at which she wears three strings of pearls. Her dress is blue. A gauzy silk, or is it muslin? Very fine. A small bouquet de corsage has been pinned against her breast. The flowers are forget-me-nots. In her white hands she holds a fan, while at her side is the cream leather of a glove she has discarded.

Theo can never see that glove without remembering the horror of Grandfather's hand of glory. Better to concentrate instead on what is on her other side. A Chinese pot containing stems of purple hyacinth, narcissi...

Can he smell their perfume now? He looks away, his clear-blue gaze (so like his mother's in the frame) is moving on across the gleam of the hallway's polished boards. Over these his footsteps echo as he turns into a passage, at last arriving at the door where he will pause and take a breath, hoping to summon up the courage he will need to step inside.

When he does the room is empty. The table is not laid. No silver dishes on the console, on either side of which the doors to the terrace have been opened. A sudden breeze catches the drapes, and there's the perfume he noticed at the bottom of the stairs, from the wisteria and lilac growing across an arched pergola, while sitting underneath it is...

'Miss Miller! You're still here.' Theo is so pleased he wants to clap and shout 'hurray'.

Meanwhile, the glass that she is holding to her lips is swiftly lowered as she cranes her neck around, and her sweetly lilting voice is replying in delight, 'Ah, there you are. My dearest boy. And look, how handsome you've become in just the past few months. Quite the young Adonis, and...' she beams '...have you grown?'

Seeing his frown, the shrug of shoulders, she knows it's best to change the subject. She motions to a jug, 'Some ginger ale? I know you like it. Or perhaps a glass of wine? The claret served with lunch today was very good. Perhaps too good.'

Miss Miller's hand touches her head, where several wisps of greying hair are falling loose from their pins. 'I had a nap this afternoon, which is unusual for me. I feared I might have been unwell. Felt very feverish and tired. But then, this weather is so warm and ... Oh!' Miss Miller is distracted as she glances out across the verdant slope of garden lawns. 'Whoever can that be?'

Her silver lorgnette spectacles are lifted from the table and pressed against her nose before she lowers them again. 'I thought I saw a man standing by the birches at the farthest boundary walls. Would the gardeners still be working? Or...' now her turn to frown '...is it a breeze in the branches? They sometimes throw the strangest shadows.'

'Is it Grandfather?' Theo asks. 'Gone for a walk before the meal?'

Her powdered cheeks are flushing pink. Sweat is beading on her brow. 'No, he left this afternoon. Gone to the Knightsbridge house. A telegram arrived. Some business needing his attention. I've really no idea. But it must have been important. He started shouting for his man to pack his bags without delay, which I did think was rather odd, because I know he'd been planning on a dinner here with you ... to discuss your future plans.'

Plans? Theo feels unsure. His voice is stammering a little. 'I ... I have another year at Eton, and after that...'

'You still have hopes for medicine? You understand there are restrictions, and that your grandfather considers the profession to be one full of charlatans and butchers?'

'I know he views the trade as below my social status.' He imitates the old man's voice: 'No one who shares the Seabrook blood will take the role of a sawbones. You might as well look for employment in the slaughterhouse at Slough.'

Miss Miller sighs. 'He has his reasons. That business with your grandmamma ... when Anne's physician had to tell him her disease had gone beyond all hopes of further intervention ... that more cutting would do nothing but prolong her suffering.' Miss Miller shakes her head. 'Very far from any sawbones! He was a man who thought of nothing but the welfare of his patient.'

She attempts to change the subject: 'There are other avenues. You have some talent as an artist. I think Lord Seabrook is more likely to fund a London art school place. Perhaps a course at the RA...'

Her words break off and, once again, she is looking at the gardens where Theo still expects to see his grandfather leap out while leering back at them in spite: *Ha! I had you fooled. I didn't go away at all.*

This is the fear the tyrant breeds, and it lingers in the house even when he's gone away. It has been present ever since an old man lured a frightened child to view the freaks in his 'museum'. Not that Theo's ever spoken of what happened on that day. Not even to Miss Miller. But for months afterwards his sleep was filled with nightmares. Merely to hear the sound of splashing from the garden pond and fountain brought to mind the withered mermaid, her monkey features grinning back as she reclined across the feet of the statue of Poseidon. Any sounds of groaning boards in the house's passageways he'd feared to be the lycanthrope, its hairy head concealed in shadows, about to bite and dig its fangs into the flesh of any child who might provide a tender morsel. The fairy baby in the jar he sometimes dreams of to this day. He'll wake to see it floating in the air above his head, a tiny finger pressed against the rosebud of its lips, as if reminding him to keep the precious secret they both share. *What can the secret be?*

More recently, different monsters haunt Theo's imagination. He is afraid of what this means, of the desires and dark compulsions that increasingly consume him. In the science labs at school when he's dissecting rats and frogs, he always seeks to understand the mechanics of the bones and how the joints articulate to form a hinge, creating movement with the tension of the muscles. When alone, he takes his pen and sketches diagrams to show the ways in which one skeleton might be fused onto another, and so create a hybrid species. He recreates the mythic beasts he has read about in classics, especially the *semihomines*. Half animal, half human. The group is vast, with many sub-sets. Theropods are represented by the hooved and goat-legged satyrs. Therocephalians have human bodies but the heads of other creatures, such as the gods of Ancient Egypt, or the Minotaur of Greece. The sphinx is an example of the set *Anthrocephalus*; a woman's features on the head above a muscular winged lion. *Cephalothorax inversus* might be depicted by a centaur. The head and torso of a man joined to a horse's lower parts.

These fantastical creations are everywhere if one starts looking. Carved in the pillars of the church he sometimes visits with Miss Miller, and – Theo strains his eyes against the sun's low slanting rays – among the gargoyle parapets rising around this house's roofs. Even in the mausoleum where the Seabrook dead are buried. Theo has never been allowed to go beyond the iron gate leading to the older tombs, but once his grandfather did take him to view the little coffins holding babies that had died before his mother had been born. The male children who Lord Seabrook said were better in their graves, where the shame of their afflictions could be hidden from the public. Not that he ever said what those afflictions might have been. Only 'Something in the blood. Skeletal deficiencies.'

Theo imagined tiny monsters lurking to watch him from the shadows. How much happier he'd been to walk on by and see the sculpted marble statue that Lord Seabrook had erected for his mother. She was both human, and an angel. She had two wings on which to fly. Were they the wings of a swan? The polished marble of the statue may have once been purest white, but now it is striated with the green and black of mould. Death will blight even perfection.

Theo's morbid reminiscing is suddenly eclipsed when he looks up to see Miss Miller's smiling face across the table. Feeling affection surge anew, he says, 'I'm glad you're here tonight and that my grandfather's in London.' He blushes as he mumbles, 'For some reason, I'd convinced myself you might have been dismissed, or even something worse. When you weren't here this afternoon, when I came home, I...'

Before he can go on, she reaches out to take his hand. Her bottom lip is trembling, but just as soon the smile returns to let him know that though they may be separated by their sexes and the difference in their years, they are the best of friends. 'You know your grandfather would never dismiss me from this house, not when I've lived here for so long, and...' she shuffles in her seat '... with your grandmama and I always having been so close, ever since we were children. I may have told you this before...'

Yes, she has told him this before, and he has always liked to hear it. He knows she's speaking out of kindness, to find some way to anchor him within a family of ghosts, from which he's always felt removed. Almost a species set apart. But today she goes much further than she's done in the past, and what she says holds bitter truths.

'My father was the reverend in a little Sussex village where Anne's parents sometimes came to holiday in summer months. In the years after she married, becoming Lady Seabrook, we resumed our correspondence, and she would very often write inviting me to Dorney Hall. But I'm afraid I felt compelled to stay at home and help my father with his workload in the parish. You see, my mother also died when I was young and, as I grew ... well I suppose I simply fell into the role she'd played before. That is, until my father joined her.' Her voice grows tremulous. 'No pain, no pain at all. It was over in a trice. We were sitting in the garden drinking tea with the church warden, when he simply closed his eyes, and he was gone. As quick as that.'

Miss Miller's eyes are closed. She is unnaturally still, and for a moment Theo fears her father's sudden end might be a trait inherited. But she revives and carries on. 'I was left homeless, with no income, so when Anne wrote to me again, to ask if I would come and live as her companion, I happily agreed. I must say I was shocked to find her frail and near to death. More than that...' Miss Miller pauses, as if debating with herself whether to carry on or not. 'She also pined for your mother, who Lord Seabrook had insisted should be sent away to school. To an establishment that specialised in "finishing" the daughters of the aristocracy.

'Your grandmamma was most unhappy, having learned the institution was renowned for curtailing the natural expressions of young women in possession of over-sentimental natures. She said that from the youngest age, Theodora had been blessed with an outgoing disposition, loving to kiss and hug her friends, the staff and family alike. Really not so unlike yourself.' Miss Miller smiles tenderly, before she heaves a sorry sigh. 'But I'm afraid her father saw that as a sign of moral weakness.

'The letters Theodora sent to her mother were discreet. But when they came to meet in person, so the truth was duly spilled. Corporal punishments were common. Being locked up and forced to fast. And hearing this your grandmamma was so upset she begged Lord Seabrook to allow their daughter home. Alas, he could not be convinced, and so perhaps must take some blame, when...' Miss Miller's fingers form a cradle on the tabletop before her '...when Theodora fell in love with a young man who'd been employed to teach music at the school, with all the shame that was to follow when—'

Theo interjects: 'When her bastard son was born.'

'It was a terrible time. I know Lord Seabrook was enraged, disinheriting your mother and insisting that he never wished to see her face again, which only left Anne more distraught, no doubt hastening her death. And after that, I left this house, being all too well aware of the gossip that might spread if I'd remained beneath the roof of a man so newly widowed.'

'You never wished to marry, to have a husband of your own?' Theo regrets his interruption almost as soon as it is made. They may be close, but this has surely been a step too intimate.

'I...' Miss Miller hesitates. 'I did once fall in love, but never with the hope of marriage. The gentleman in question ... he misled me, very cruelly. But living as a spinster has not been without rewards. And Anne did leave a small bequest. Enough for me to buy a cottage.' Miss Miller nods contentedly. 'Back in my childhood home of Bosham.'

'But you returned ... to Dorney Hall. To be my governess.'

'Yes,' she nods. 'After three years, when Lord Seabrook wrote to tell me of your mother's tragic death, although' – she frowns – 'I must admit I've always thought it rather strange the way your father gave you up.'

'It doesn't matter,' Theo says.

'Well, don't you think perhaps it should?' Miss Miller's brows are slightly raised.

'If my father cared for me, why *did* he give me up? Why has he never come to visit? He must have known where he could find me. I don't even know his name. I did ask Grandfather once, but he refused to discuss it.'

'I wish I knew.' Miss Miller sighs. 'But I'm sure the arrangements were only made with good intentions. A man alone, without the funds to ensure his child was cared for. A man who may have hoped that you would have a better life if you lived here at Dorney Hall, where you would also then become the heir to the estate. And, as I'm sure you are aware, when he sets his mind to something Lord Seabrook is persuasive ... such as when he sought my help to come and be your governess. I will admit my first response was to decline the invitation. But then I met you for myself. Such a sweet cherub of a child. That lovely mop of golden hair.'

'Am I so different today?' Theo's smile is full of charm.

'You still have an angel's face, so like your mother in her

portrait.' Miss Miller pulls a handkerchief from her sleeve to dab
her eyes. 'Oh, do forgive my foolish musings. My nerves are
somewhat frayed, too often thinking on the past. But...' Her
composure has returned, back to her sprightly self again. 'I'm sure
you must be feeling hungry, but I assumed you wouldn't want a
stuffy meal in the house. That's why I took the liberty of asking
for a cold collation.' She turns towards a table that's been brought
onto the terrace. 'For dessert there's apple pie, with some of Cook's
vanilla cream. I thought we'd simply help ourselves without the
bother of the staff. And then...'

A liver-spotted hand reaches down to lift a news sheet that is
lying in her lap. The paper rustles as she searches through the
pages, finger tapping at a large advertisement. Little dancing
specks of light glint at the corners of her mouth when she asks,
'Did you know, it's the summer Brocas fair? What do you say, we
eat our meal, then walk across the meadow paths? The cat may be
away, but that's no reason why the mice can't leave the house to
go and play.'

'Oh yes! That would be...' How Theo loves a fair. He feels such
stirrings of excitement. But his reply is interrupted by the
humming thrum of wings. He glances up to see two swans flying
low across the gardens, and then the wall that meets the common.
On from there towards the river and green acres of the Brocas.

FOUR

PROFESSOR LOVELL'S ELIXIR

Miracle Cure for Every Ailment & Affliction Known to Man

The seed from which Pa's enterprise expanded to fruition was planted on the morning when he dribbled Betsy Jones' potion in my sister's mouth – when, just like Lazarus himself, Tilly sprang up and was reborn.

Inspired by such a miracle, Pa spent the coins that Ma had hidden on intoxicating liquor, but never ended up so blootered that he left his girls to starve. Her rings were doubtless pawned or sold, and with the profits Pa acquired himself a fancy new brass bedstead and expensive feather mattress, to replace what he had burned in the garden when she died. Other items were delivered, and often in great quantities. Crates of empty bottles, sacks of sugar, kegs of whisky, flasks of gin and tins of treacle. There were also little phials in cardboard boxes which contained a viscous dark-brown liquid. We opened one of them on a day when Pa was out. What it held tasted bitter on our tongues and made us cough. But more alarming were the two big iron pots that had been placed on the floor beside the range. Had he bought them from a witch, such as the one we'd read about in Ma's old book of fairy tales? The one who lured away small children who had strayed from forest paths to come and shelter in her house, where she locked them in a cage, fed them on sweets to make them fat, then boiled them up inside a pot so as to nibble from their flesh till there was nothing left but bones.

To tell the truth, beyond such fears, we had no inkling of what these acquisitions might suggest; though soon enough we would find out – beginning on the day when me and Tilly were awoken by a sweet and malty smell. The morning 'sounded' sweet as well, for we could hear a woman singing in a gay and lusty voice, and as we knew it wasn't Ma, then ... *Whoever could it be?*

That was the question in our heads as we got up to creep downstairs and peer around the kitchen door, where Betsy Jones – for it was she – was warbling beside the stove, and it was the very song our ma last chanced to sing to us. The one about a blacksmith who wore a hat with marigolds. As if that hadn't been enough to raise the hackles on my back, the golden hoops Betsy had hooked into her ears were very like a pair our ma had often worn. Around one wrist we couldn't fail to see our mother's amber bracelet. The beads were clicking like a warning when Betsy raised a hand to push away the frizzled curls clinging damp across her cheeks. Meanwhile, she crooned through burring vowels, 'Well, here you are. The sleeping beauties. I thought you'd never wake. Why are you standing in the door, mouths gawping open, catching flies ... looking like you've heard a banshee?'

I was about to say she'd hammered the nail upon the head, but Tilly beat me to it, and most solicitous to boot. 'I like your singing, and that song. Do you know the other verses?'

'I'll tell you what,' Betsy replied. 'You carry on with the stirring of this pot, and I shall sing a little more ... and take the weight off these poor feet.'

Before you'd even think to blink, Tilly had pushed a stool across the tiles towards the stove, and what a scraping din it made, all but drowning the sirens blaring off inside my mind when I remembered how our ma had rested her own legs upon the very chair Betsy was sitting in right then, and where her singing carried on:

'Why did he promise me so gladly he would marry, then deny me?
I only have God as my witness that he had his wicked way,

Then left me lost, and pale and white, and with a trembling in my heart,
To think he'd said he loved me only, but turned out to be deceitful.'

When she was done Betsy looked sad. To be fair I felt the same.
It was not a happy song, even if I was too young to comprehend
the subtleties. But Tilly, on her stool, veiled in the plumes of rising
steam, she turned her pinked-up face to Betsy and continued
happily: 'Did you know about our pa being a blacksmith once
himself? Ma said he went around the farms, even the houses of
the gentry, to do the shoeing of their horses. But then one day
some spitting sparks of white-hot metal hit his eye, and after that
our pa was blinded, and...'

Despite my own antipathy to finding Betsy in our house, I
joined the spinning of the thread: '...And after that he gave up
smithing, and the horse that pulled the van that Ma and Pa had
travelled round in was unhitched and put to pasture, although
they'd only ever meant to rent this cottage for one harvest, picking
hops throughout September, moving on in the next spring...'

'...Which was lucky.' Here, my sister muscled back into the tale.
'Because some townies had concocted wicked lies about their
tribe. Two men were sentenced to the gallows. But, our pa, he was
all right, because...'

'...Of working on the farm, where he was helping Mr Kenton
with the harvest at the time when the offences all took place, and
so...'

'...He wasn't sent to gaol. And then Ma found that we were
coming, and...'

'...She didn't want to move from where she'd settled happily,' I
concluded, just before an altogether deeper voice burrowed
through the conversation.

'Well, you can get a move on now!' Pa was standing in the
doorway leading out to the back garden. His shirt and trousers
had been splattered with some green and yellow paint, more of it
smeared across his cheeks, as round as apples when he smiled. 'You

girls leave Betsy with her brewing. Go and dress, and you can come and help me working in the barn.'

Tilly was the first to ask, 'What are you doing out there, Pa?'

'Scrubbing and sprucing up the van in readiness to do some touring.'

'Touring, Pa?' My turn to question, suspicion churning in my belly.

'I'll be setting up my stall around some of the local fairgrounds. That's right now, ain't it, Bet?' Pushing back his dusty cap, Pa strode across the red stone tiles and bent in close so as to slobber kisses over Betsy's mouth, which turned my stomach inside out and only led me to complain.

'Pa! It isn't right. Betsy has stolen Ma's gold earrings. How can you want her in the house? How can you...?' I couldn't bring myself to say – *How can you bear to kiss that woman?*

My mind went back to a time Betsy had visited before, when she came to sit with Ma, with the new baby on the way. Tilly and me had tried to peep in through the keyhole of the bedroom, but Betsy opened up the door and left us terrified to see the expression on her face. Too crazed her eyes, too big the fortress of her bulk for us to pass and reach our mother's bed. Too hot the simmer of the temper when Betsy's arms were flapped about to shoo us both back down the stairs – 'On your way, you nosy rascals! Why don't you go and find your father? Go and pester him instead. And don't come back until you're called.'

As Pa was in the parlour, drinking a jug of Black Rat Cider, we ventured out into the garden and placed some stones upon the grass to mark the squares for playing hopscotch. Soon growing tired of that, we took some carrots from the basket in the kitchen and set off across the lane towards the paddock where Pa's mare was put to pasture. Her big brown head nuzzled between us. Our fingers stroked her rough-haired mane. And then, as dusk began to fall, we made our way back home again, sitting down on the bench below the roses that were growing all around Ma's bedroom window – from where we heard some awful groans, and then a silence, which was worse, only broken by another squawking shout from Betsy Jones.

Creeping through the kitchen, we made our way into the hall. Looking up the narrow stairs we saw our pa and Betsy Jones bathed in the shimmer of light that shafted through the bedroom door. Betsy's hands were freckled red. There was a sharp, metallic odour wafting down into our noses, which only filled us with a dread impossible to comprehend. We saw Pa slump in Betsy's arms, as limp and lifeless as a doll that's lost all remnants of its stuffing. We saw him pull away again, while Betsy turned and lifted up a little bundle of white linen. Wrapped inside it was a baby. What we could see of its face was an unnatural mottled grey.

Betsy is a devil. She's a thief. She's killed our mother and our baby brother too – So I was thinking in the kitchen all those weeks after the event when, quick as swallows in the wind, Pa raised his hand and cuffed my ear.

Through the jangling of the pain, I could hear his muffled shout: 'If I were you, I'd take some care to button up that spiteful mouth. But not before you make apologies to Betsy here as well. I gifted her those trinkets after she'd done her best and more to try and save your mother's life. I don't know where we would have been without her kindness these past months.'

'Kindness to you, but not to us!' I stamped my foot and was about to run upstairs, when Betsy rose from the chair and called my name.

'Stop right there, now, Miss ... Keziah?'

'Yes, that's me!' I all but spat. 'I'm the one without the mole, which is still there on Tilly's cheek to prove your spells contain no magic.'

'My cures will work, for those with faith.' Betsy's reply was calmly spoken. But I heard the seething anger that was running underneath it, much relieved when she turned to look at Tilly once again.

And what was Tilly doing? She was still standing on her stool next to the pots upon the range. She was tasting thick black dribbles from the spoon she'd used for stirring, blooming up in a smile when Betsy's tone became more kindly:

'Tilly, dear, it does appear my charm has failed to fade your mark. I should think there's a good reason. Snail slime is good for warts, but what you've got there on your cheek is far from any such affliction. It is more likely a sign left by the fingers of the fairy folk who blessed you in your crib. It tells the world that you are special, and altogether different from...' Betsy did not speak my name, but her glance said everything. 'You know that oftentimes the fairies will steal a human child and leave a changeling in its place. Perhaps they brought a changeling here, but then forgot to take you off. That might explain why there's one twin as sweet as honey in this house. Another sour as vinegar.'

Could Betsy see into the future, like our ma's Bohemia? Did she know that all too soon Tilly was doomed to stop her growing, destined to look more like a fairy than a normal human person?

Meanwhile, the woman carried on: 'Tilly can stay with me today. She's got the knack for steady stirring, while Keziah goes outside to give her da a helping hand.'

Tilly glanced at me. Was she seeking my approval? But then her eyes moved back to Betsy. She licked her lips as she proclaimed, 'It tastes like liquorice. It's nice.'

Betsy's reply was stern, 'It's not a pot of bubbling toffee. A sip or two will fire you up. But take too strong a dose and you'll be sleeping for a month, that's if you ever wake again.'

'And it's for business, not for pleasure,' Pa interrupted with a warning. 'Every drop spooned in your mouth is money stolen from my profits. Is that clear ... to both you girls?'

I saw my sister nod, then lift her shift to wipe her chin.

I ran upstairs without a word, tears scalding hot across my cheeks.

And so, it went from that day on. Tilly seemed to have no qualms about the cuckoo in Ma's nest, even when Betsy shared Pa's bed. And what a racket they both made with all their shrieks and whoops of laugher, the bedstead banging on the wall – until Pa came to shake our own to wake us up for morning chores.

Tilly would stir Betsy's pots, then help with filling up the bottles, which would be corked and sealed with wax, with printed labels on the fronts. Meanwhile, I rubbed my fingers raw, and ended up with many splinters, helping Pa with all the sanding and re-painting of the van that he more often called the vardo, and which, until that point, had been locked up in the barn.

Tilly and me, we were enchanted by the yellow slatted shutters drawn across the small side windows, and the door that split in two, like the ones you find in stables. When the vardo rolled along you could open up the top and swing your arms across the bottom to watch the whole wide world go by. But once you were inside, it was a home in miniature, with everything that might be needed for the activities of lounging, cooking, eating, or else sleeping on the mattress of the bed boxed in at the far end. On the floors were patterned rugs, very bright and colourful – once we'd hung them on the washing line to beat them clean of dust. Same with a lovely patchwork cover, although the rest of the bedding was so moth-eaten and mildewed, Pa had to throw it all away.

On the walls were shelves and mirrors, and the blackened brass of brackets to support the etched-glass orbs in which oil burned during the night to give a soft illumination. There were candle-holders too, protruding through the clutter of the china figurines arranged across some narrow shelves. Tilly particularly liked the shepherdess and her two lambs. The matching shepherd with his hat adorned with flowers and bright ribbons.

What else can I recall? Well, there were fancy painted plates, and a clock no longer ticking. There were floral, chintzy curtains, and an ornate gilded hearth with little drawers set in the uprights filled with cutlery and spices. Copper pans and iron kettles dangled on chains beside the stove, its chimney poking through the roof. When the van was stationary it would be lit for cooking food, or boiling water for Pa's tea. Apart from that, it was the source of any heat on colder nights, though when the weather was more clement Pa preferred to sleep outside, so as to be on the alert to any thieves who might creep up to try and nab his merchandise. More than once, we'd seen him floor fully-grown men with his bare knuckles.

Tilly and me would also feel those punching fists in years to come. But for then, our pa was nothing more than cheer personified. How gaily he'd waved as we'd stood on the cottage step when he drove off on his first foray for the selling of elixir – which was at Hereford Spring Fair, a place so near that Pa was home even before the first few stars began to twinkle in the sky.

Some weeks after, on a day when Betsy wasn't in the house, we rose from our bed and went downstairs to find the table laid with plates of scrambled eggs and piles of greasy, fried-up bacon. Pa, the source of this great feast, first looked at Tilly, then at me while pronouncing with some gusto, 'Girls, I see you sitting there, and it's putting me in mind of a business proposition I would like you to consider. I sold some cures at Hereford, but nothing like the quantities needed to turn a profit on my considerable investments. However, I did make a special study of those showmen most adept at drawing crowds, and what I saw gave me the notion that I needed to employ a little drama in my act. Something unique to tantalise and lure the punters in.'

There was a pause while Pa chomped down on a lardy slice of bread, then mumble-chumbled his next words. 'Recently, Betsy's been drawing my attention to the fact that' – he fixed me with his gimlet eye – 'Keziah here's been spurting up like she's been shovelling great heaps of manure in her boots, whereas *you*' – he looked at Tilly – 'don't appear to have been moving with the same velocity.'

I stared at Tilly. She at me. Could Pa be right in what he said? Now he'd mentioned such a thing I realised there *was* a difference, and not only in our heights. Tilly's face was very thin. Her chin and cheekbones were protruding sharp as razors through the skin. There was an odour to her breath, which I could smell when we were sleeping face to face upon Ma's pillow. The scent was herby, slightly woody, with a hint of aniseed. It was what lingered from the tonic Pa would often come upstairs and spoon onto my sister's tongue, claiming the medicine would aid her frail constitution.

Was it the bang on Tilly's head that had somehow stopped her growing, or was it due to the quantities of gin and opium in Lovell's patented elixir; which in turn begs the question – what was the nature of the father who so willingly encouraged his own child to drink it down, night after night, month after month? And, in the end, year after year?

Now, to think of such a thing, it fills my blood with raging fire. But in those days, how could I know or suspect our pa's intentions? Tilly and me, we were all smiles and open ears as he went on – 'Now, listen up, and here's the scheme...'

There wasn't much for us to do. The art of his deceit was to take us to the fairs where we would pose upon a stage. Meanwhile, the audience who'd gathered would be told the sorry tale of how, in infancy, we'd suffered from the wasting of consumption. During this illness, one of us had dutifully sipped elixir, while the other one refused and, as was all too clear to see, had now been stunted in her growth by the malingering disease.

What an irony it was, that I had rarely touched a drop of what our pa was boldly touting, finding the taste to be too sour and very numbing on my tongue, never mind the addled feeling lingering for hours after. But Tilly liked it, and so much it became an addiction. If she ever went without, she would explode into a tantrum. Her face would burn a purple red, and she'd be choking on her screams, limbs thrashing out in all directions. A night or two of that palaver sent us all into distraction, after which our pa ensured she was kept constantly supplied.

Meanwhile, he was as happy as a pig in clover, growing fat on all the beer and gourmandising of the fairs. But in the colder winter months, when we'd be back inside the cottage, he would be restless and announce, 'This house is like a prison. It positively makes me ill. Why, it was only for your ma that I remained here in the first place. But now she's gone, and I am free, and I have seen another world. I can cure, or I can smite...' Etcetera, etcetera.

Oh, how he loved the grand orating and the quoting from the Bible, even if he'd not been moved to take one step inside a church since our mother's funeral. It was the same with William Shakespeare and the encyclopaedia of every ailment known to man. The books he'd found in a pawn shop of a town not far from Oxford. So splendid was his memory, sagacious medical advice would drip in torrents from his tongue, always concluding with prescribing his own potion as a cure. Why, even if a customer had been as healthy as a horse before Pa started pontifying, they'd leave the shows wholly convinced that they were standing at Death's door, its imminence only prevented by the bottles they were clutching.

He did so well, it was astounding. And every spring, when he and Betsy brewed new batches in the kitchen, Pa would say, 'Just one more year, and we'll be rich beyond our dreams. We'll find ourselves a fancy house. I'll dress you three in furs and diamonds like the world has never witnessed. Just you wait, my pretty chicks...' Alfred would kiss his Betsy's lips, then pinch the cheeks of his two girls. 'I've seen the future in my dreams.'

But, for all his other talents, Alfred Lovell was no prophet. He may have dreamed about his riches, but not the dramas soon to follow when his vardo chinked and clattered on the roads leading to Windsor – where he rolled up to pitch his stall at the Brocas Summer Fair.

FIVE

ONCE WHEN SLEEPING in the woods the girls awoke to see a boy dressed in clothes of shining white. He looked down on them so kindly, without uttering a word. They woke again at dawn and realised they had been resting on a precipice's edge, and would certainly have fallen to their deaths if they had chanced to wander further in the darkness.

When their mother heard of this she said they must have seen a vision of the guardian angel who watches over all good children to keep them safe from any harm.

From *Snow-White and Rose-Red*

Theo turns towards Miss Miller. Her face is drawn and very pale. Has the walk across the meadows to the Brocas been too much? When he was younger, they would stroll for miles around the house's grounds, but she is frailer than she was – unless it is this evening's wine that slows her pace and stifles breaths.

Here comes another gasp, but only due to her excitement when the path on which they walk emerges through a clump of trees. To the left, and misted grey in the fast-descending dusk, are Eton's medieval spires, while on the right and rising high above the rooftops of the town is the great sprawl of Windsor Castle. At any other time they'd also see the River Thames as it runs below the bridge connecting the two towns. But tonight, it is obscured by the clutter of the fair. All the brightly coloured lanterns strung around the showground stalls, luring them on to join a world filled with the merry sounds of fiddles, pounding drums and barrel organs played below the painted showboats.

'Oh, to be young!' Miss Miller laughs as the boats soar high above her, hearing the passengers halloo down to their friends still on the ground – before she flinches at the sudden whip-crack *rat-a-tat* exploding from the rifle galleries. The smell of sulphur from the shots has a sharp, metallic zing. She holds a cloth against her nose, then wanders off, leaving Theo on his own amid the chaos of what his grandfather would call 'the cesspit of humanity'.

Theo is happy to wallow in this world of wondrous filth, and he is smiling yet more broadly when distracted by the muscles of Achilles the High Striker. What a god of a man in his belted leopard skin, while an educated voice challenges any contenders to take the hammer from his hand and strike the target that will send an iron weight careering up towards the summit of a pole, perchance to ding-a-ling the bell that will result in a reward.

Theo is tempted to try, but Miss Miller's back again, nibbling on the gingerbread extracted from a paper bag, before she asks, 'Would you like some? I simply couldn't resist. I do adore the fiery taste.'

He takes a piece, and they push on, pausing a while to watch a woman in a harlequin concoction of crumpled velvets, silks and satins, who's throwing balls into the air with an assured dexterity, while a magician at her side snatches a goldfish from a hat.

'What an ingenuity,' Miss Miller beams, before she turns towards The Educated Porcine that, for a penny, calculates simple additions and subtractions. Theo is less impressed, but then he knows the trick of it, having crouched down the year before to see a boy direct its snout towards the brightly coloured numbers painted on a wooden bar. Another miracle debunked to the realm of the mundane. And now, Miss Miller's bored as well, rummaging inside her bag to pay a sixpence to the showman advertising dioramas: *As marvellous as any waxworks you'll observe in Madam Tussaud's.*

'What do you think we'll see tonight?' She is bustling ahead before an answer can be made. 'The Battle of Waterloo is always very popular. Or the antics of Lord Byron?' Eyes twinkle at the thought, before they grow more serious. 'I hope it's not the re-enactment of Prince Albert's funeral. So very tasteless and depressing.'

Good taste or not, Miss Miller fizzes with renewed anticipation as they're directed through the flaps of the tent to find themselves crammed in among the audience already waiting patiently. The atmosphere is tense as every face is turned intently to the cabinet before them, which is at least five feet in height and maybe ten in width, and where a skinny boy assistant lights a lamp at either end. The flames shoot up alarmingly before they dip into a sizzle, and then the crank and the whine of the machine's concealed mechanics as the man who took the fees slides back the shutters and proclaims, 'Behold the ancient tale ... Daniel in the Lion's Den!'

'Is this to be a Bible show?' Miss Miller whispers as the bulging marble eyes of a wax puppet spin around so as to demonstrate its horror at approaching wooden lions. By the clicking of their jaws, they demonstrate that they intend to make a meal of the man. But, lo! The Lord has intervened. With flowing robes, and hair and beard of cotton wool stuck on his head, he only has to give the nod and the archangel is descending. Daniel's fate has been averted. The shutters close. The showman's booming hallelujahs rise above the less enthusiastic clapping from the crowd – till expectation looms anew in 'The Wondrous Tale of Jonah!' This is an underwater scene, with the puppet playing Daniel now to be swallowed by a whale. The leviathan is squeaking back and forth across the stage behind a rack of cardboard waves, finally opening its mouth to vomit Jonah out again.

Never have the minutes of Theo's life dragged by so slowly, and he's relieved to hear Miss Miller say she's also had enough. Outside again, they're somewhat dazzled by the flare of nearby torches, before she tugs at his sleeve and says, 'Oh, look ... Lovell's Elixir. Cook was telling me about it. She bought a bottle Henley way. She says the medicine worked wonders for her nasty yeasty rash. Not only that, she said she had the best night's sleep in several years. She asked if I would keep a look out, and if I chanced to see the stall to get more bottles for her shelves.'

As Theo fears he'll never feel the same about Cook's food again, Miss Miller rushes off towards the swarthy, dark-haired man who is orating from a stage set before a caravan. Caught in the glimmer of the flames the van is glowing emerald green. The legend on the side, in gaudy red and shadowed gold, spells out the name of the performer and the merchandise he's selling: *PROFESSOR LOVELL'S ELIXIR*.

Has the professor seen Miss Miller join the audience and winked? No, he's missing his left eye – which must be the one affliction his cure has failed to remedy, for on a board below stage is a plethora of claims...

THE CRIPPLE WILL BE MADE TO WALK,
THE DEAF TO HEAR,
THE BLIND TO SEE
The dying man will live again, with every other known affliction
incidental to the human predisposition being slain.
Suffer no more the miseries of
Gout, Jaundice, Indigestion, Rheumatism, Cholera,
Want of Appetite, Dry Skin, Flatulence, Palpitations, Diarrhoea,
Deprived Vision, Coughs, Nausea, Frightful Dreams, Piles,
Convulsions, Ulceration of the Breasts,
Burns, Bruises, Itch, Heartburn, Quinsy, Headaches...

'Headaches! Do you see that?' Miss Miller speaks so loudly that the showman surely hears, because he's pointing straight towards her, smiling broadly as he calls, 'Madam. You, over there, with the cherries on your bonnet.'

'Can he mean me?' Miss Miller asks, her fingers rising to the hat that frames her face, and where there is indeed a cluster of silk cherries.

Still not convinced that she could be the object of the man's attention, her eyes flit nervously around other people in crowd, until – 'Yes, you!' the showman calls. 'Clearly a lady of distinction, and I knows one when I sees one. Come and introduce yourself.'

Caught up in the excitement, Theo's old governess steps forward. Much like Moses when he raised his wooden staff to part the sea, the crowd dissolves before her, forming an aisle through which she walks to take the showman's hand.

Once hoisted up onto the stage, the professor asks Miss Miller, 'My dear, you look unwell. What be the nature of your ailment?'

At first Miss Miller seems struck dumb, but then the wittering begins. 'I've been having dreadful headaches. Perhaps it is the weather. So hot and muggy these past days. I had to spend this afternoon confined to bed, the curtains closed. I—'

Here the showman interrupts and seems to mock her when he asks, 'Could it be you are you afflicted by a worm? You're very slender. I met a lady recently who suffered such a ravager. But then one dose of my elixir and she expelled the parasite. A monstrous thing it proved to be, more of a wolf than nematode, and measuring near twenty feet, with giant suckers formed like grappling hooks extending from its body. How that poor woman stood the pain of all those claws, I cannot think. And...' his voice is raised above the sounds of jeering from the crowd '...for all of those who doubt my word, the specimen is now preserved in her local town museum.'

'Oh no. Nothing like that.' Miss Miller looks appalled. 'This is a headache. Just a headache.'

The quack goes on: 'Accept this cure and you'll soon be as right as rain. But you don't need to take my word for what the potion can deliver. Stand aside and I shall demonstrate its wonder in the form of the twin sisters who were born identical in every way ... and so they did remain until their ma took with consumption. At only five years old, and with no soul to take them in, these orphaned girls were destitute and doomed to begging on the street.'

He stops to wipe his brow in a show of consternation. 'How could I see the sisters' plight and not find pity in my heart? From that first day, and unto this, they have been raised in my own home. But there the story does not end, for when they both developed morbid signs of the same ailment that had claimed their mother's life, I pressed them urgently to take a dose of my elixir, being sure that I should drive the fearful malady away. Now...' He pauses and is frowning as he looks out around the crowd who are still rapt in this performance. 'The sister who exhibits the more compliant personal nature imbibed the tincture she was offered without a moment of complaint. But, regretfully the other, of a surly disposition, refused to take a single drop, falling into fits of rage on those occasions when I tried to force a spoonful on her tongue.'

A thick black brow is arched above his one remaining eye. 'Well, yes, I hear you thinking. She was a poor pathetic child, and here am I a full-grown man who surely must have had the strength to pinch my fingers at her nose and therefore force the potion down. In my exasperated state, that is exactly what I did. But, all in vain, for the next moment she would spit it out again.' His head is shaken mournfully during another lengthy pause, presumably to ratchet up yet more anticipation. 'The change occurring in the health and constitution of those girls was all-too subtle at the start. But now, at fifteen years of age, it is remarkable to see the ruddy health exhibited by the child who drank elixir.'

His hands are raised above his head, like a preacher in a pulpit. 'Prepare, my friends to be amazed, when you observe the benefit

that was produced by the cure. Ladies and gentleman,' he cries
with a manic, grinning gusto, as a girl steps through a gap in the
canvas draped behind him, 'I introduce you to Keziah, the finest
specimen to demonstrate my miracle elixir! Did you ever see a
child with so fine a corporation, and in the ruddiest of health?'

The crowd, which has been hushed, is now a buzzing rush of
murmurs when it sees – what does it see? A pretty, dark-haired
girl upon the cusp of womanhood, whose expression is blank
above the floral cotton dress falling against the well-shaped calves
rising from her leather boots. She is staring at these boots, looking
as if she'd rather be anywhere but on that stage. Somewhere she
doesn't have to hear...

'Now,' the showman cries, 'observe the child who did not thrive.
The one who took no medicine and is in consequence afflicted by
a stunting of her growth. Despite my very best endeavours, too
many years have now elapsed for any cure to take effect. In many
ways, I can work magic, as displayed in the marvellous condition
of her sister. But where this child is concerned, the time for
miracles has passed. Miss Matilda...' he lifts an arm and is
beckoning again, 'It is time to show yourself.'

There are cries of consternation when a second girl emerges
though the folds of drapery. Theo is blinking in amazement, and
he has that slightly spinning, out of time and place sensation only
experienced before when in a tented hall of mirrors. How
confusing it had been to see the walls on either side creating topsy-
turvy worlds, when what was crooked became straight, the
beautiful turned into ghouls. Where Theo saw himself stretched
out to more than twice his normal height...

This demonstration, in its way, is just as discombobulating. The
girls are mirrors of each other, but the first appears as Alice before
she tumbles down the hole to find herself in Wonderland, whereas
the second is the girl who found the bottle with a label saying
Drink Me – and she did, and in consequence she shrank. Only
here the tale's reversed. The girl who drank went on to grow.

The comparison is stark, at least for any fools who are gullible enough to believe this is the truth. But the crowds are surging forward, and many coins are being pressed upon the god who holds the secret of eternal health and vigour. Even Miss Miller, who still stands on the showman's other side, is opening her reticule.

Theo remains quite motionless, as do the girls, who stand apart from the vendor and his crates. How astonishing the smaller, looking more like a doll than a real living person, and could that be a tear spilling down across her cheek to pool around a heart-shaped mole? How perverse, the way the shimmer of that tear puts him in mind of a snail's silver trail.

The larger twin who, until then, gazed at the chaos of the fair has surely noticed Theo's stare. The corners of her mouth are lifting. Such seductive, full pink lips that leave him charmed and smiling back – before he comes to realise that look was never meant for him.

Glancing around, he sees a man who is striking in appearance. A good head taller than the rest, who are still thronging round the stage, he has grey hair that gleams like silver, worn loose and long about his shoulders. This alone would be dramatic, but is enhanced by the addition of a spangled top hat. And his jacket, velvet green, has braids sewn onto the lapels. The type of garment that a gentleman puts on when he is smoking. Meanwhile his legs are adorned in some black-and-red striped trousers that look as if they might have come out of a circus costume box.

Theo admires the jaunty look. Could he ever dress that way, or would he be a laughing stock? No one's laughing at this man with his jaded air of glamour, and whose smile, to which the girl up on the stage has been responding, is eclipsed when he bows, tipping his hat across his forehead in a wordless act of greeting. Could he be an entertainer from another fairground show? Something about him is familiar. But if there'd been the slightest chance to seek an answer to this question it has melted in a moment. Mr Spangled Hat has disappeared into the crowds.

In his place, here is Miss Miller, looking flustered as she stuffs some small green bottles in her bag. 'Whatever was I doing?' She shakes her head in disbelief and sets the cherries wobbling. 'Standing up there, on the stage for everyone to see? But when Professor Lovell reached down to offer me his hand, I simply felt compelled to take it. Do you know...' She leans in closer, voice coming low and confidential. 'I swear I felt some current of connection pass between us. And, those two girls he introduced ... how remarkable it is what the elixir has achieved. You'd almost think that one was boiled and took a shrinking in the wash. Speaking of which, I feel as if I've had a wringing through the mangle. I fear my headache is returning. Would you mind so terribly if I went home to find my bed? You're very welcome to stay, and—'

'No. You must let me walk you home.' Theo is sad to leave the fair, but if Miss Miller goes alone she would surely be a target for any fool mug-hunters who are lurking in the bushes.

❖

It is a pleasant night-time stroll. Insects buzz. A warbler sings, and with a moon bright overhead they need no lamp to guide their path – although Miss Miller is concerned to see the mists begin to rise like wraiths above the grasses.

'We really must get on. I once read that Mr Dickens lost his way upon this path. He'd been visiting his mistress, Ellen Ternan, or so they say. He'd set her up quite near to Slough, hoping that way to keep the news of their affair from all the gossips. Well, he must have been to see her and was walking though these meadows to catch the train back home to London, but with it being the depths of winter, and such an icy fog descending, he ended up completely lost, going round and round in circles until he caught a dreadful cold. They say it laid him low for months and that he never quite recovered.' She heaves a sigh of deep regret, for Mr

Dickens is her hero. She even has an oval frame that holds his likeness by her bed.

'It's not winter, cold, or wet, so I don't think we need to worry,' Theo tries to reassure as she is reaching for her skirts, throwing one leg across a stile – still remarkably lithe for a woman of her age. But there's a moment when Miss Miller appears to lose her balance, and the reticule she's holding falls and rattles to the ground. Theo stoops to pick it up but fears the bottles of elixir have been smashed to smithereens. Black liquid seeps through the bag, and must be quite the humming compound for the reek is very strong. But luckily a good clean break has only snapped one bottle's neck. Any objects that are covered in the syrup are wiped clean on Miss Miller's handkerchief. First, there is her lorgnette case, and then a jar of smelling salts. A silver phial containing perfume and her set of household keys. But she cannot find her purse.

Already on the verge of tears, she clambers down from the stile and cries, 'Oh no! It can't have gone. I only took it out for...' Her brow is creased as she considers. 'There was the bag of gingerbread, and then the dioramas, and...'

'The elixir.' Theo's words drop through the silence she's left hanging. 'Or do you think you may have dropped it somewhere on the meadow paths? We could go back, retrace our steps.'

Not for a moment does he think the latter is the case. He is convinced that she's been robbed by that quack, Professor Lovell. If not him, another punter who was crowding round the stage. What better opportunity for any practised fingersmith?

As Miss Miller starts to weep, Theo takes her by the arm and is speaking with a calmness that belies his growing anger. 'Please, you mustn't be upset. I'm sure you're not the only person who's gone home from Brocas Fair to find their pockets have been picked.'

'But, my purse.' Her voice becomes almost hysterical with panic. 'I don't care about the money, but what about my lucky heather ... and the miniature in oils that showed my parents in their youth? I cannot bear to think them lost.'

When she has finally recovered, after two doses of her salts, they resume the journey home. It feels like hours before they get there, and several more that they sit in the empty, night-time kitchen. Cast in the melancholy flicker of a candle on the table, Miss Miller looks dejected and is continuing to sniffle as she drinks the cup of tea that Theo's fortified with brandy from a bottle in the larder – to which she also adds several drops of her elixir.

As Theo sips from his own cup, holding more brandy than tea, he comes to the decision that when Miss Miller's gone to bed he'll make his way back to the Brocas. He still has money in his pocket, and if the stalls have been shut down then he'll pursue his higher mission – which is to find the stolen purse. At least to search in the location towards which every clue is pointing, and where – if truth be told – another magnet tugs his heart. Those girls, so eerily alike. The one so stunted in her growth.

❈

It is later than he thought, and the romance, the glitz and glitter of the showground has been doused in the night-time's heavy gloom. The painted booths and tented stalls that run along the grassy aisles have all been locked and shuttered up. No more laughs and shrieks of panic from the swing-boat passengers. No more dinging of the bell as Achilles strikes his hammer.

The fairground dogs lope through the shadows, some of them growling as they scent Theo's odour on the air. Fortified by alcohol, he tells himself they're only interested in nosing through the bones lying discarded on the ground. The spat-out nuts. The half-chewed toffees. The liquor left in oyster shells. One of the dogs is even lapping at a pool of frothing vomit. The attractions may be closed, but the stench of stale beer pervades the desultory sprawl of these tented backstage realms, where giant engines are still wheezing plumes of steam into the air. The acrid smoke of burned tobacco wreathes the posturers and gamblers shuffling cards or throwing dice. Hands are waving paper money. Voices are whooping with delight at the man who is holding a rat by its tail, before he opens up his mouth to snap his teeth around its head.

Sickened at the sight, Theo turns to see some women huddled round a brazier. He wonders why. It isn't cold. But then he notices the feathers. The pure white down of two swans that have been slain to make a meal.

Further on, another group clap to the beating of a drum. A fiddle plays. One couple dance. Theo's own feet begin to tap, but then he hears a different music with a beat less regular.

Curious, despite himself to hear loud grunts and stifled cries, he moves on through the closed-up stalls and comes across Professor Lovell, his forehead pressed against his van, where letters form the word of *CURE*. His shirt and jacket, now discarded, show a broad and muscled back. His braces, cavalierly dropped, are hanging loose around the trousers also fallen to his knees. Higher up, his naked arse is thrusting hard between the legs tightly wound about his waist. The thighs are doughy, pocked with dimples, spilling over wrinkled stockings.

As Theo mutely stares, feeling repulsed yet mesmerised, a new idea begins to fester. *Right now, I'd pick your pockets and you wouldn't even notice.* Or could he climb the ladder steps and look inside the caravan for any signs of stolen purses? But the professor's raucous breaths are growing ever faster, surely driving to a climax, and how can Theo guarantee that he will find the vehicle empty. Those two girls might be inside. What if they see him and cry out? No, when the pumping is completed, he'll introduce himself directly to the showman, and he'll ask...

Another problem is arising, as the brandy Theo added to his tea an hour before begins to weaken in his blood and his thoughts are sharpening. If the professor turns around and sees him there, what will he do? If Theo was attacked, he wouldn't stand a chance.

Giving up on the purse, he looks about for an escape and walks across a stretch of grass, towards the river's ribboned black. In the water he can see reflections of the moon and stars, also the spread of Windsor Castle, the silhouetted towers and turrets looking like a sleeping dragon. Nearer to the water's edge, willows drape across the path. The path that leads towards the meadows, and from there to Dorney Hall.

But his journey is diverted. First, there is the sudden aching of a fullness in his bladder and, still feeling slightly tipsy, he has to fiddle for so long with the buttons at his crotch, it is more by luck than judgement that his prick has been released before the water fountains out. The stream cascades in a great arc. Some of it splatters on the pebbles of the shore below the bank. The remainder finds its way into the ripple of the water, where at least there are no waterfowl to squawk and raise complaints. Not a single breath of wind to stir the bushes on the bank – until Theo hears a voice...

Afterwards, looking back, he will smile and tell himself that was the moment he first heard the sweetest voice in all existence. In a less romantic version, he will recall more of a screech, before the angry reprimand – 'Not again! How many times? If you will persist in waving that monstrosity about, I swear I'll find myself a knife. I'll come and cut your todger off and I'll wear it like a trophy round my neck for all to see. Better still, I'll have it fried and feed it to the fairground dogs.'

Where to hide? Mortified, Theo tries to dive for cover, but he trips and ends up rolling through a clump of stinging nettles. Biting against his bottom lip to supress a cry of pain, he can only hope he's hidden by the caging of the willows. And, thank the Lord, he has managed to button up his flies, and hopefully what lies behind them is at no risk of slicing blades.

Another deeper voice is honeyed with concern when calling out, 'What is it, Tilly?'

'It was that boy, come back again. The one who works the

fairground engines ... when he's not pulling out his thing to wave about like a flag, as if he thinks that's entertaining. And now, he's found himself another skill to add to that performance, which is to piss like he's a cannon. I swear, he only missed me by an inch. Mind you...' There is a pause, followed by a tinkling laugh. 'I've never seen it quite so close. When I looked up, I thought it must have been a barge pole sticking out. He could start up his own act, stand inside a curtained booth and charge a sixpence for a look. Mr Elephant's Lost Trunk.'

'Not lost enough.' The deeper voice is joined by sounds of splashing water.

Peering through the willow leaves, Theo sees the larger girl from the snake-oil salesman's show as she emerges through the mists swirling above the river's surface. Her face is silvered in the moonlight. Her neck is pale as a swan's. Tangled weeds of long black hair are clinging to her naked shoulders. Her body glistens with the diamond beads of water dripping from it.

Theo is mute with admiration. *She is a sprite. She is a mermaid...*
No. She's human after all. She has two legs on which she rises to paddle through the shallows. From there, she walks across the shingle towards the sister who's still clothed, just as he saw her on the stage, and who now helps the larger girl step back into the shift discarded for her swim. It is pulled up across her thighs, her hips and belly, then her breasts – which is the moment Theo thinks it's safe to make his presence known.

He coughs as if in introduction, and then calls out, 'Can you forgive me. I didn't mean to spy. I was walking by the river when I took the opportunity to sit and rest here on the bank, only minding my own business, when...'

As Theo thinks that even saints may tell white lies from time to time, the smaller girl responds, 'Now, we've got a peeping Tom, and a posh one by the sound.'

Her sister grabs another garment hanging on a nearby branch, thrusting her arms into its sleeves and pulling skirts over her head before she calls her response, 'Will he dare to show his face and properly apologise?'

Nothing ventured, nothing gained, and it isn't every day that Theo's had his prick described as being like an elephant's? Crawling between the willow curtains, he kneels down among the grasses so as to get a better view, and hears the bigger girl exclaim, 'Well, I never did. Is it the pretty cupid boy from the audience tonight?'

So, she did notice me. It wasn't just The Spangled Hat. Theo feels immensely buoyed by this small kernel thrown his way, and though he tries, it is impossible to stop a foolish grin from spreading on his face as she continues questioning.

'Whatever are you doing, hanging round this late at night? I hope you haven't come here wanting more of Pa's elixir, because the bottles are all sold. And, even if they weren't, you can't believe a single word that slips through Alfred Lovell's lips.'

Pa. Did she say Pa? Theo's eyes are blinking as he stammers disbelief: 'He ... he is your father?'

Why is he surprised? The Lovell man was darkly handsome, in a florid sort of way. These girls, they also have that look, though somehow purer and more polished. Far less rough about the edges. In some perversely odd connection Theo sees them with their hands plunged in a bowl while using soap. Could it be Pears? The advertisement he'd noticed in Miss Miller's newspaper during their dinner earlier: 'To Keep Their Pretty Fingers Clean. The Softest Whitest Hands.'

The smaller sister glances up and with a note of some dismay, she says, 'Yes, he is our father.'

'More's the shame,' the other adds. 'And if you believe his tales, then you're a dupe like all the rest. My sister Tilly is the one who has a liking for the tincture, whereas—'

'Please Keziah, not again. You know how hard I try to stop ... that I don't want it anymore.' The smaller girl's appeal is plaintive.

In return, looking ashamed, the girl who's called Keziah

crouches down and enfolds her sister in her arms. Theo can't hear her muffled words, only the tone of wretched sorrow. And then, in a reprisal of the show in which they starred only a few short hours before, he sees the glitter of tears spilling out from Tilly's eyes.

How he is touched to see her sadness, to sense the vulnerability, and this is why, after Keziah has released her smaller sister and is standing once again, he dares to tell them why he's there.

Hearing about Miss Miller's purse, Keziah hangs her head in shame. Tilly speaks, but in a voice that is so hushed he barely hears it: 'Pa marks the wealthy-looking people who are standing in the crowds and then he calls them up on stage. When it is time to sell the bottles, he takes his chance, and should there be the slightest element of doubt that his deceit has been observed, he'll simply slip the stolen goods into another punter's pocket. Which means some innocent bystander will be blamed for sticky fingers, only able to look on while Pa creates a song and dance as he accuses *them* of stealing.'

'You're not concerned that he'll be caught?'

'We are,' Tilly says, her voice now clearer and more strident. 'And if our pa should be arrested, clapped in irons and sent to gaol, then there's a chance we might be too, as his accomplices in crime. And what will happen to us then?'

'It's not just thieving at the fairs.' Keziah's voice takes up the story. 'If there's some mischief to be had then—'

'Alfred Lovell will be there,' Tilly interrupts. 'He's like a moth drawn to a candle at the slightest sniff of trouble, especially if he's been drinking. Why, you never would believe what happened on our way to Windsor, when we stopped off outside an inn for him to take his fill of ale. Out he came, eventually, with these two strangers following, both of them looking very grubby, and such a stink they had about them, as if they'd bathed in a sewer. If that wasn't bad enough, Pa opened up the vardo door and announced, as if he'd known these bosky rogues for all his life...' She pauses for a breath. "'Can you girls move up the bench and make some space for these two gents who are requiring a ride, for which they've generously paid.'"

'Paid for what? We were afraid.' Keziah's deeper voice again. 'No way would we agree to being locked inside the vardo at the mercy of their whims. We bolted up the doors and windows, and made it clear we'd not succumb to any oily, wheedling words ... which meant the passengers were forced to drag themselves and any baggage onto the roof to sit with Pa for the duration of the ride.'

Tilly spoke again. 'We could hear them all conversing. Very convivial it seemed. But, as the twilight hours passed and the night became yet darker, the voices slowed, and we assumed the passengers had gone to sleep. Maybe Pa was dozing too, for his old mare, she never needs more than occasional soft clickings of his tongue to keep on plodding. Meanwhile, Keziah and myself were in no mood to go to sleep, but only lay upon our bed, and ... it's hard to quite describe ... felt oddly scratchy in our blood. To try and soothe the eeriness, we started singing to each other, only pausing now and then to say how bright and full the moon appeared beyond the window.'

'That moon' – Keziah now – 'so oddly big and low as it was bobbing there before us, and never even disappearing when the road changed its direction ... which didn't seem quite natural.'

At this point there is a lull before Tilly carries on, 'You'll never guess what happened next.'

Her sister grabs her tiny hand and continues to explain: 'Have you ever seen the moon and visualised the eyes and nose and mouth of a man? Well, that's exactly what we saw when we knelt upon our bed and pressed our noses to the glass. But even more alarming was the way the moon continued slipping from the sky, until ...'

'We've never yelled so loud,' Tilly butts in dramatically. 'Those passengers of Pa's, they were resurrection men, and in their baggage was a corpse recently stolen from its grave. It must have fallen from its wrappings, and what we'd thought to be the moon was in fact a dead man's face, as clear as day for any travellers out on the road to witness! Afterwards, Pa did protest his ignorance of the matter, and for once we did believe that he was telling us the truth, for when he heard our frantic cries and turned about to see the horror, he pulled his mare up pretty sharpish and was yelling frightful curses. His passengers soon clambered down and dragged their merchandise behind them, disappearing through some hedging, where no doubt they planned to wait and trick some other drunken fool into giving them a ride.'

'It was a ghastly thing.' Keziah's voice is trembling, half a sob and half a laugh as she looks up towards the moon shining bright in that night's sky. 'But whenever Pa's in drink, he is susceptible to schemers and illicit temptations. These last few nights it's been the grifters who join the gambling that goes on when the fair has been closed up. Some of them pester us as well, calling out lewd suggestions, leering after us like wolves, which is why we've come down here, so as to hide until we're sure all the roisterers are sleeping.' Her eyes are fierce, like burning coals. 'Tilly and me have realised that we must seek a different life. We cannot bear to go on acting out our pa's immoral lies ... or to face the other dangers he's now bringing to our door.'

'What would you do? Where would you go?' Theo is surprised at the depth of his concern. The twins' peculiarity, of being so alike and yet quite different in size, is bound to draw undue attention, and perhaps for the wrong reasons. Tongues can be cruel, and that's not all. He has read some of the novels Miss Miller leaves about the house. Stories that tell of tragic fates suffered by innocent young women who flee the safety of their homes, only to end up being ruined at the hands of libertines.

Why does the image of his grandfather loom large inside his mind? But as Lord Seabrook is away Theo feels free to suggest: 'You could come home with me tonight. Miss Miller – that's the woman who was with me at the fair – I'm sure she'll offer you a bed. There might even be some jobs available around the house. It is quite large, and there are servants, and of course you would be paid. That is until you find some work more suited to your interests.'

What interests could they be? Even as he speaks, he is doubting the plan. He knows so little of these girls. Are they honest, or corrupted in the manner of their father? Miss Miller *might* agree to let them stay at Dorney Hall, but there is no guarantee. Worse still, what if Lord Seabrook reappears in the morning and decides to take against them? Theo knows only too well the spiteful hatred the old man directs at travellers and showmen.

Some years ago, when he'd been walking on the common with Miss Miller, they'd come across a gypsy woman in the act of picking heather. A child was at her side, its fingers grabbing at her skirts. A smaller baby was bound in a shawl around her breast.

Miss Miller, who could easily have gathered some herself, for the flowers had been growing in abundance on the common, asked the woman if she'd sell a sprig or two from her basket.

'God bless the goodness of your heart,' the gypsy woman smiled and took the shilling she'd been offered, before she pinned a small bouquet against Miss Miller's coat lapel. But what came next was far less pleasant, for when the woman raised her head towards the gates of Dorney Hall, she spoke with fierce intensity. 'You and this boy should get away from the prison where you live, where neither one of you belongs. What lies behind those walls, and what is buried in its soil...' she paused and touched her baby's head '...is forever dead and gone. You should both seek a life elsewhere. But while you're here, my dear sweet lady' – her eyes fixed firmly on Miss Miller's – 'this sprig of heather will protect you. Make sure you always keep it close.'

Barely had she finished speaking when there came the distant clattering of horse hooves on the road. Looking back towards the source, the woman frowned and then more rapidly continued on her way. But she had not gone far enough to escape Lord Seabrook's wrath, for as his carriage reached the gates, the wheels slowing to halt, his reddened features protruded through a window as he shouted, 'Trespassers! Get off my land! I won't have gypsies camping here. No roots. No honest souls. Never adhering to the rules of decent, law-abiding men. I'll have you locked in chains if you're not gone before the morning!'

Where had the gypsy woman gone? Theo often wondered in the months and years that followed, always looking out in case he saw her there again, always hoping that his grandfather's cruel words were empty threats. But he could never be sure, and it's this fear that is now causing him to stumble as he says, 'Even if you would prefer to find some other place to stay, I know Miss Miller would be grateful ... might even offer some reward to see her purse returned again. It holds a picture of her parents and a sprig of lucky heather.'

Does the thought of a reward stir some interest in Keziah? 'We can look inside the box where Pa conceals his pilfered loot. But' – her pleading eyes are raised to his – 'how do we know that you won't harm us? What if this woman, this Miss Miller, then accuses *us* of thieving?'

'You must have seen her earlier, on the stage beside your father? She is a sweet and gentle soul, and...'

'The one with cherries on her hat?' Tilly nods. 'She did look kind.' She stares intently at her sister. 'Why don't we take this chance? Go back and find this purse, collect our things, and run away with...' She glances up at Theo. 'We don't even know your name.'

'Theodore,' he says. 'But everybody calls me Theo.'

'What does it mean?' Keziah asks.

'It's Greek. It means God's Gift.'

She laughs, and Theo's cheeks are burning with embarrassment.

But her sister is more gracious: 'I do believe you have been sent from God to help us in our need. That is...' he sees the doubt begin to flicker in her eyes '...if you *really* will be waiting? If you mean the things you promise?'

'I'm not going anywhere.' Theo hopes he's reassured them, watching as they scrabble up the bank, as sleek as otters, and emerging not that far from where he's kneeling, half submerged among the willowherb and hogweed. Their skirt hems brush against the grasses as four quick feet go speeding off, across the meadow to the fair, though there's a moment when they stop and turn to look at him again. One face is anxious. One is smiling. They both have eyes so very dark they could be made of glinting jet.

Only when the girls have gone does he turn back towards the Thames, where the water's glug and lapping weaves a slow hypnotic magic – until it's broken by a deafening crack of thunder in the air, the quaking of the ground below. The lightning's flash is very near, and as the first fat drops of rain fall from a sky that's rent in two, he hardly notices the wet; not until his shirt is drenched, eyes almost blinded as he crawls back to the shelter of the trees. This is where he spends the night, until at dawn he hears the bells of the churches of two towns tolling out the hour of five. He sees the sun's first golden rays filtering between the leaves, and he admits he has been duped.

The sisters won't be coming back.

SIX

THE TOSSING OF A COIN

We so often thought of Theo, who we'd met on Windsor Brocas, who was to be our gift from God – that is before God changed his mind. We used to wonder if he'd waited very long in all the thunder and the rain that came that night? Well, I'd wonder. Tilly would sigh and grow embarrassingly swoony when she pondered on his voice, which she called cultured and melodic, or his strong-jawed handsome features, and his halo of gold hair.

I'd generally reply, 'You do know he was a boy and not an angel, don't you, Tilly? As far as I could tell, and I admit I couldn't see him all that clearly at the time – not with him crouching in the grass growing so tall above the bank – but I would bet a thousand pounds he didn't have a pair of wings.'

Well, at least one Lovell sister had the sense to look around and see the world for what it was. A world so wicked that a father would sell his daughters to a stranger.

When we'd arrived back at the vardo, Alfred Lovell wasn't there. No doubt off squandering his takings. Not that the details are important, only the fact that in his absence we were free to gather up the personal items we might wish to carry with us when we fled.

Soon we'd filled a carpet bag, to which Tilly also added the china figurines from which she could not bear to part. Meanwhile, I searched for the purse our pa had pilfered earlier. It didn't take me long to find it, and to add it to our luggage, for it was lying at the top of the box in which he stored most of the goods he chose to steal. If only I had not continued digging down through the rest – through coins, and gloves, and lace-edged clothes, even a golden chain and time piece – because my curiosity delayed our leaving by some moments. Long enough to be surprised by the sound of heavy feet thudding on the vardo steps, then by our father's florid face as it appeared around the door.

There was no protest we could make, for he'd already seen our bag, and hadn't I been caught red-handed with my fingers full of money I'd decided we were owed as compensation for the years of our parades around the fairgrounds? But, as you might surmise, he did not see things in that light. Already fuming at the fact that he had gambled and then lost most every coin of that night's takings, now he'd discovered his own daughters busy stealing what remained. How the metal in my hands shone bright with guilt when lightning streaked like molten gold across the skies, as if the whole wide world was set alight with dragon fire. The shock was swiftly followed by the roaring of the thunder, of such a force the very ground on which the vardo had been parked began to tremble violently. While this went on our pa stood frozen, as if he sought to hear some music in the wild cacophony of every pot and ornament rattling in the van around us. The coins I dropped to the floor set up another clattering, before I reached for Tilly's hand, meaning to make a dash for it. But with Pa's bulk blocking the door, there was no way for us to pass. No way to avoid the alarming manic stare on the face that turned yet darker as his fury boiled over and exploded in a great volcanic punching of his fists.

Luckily, he was so addled by the ale he'd been imbibing, most of his blows missed their targets. But, even so, despite our shrieks and all the scratching of our nails in an attempt to fend him off, he proved to be a great deal stronger, forcing us back towards the bed on which we fell, and where I wrapped my larger body over Tilly's in an effort to protect her.

How long we lay there, I don't know. But the fury of the storm continued raging for some hours, rain battering the vardo roof as we were battered by our pa, until, at last, he slumped, exhausted, on the velvet-cushioned bench – where by the light of the moon that slanted through unshuttered windows, we saw the white of his good eye, still open wide, still fixed on us as we cowered on that bed and didn't dare to move an inch

When the morning came around and the storm had blown away, he was on his feet again, casting a shadow of such gloom as he grabbed us by the hair and all but flung us through the door, down to the puddled grass below. Towering on the steps above, looking like some mad King Lear, he raised his head and bellowed out to all the other fairground wagons: 'How sharper than a serpent's tooth it is to have a thankless daughter, and I am cursed with two of them. Two wicked girls who plot and scheme to betray their loyal father. Who will take them off my hands? Come on. Get up, out of your beds, you lazy sods. You drunken oafs...' His voice became more plaintive, 'Won't anyone make me an offer?'

'Here's my offer, if you'll take it.'

Pa heard those words and looked askance. To this day I don't believe he was expecting any answer. But there it was, a clear, deep voice that held a hint of foreign accent.

Wiping the mud from my eyes, I turned around to see a wolfhound, its fur a pale silver, and at its side there was a man, his own grey hair worn long and loose below a showy spangled hat. He wore a dark-green velvet jacket, over which his arms were folded, and as he stood there, quite at ease, so my senses burrowed up through the exhaustion and the shock to realise that I had seen him at the show the night before. He'd been distinctive in the crowd due to his height and fancy clothes. He'd lacked the usual dull gaze of any dupes in thrall to Pa. Neither did he have the look of the fairground's leery men who sometimes wished to offer me a dose of medicine that had nothing to do with Pa's elixir. No, his eyes did not hold lust, and yet they left me queerly giddy. Not any physical response. More like a kind of understanding. A prickle in my blood that made me feel as if I knew him. Such a certainty it was. If not in the past, or in the present moment, I *would* know him in the future.

In the dreary dawning light, the stranger smiled at Alfred Lovell and replied, 'I've heard from friends around the camp that you're a man who likes to gamble now and then, although of late you may have lost somewhat more than you have gained. May I suggest another bet? We toss a coin. The best of three, and if you win then I will press one hundred guineas in your hand. If *I* win, I'll give you double, and...' he left a hanging pause '...I'll take your daughters as you ask.'

'What sort of game is that?' Pa scoffed. His voice was gruff, as rough as any badger's arse. 'Are you some vazey-minded fool recently fallen off his rocker, thinking you have the wit to try and twit with Alfred Lovell?'

'I suppose that some might call me a showman, like yourself,' came the silkier reply, just as the wolfhound started growling, before its master touched its head and softly murmured, 'Dolce, hush.'

Alfred Lovell was not hushed. His face was livid, glowering, when he offered his response: 'In what area of trade?'

Pa's fists were clenched against his sides, his lips drawn back to bare his teeth when the grey-haired man replied, 'I am a musician of the itinerant persuasion. I frequent the Thameside towns, down to Reading in the west, and heading east as far as Gravesend. At other times I am more prone to ply my trade in London theatres.'

As if to prove that what he'd said contained some element of truth, he reached a hand into his coat, drawing out a silver flute which he then pressed against his lips. Such a sweet melody it was, weaving some net around my heart; until Pa went and broke the spell, calling out contemptuously, 'I doubt you haunt enough grand theatres to afford to pay the fee you've offered me today.'

The man removed his spangled hat and tipped it upside down to reveal a wad of notes secured within the inner band.

'Hmm,' Pa said, his interest piqued, as the stranger cast his eyes across the sprawl of the fairground where, already, there were signs of people waking from their beds. Waving the flute above his head, the stranger whistled through his lips, and then called out, 'Hey, you ... you, boy! Do you chance to have a penny in your pocket you could loan us?'

'Might 'ave. What's the deal?' A corny-looking youth, about the age of me and Tilly, removed the stub of cigarette that had been pursed between his lips. Throwing that down, he carried on, splashing towards us through the puddles as the stranger offered thanks. 'If you'll toss it just three times, I shall make it worth your while.'

'S'pose I could.' The sulky boy, not in the least bit prepossessing, stooped down to pull a penny from the lining of his boot. Clearly warming to his task, he flipped it over in one hand and asked, 'What's yer choice then. 'Eads or is it tails?'

With an easy elegance, the stranger placed his flute back in his pocket and replied, 'Oh ... I don't know. You decide.'

'Fair 'nough,' the boy decreed, a knowing twinkle in his eye. 'You takes the bottoms. Him the tops.'

'Is that acceptable to you?' the grey-haired man enquired of Pa, a strange, long emphasis on 'is', so that it sounded more like 'eez'.

With another surly grunt Pa nodded his assent and was soon grinning like a loon when heads came spinning up three times, whereas the man he'd played against wore but the twitching of a smile when he flicked the skinny boy a bright new shilling for his labours.

I did think that somewhat strange, though Pa appeared not to have noticed, or to question why the stranger called the boy to show a coin, when all the while he had been in possession of his own.

Now, as the lad went running off, the wad of money that the

stranger had revealed beneath his hat was exposed a second time. With the dog close at his side, he strolled towards the vardo steps, where the notes were counted out, one by one, into Pa's palm. After that, without the slightest remonstration of remorse, Pa stuffed the money in his pocket, then dipped a hand into the vardo for the carpet bag we'd packed for our flight the night before. This he threw down the steps towards us, after which he turned his back. The door was slammed as a full stop, and it seemed that that was that. No fond goodbye. No fare-ye-wells. More like, *Fuck off, and go to Hell.*

Not knowing what to say, I watched the stranger place his hat back on his head and then stretch down to lift our luggage from the ground. His other hand reached out for Tilly's. Her tiny fingers twined through his, and off they went, across the steamy morning grasses of the Brocas. The dog did linger for a while, gently nosing at my skirts before the rain set in again, when it followed in their wake, leaving me standing there alone, realising that my future would not take the stranger's path. Not in the present, or the future. It was Tilly. Only Tilly he had wanted. Never me.

Some time I dithered by the steps, feet glued in mud while getting drenched, and wondering to myself, *Should I knock on the door and ask to be let in again?* A moment later I was looking through a gap around the side, seeing Pa slouched across the bed on which I'd lain so recently. Already he was snoring, fast asleep, no guilt to see in the smile upon his lips. Almost as if he was no longer my own father but a stranger, I saw anew the ugly red of the grog blossom of his nose, the spittle drooling from his mouth – the dullish glinting of the blade of the knife held in his hand.

Why would Pa be clutching that? Did he have reason to suspect the grey-haired man would be returning with intent to do him harm, or to reclaim his wad his money? What if he woke that very moment, saw me standing at the door, and in a madness of confusion swung the knife in my direction?

Not knowing what to do, my eyes went searching through the
van – and saw the crystal ball inside its box above the bed. It might
have been the very one our ma had mentioned in her stories of
Bohemia the Gyptian, in which Bohemia had dabbled in the arts
of prophesying.

Ma once said she'd seen a gruesome-looking thing beside that
ball. The heart of a dead cow pierced with countless rusted nails,
which Bohemia then told her had been used to curse a farmer
who'd set fire to the vardos owned by travellers who'd hoped to
make their camp upon his land. One little boy, no more than two,
had perished in the blaze. With no hope of any justice from the
law to set things right, Bohemia swore to take revenge. Within a
month, word arrived to say that milk from every cow set out to
pasture by that farmer could not be sold because it curdled. Next,
the herd became diseased and almost all the creatures died. Finally,
the man himself collapsed in a seizure, never to speak another
word. His every limb was paralysed.

Emboldened by that tale, my eyes dropped down to Pa again.
He looked fair paralysed with booze. Could I creep towards the
bed and prise the weapon from his hand, then use the blade to cut
his throat? Wasn't that what he deserved, having beaten his own
daughters to a pulp of dread and terror, before he sold them to a
stranger with no question of intentions? Tilly and me, we might
as well have been two lambs sent to the slaughter. Why should I
not slaughter him?

Realising how near I'd come to murdering the man, I doubled
up. I thought I'd vomit. But if the horror of last night had taught
me anything at all, it was that I could not remain another day with
Alfred Lovell. Nor could I ever go back home to the cottage where
his Betsy had usurped our mother's life.

With a pounding in my head, I slowly turned and, inch by inch,
headed back down the ladder steps. I looked on past the maze of
wagons towards the empty stretch of common, and I felt as if my
heart might break in two when I could see no further sign of Tilly

THE FASCINATION 75

Lovell. But there was still one hope to cling to. And that was Theo,
by the river. Hadn't he promised he'd be waiting? If only I still had
the purse Pa had pilfered from his friend. But that was in the
carpet bag. The bag the stranger carried off.

The rain came down yet heavier as I walked towards the river.
I searched the banks, but it was hopeless. I thought, *Keziah you
are mad. He will be gone. Of course he's gone. Who would have
stayed out here all night in the thunder and the rain?* But for a while
my hopes persisted. I poked my head beneath the willows where
they formed the emerald curtain through which he'd first
emerged. I told myself he might have crawled back underneath in
search of shelter, and – how desperate were the notions of my wild
imaginings – that he'd drifted off to sleep, like some new Ophelia
among the willowherb and comfrey.

Well, God's Gift might well have gone, but someone else *was*
very near. Someone who reeked of nicotine, who poked me
roughly on the shoulder as he asked, 'You coming then? We're
about ready for the off. Can't dilly dally 'ere all day. What if your
old man sobers up and then decides he wants you back? You need
to make yer mind up. Is it us, or is it 'im?'

Spinning round, I saw a face I recognised and then replied: 'You
again? Leave me alone. Go and spend your silver sixpence.'

'Maybe I will. Maybe I won't ... spend me winnings that would
be. Mind you...' he squinted back through the thinning mists of
drizzle '...that fair looks very tawdry in the cold 'ard light of day,
wouldn't you agree? Like some old whore, all painted up, she
shines as bright as Christmas glitter in the hours of the night, but
come the dawn she drops her drawers and what is lying
underneath is not the most alluring sight. Better take yer chance
elsewhere. But, it's only right to tell you, that penny in me boot,
it is a coin that 'as two heads and never any tail to show. Comes
in useful now and then, should Captain 'ave a need, though most
occasions he plays straight, as you will see with your own eyes ...
if you'll only shift yerself and join the boat before she sails.'

He smiled to show his crooked teeth, most of them brown from nicotine. Some as black as Tilly's after drinking her elixir. I rubbed my tongue across my own and could taste the acrid vomit that had risen in my mouth during the height of Pa's assault. The stink it left upon my breath made me clamp my lips tight shut. But then, I had no need to speak, for it seemed this boy considered me to be some senseless fool as he grabbed me by the hand and dragged me off along the bank – until we came upon a boat that could have been another vardo; rather shabby in appearance, but painted up in such bright colours, and poking through the roof a chimney flue was puffing steam.

'Come on.' The boy now motioned to a door upon the deck, where the upper part was opened and another head extended. In that head were two brown eyes amid a mask of thick, dark hair, which caused my mind to wander back to *Snow-White and Rose-Red* – the scene in which, one winter's night, someone knocks upon their door, and when Snow-White goes to look she finds the most enormous bear. Snow-White screams in mortal dread. Snow-White tries to run away, to hide beneath her mother's bed. But the bear comes in and finds her, kneeling down as it says –

'Don't be afraid. I have not come to do you any harm! I am half-frozen in the forest and only want to feel some warmth. If I could lie at your side and hold you in my arms, then...'

Then what?

The story was reversed. *I* was outside and shivering, and very near delirious due to the lack of any sleep. So, when the cabin door was opened, when the bear nimbly ascended the ladder steps to stand before me, my head began to spin. The world turned black. I was quite blind, but still aware of being lifted...

I knew no more until I woke, lulled by the motion of the boat as it was sailing up the Thames. And wasn't that a strange commotion, with all the washing and the splashing as we rocked upon the water, yet more precarious each time another boat went surging past and trailed great eddies in its wake. I heard the clanking of chains. The snaps of sails. The fearful screeching of the gulls, which seemed so near that I supposed they must have perched upon the roof above our heads. Horns were tooting. Men were whistling, shouting greetings from their vessels. Somewhere a dog was barking. A low deep bark, that could have been the wolfhound seen upon the Brocas. And, in amongst all these distractions, which were really not so different to the pounding raucous clatter of the fair's machinery, it was the nicest thing on earth to hear my sister's soothing voice. 'Keziah. Dear Keziah. Can't you hear me? Won't you wake?'

I felt her hand upon my brow, soft as the wings of butterflies. Her fingers pushed away the hair that had slipped across my eyes. And when that barrier was gone, what a shock it was to see Tilly's bruised and swollen face.

'What has he done to you this time?' My mouth was parched. My voice was weak. I had a throbbing in my head, and many other aches and pains reminding me that there had been more than the one punching bag for Pa.

'Please. Do not try to move.' The bear, who was a man – was I still dreaming, or gone mad and lost in wild hallucinating? – was standing not far off, and he was speaking in a deep and mellow voice which, to my ears, also held a foreign accent. Although it lacked the softer music of the man with silver hair, still it seemed no less exotic.

'Stay there and rest,' he carried on. 'It is not so very long before we are at Captain's house.'

I strained my neck to look around, and even though my eyes were blurred I thought again how odd it was, the way this river boat resembled the old vardo I was used to. There was a little iron stove, and rows of bunks behind thick drapes, such as the one on which I lay, and from where I tried to rise as I asked, 'Are you ... the Captain?'

'I am Aleski Turgenev. Captain is at the helm. You are safe with him. With me. With Ulysses as well. None of us will do you harm.'

'Ulysses?'

'That'll be me,' announced the boy with baccy breath, a ciggie dangling from his lips as he continued to explain. 'Gave me the moniker, did Captain, when I was nothing but a scrap found lost and 'ungry on the streets. Said no other name would suit, due to my brave, intrepid nature and my love of wandering.'

'Oh, I see. I ... think I ... see.'

Again, my eyes were dimming, only aware of smells of coffee, toasting bread, and marmalade. It made me smile and picture Ma making our breakfast in the kitchen. It made me think that I was sleeping, that I was dreaming. Happy dreams. But soon enough I would wake up and find myself back in the vardo. Back on the road with Alfred Lovell.

SEVEN

LORD SEABROOK'S LETTER

This is set to be a day of dramatic revelations for which Theo is not equipped. He's only had a few hours' sleep, and someone's shaking his arm, calling his name repeatedly. Brass curtain rings are jangling as the bedroom drapes are opened, leaving him dazzled by the light, through which he sees Miss Miller's blurring silhouette beside the bed.

What is she doing in my room? Still half asleep, his head is thick and feels too heavy on his shoulders. He drags the sheet a little higher to conceal his naked body as she breathlessly exclaims, 'You must get dressed and come downstairs. There's been a theft. A dreadful theft.'

'A theft? Oh ... yes. Your purse.' The Brocas memories flood back. The girls. Those dark-haired girls who'd left him waiting by the river.

Miss Miller wrings her hands. 'Not my purse. Lord Seabrook's study. The kitchen door was left open. Did we forget to lock it up?'

Did I forget to lock it up after returning from the Brocas? This is the thought in Theo's mind as he flings on his dressing gown and follows Miss Miller down the stairs towards the study. Still in the hall, he takes a moment to knot the cord at his waist – and senses something else is wrong. He turns around in consternation, looking back towards the staircase, where the aged and po-faced portraits of his Seabrook ancestors are staring blankly from their frames. But his mother's eyes aren't there. Where her likeness hung before, there is nothing but an empty, faded square upon the wall.

He feels unsteady on his feet, almost as if he's being sucked into the vacuum of her absence. His mother may be dead, but through that picture he had known her. It was as if she'd still existed in the paint upon a canvas. And now she's gone. His mother's gone.

Was she still there when he'd come home, already dawn and light enough to notice anything amiss? And – Theo stiffens as he wonders – had he played the fool accomplice when he mentioned Dorney Hall by its name to those two sisters? Any house employing servants would be a source of valuables. What if they'd followed him back home? What if they'd told their thieving father there were bigger fish to fry than stolen purses at a fair?

'Theo!' Miss Miller calls from beyond the study door, the wooden frame of which is fractured where the rim lock has been forced. Wary of splinters in bare feet, Theo gingerly steps past any debris on the floor and enters the room where Cook is at Miss Miller's side. Both are staring at the desk where every drawer has been pulled out and left suspended at odd angles. Lying on the boards nearby are crumpled heaps of correspondence, and many formal-looking papers. Also pornographic pamphlets showing bawdy cartoon whores posed in the most indecent acts with men and animals alike. Books on biology and science have been taken from the shelves and left discarded over tables. Many pages still lie open, as if the burglars had been searching for specific information. *Educated thieves?*

Someone has opened the shutters where all the windows are intact, so why is there a maid sweeping glass shards into a pan? None of the study's display cases appear to have been damaged. But what about the rarer specimens? Lord Seabrook's private collection? Theo glances round and sees the book-lined door swinging open on its hinges. Only an inch or two ajar. Unless you knew of its existence, you'd be unlikely to notice. But he knows, and now his ears are filled with sounds like rushing water, through which he hears Cook prattling. Something about having sent the gardener's boy into town to organise a telegram to reach Lord Seabrook's London house. Something about not being sure if they should wait for a reply before they call in the police.

Is she speaking to him? If so, he doesn't answer. No longer caring if he cuts his naked feet on broken glass, Theo steels himself to enter the nightmare of his past. But is it relief or disappointment he feels to find the monsters gone? As a hazy moted light shafts through the open door behind him, he sees no hand of glory. No child with a tusk protruding from its forehead. No withered monkey mermaid. No fairy floating in a bottle. Only one object still remains. The densely furred and lupine features of the lycanthrope's large head is lying on the floor. The glass the maid is sweeping up may well be from the broken dome that once protected it from dust. One marble eye has slipped its socket. Theo kneels down and picks it up. For a moment he is lost in admiration for the artistry involved in its creation, where the tiniest of brushstrokes replicate flecks of light glinting in the irises.

He lets it drop. There is a clomp and it rolls across the boards. Miss Miller must have heard, and now her footsteps are approaching as she nervously cries out, 'Where have you disappeared to, Theo?'

Luckily, she does not enter. She is distracted by the maid, which allows sufficient time for him to edge back through the door and draw it closed before he says, 'It's just a storeroom. Thought I'd check, but nothing seems to be disturbed.'

Reaching for her arm, he steers her to the leather chair positioned close beside the hearth. The tiger skin still lies before it, looking as threatening as ever. *A shame the thieves left that behind.*

She sits and says, 'I do feel queer. Such a headache again. It must be all the stress ... waking up and finding this. What an act of desecration!'

Theo thinks about the brandy and the tincture that Miss Miller drank so eagerly last night. Turning to Cook, he suggests, 'Do you think you could make a pot of tea for Miss Miller? Something sweet and strong, to help with the shock.'

'A grand idea is that, young master,' Cook replies, and makes a start on bustling back to her domain, where every pot and pan and spoon remains precisely in its place. And on the table are there still the bottles of Lovell's Elixir? But, before she's had the chance to even reach the study door, the front-porch bell begins to chime, and she exclaims, 'Good Lord. Who's that?'

Miss Miller rises from the chair and heads towards a window bay. She says, 'I'm sure it's not Lord Seabrook. Even if there had been time for him to get the telegram, how could he possibly arrange to travel home again so quickly?'

As she continues staring out, her fingers plucking at her skirts, Theo is alarmed to see the strain upon her features. Cook is much the same, even releasing a small shriek when the bell rings again. This time she calls to the maid, 'Chop, chop, girl. Are you deaf? Put down that pan and answer it. And you can give your hair a tidy in the mirror on the way. Your cap is all skew-whiff, and your apron's coming loose. We do have standards in this house, even after such a morning.'

All of this is being said as Cook stares pointedly at Theo. He's hardly dressed for visitors. But what to do when he can hear the heavy rattling of chains, and then the maid's slow lilting tones, met by some deeper mumblings. However, when she reappears there is no guest to be announced. Instead, she holds an envelope.

'Well?' Cook demands.

The bullied girl speaks sullenly. 'Only the postman, with this letter. It's addressed to Master Theo.'

Whether or not his grandfather has yet received the telegram with information of the theft, this correspondence from him, penned and dated yesterday, refers to quite a different matter, and one that is no less surprising –

To Theodore,

My departure from the house this afternoon was due to hearing of the happiest event. In short, I have become the father of a healthy boy, perfectly formed in every way. He will now become my heir and carry on the Seabrook line. The mother, who has been a close acquaintance for some years, has agreed that we shall wed and legitimise his name just as soon as I am able to obtain a marriage licence.

I mean to bring my family to reside at Dorney Hall. Zephyrina is already making plans for renovations. As I'm sure you can imagine, the expense of such works will be a drain on my finances. With this in mind, I shall no longer be providing any monies for your continued education. I understand that this may come as something of a disappointment, but on the whole your expectations should not be that ill-affected. Up to now you have received more advantages than most, all of which stands you in good stead for an independent future.

My man, Clements, will arrive at Dorney Hall later this week to oversee the arrangements I have made for your departure. He will provide you with funds more than sufficient for your travel and to secure yourself some lodgings. For this new era in your life choose whatever name you will, but I suggest you refrain from employing that of Seabrook. After all, you are a bastard. It was never yours to take.

Would you also please ensure that Miss Miller understands she must vacate the house as well? She does not leave it unrewarded, already being in receipt of a generous bequest gifted in my first wife's will.

And, with that, I do believe every matter is concluded,
Yours respectfully, etc...

Theo has scanned the letter swiftly and now he stands in a daze. *'Every matter is concluded'? What will I do? How can I live? I have no skills for anything. What sort of name is Zephyrina? Who is this whirlwind of a woman who has blown into my life to cause such chaos and disruption?*

He folds the letter and he slips it in the pocket of his gown. No matter how distraught, he must compose himself and find some way to let Miss Miller know of his grandfather's decisions. But the task will have to wait, because the doorbell chimes again. This time a telegram arrives. A reply to the one sent off to Knightsbridge earlier.

Miss Miller takes it from the maid and reads the words for all to hear:

"'DO NOT INVOLVE POLICE AND CAUSE UNNECESSARY SCANDAL. CLEMENTS WILL JUDGE IF ACTION NEEDED. MEANWHILE INSTRUCT THE STAFF TO MAKE ALL PREPARATIONS FOR THE IMMINENT ARRIVAL OF MY WIFE AND NEWBORN SON.'"

'His wife? His wife and son!' Miss Miller lets the paper drop.

Cook shakes her head. For once she's speechless.

Theo is numb, his fingers reaching in his pocket once again to touch the news that it contains, to somehow prove that it is real and not the figment of a dream.

Silently and stiffly, almost like an automaton, he leaves the room and walks upstairs. He'll wash and dress, and pack whatever things he'll need for his departure. Some clothes. His favourite books. The sketchbooks filled with hybrid freaks imagined in his darkest dreams, though what deformity is worse than a man who has no heart? How could Lord Seabrook be so callous?

He does not go downstairs for lunch. He cannot eat. He feels sick. How can he sit beside Miss Miller and not tell her of her fate? But he *must* find a way to do it, and before the day is out. She also needs to make arrangements, and before the valet comes to see them off the premises. That is one indignity Theo hopes they'll both be spared. He may be foolish in his pride, but he refuses to accept a single penny from Lord Seabrook.

He and Miss Miller meet at dinner. As before, they sit outside. Despite the upset of the theft, and the shock that there will soon be a new mistress in the house, Cook has rallied and produced an iced pea soup, a salmon tarte, and then a cake. Strawberries and cream. All are dishes he would normally devour greedily, but tonight he cannot taste them. He might as well be eating dust, and Miss Miller is the same. Her silver cutlery is chinking on the gilding of her plate, but not a morsel finds her lips. She looks too tired. She is too quiet. The energy that flows between them is too heavy and oppressive, almost as if another storm might erupt at any moment. And yet the rain has cleared. The skies are blue, barely a cloud. The air is calm. The birds are singing.

Only when sipping at their coffee, when the maids have cleared the table, does Theo swallow anxiously, and then begin to explain. 'The letter I received before the telegram arrived, it was to say that Lord Seabrook wants me gone from this house.'

'Gone? Oh, my dear boy!' Miss Miller's hands are trembling. Her cup is tipped. A large brown stain spreads across the linen cloth. Not that she seems to notice. Instead, she looks from left to right as if ensuring no one's near, and then goes on in hurried tones. 'Surely, that can't be right? Have you mistaken his intentions?'

He shakes his head and then removes the letter from a trouser pocket. Silently, he hands it over. Silently she reads, and the flushing of her face reveals the rising of emotions when Miss Miller shuts her eyes and lays the page down on the table. There, coffee seeps into the weave and the ink begins to blur. Lord Seabrook's words are disappearing, but his malice remains.

She takes a breath, exhales again, opens her eyes and stares at Theo. 'I suspected yesterday. Indeed, I have for several months. When he went dashing up to town, I guessed that something was afoot. I have already packed my bags and said goodbye to the staff. I've asked the grooms to organise a horse and trap first thing tomorrow. I mean to go to Windsor station, and from there back home to Sussex.' Her slender fingers twine through his. 'My Bosham house is very small, but large enough for two to live in. What do you say?' Her smile is bright, and though her eyes are filled with tears there is the glimmer of some hope – before she turns towards the gardens and her expression grows more desperate. 'But first, there is a task I must perform before I leave. I wonder, Theo ... will you help?'

❈

It is not fully dark when the clocks are striking ten, and so they wait until it's twelve, and in that hour of ghosts and witching they leave the house by the front door, that way avoiding any servants who might not yet be in their beds.

Theo follows Miss Miller through the shadows of the gardens towards the grove of silver birches. Among the trees there is the ornamental statue of a child. In its hands it holds a bowl that Miss Miller very often fills with seed to feed the birds. But tonight she only carries a folded cotton sheet, a ball of string, and some brown sacking. Meanwhile, Theo has a spade found in one of the gardeners' sheds. She is precise about the spot where he is asked to dig a hole, and though at first the ground is hard, riven with roots and heavy stones, he persists, and gradually the spade edge meets with something solid. There is a dull metallic clang.

'Stop!' she cries, before she throws her body down on the ground, plunging both arms into the hole, her fingers scratching at the soil still covering what looks to be some form of storage box. It is about twelve inches wide and perhaps two feet in length.

Theo helps to drag it up, and then employs his spade again, this time to strike the rusted lock and free the lid, and, as it lifts, Miss Miller sobs, 'I've come to find you ... to take you home with me. Didn't I promise I would never leave you here alone again?'

Has Miss Miller gone quite mad? Theo is shocked at these hysterics. He supposes this must be the grave of some beloved pet. He remembers her once speaking of a cat in the house, although apparently Lord Seabrook often kicked the creature cruelly, disapproving of the way it always hissed when he approached. And then, there was the day it was found dead, for which there'd never been a thorough explanation. Or did she know, and never dare to point the finger at the villain?

But what Miss Miller now confides contains no mention of a

cat. 'My child. My precious child. He didn't even live a day. There was something wrong. They said his bones weren't fully formed. They were too delicate, too brittle. Some had ruptured through his flesh during the trauma off the birth. To hear his cries, it was a torment. Such a blessing when the midwife came to give him ... well, whatever had been needed at the time to ease his passage from this world into the mercy of the next.'

Miss Miller ... had a baby? Theo's thoughts are fizzing. 'Why was a child buried here? Why in the garden, with no gravestone?'

The words are barely off his tongue when she reveals the awful truth.

'Lord Seabrook was the father. Long before Anne's death, he'd started visiting my bed. I should have left when it first happened. His needs were selfish and depraved. I can't say why it carried on. There must have been something as base in my own soul as in his own, and for that sin I was then punished.' Suddenly, her voice is pleading. 'Please don't judge me. I believed he only wished to be consoled. I trusted him when he insisted he would never let me down if our affair should chance to lead to...' she can hardly say the words '...to any natural consequence. But when that happened, he demanded I should have the child aborted. He made me swear never to tell another soul of my condition, for what about his dying wife? Did I wish to break her heart?'

She heaves a sigh, then carries on: 'Anne died three months before the birth, after which I started suffering appalling bouts of sickness. That in itself did not seem right. I thought it could have been my grief, but then I came to fear it must be caused by all the powders your grandfather provided as an aid for my digestion. I have no way to prove it and, God knows, I may be damned to entertain such wicked thoughts, but I did wonder afterwards if my baby's tragic fate had been decided by its father. Although, when the child died, he did show some remorse, bringing me here to lay the body in this grove, where I could visit. Where it would never be suspected that...'

'None of the other staff had guessed?' Theo is struggling to stay calm and not distress Miss Miller further.

'I never did grow very large, and corset stays concealed the swelling. Only the midwife who'd attended me in labour knew the truth, and she was paid for her discretion.' Miss Miller gives a bitter laugh. 'Once the baby had been buried, I went back home to Bosham. It was after your birth that Lord Seabrook wrote to ask if I'd return in the role of your nurse, then governess. I suppose I was a fool, but he professed to having missed me, and I believed that in some way he felt you were the consolation for the loss of my own son.'

'I would be proud to be your son.' Theo takes her hands in his, and as the words spill from his lips he realises they are true.

'Dearest Theo!' She is smiling, hands wiping at her eyes, smearing her cheeks with mud. 'For all the upsets in the past, your grandfather did one good thing in introducing me to you. And living here in Dorney Hall, I could still be near the grave of the child I'd abandoned. But I won't leave him this time. I mean to take him back to Sussex, where I hope to find some way to bury him in hallowed ground ... even if I have to creep into the graveyard in the night and dig the hole with my own hands.'

Miss Miller's eyes are lowered as she peers beneath the lid into the darkness of the box. Very cautiously and slowly her fingers reach inside, but what she draws back out has no solidity whatever. Held in her shaking hands is a flimsy piece of cloth that simply crumbles into dust when it meets the open air. She's picking through the scraps and crying out in her confusion. 'He isn't here. There's nothing here? Oh...' Her eyes are wide in desperation. 'Could it have been the thieves ... the ones who broke into the house? I *did* see someone in the garden.'

'But the ground was undisturbed.'

Miss Miller nods, 'Of course, you're right. I can't think clearly anymore.'

Somewhat stiffly she rises to her feet, craning her neck so as to look up through the trees towards the brightly shining moon. She appears to be quite calm, until the wail escapes her mouth: 'Where are my precious son's remains?'

Her breaths are sawing, struggling as Theo holds his arms out wide to draw her into his embrace. His eyes are closed to try and shut the awful image from his mind. But it's no good. He clearly sees the newborn baby with the shards of splintered bones poking out through its near-translucent flesh. The specimen in the bottle he'd been shown as a child. The one he'd thought to be a fairy.

And now, it's gone. It has been stolen. But who has taken it, and where?

PART TWO

Come Unto Me ...

EIGHT

INTRODUCING
HARE-LIPPED MARTHA

Whenever thinking back to that first night in Captain's house, it is a memory that flutters like a candle in a wind. Some of the images are hazy. Others remain as clear as day. The softness of the sheets. My fingers wrapped round Tilly's hand. Her forehead resting on my breast. And then the morning when we woke and somewhat stiffly left the bed, walking towards a large gilt mirror propped against a re-flocked wall. Dressed only in our shifts – *where had our dresses gone?* – we stood there, side by side, and through the oddly blackened speckle of the glass we saw two ghosts. Where the flesh had not been bruised our skin was white as alabaster, which only emphasised the more the darkness of our hair and eyes, and my sister's heart-shaped mole.

Of course, we'd seen reflections of ourselves at other times. In the small mirror that our ma used to keep next to her washstand. In the distortion of the diamond panes of glass in casement windows in the cottage in the lane. But we had never been so visible as this, with every inch of us exposed from head to foot, and I confess it was a shock. Tilly, so delicately formed, could be a child of half my age. Or a living china doll, her eyes too large and glittering, just the way they always were after a dose of Pa's elixir. But at the time that was a fact I didn't pause to comprehend, being caught up in noticing how I looked lumpy and misshapen. My arms and legs were long and coltish. My breasts had started budding, the nipples prominent and brown below the cotton of my shift.

Breaking through my consternation came my sister's plaintive cry. 'Kezi, why am I a shrimp? Who would believe that we were twins? Might there be some medicine that I could take to make me grow ... to make me look like you again?'

An unknown voice with nasal vowels, consonants lisped and indistinct, surprised us both with the reply. 'Don't waste your breath or expectations on any miracles of science.'

Neither one of us had noticed the buxom, dark-skinned woman who had joined us in the room. But, she wasn't quite a stranger, for at that moment I remembered I'd seen her there before, during the fug of night-time hours – when her brown eyes had glittered brightly in the flames of candlelight, although that gentle radiance had not concealed a sneering mouth, which I confess had frightened me. However, in the light of day, I realised that her expression was not due to any cruelty but a deformity of nature, whereby the upper lip did not join below the nose, but rather split into two, forming a cleft through which I saw her teeth and gums, even her tongue – to which she often raised a cloth to dab the dribbling of spittle when her talking carried on:

'Leastways, you waifs and strays are up and on the mend. Are you hungry? There's a beef and carrot stew down in the kitchen. First, I'll show you to the rooms where you'll be sleeping in the future. Aleski kindly gave his up when you were both in such a state and we had no others ready, but I imagine he would like to have his comforts back again. Wouldn't you agree?'

'Oh!' Tilly said when hearing this, all wide-eyed innocence and smiles. 'I would have thought the bed in here is big enough for three of us.'

The woman gave her short shrift. 'Well, wherever Captain found you ... and by the look of all those bruises it's a good thing that he did ... this is a decent house.' Another pause to stress that fact before she carried on again. 'There are more rooms along the passage and they should do you very well. They both have pretty papered walls. One with red roses. One with white.'

Roses, red and white? What a serendipity. But even so, I felt reluctant at the thought of separate beds, for I had never spent a night apart from Tilly in my life.

Meanwhile, the sneering woman opened up this bedroom's wooden shutters, raising the sashes of the window to let the fresh air flow inside, before she wryly announced, 'I don't suppose you'll try to jump and run away, unless you're mad. If I were you, I'd say a prayer to thank the Lord that you've been blessed to have this chance to come and live with Captain and his crew.'

What was this crew? I was beginning to suspect that me and Tilly might have been stolen by a sect of religious maniacs. Was this woman one of those wild evangelisers, the ones who turned up at the fairgrounds, bellowing their soapbox sermons, quoting the Bible át one moment before then bursting into song?

Well, singing hymns and chanting prayers was the last thing on my mind. Right then my main concern was what I'd spied beside the door. 'Our bag!' I rushed towards it, opening the big brass clutches to plunge my hands deep down inside, where, as far as I could tell, nothing we'd packed had been disturbed. There was the stolen purse we'd been hoping to return to Theo by the river. And Tilly's china figurines were still miraculously intact. As were the bottles of Elixir chinking together in the folds of some of Tilly's clothes, and one of them already opened. The cork was stained a gluey black.

I couldn't think of what to say. I'd hoped that leaving Pa behind would also mean my sister leaving her addiction in the vardo. Now, in a stupor of my own, I stood and walked towards the light of hazy green cast by the trees growing so tall outside the window. I leaned across the open frame and pressed my palms flat on the sill. The stone was crumbling in places. It was sticky with a residue of silky silvered threads, and the desiccated grey of tiny wings of ... dying moths? I saw a maggoty white worm. I picked it up between two fingers, and then – I don't know why – squeezed and squeezed until it burst. Nothing left of it but pus.

Wiping my hand on my shift, I stared on downwards through the leaves and caught a glimpse of gravel driveway, though for the most part it was hidden by the tangles of the weeds obscuring borders either side. Further away I saw the chimneys of some other large brick houses, and – could that be a road, and people walking on a pavement? I heard the drumming sound of hooves. First a carriage, then some wagons trundling past tall iron gates closed against the outside world. I wondered, were they locked? And, if they were, did that mean we'd been imprisoned in this house, just like two fairy-tale princesses?

What sort of scrape had we got into?

After our journey up the Thames, I could recall leaving the boat and being lifted in the arms of the bear man once again. Somewhere below there'd been the thudding of his feet on solid ground. The rising smell of dew-damp grass. Overhead, branches of trees were drooping with the weight of apples. Plums bloomed purple in the glimmer of the lantern being carried by the boy called Ulysses. There were some vegetable gardens, then a door through which the lamplight fell across a great expanse of a kitchen's stone-flagged floor. Rows and rows of gilded china laid across a vast oak dresser. The most enormous iron range. Another door. Another room. The burnished turnings of dark stair-posts. Turkish rugs in jewelled colours, and even crystal chandeliers with drops like stars up the heavens. All so mysterious and strange that I heard myself enquiring in a low and slurring voice, 'Am I in Arabia?'

I was soon to realise that in the harsher light of day this new, exotic world was in a state of some decay. Many furnishings and fabrics had been frayed by use and age. And with the ceilings built so high, spider's webs were trailing down like tangled lace from cornices – which was too poignant a reminder of our old bedroom in the cottage. The make-believe of gauzy veils through which we'd told ourselves so often that our mother's face was smiling from the kingdom of the dead.

Whereas before I would have yearned to touch what lay beyond those veils, now my fingers were content to stroke the dusty, dark-red velvet of this bedroom's window drapes. While doing that, I looked around, noticing a violin case, and some music on a stand. And then, the bed in which we'd slept, very large and made of brass – which caused another jolt of memory to drag me back to Pa, thinking again of the bed he'd bought to share with Betsy Jones.

How glad I was of some distraction from that bitter reminiscing, hearing the hare-lipped woman say: 'As we're alone here in the house, for the next few hours at least, I'll fill the bath down in the kitchen. I'd say you're both in need of a good scrub to get you clean.'

Oh, the tin bath down in the kitchen, back in the cottage in the lane. Another memory of Ma filled my mind as she went on, 'I see you've got some extra clothes in the bag you brought along. What you arrived in has been laundered. But if you'd like to choose the fabrics, I can make you something new ...' At this her eyes glanced back at Tilly. 'The prettiest of girls deserves the prettiest of dresses.'

'Oh, yes please!' Tilly smiled, sounding altogether brighter. My sister always had a yearning for the fripperies of fashion.

At this, the woman pushed aside the plain-white apron she was wearing, so as to show the ruffled blue of the dress worn underneath it. After giving us a twirl – and very nifty on her feet, despite her being what you might have called well-fed and better favoured – she resumed the conversation. 'I've never had such lovely things since I started living here. We all pitch in with our fair share of the skivvying and cooking, though no one's really all that fussy, which leaves me time to make my costumes, using the lace and draperies that I find stored about the house, and—'

'Costumes?' I butted in. 'Like in a fancy-dress parade?'

'I'll turn my hand to that as well. Captain and Mr Turgenev, they are performing gentlemen. They used to travel round the fairs. But now they've made more of a name, their work is mostly done in London. Sometimes, their theatre friends will come and visit Linden House for—'

'Linden House?' Tilly exclaimed. 'I like the sound of that.'

'Theatre friends?' I parroted.

'I dare say,' the woman said, 'you will both be introduced, if you intend on sticking round. It'll be hard for you to miss them. Sometimes the parties last till dawn.'

'I think I heard them in the night,' Tilly said more thoughtfully. 'Someone was playing a piano, or something very like it, although the notes did sound a bit more jingle-jangly. There was some singing too? Such a lovely voice. I wondered if it was an angel, if I'd died and gone to heaven.'

'Well, that won't be Ulysses. When that lad decides to sing it's like having two sharp pencils being poked inside your lugholes. I dare say it was Aleski. He has a counter tenor, and I know he's been rehearsing for—'

'Where is he from?' I bluntly asked, interrupting her again, at the same time feeling sure that I'd heard no sound of singing, and deciding it must be a case of Tilly's black-drop dreaming.

'Well, not from here. Neither is Captain, although these days this is their home as much as it is yours and mine. Indeed, I hope they'll always stay, for wherever should we be without our pair of guardian angels?'

'Then they really *are* from heaven!' Tilly's eyes were twinkling.

The woman sniffed and arched one brow. 'I can see that *you'll* be lively. I hope you won't be causing trouble. No, Captain comes from Italy, and it was there he studied music, and from no other than the famous Mr Signor Rossini.'

Did she see our blank confusion? She tried to clarify the matter. 'All right, I must admit I'd never heard of him myself. But Rossini must be famous, because he wrote a testimonial to praise the Captain's worth, which proved to be the greatest help when he first travelled here to England and was seeking some employment.

He ended up teaching music to the daughters of the gentry, although his present occupations are less conventional in nature. But it's the music that's his passion, and main source of any income. Why, last year he wrote the songs for a Christmas pantomime. The one put on in Drury Lane. Aleski had a starring role.'

'A pantomime!' Tilly gasped.

'Aleski is an actor?' I asked in some confusion. 'What sort of roles does he perform?'

'The sort you might imagine. Last year he played the wolf in *Little Red Riding Hood*. I believe it is beneath him. But he and Captain say the money is too good for them to sneeze at. Frees them up for all the months when they can work on making music of a more serious persuasion.'

'Is Mr Turgenev Italian as well?' I intervened. 'Only he doesn't sound like Captain.'

'No, Aleski comes from Russia, although his accent is mixed up with all sorts of other lingos. All the countries he has visited in childhood I suppose.'

'Was he travelling for long?' I imagined him to be on some Grand Tour as an aristo, for, despite his bearish features he did exude such an air of nobility and grace.

'I think he started very young.' She sucked the spittle from her teeth. 'But then again, with all that hair across his face it's hard to guess what sort of age he might be now. He could be wrinkled like a prune and you still wouldn't have a clue. Which is one benefit he has over everybody else. And, as *you've* obviously heard' – she turned to look at Tilly – 'Aleski really has the most attractive singing voice.'

'Oh no!' Tilly was strident. 'I heard a woman, not a man. I didn't recognise the song, but I *can* remember this.' She raised her head and started singing: *'Shadows are falling. I am sleeping. Love, I am dreaming of thy face. Of thee, only of thee.'*

'Well, well,' the woman said. 'Sweet as a bell and clear as crystal.

Won't Captain be delighted. Next thing you know you'll be on stage and entertaining at his soirees.'

I didn't know what soirees were, but I could hardly disagree that Tilly had a pretty voice. Even so, I'd never heard the words or melody that she had just that moment been recalling. And, as I pondered over that, another quandary filled my mind. 'We met Captain at a fairground ... but you say he doesn't do that sort of travelling these days.'

The woman blithely answered, 'No. The boat they used to sail about the Thames for all the shows rarely leaves the moorings now.'

'But ... they sailed to Windsor.' Tilly also looked confused.

'I wouldn't know the ins and outs, but from what Ulysses let slip it must have been some private matter that Captain was intent on. And then, well, blow me down, if they don't bring you both back home.'

'A surprise for us as well!' My tongue was sharp as acid.

The woman held my gaze. 'He has a thing for waifs and strays, a sort of charitable mission.'

'Were *you* a waif and stray as well?'

'Suppose I must have been.' She sat down upon the bed, and related how she'd also come to live in Captain's house ...

'I had a decent job up west. A milliner's it was, where I'd been 'prenticed as an orphan from the Foundling Hospital. Now and then, the owner let me choose whatever I might like from any scraps of the fabrics left over from the work. I'd make them into flowers, and when I had enough I'd spend my nights pushing a barrow all around the West End theatres, in the hope that wealthy gents might buy a token for their sweethearts. That way I could afford the rent required for my lodgings, in a house up Holborn way, and recommended, if you will, by my employer at the time. It was nothing all that fancy, but respectable and clean, and I had suffered other rooms that were little more than squalor. But what a struggle it had proved to keep that roof above my head. I was thoroughly despondent come one bitter winter's night when there were barely any folks out on the streets to buy my wares until, or so I thought, some lucky star was shining down, sending along a kindly lady who said she wished to purchase every item I possessed.'

She paused to dab her mouth. 'I didn't doubt she could afford them. She smelled so nice. The scent of violets. She said those flowers were her favourites. She spoke with such a cultured voice, and her clothes were finely made. Something strange about her eyes though...'

Her voice trailed off, and she was lost in a moment of reflection before she started up again. 'When she asked if I would walk a little way along with her, to deliver what she'd bought to the steps of her own door, well, I didn't stop to think. What's more it was in Bloomsbury, on the way to my own lodgings. Except I didn't get to find my way back home until much later, because...' she paused to swallow '...the woman asked if I would like some hot chocolate by her fire, and how could I resist such a luxury as that?

'As we drank, she was companionable, and showed the greatest interest in my day-to-day employment. She said she'd once been poor herself, thrust from a comfortable world to one of shame and destitution when her drunkard of a father gambled away the family wealth. Living on nothing but her wits, but always favoured with good looks, she had at first found employment as an actress on the stage. Since then, she'd risen up as a society hostess, whose private club was now attended by a carefully selected clientele of wealthy men. Men with sophisticated tastes that she was happy to provide for.

'Well, there I was imagining the fanciest of dinner parties. Silver dishes. Champagne flutes. People spouting poetry. So when she asked if I'd return another night to do some work on her own hats and evening gowns, for which she'd pay me twice as much as I would normally receive, I very nearly snapped her hand off.'

'That *was* generous,' said Tilly.

'Generosity is judged in deeds as well as words. I was nothing but a fool, and she must have seen me coming. The second time I visited, she poured me out a glass of wine, but I fear it had been doctored with some potion of sedation. I woke again to find myself locked in a room, and with a man who the procuress must have known had a liking for a freak. You see, deformities of nature ... *that* was her speciality.'

She turned her face away from us, as if ashamed of what came next. 'She imprisoned me for weeks, forced me to stand like a waxwork on a plinth in Madam Tussaud's while her gentleman friends paid to come and have a gawp, and to do much more as well. When the interest waned away, I was told it was due to my "surly disposition". I was thrown out onto the street, and when I finally got home it was to find that my lodgings had been leased to someone else. All my possessions had been sold to pay the rent that I'd left owing. Same story at the milliners, where they'd found another girl to come in and take my place. I was feeling so despondent at that news, I walked and walked until I reached the Thames Embankment, where I decided it was best to end the misery for good ... within a whisker of jumping when someone tapped me on the arm to ask if I required assistance.

'I must have looked a dreadful sight. Even so, as you'll imagine, I was not inclined to trust another stranger bent on comfort. Still, as it happened, Captain never had such sinister intentions. And here I am, seven years later, counting my blessings every day. If not for him, I would be dead. Drowned, or frozen in a gutter.'

'Oh, I'm sorry.' Me and Tilly said the words at the same moment.

Hard to tell if she was frowning, or if she smiled to hear our pity. The grimacing on her face was something horrible to see, and I fear she must have noticed the revulsion on our own, for before we'd had a chance to try and wipe those looks away, she'd raised a hand to her mouth to conceal it from our vision – at which point it was remarkable to see how an appearance could be immeasurably enhanced. We only saw her small snub nose, her shining eyes, her dark-brown curls burnished in the summer light that shimmered through the garden trees. It was then I also realised how young this woman was, barely even in her twenties, and with a sudden sense of kinship I reached out to take her hand and simply said, 'I am Keziah, and I'm very glad to meet you.'

'I am Martha,' she replied. 'And I believe this is Tilly. Or so I heard from Ulysses.'

As her hand dropped from her mouth, her voice contained a note of warning. 'A right rascal is that boy. Far too full of cheek these days. You'd be advised to watch him closely, though he's rarely in the house. Where he likes to hang his hat and lay his head these past few years he never says, but I have doubts. For all of Captain's hopes of nurture triumphing over nature, I'd say he's lost the battle there. Ulysses only shows up when he's in hiding from some trouble, tapping Captain for tin, or filching items from this house, before ... puff! He disappears, like a genie from a bottle.'

'He steals?' Tilly asked, as shocked as me to think we'd managed to escape our father's clutches, only to find ourselves immersed inside another den of thieves.

Martha gave a nod. 'I fear that boy is too engrained in whatever life he had before he came to live in Chiswick. Such a skinny little scrap. But even then, he could be sly. Ever since he started growing, sprouting that bumfluff on his chin, he has shown a jealous streak. He'll even take against the dog should Captain deign to give it treats. The fur's grown back more recently, but for a while Dolce's flesh was suppurating with the sores, from all the times when Ulysses stubbed his burning cigarettes out on her nose or her ears. He may deny it, but I've seen him, and I've heard the poor beast whine from other tortures just as wicked ... though whenever he's been challenged, Ulysses will always claim the dog's been scrapping with the rats on the path down by the Thames. Well, Captain may have been persuaded due to his fondness for the boy, but I am far from blind. And I'll tell you now for nothing,

if a child torments a mute, defenceless animal like that, what will
he grow to do to men?'

Martha stood up and left the bed, patting the creases from her
apron. 'I only say these things to warn you. Watch yourselves with
Ulysses. Captain might think he is a sparrow, always flitting here
and there, and who'll eventually be tamed, but...'

'What about the bear?' Tilly butted in.

Martha sounded peeved. 'By the bear I must assume you mean
Aleski Turgenev, who is a man, like another other, only he grows
a deal more hair.'

'Why does he have so much of it?' my sister carried on.

'Why is my mouth like this? Why are you so small? It's the way
we were born. Nothing to be done about it.'

Ignoring jibes about her size, Tilly's questioning went on.
'Where is he now ... the others too?'

'Well, Ulysses went off at dawn, not long after you arrived.
Captain and Aleski left for London after breakfast. No doubt
they're visiting the traders who will buy the merchandise carried
back from their excursion. Mind you, I can't help thinking, what
would anybody want with those decaying specimens? Enough to
give a person nightmares. Wherever did they find them?'

Of course, we were intrigued. What were these specimens she
mentioned? But Martha's mind was moving on, and we were
bustled down the stairs into the kitchen for some food, while she
busied herself with boiling water for our bath. Afterwards, with
towels wrapped around our heads like maharajahs, and with our
modesty preserved by the same shabby shifts we'd been wearing
earlier, we trailed in her wake across the hallway's chequered floor,
where Martha stood before a pair of panelled doors and pushed
them open.

'Ta da!' she announced. 'What do you think? Now, ain't that
something? Have you ever seen the like?'

We most certainly had not, and as I heard my sister's gasp, I also
stared in awe at what appeared to be three rooms, each divided

from the others by a wall of dark-wood shutters that could be closed for privacy or, as we saw them at that moment, thrown open to reveal a space some forty feet in length. As in the bedroom above, the air in here was permeated with a vivid emerald glow from all the untamed foliage pressed against the window glass. It cast an otherworldly hue across a big, black grand piano and an old-fashioned harpsichord painted up with pretty scenes of nymphs and satyrs frolicking. In the middle area were cluttered desks and leathered chairs. Set to one side were smaller tables, still holding cards from games abandoned. Around the walls were shelves of books that I was itching to explore, already missing the old Shakespeare and Ma's book of fairy tales that we'd abandoned in the vardo. Wonderstruck, my eyes skimmed on, over tapestries and rugs, stopping to linger for some time on the sculpted naked forms of marble women who supported the mantle of the hearth, and who would surely look at home in some etchings I'd once seen of the Parthenon in Greece.

'The Captain must be very rich.' Tilly was first to find her tongue. 'To live in such a house.'

'Oh, it's not his,' Martha replied. 'He rents it on the cheap from a family who have no wish to live here anymore. They've often tried to sell, but the transactions always fail. Most likely due to all the rumours of the hauntings, and the scandals.'

'Hauntings?' Tilly asked.

'Scandals?' My ears pricked up.

'Well, mainly it's the murders, as carried out by a gentleman who lived here in the past. He was quite the Georgian dandy. There's his portrait over there. Thomas Wainewright was his name.'

She pointed out a small-framed watercolour picture by the door. It showed a kindly looking man, with plump pink cheeks, and a quizzing glass held up against one eye, through which it seemed that he was staring as intently back at us. But, honestly, without the news that Martha had imparted, you'd never look upon that face and think the man who'd owned it could be capable of murder; which I was just about to say when the lecture carried on:

'He'd inherited his money from a relative who'd published a book called *Fanny Hill*. By all accounts it sold like hot cakes, and is still doing so today. Or so I'm told. I wouldn't know. From what I've heard it is indecent, and I saw more than enough of such blasphemy and filth when I was trapped in Bloomsbury. But even having all the wealth provided by its sales, Mr Wainewright never seemed to have the means with which to cover the expenses he incurred. That's when the murders started up, when certain members of his kin who came to stay here in the house would then depart it in a coffin. There were three of them at least, and in each and every case Mr Wainewright was the heir to any will they might have made.'

'How did he...' Tilly started, while I finished off the sentence: '...go about the killing?'

'He used to wear a ring. It had a secret compartment hidden underneath the stone. And that was where he kept it.'

'Kept what?' We spoke as one.

'Strychnine. For killing rats. The ones that come up from the river here can grow as big as cats, and they are often twice as bold. I found some poison in the larder, thought I'd use it to deter them. But, of course, that had to stop when Ulysses got his white mice. They were a present from Captain. Ulysses kept them in his pockets ... had ideas of teaching them to do a set of circus tricks to demonstrate around the fairs. I even made a small marquee out of some red-and-white striped ticking. But then, one day they disappeared. Every single one. Neither a trace of hide nor hair. Ulysses blamed Dolce. Said the dog had eaten them. But I fear it was a rat.'

'Was he caught? He must have been?' Tilly sounded breathless, any flesh around her bruises now becoming even paler.

'What, the rat?'

'*No*, Mr Wainewright.'

'Well, that's the thing,' Martha continued. 'The so-called poisonings were never really proved until much later. The victims were old, and the doctors who were called to write the death certificates had been duped into agreeing they'd all died of natural causes. No, what Wainewright had been charged with at the start was – wait for this – diddling the Bank of England! Have you ever heard the like? He'd forged the signatures of other wealthy family members, so as to try and lay a claim to a trust fund in their names. He was tried, and he was sentenced, then transported on a ship that sailed halfway around the world until it reached Van Diemen's Land. To you and me, The Devil's Isle.' As Martha said that name she gave an ominous slow nod, indicating it must be the very worst of destinations.

'What do you think ... about the murders?' Tilly anxiously enquired. 'Could this house have restless ghosts?'

'I believe that's nought but bunkum. I've never once experienced more than a creaking of the floorboards. Now and then a window slamming due to sudden gusts of wind can tend to make a person jump. But if there are any screams, or strangely melancholic music heard by those who sometimes loiter on the road outside the gates, it is as likely to have come from the parties Captain holds, and inside these very rooms. I suppose if that will help dissuade the opportunist looters, or any others with a hunch to buy the property themselves, then we must kneel and thank the Lord for his kindly charity. Why, now and then I come in here before I take myself to bed and I raise a glass of port to Mr Wainewright in his portrait. Without his sin and infamy I might be living in the workhouse instead of such a world of splendour. Speaking of which...'

She motioned to a cabinet that stood on curving lions' feet, an arching crest upon the top. And when she opened the doors...

'Oh!' Tilly gasped to see the folded piles of fabrics, rolls of laces. The coloured ribbons, and the buttons.

Meanwhile, Martha explained, 'All of this must have belonged to other Wainewrights in the past. Some of it is very old and has been eaten by the moths, but most is well preserved. Captain's lady friends will choose the fabrics they like best and hire me for their "everydays". I keep the better samples here, being easier to show them when they visit for the soirees.'

As Martha rattled on, I fancied being in a shop, but a shop where everything we might have liked was free to take, so long as Martha judged the goods as enhancing to our looks.

'No, not that pink, Keziah.' She tapped my hand when I reached out to stroke a velvet's lustrous nap. 'Much too sugary for you.'

I followed where her finger led. I said, 'I don't like bottle green.' My sulky tone was mainly due to never wanting to resemble any colour of the vessels used to hold Lovell's Elixir.

'What about this?' Martha enquired, as she displayed the finer shimmer of a dark-red sateen, which was a colour she would very often use for me in future – when she was in her attic bedroom, working away on the machine Captain purchased for her use, and where the racket of mechanics failed to be quite so disturbing to the residents below. How I loved to watch her work, or to see her sketch designs for her wonderful creations. It was miracle to me, the way she conjured up such things. It left me awed, and very often also greatly irritated, for when I tried to do the same I ended up with cobbled stitches, baggy seams and fraying hems. Nothing ever hanging straight.

But such frustrations were to come. On that day my main concern was in the frowning disappointment when Martha rightly said I wouldn't suit the fuchsia pink, although I soon forgot my yearning when she led me to the mirror fixed within the cupboard door. Perhaps it was the turban I was wearing at the time that lent a look of mystery, but I was awestruck to behold the way a colour can contain the magic spell that might transform a person's dullness into glamour, even when that person has a pair of blackened eyes. Only now am I ashamed to confess that in that moment, I thought nothing of my sister or the pain she might be feeling, so rapt I was to see myself reflected in that glass, and blushing with delight when Martha said, 'My word, Keziah. A few more years of growing and what a beauty you will be. Won't you be turning all the heads.'

Was that when Martha experienced some pity for my sister? All at once her voice was brusquer: 'Well, that'll do for you. Come on, Tilly. It's your turn. What do you think about this yellow? And there's a fine Brussels lace. You'll look as pretty as a daisy. Climb up here, look in the mirror.'

Martha's hand patted the tapestry surface of a footstool, from which a fine white plume of dust was carried upwards on a draught and towards another door. Covered in silk, just like the walls, it gave off the faintest whine as it swung open on its hinges.

'Where does that lead to?' Tilly asked.

Martha's eyes narrowed in confusion. 'That's the door to Captain's room. I'm surprised it isn't locked. It usually is.'

'Does he keep his dog in there?' Tilly sounded nervous.

'Dolce?' the woman said. 'No. She'll be at Captain's side or kennelled in the yard.'

As she spoke, I wandered past her, only stopping at the door to see another standing open at the end of a short passage. Through that, I clearly viewed a fancy frame hung on a wall. And in that frame, there was the portrait of a woman dressed in blue, a shade exactly like her eyes. Her golden hair was worn in ringlets and appeared somewhat old-fashioned, but...

'She is lovely,' Tilly said, pushing the door a little wider, and thus enabling us both to see more of the room ahead, where on a table in one corner a large glass jar was on display.

'Come away from there at once!' Martha gave a shriek. 'Oh, my good Lord, and all the saints who sit around his throne in Heaven, whatever is it in that bottle?'

Tilly and me remained in silence, both continuing to stare at what was floating suspended in a murky yellow liquid. It made me think of years before, when we'd first travelled round the fairs, and one day we'd wandered off to find ourselves near mesmerised to see the taxidermied body of a calf born with two heads. Next to that, there'd been a cat labelled *The Feline Octopus*, which had eight legs instead of four. But *this* freak in Captain's house, which was a tiny human child – well, it only had one head, the normal quantity of limbs. What made the thing so queer to see was the way the shoulder blades seemed to have fractured into splinters, from which the flesh frayed out like ribbons. Almost like a pair of wings.

NINE
DR SUMMERWELL'S MUSEUM

My dearest Theo,

I can hardly believe it's been three years since I stood waving as your train steamed off to London. Despite my sadness at your leaving, what a success you have achieved! I am immensely proud, and always make a special point of telling any Bosham friends about the work you are involved in at Dr Summerwell's museum.

What a collection it must be. And what remarkable acclaim, to have been mentioned in the pages of The Lancet *recently. 'A valuable provider of erudition of the masses'! I intend to frame the cutting you sent in your last letter. For the present it is pinned to the wall above my desk as a reminder to come and see with my own eyes the place in which you are employed. I know you are concerned about me travelling alone. But, rest assured, the Reverend Price has volunteered to be my escort. He'll play my knight in shining armour should the need arise for battle – even though his umbrella must take the place of any sword. Still, I am sure its metal tip could give a more than useful prod at any rascals set on mischief!*

As I am writing of the Reverend, I must tell you he has asked if I will share his Christmas Day at the vicarage this year. How nostalgic it will be, back in my old childhood home. I do hope you'll join us too.

Until we meet again in person,

I am, as ever, sending love to my dearest bravest Theo,

From your most devoted friend,

Miss Miller (Agnes)

After all these years, must Theo call Miss Miller ... Agnes? He isn't sure that's possible. But is her surname soon to change? He smiles at the thought. What does it matter if a genuine romance has only found her in the twilight of her years? It is no less than she deserves. The Reverend Price is some years younger than the woman he's been courting, but with his straw-like yellow hair, the jutting jaw below his beard and a heavy furrowed brow, he's more Neanderthal in build than any homo sapiens. Still, belying this appearance, he is a kind and learned man who clearly makes Miss Miller happy, and that is really all that matters.

What to do about this Christmas? Theo sighs, and the air becomes a mist of feathered white. He drops the letter to the crumpled hills and valleys of his bed. Perhaps it would be best if he spends the day in London, leaving Miss Miller to indulge in her affair with no disturbance. But, if he fails to go to Bosham, will that only spur her on to make a visit to his lodgings, where she would surely be appalled to find him living as he does.

His bed's low iron frame almost fills the narrow room. It would be hard to swing the slothful fat grey cat presently snoring on the cushions of the chair drawn up close beside the fire. It continues to sleep as Theo heats a kettle on the coals to fill his wash bowl. The briefest splashing of his face, and his bristled chin is shaved. His childhood curls have now been shorn. They need no more than the briskest passing over of the comb and he is ready for the day.

But first, he crouches down to stroke the cat's big, ragged ears and, as it purrs, he murmurs back, 'Wake up now, Pumblechook. Isn't it time you earned your keep?'

He scans the room and sees more droppings near the skirtings by the door. This premises is plagued with mice. *This* cat – he chucks a finger underneath its chin again – is absolutely useless, spoiled on the scraps of butcher's meat Eugene Summerwell will feed it. Apart from that, its only interest is in the shedding of its hairs on this chair, or the bed. Still, hair is more appealing than the bedbugs encountered on the night of his arrival, waking next day to find his flesh a mass of bites and itching welts.

At least his new employer did apologise profusely, muttering about the habits of his previous assistant. 'A most unsavoury, disreputable young character he was...'

Within the hour, Doctor Summerwell thud-thudded back upstairs so as to deal with the bugs. (He has a wooden leg, the real one having been blown off when he was working as a surgeon during the Battle of Balaclava.) He'd brought a bucket holding sulphur dissolved in alcohol, and the pungent-smelling potion was as good as any bomb when lit to fumigate the room. Not only did it kill the pests, it bleached great streaks of yellow on the clothes Theo had pegged on the hooks inside his door. The boards on which the pot had stood were scorched and badly blackened. Wooden panels tacked against the chamber's walls were split or warped. Despite the window being opened to dissipate the fumes, the stink had lingered for days, and Theo suffered fits of wheezing so intense he'd feared that he would also die from poisoning.

After a week, when he still lived, he made the room his own, covering the ruined walls with some brothel *carte de visits* found in a box of random lots Eugene once bid for at an auction – which he does from time to time when seeking objects suitable for his museum, or the shop. One has a muscular man posing as a gladiator. Could he be the same Achilles Theo saw at Brocas fair, wide leather belts strapped at his chest and carrying a mirrored shield, while a sword is firmly anchored in-between his sturdy thighs? Another photograph is set in a formal drawing room, where a maid is pouring tea from a gleaming silver pot. Her mistress holds a china cup. She looks demure and elegant, but underneath the table top her skirts and petticoats are raised. There for all the world to see is the tackle of a man.

Truth be told, Theo rarely feels the stirrings of desire, though the streets around the shop have a vibrant night-time trade. Something to suit every taste. But he prefers to sit alone, with the

walnut writing box Miss Miller gave him as a present on the day
he left her cottage. It has a sloping, leathered lid that opens up to
show compartments holding pencils, pens and inks, and the
notebooks that he fills with the most intricate designs of his
imaginary hybrids. It is the only way he knows to exorcise the
demons that have haunted his dreams ever since he was a child.
To fix their likenesses on paper is to tame, if not destroy them. To
try and render what is ugly into something beautiful.

At other times he writes replies to Miss Miller's weekly letters,
in which he does not so much lie as embellish any truths about
his life and work in London. He has told her he is happy, which
indeed he mostly is. He has told her that his room has a view of
Oxford Street. If he was at the window now, and if he used his
sleeve to rub away the blur of condensation and form a spy hole
in the glass, he'd see the world coming to the life in the glimmer
of the gas illuminating other shop fronts. He'd see the foggy
breaths of horses drawing carriages and trams, or else pedestrians
wrapped warmly in their mufflers, hats and capes, heads hunched
low as they struggled against blasts of sleety wind. ·

Working in the shop downstairs, he has no need to face the
weather. His weekday mornings are employed in serving
customers who come to peruse the unique objects made available
for purchase – such as the rows and rows of skulls, from the tiniest
of voles, to an enormous buffalo. Gallstones are stored in jars and
almost look like sugared bonbons. Stuffed white mice have been
attired in tailored evening suits and gowns. (Why are they so
popular? It is a mystery to Theo.) Glass-fronted drawers are
opened up to show a range of human teeth, in great demand with
local dentists. Trays are filled with fake glass eyes, and hanks of
hair are sold for wigs. Dried frogs are pegged on strings, like so
much washing on a line. There are snail and turtle shells, and
endless boxes holding beetles, reminding Theo of the specimens
inside Lord Seabrook's study. On other shelves are stacks of books,
many with vivid illustrations of the organs of the body. Foxed and

yellowed pages chart astrological alignments. Almanacs hold country cures in the form of riddle verses. And on the shelves behind the counter are apothecary potions, patent pills, and the bottles stuck with labels that proclaim: *Professor Lovell's Elixir*.

Even though five years have passed since that night at Brocas fair, every time a customer mentions the medicine by name, Theo's mind goes drifting back and he cannot help but wonder what has happened to the sisters.

For the public exhibitions held each weekday afternoon, eager visitors are shown between the heavy brocade curtains draped across a single door in a back corner of the shop. As they emerge into the drama of Summerwell's Museum, the doctor greets his audience with smiles and open arms – 'Come!' he beckons grandly, looking for all the world as if he is about to lead them on a tour around the tulips in his fragrant spring-time garden; instead of which they will be lured along a dingy narrow passage where human skulls are lit with candles and the doctor carries on with his well-rehearsed routine: 'Prepare to see the wonders of the structure of the body, beginning with the processes of human reproduction...'

Which will be the blond-wigged 'Venus'. Seventeenth century, and French, and acquired at great expense. Reclining naked on a couch with one arm draped behind her head, she looks sublimely unaware that her abdomen is opened to expose its inner workings. Her heart, her lungs and liver, mammary glands, kidneys, and spleen, even the ropes of curling guts, have all been moulded out of wax. Also a uterus and baby.

Miss Miller must not see this, or the genuine cadavers preserved to demonstrate the grossest of the ailments and contagions that affect the human body; what Dr Summerwell describes to titillate the visitors as, 'Those poor wretches who have died due to the sinful consequences of distorting or defiling the sacred gift of human love...'

Which is venereal disease, and another of the reasons why Theo does not dally with the warmer living flesh up for sale in the West End. He imagines pretty faces afflicted by the pox. He sees black holes in place of noses. He fears the sores and rotting lesions eating through the mouth and jaws to show the white of bone below. And that is not the worst of it. The museum also has a vast array of human organs riddled with every form of tumour, even – what a surprise when Theo first encountered it – the head of a child with a twisting growth of cells protruding from its brow. And, after that, something else all too vividly remembered from his days in Dorney Hall:

'Where did you get this, Dr Summerwell?' Theo had asked as he'd pointed towards the hand of glory, in that moment wondering what fate had brought him to this place in which the trade bears little likeness to the medical profession for which he'd once held aspirations.

No. Not fate. More like contrivance, and it had started on the day when Miss Miller had received a letter with a London postmark. One she'd opened over breakfast in her Bosham harbour cottage.

⚜

'Theo, you'll never guess!' Lifting her lorgnette to her face, her eyes and sight thus magnified, Miss Miller beamed across the table. 'I took the liberty of writing a letter of enquiry to Doctor Eugene Summerwell ... the physician who'd attended your grandmama at Dorney Hall. I really didn't know if he'd remember who I was, but I addressed my correspondence to the Harley Street address where I recalled he'd once had rooms, and...' She drew a hurried breath. 'Well, it seems he's moved away, but someone forwarded my post.'

'Why did you write to him?' Theo asked suspiciously.

'I mentioned your relationship to Anne, and then enquired if he could offer some advice regarding your own interest in the medical profession. Anyway, he has replied and – would you believe the luck? – is in need of an apprentice. Not only that, but he's included an advertisement he posted in *The Times* just recently.'

Theo set down his knife and took the cutting from her hand, quickly scanning through the smearing print of letters as he read —

GENTLEMAN ANATOMIST SEEKS ASSISTANT. – The successful applicant will aid the doctor in the study of anatomy and physiology. Demonstrations of procedures to the medical profession will be regularly made to interested members of the public. Applications should be sent to: — Doctor Eugene Summerwell, The New Museum of Anatomy, 315 Oxford Street, London. (Board and lodging both provided to the successful candidate.) NB: – No-one of a squeamish disposition need apply.

'Should *you* apply?' Miss Miller asked when she was sure he'd finished reading. 'I know it's not quite what you'd hoped for, but a position such as this will provide experience. You never know where it might lead.'

In the two years since leaving Dorney, Theo had grown reclusive, even more so than before. For months on end he could not sleep and often left the house at dawn to go and watch the rising sun across the waters of the quay, with no disturbance but the screeching of the gulls, the chink and snapping from the riggings of the boats moored against the harbour walls.

For the first winter, when the ground, even the water, had been rimed in crusts of thick black ice, he'd rarely left the fireside chair where time was passed in reading books taken from Miss Miller's shelves. Dickens, of course, always her favourite, although Theo much preferred the Wilkie Collins' sensations. Especially *The Woman in White,* a mystery in which two women looked so alike they could be twins – which only made him think again of the girls at Brocas fair.

Gulliver's Travels had obsessed him, in particular the scenes taking place in Brobdingnag, where every animal and human the stranded Gulliver encountered was gigantic in its form. This story spoke to Theo's soul, to his own crippling sense of smallness. The Sussex coast seemed too big. The fields and ocean were too vast, and in a land where many locals would so often stand and stare at any stranger in their midst, he felt too obviously 'other'. *Was* too obviously other.

Previously, he'd been protected by his wealth and privilege. Now, all confidence had gone. One Sunday morning after church, only attended because he knew how much it pleased Miss Miller, he'd left the crowds who stood and chatted in the gardens by the porch and went on walking, walking, walking, until, at last, he reached the coastline. There, he decided he'd be happy to have shared Gulliver's fate in his last hours in Brobdingnag – when he'd been standing on a beach and was surprised to find himself grabbed by the talons of an eagle, carried high into the sky and then discarded far at sea, plunging downwards through the clouds, into the waves where he might drown.

Theo *would* drown if he remained with Miss Miller for much longer. She never made him feel unwelcome. Really, it was the opposite. But she had her other friends, her other interests – and expenses to which he made no contribution. Added to that, the constant ticking of the clock above her mantle was a perpetual reminder of all the days and weeks and months during which he had become a creature lost in hibernation, afraid to wake and go outside, to feel the sunlight on his face.

Surely Miss Miller also suffered and was haunted by the life she'd known before at Dorney Hall. Since the night when she had wept beside a child's empty grave she had not spoken of her grief, though Theo often saw it, etched in the furrows that had deepened around her eyes and in the grooves at the edges of her mouth; especially on those occasions when she forgot to wear her smile. But she had smiled more frequently since Reverend Price first started calling, which meant she wouldn't be alone if Theo took this job in London.

How Dr Summerwell's advertisement rekindled his ambition. Such was his hope, he'd left the table with his breakfast still unfinished so as to write an application. Within the hour his own sealed letter was posted in the box towards one end of the Shore Road. After that, he walked the path that led around the harbour walls, and from there towards the point where the inlet met the ocean. A cold east wind made him shiver. The winter sun was hazed and white against the lowering of clouds as he imagined setting sail across the freezing, steel-grey sea, and thought *if* he could be so lucky as to be chosen for the role of an anatomist's assistant then, much like Lemuel Gulliver, he might begin his own adventures in unchartered continents – whatever perils they might hold.

As it turns out there have not been any perils since the bed bugs, though nothing quite dispels the gloom of Summerwell's museum, and even worse these last few days due to a heavy fall of snow that has settled on the city. But despite initial doubts about the doctor's moral values, after seeing certain items once belonging to Lord Seabrook, Theo is sure that Eugene is not the sort of man who ventures out at night to go and burgle country houses. He has no need, being well known among the thieves who come offloading their own stolen artefacts of morbid curiosity.

Many of these acquisitions, not always in the best condition, are stored in the parlour across the hall from Theo's room. Last summer they gave off the most dreadful smell of rotting, and the constant drone of flies had almost driven him insane. But now the winter has arrived, and only odours from the street rise up to fill his nose. Through the freezing sleet and snow that settles on the window panes comes the acrid stench of gas, mixed with the headier concoction of manure from the gutters.

Far more pleasant is the smell of bacon, eggs and oyster toast that his employer leaves the shop each day to purchase for their breakfasts. Theo's mouth begins to water when this morning's greasy odours are wafting up the stairs. Still shivering against the cold, his belly grumbles as he fumbles with the buttons of the jacket worn whenever he is working, which has been fitted to perfection by the tailor opposite. For the first year at Summerwell's, Theo saved his meagre wages and sent most of his money back to Bosham for Miss Miller. But since last Christmas she's refused to accept another penny, and far too many have been squandered on his fashionable appearance. He has a fervent love of colour, although his tailor has succeeded in restricting his excesses to his waistcoats and his ties. Today's are silk. Both peacock blue.

Emerging through the door behind the shop's long marble counter, Theo peers above it, to where his breakfast bag is steaming next to a box of shells and feathers, and the stuffed kakapo bird. A type of parrot, feathers green, with those that tuft around its beak making the creature resemble a whiskery old man. It looks a little like Lord Seabrook.

Perched on a stool across the counter, Eugene could be a crow, nodding his head in silent greeting. He cannot speak because his mouth is chomping on his roll. This mastication is joined by the sound of water dripping from his hat and long caped coat, both hanging from the stand beside a human skeleton. The doctor's own dry flesh and bones are immaculately dressed in his black four-buttoned jacket, black stock and grey striped trousers. Only the glitter of a heavy golden chain fixed to the watch concealed within his waistcoat pocket throws any light into the shade of this funereal appearance. His hair follows the theme, flat and heavy with the bear grease. The same with his moustache, which provides a ghoulish contrast to the pallid doughy face in which a pair of smiling eyes – he is by nature ever cheerful – are somewhat overshadowed by two densely bristled brows. Today, whatever dye – or is it polish for his boots? – the doctor has employed has been erratically applied, or else dissolved out in the snow. The colour smears around his hairline and is running down one cheek, where it merges with the bacon fat he dribbles from his mouth.

Theo is wondering how best to tactfully suggest the doctor look in a mirror to address the situation, but before he has the chance there comes a knocking on the door.

The sign for Summerwell's says *CLOSED*, but the door has been unlocked due to the doctor's breakfast outing – and now it opens again, causing the bell above to jangle as a stranger steps inside.

At first Eugene seems disgruntled at the thought of any customer arriving prematurely. Gulping down a final swallow of hot bread and melting lard, he cranes his neck at such an angle that the tendons of his throat are drawn as taut as bulging wires. But they relax, as does his face when he leaves the counter stool, his wooden leg tapping a beat across the boards as he propels himself towards the visitor.

'Why, it's Captain! My good friend' – he holds his arms out wide in greeting – 'it's been too long. What brings you here, on this most dismal of days?'

'*Me scusi*, dear Eugene.' This so-called 'Captain' wipes away the dampened strands of silver hair that have blown across his face. More than average in height, he has to duck and so avoid the dusty alligator hanging from hooks fixed in the ceiling. The creature sways, and razor teeth in open jaws appear to snap at the visitor's top hat – before it is removed and placed down upon the counter, only narrowly avoiding the pools of grease still remaining from the doctor's sloppy breakfast. Meanwhile, the icy sleet furring its felted beaver surface begins to melt and forms another separate puddle of its own.

After some time observing this – is it a second or a minute? – Theo climbs the counter stool, takes a deep breath, puffs out his chest and hopes to make himself impressive. Meanwhile, he's staring at a face somewhat battered by the years, although the man is far from old. No more than five and forty, his body's lean and muscular and, through the lens of his profession as trainee anatomist, Theo can easily imagine the femur, fibula and tibia being perfectly aligned with the patella of the knee. Not only that, there is the voice, which is deep and charismatic. Italian, he thinks, although without the swarthy looks that would suggest that origin. Is he an entertainer? His apparel is distinctive. Beneath the bulk of a coat so long it reaches to his boots, the street's wet filth has soaked and stained a good three inches up the hems of ... his black-and-red striped trousers.

All at once, Theo remembers. The trousers he admired, worn by a man at Brocas Fair. And here he is again, and how he makes himself at home, sitting down upon the stool the doctor's recently vacated, even reaching out a hand to tear a piece from Theo's roll. He chews this at his leisure, before he deigns to tell the doctor of the reason for his visit – 'Something to help complete a costume.'

'For your travels, or the theatre?' the doctor enquires.

'Drury Lane. The pantomime.'

Saying this, the so-called Captain dips a hand into a pocket, from which he takes a handkerchief. He spits to dampen down one corner, then rises from the stool, using the cloth to clean the stains smeared across the doctor's cheek. While doing this, he's also murmuring in confidential tones, 'More on your face than on your head. Do you need spectacles, my friend? You should not always be so vain.'

The doctor looks embarrassed and snatches at the cloth, walking towards an oval mirror near the trays of mourning jewellery. As he dabs, and then more earnestly is rubbing at the stains, the other man turns to Theo with a most disarming smile. 'Who is this behind the counter, Signor Summerwell? Have we met before? There is something – how do you say? – *Mi sembri familiare.*'

Eugene, who is still flustered, but no longer quite so blemished, looks through the glass as he replies, 'This is Mr Miller. He's my assistant, and he's living in the room where you once stayed.' His gaze moves on to Theo. 'Captain did *not* bring the bed bugs. He was here some years before, around the time I first moved in ... after my name was cruelly smeared and I was forced to change profession.'

'How kind you were to me back then, when you had troubles of your own.' The Captain's voice is edged with – what? – the trembling of some emotion?

'Troubles shared and bravely borne,' Dr Summerwell replies before he glances back to Theo. 'Mr Miller has been working here with me for...' Eugene pauses as if straining to remember.

'Three years.' Theo speaks up, before the doctor's eyes flick to the Captain's, and he says:

'Mr Miller is a godsend. My last assistant did no more than fiddle money from the till to spend on drink and bedding whores. Theo is not that way disposed. In fact, I sometimes wonder if he aspires to be a monk. And yet such talent for the business, even starting up a scheme for cataloguing the stock, or suggesting new arrangements for displays in the museum. As I am sure you will have noticed, he has the most enchanting manner. If I am ever absent, such as when bidding at the auctions, I rest assured he'll lead the tours with mastery and aplomb.'

Out at the auctions, or perhaps indisposed in other ways? Eugene Summerwell is fond of the oblivion he finds when he is smoking opium, though never on the premises. Instead, when he's afflicted by what he calls the phantom pains from his amputated leg, he'll disappear for days on end, taking his 'East End holidays'. From these he comes back home looking raddled and exhausted. Even so, he will insist that the cure has calmed his mind and worked great wonders on the nagging discomfort of lost bones.

'Miller?' the Captain muses.

'Yes,' Theo replies, before the doctor has a chance.

'Not a name I know. But I'd swear we've met before. And your voice, it is distinctive. Such a warmth within its timbre ... also deeper than expected, coming from one so very young. I wonder, do you sing? Or, musical in other ways?'

Theo shakes his head. Meanwhile, the clock behind the counter starts to whir as cogs are tensed, before the hammer strikes the chimes that mark the hour of ten o'clock. Mornings start late at Summerwell's.

At the same time the doctor draws the fob watch from his waistcoat pocket, opening the lid so as to check it is correct before announcing, '*Tempus fugit*. Cometh the hour, cometh the customers ... which means that I must ask anew, what brings you here this morning, Captain? I would not be so deluded as to think it is due to my own scintillating presence.'

The Captain looks around the shop, the slightest frown upon his features. 'You used to keep a stock of feathers. I need wings. Wings of a swan. The wardrobe at the Drury do have some in the props room, but they're so old they've starting moulting on the stage during rehearsals. As we're opening next week, short of sailing down the Thames looking to find a bird to shoot...'

As this exchange goes on, it is as if the clock continues to chime in Theo's brain – because *if* Eugene's Captain friend was at the Brocas on the night when someone burgled Dorney Hall, then could *he* have been the thief who stole the horned child's head, or the withered hand of glory? Or the painting of his mother?

Is Theo going mad, imagining conspiracies where surely none exist? Better if he trusts to his original suspicions – at which point his eyes are turned towards the shelf that holds the bottles of *Lovell's Elixir*. Another person who'd been present at the summer Brocas Fair, and whose nefarious intentions have already been well proven.

The Captain follows Theo's gaze. There is a 'hmmm' low in his throat as he steps behind the counter to touch the ribbing of one bottle. 'This man, Lovell, do you know him? Does he ever visit here?'

Dr Summerwell replies, 'No. I met him at a show down Stepney way, some years ago. I should write to order more. It does sell marvellously well. Why not try some for yourself?'

The Captain answers sternly, 'Only the swan's wings for today, although...' His eyes rove to another shelf where, among the 'antique' items supposedly connected to beliefs in the occult, there is a set of battered cards. He lifts them down, turning the box in his hands before he asks, 'What would you charge me for this?'

The doctor runs a hand through his sheen of drying hair. 'For you, it is a gift. To tell the truth I've had that box of cards about the place for years. But, getting back to feathers...' He gives his chin a scratch, and Theo can't help worrying: *Not bed bugs again.*

The doctor carries on, oblivious to this concern, 'Most were taken by the milliner who works a few shops up, using the plumes to dress her hats. Nonetheless, I do believe I may have just what you require in the storage room upstairs. Theo,' the doctor smiles, 'would you go and have a rummage?' Then, to his customer again, 'It might take a little time for him to sort through all the stock, but I'm sure Mr Miller wouldn't mind a short excursion. We'll wrap them up and he can bring them to the theatre door in person. The back-stage entrance, I presume?'

'*Perfetto!*' The Captain stands, setting his hat back on his head, and while smiling Theo's way he says, 'The Royal, Drury Lane. This afternoon. Shall we say two? *Fino a quando incontriamo di nuovo.*'

Theo is far from fluent in the language of Italian, but he has enough of it to comprehend the Captain's words. *Until we meet again.*

TEN

THE BEAR STRETCHED himself by the fire. He growled contentedly. It was not long before the sisters felt at home with their new friend. They tugged his hair, and tickled him, and even rode upon his back. But the bear was kind and patient, and only when they were too rough did he call out: 'Leave me alive! Children, I beg you. Do not hurt me!'

From Snow-White and Rose-Red

Another Christmas came around. It was our fifth in Linden House, and what a mood of expectation fizzing in the atmosphere, not least because Aleski and my sister were both starring in the panto at the Drury, due to start on Boxing Day.

It wasn't only Tilly's size that made her perfect for the role of the production's Fairy Queen. My sister had the sweetest voice, and much improved over the years, when she would sing alongside Captain as he played his grand piano. The music was her passion, and yes, I loved to hear it too, but in the lonely sort of way of one who always stands apart – something I felt yet more acutely since Tilly had been busy with the pantomime rehearsals.

In fairness, she had asked me, and on more than one occasion, if I would like to go along to meet the members of the cast and see the backstage preparations – such as those she had described for at least the hundredth time when we sat down to eat our lunch of roasted goose and spiced plum pudding. Everything had been delicious, and my belly was so stuffed I feared I'd never eat again. But Tilly barely touched a morsel, and such a hectic flush of colour in her cheeks as she announced, 'Oh, Keziah, I can't wait for you and Martha to come and see the show in all its glory. The settings are a dream. What they've made from planks and sawdust, you never would believe. And wait until you see me fly!'

'You're going to fly?' Well, this was new. Not a thing I'd heard before.

'Can it be safe?' Martha enquired.

'Oh, yes, perfectly safe. I rise up through nets of gauze that look as if I'm steeped in fog. And they've cut all these holes from the canvas of the backdrop, with the lights that shine behind it looking like a real moon and a thousand little stars twinkling in midnight skies. And then there are the costumes. I know you're going to love them. Martha, if you like, after the show I'll introduce the wardrobe master. He so admires all the clothes that you have made for me. Secretly, I think he's scheming to employ you at the theatre. He wants to meet Keziah too.'

I had no wish to meet with strangers. I did not want to think about my sister in a world beyond the walls of Linden House. It was illogical and foolish, but I felt myself abandoned, just as I had so long ago when she had taken Captain's hand and left me standing on the Brocas. I felt as if I was the snail that Betsy Jones once gave our pa. The one he'd buried in a box, in which it shrivelled up and died so as to leave an empty shell.

I wasn't really alone. Martha was with me in the house. But of late she'd grown immersed in the creation of the gowns for us to wear to the show and very rarely left her room. Her own design was to be black, to look as if she was in mourning, so that a veil across her face would not appear conspicuous. Although I wondered just how common it might be to see the grieving gadding round the London theatres.

Over the years she'd made so many lovely gowns for me and Tilly to wear to Captain's soirees. Primped up and 'afternoon-ified', we'd walk into the music room just like a pair of Queen of Shebas as we mingled with the guests; mostly people from the theatre who, at the dropping of a hat, would clamber onto chairs so as to spout soliloquies. I knew a lot of them myself, having learned them from the pages of the Shakespeare in the vardo. Did Pa still flick through its pages, looking to find expansive passages pertaining to good health, which he would stand and orate for the punters at the fairs? I often wondered if he did. I felt sure he would admire Captain's ebullient acquaintances who came to sing the latest ballads popular around the halls, all with such lewd and bawdy themes. Or the musicians who would play on clarinets, or pipes and fiddles while we all kicked up our heels and cavorted round the room, quite as wild as any jigs I'd ever known about the fairgrounds. But that would only last so long, for the time would always come when the dusk had turned to night – when Captain would stand and raise his hands, demanding silence while announcing it was now Matilda Lovell's turn to sing.

If Pa could have seen her then, I think he would have been amazed. She never showed a hint of nerves. No one would think she was so small. She didn't sound it with that voice, and being lit by the candles burning in the chandeliers, how she would shine, how she would sparkle, bubbling up and overflowing like champagne in crystal glasses. She was no less intoxicating, the very darling of the guests, who would exclaim that she was born to entertain upon the stage. And among the very loudest was Mr Augustus Harris, the balding and exuberant manager-impresario from the Royal in Drury Lane – to whom Captain would reply that there was no need to rush. He would not see Miss Lovell's character and talent being spoiled by exposing her too early. It was enough for her to hone her craft and sing to them in private: '*Fino al momento giusto.*' Until the time is right.

Was this the trick I'd once observed in Alfred Lovell's own productions? Anticipation and suspense leading to the grand reveal? And now, at last, the time was right for Tilly's debut on the stage, although the letters of her name were nowhere near the banner tops of the posters advertising *La Belle et La Bête*. It was some way below Aleski's, who'd been hired to play the prince transformed into a monster by a wicked witch's spell – until my sister came along to dance and wave her magic wand, and in a puff of coloured smoke restore him to his 'human' role. However, *that* was a part taken by another actor, which I did think a dreadful shame, because Aleski Turgenev was Magnificence itself...

But I am running on ahead. Back to the meal on Christmas Day, when my sister was the one to find the sixpence in the pudding. She closed her eyes and made a wish, then Captain stood and clapped his hands, lifting his glass to make a toast to the pantomime's success – after which it was agreed we should all go and find our beds, for the actors in the house must be their bright and breezy bests when the morning came around.

Not the least bit tired myself, I stayed downstairs and cleared the kitchen like some Christmas Cinderella. When that was done, I took a candle into the music room, where I settled on a chair to play a game of Solitaire. Soon growing bored with that, I shuffled through the deck again, and this time I laid the cards down on the baize so as to form a fanning arch across the table. I turned them over randomly to try and read the hidden patterns in the numbers and the pictures. I wondered if our ma had ever done the same, or did I simply have a yen to try and muster up the talents that Bohemia possessed for the interpreting of fates? Oh, but who was I deluding? I had no gift of second sight, and in a burst of sheer frustration I thumped my fist on the table, making the cards flutter up and then go falling to the floor.

Staring down in stark dismay, my mood was even more depressed by the distant melody from Aleski's violin, which he very often played before he went to sleep at night. Such stirring, melancholy notes, and how they tugged upon my heart. Meanwhile, I muttered to myself, 'Keziah Lovell, you are nothing but ridiculous and worthless!'

No sooner had my anger vented than I heard the sound of creaking from the boards not far behind. Looking back, I saw the handsome face of Captain, who was asking, 'My *bella* Keziah? Why are you sad this Christmas night?'

Without the guile to try and lie, I said, 'I'm lonely, and I'm useless. I'm so unsure about my future. I wish I knew what it might hold.'

'Ah!' he smiled. 'But there are times when ignorance is for the best, wouldn't you agree?'

In for the penny, in for the pound, I sniffed back tears and carried on, 'I suppose ... well, what I mean is, if I could only sing like Tilly, or sew fine clothes like Martha does ... or play some kind of instrument. Perhaps, if I applied myself to learning the piano?'

There was a time some years before when Captain beckoned me to come and sit beside him on the stool. He'd placed my fingers on the keys, pointing his own towards the music that was open on the stand. But all those tiny dots and squiggles only squirmed before my eyes, like tadpoles swimming in a pond. My hands were clumsy as a giant's. Far too big and uncontrolled, bashing away on the wrong notes.

'Spare us that torture, *mia caro*. Once was enough,' Captain laughed, and there I was just like a fish caught on his hook when, all at once, he became more serious, 'I know your sister is enjoying her new life in the theatre, but there are times when I have wondered, was I right to bring you here?'

Something cold ran through my blood. My voice came dull with accusation, 'I've always known that was the truth, that you only wanted Tilly.'

'No, *mia caro*! I would never have left you on your own. That's why Ulysses came searching, so as to show you the way. But was I right? Would you be happier if you *had* stayed behind?'

'No!' I cried through my distress. 'You saw my father, and the bruises from the battering he gave us. I don't suppose he would have stopped once he'd started on that course. I hated him. I always will. If only...' *If only you could be my father. If you were, I should be blessed.*

The realisation of that fact took me by surprise, sitting motionless as Captain tried again to reassure me, 'When it comes to any talent, it is simply that your own have not yet risen to the surface. I've often watched you sitting here and playing with these cards, and now I think the time is right for your Epiphany gift.'

Most of our gifts had been exchanged earlier that afternoon. Using some of Martha's offcuts, I'd made silk stars for everyone, embroidered with their own initials. Not very well, I must confess, but they looked pretty on the tree next to the sugared nuts and tinsel. Tilly had produced the most enormous box of chocolates for everyone to share. Such a lovely ribboned box, purchased from Samuels Emporium, a grand department store in Knightsbridge. (When had Tilly found the time to visit such a place? She'd never mentioned it to me.) Martha's contribution was the gown for me to wear for the show tomorrow night. And from Aleski I received a book of Shakespeare's sonnets. But Captain's gifts always came later, being presented on Twelfth Night in the Italian tradition, when it was said that La Befana (some kindly witch who flew around the world while sitting on a broomstick) bestowed largesse on all good children.

Whether or not I had been good, and I was surely not a child, being a score in years by then, I felt a frisson of excitement as I wondered what could be inside the box that I'd been given. Once the ribbon was undone, I saw the lid was illustrated with a rose, a single eye, and then the body of a snake which formed the sinuous green letters spelling out the word of *TAROT*.

That alone caused me to shiver. Had Bohemia once used cards such as these for prophecies? My hands were shaking as I lifted the lid and looked inside, to see a deck with corners turned, and here and there the varnish worn so that in places all the inks of printed colours looked uneven. But, somehow, the fading lustre only added to the glamour, in which the spades, hearts, trumps and diamonds to which I'd grown far more accustomed were replaced by images of wands, and swords, and cups, and discs.

Many other things as well. Here was a world in miniature in which I'd never be alone, for within the twirling borders of exotic foliage, among the foreign-looking scenes containing pyramids and palm trees, there were figures representing the Hierophant, the Sun, the Moon, the High Priest, the Priestess, and even the Magician. There were the courts with emperors, empresses, kings, and queens, and all the princes and princesses. There were The Lovers, and The Hermit. The blazing Star, and The Hanged Man. The Devil card, The Fool, and Death, and … what did the pictures mean? I spread them out across the table and was thoroughly engrossed, so much so I didn't notice when Aleski's violin fell into silence for the night.

At last, I dragged my eyes away so as to offer blushing thanks to the man still at my side, whose hand was placed upon my shoulder as I heard him softly murmur, '*Il piacere e tutto mio.*'

I suppose I'd looked confused, until he clarified the words: 'It is my pleasure, dear Keziah. I hope you'll find them of some use.'

'I will treasure them forever!' My words came rushing out. 'But who did they belong to, before you gifted them to me? It's just, they look to be quite old. Not that I mean to be ungrateful. Really, I'm not. They're wonderful!'

'I found them in a shop belonging to a friend. I knew at once they were for you. But I believe there is a rule. If such a pack of cards has been owned by someone else, you must only pass them on to a new owner who is worthy; who will respect the mysteries embedded by the other's spirit.'

'I will respect them. Thank you, Captain.' My words were followed by a yawn, after which we said goodnight and I made my way upstairs.

✠

However tired I might have been, once in my room I could not wait to shuffle through the cards again. But how to try and concentrate with such a racket overhead? The thumps and clattering vibrations of Martha's sewing machine made my bedroom's chandelier sway about alarmingly. I must confess there'd been a moment when I'd looked up to see the dust and bits of plaster falling down and truly feared she might come crashing through the ceiling any moment to leave me flattened as a pancake.

Placing the cards upon the mantle next to Aleski's book of sonnets, I thought that if I dragged my bed across the floor towards the door, then I would surely feel much safer.

While in the act of doing that, I saw three things quite unexpected. The first one was a ring, previously hidden in the darkness of the space below the bed. Crouching down to pick it up, once I'd wiped away the layers of dust that furred the stone, I saw a large and lustrous opal. Also, some fine white powder spilling across my palm, having leaked through a hinge between the casing and the gem, which I then opened to reveal a little box in miniature. I clicked it shut. The catch held well. I wiped my hands across my skirts and then I tried the ring for size. Meanwhile, glancing back at the boards I'd just exposed, I gasped in shock at the sight of a mummified white mouse, very stiff with dull red eyes, and it was lying on its back in the middle of more grains of the suspicious-looking substance. Could it be one of the mice Ulysses had kept as pets? I felt a shuddering revulsion when I stooped to pick it up, then went to raise my bedroom sash so as to cast the withered husk into the darkness of the garden.

I didn't waste another moment in removing the ring, placing it in my washing bowl and using water from the jug to scrub it clean of any powder – which I suspected might be poison. *If* this was Mr Wainewright's ring? And, if it was, what on earth was I supposed to do with it?

For a good while I stood there feeling inordinately confused, only distracted by the racket Martha was making overhead. And during that, the third surprise, for as I gathered my strength to

give the bed a final tug, so a pillow was dislodged, and thudding
after it, a book.

I thought how strange for that to happen, because I'd only
stripped and changed the linen in the past few days. Surely I would
have noticed something as solid as a book bulging underneath my
head? Taken with curiosity, I snatched it up, and flung myself
down on the bed to see what lay within the plain brown cover –
the words so scandalous and lewd that I entirely forgot about the
ring and the dead mouse, so rapt was I in the confessions of *A
Woman of Pleasure* as described by Fanny Hill, which was as
thoroughly indecent as Martha warned some years ago when I'd
first come to Linden House. Why, the descriptions I was reading
could have brought a long-dead parrot back to squawking life
again, never mind any white mice. And that was saying
something, for after witnessing the antics of my father, Alfred
Lovell, I'd presumed myself immune to such immoral behaviour.
But once I'd started on the story of an innocent young girl who
had travelled up to London from the country seeking work, and
was then lured into a life of ill repute inside a brothel, well, I
simply could not stop. I read of Fanny Hill's seduction by a fellow
prostitute who used her fingers and her tongue in the most
outrageous manner. The languid sighs and 'I am comings' of those
passionate embraces left me blushing to my roots. And then, the
scenes when Fanny spied on the hideous debacle of the brothel's
aged madam, with her pendulous breasts swinging down below
her naval as she engaged in a frantic copulation with a soldier, *he*
in possession of a member of the most prodigious size. More of
the male anatomy, when Fanny later on recounted her own bliss
at the first sight of the young man she came to love. How vividly
was portrayed his organ's pale and silky skin with its protruding
purple veins, and then the pleasure of the thrusts of this machine
when it was plunged into Fanny's 'nethermouth'.

Why, I am blushing even now, and at the time I felt worn out
with all the passion and excitement, having discovered certain

parts of my own anatomy that corresponded very well with those described by Fanny Hill. At least my headache from the noise that Martha made was much improved, and better still the awful racket from the attic had now finished – which left me safe to drag my bed back from the door it had been blocking.

After such an exertion, which left me yet more hot and bothered, I pondered yet again: who'd placed the book below my pillow? I doubted it was Martha. I'm sure she'd rather see it burned. Could it be Captain? Surely not. Although, it's true I'd sometimes pondered on the nature of the man who kept a pickled baby in the room in which he slept. It was such a morbid thing. It did not fit with him at all. What other secrets did he hold?

Perhaps I'd ask the Tarot. Lifting the box, I spread the deck across my bed and closed my eyes. Strange to say, but as I laid the final card down in its place, I felt the greatest certainty about what chimed inside my mind. *Ulysses?* It *must* be him. *Fanny Hill* was just the sort of book I knew he would be drawn to. But when had Ulysses displayed the slightest interest in reading? Come to that, when had he last paid any visit to the house?

It would have been a few months back, when both Captain and Aleski were on another trip to London. He'd ambled through the kitchen door, where me and Tilly had been sitting watching Martha making pastry, and there he'd settled on a chair and placed his boots up on the table as he spouted filthy jokes that nearly set our ears ablaze – until Martha used her rolling pin to clout him on the head. After that, he'd changed his tack and presented me and Tilly with some bits and bobs of jewellery. Things he said he'd found discarded on the pavements up in London. As if! Wasn't it strange that he should have the eagle eye to spy so many valuables where normal folk walked blindly by? But then of course, I guessed his game, and warned that he should be more careful, or end his days hanged as a thief, doing the dead man's dancing shuffle.

Well, blow me down, but on that night as I'd looked at the

cards, there it was – The Hanged Man. A youth suspended by his feet from the branches of a tree, his head but inches from the ground.

I arranged the cards again. This time I turned the Prince of Cups, a golden goblet in his hand as he rode a large white horse across a flowing silver stream. Such a romantic and Arthurian-looking image of a knight, which was ... Aleski Turgenev? Could *he* have been the culprit? He was a great one for reading, which would have made him far more likely to have found the book at all. There was – I could not help but admit this to myself – something intensely sensual emanating from the man, with his pelt of thick dark hair, and those endearing, large brown eyes.

Wasn't it strange that Ulysses could leave me prickling with revulsion whenever I should find his gloating eyes upon my person, whereas if it should be Aleski I never minded in the least?

Feeling more restless and confused I went and stood beside the window, rubbing a spyhole though the mists my breaths had formed upon the glass. Outside, the drifts of snow formed a luminous white blanket on the branches of the trees. Beyond the silvered iron railings where the streetlamp faintly glimmered, more flakes of ice could still be seen swirling about in gusts in wind. How long I stood there shivering, I really couldn't say. But when my candle sputtered out, and with only cooling embers still remaining in the hearth, I decided I would go into the room next door to mine, to share the warmth of Tilly's bed – which I still did from time to time, when I felt lonely, when I longed to feel her body next to mine.

But surely Tilly would be angry and resent the interruption, needing every ounce of sleep for tomorrow's pantomime? If not that, she might be sitting with her back against the bolster, looking pale and whispering that she could hear the phantom singing from the music room below; the voice of the woman only Tilly ever heard, conjured up in black-drop dreams. And though she swore she never drank the tincture any more, I suspected that she did. I simply didn't have the heart to lie beside her in the bed and smell the sweetness on her breath – which is why I went instead to the room with red-flocked walls.

⁂

'Good morning, Bear.' The words were whispered through the smile of my contentment. His face was turned away from mine, so I couldn't see his eyes. But by his slow and even breaths I guessed Aleski must be sleeping, and I knew that I should leave before he woke and had the shock of finding me in his bed.

Above the sheets the air was bitter. The cobwebs hanging from the ornate plaster covings overhead looked more like tapestries of ice. I thought how beautiful it was, the thick, grey glimmer of that lace, the faded grandeur of the house. Filled with such notions of romance, I started whispering the lines of a sonnet from the book Aleski gave to me for Christmas...

'If I should think of love
I'd think of you, your arms uplifted,
Tying your hair in plaits above...'

I had stop, for that was when Aleski opened his eyes, and began reciting back:

'I think of this,
And all my universe becomes perfection.
But were you in my arms, dear love,
The happiness would take my breath away,
No thought could match that ecstasy...'

I don't know about ecstatic, but I was feeling very dizzy to see him rising on an elbow, looming above me as he smiled, 'Good morning, Keziah. I trust you slept well?'

What could I do but start to blurt the first excuse that came to mind. 'I was just practising the Shakespeare. It's rather lovely, don't you think? But ... in truth, I only came in here because, well, I wondered...' the silly lie rushed through my lips '...if you chanced to be awake, and if you were, then would you like me to fetch a cup of tea?'

His accent rolled across his tongue. 'Was it not a little strange to think of making cups of tea in the middle of the night?'

'It's morning now ... but oh, I see. You knew that I was here before.'

'Yes. I was awake.'

'I'm sorry I disturbed you. I was cold. I only thought...'

'There is no need for explanations.' He glanced away, in the direction of the window, where Jack Frost had drawn his flowers on the glass. When he turned to me again, I felt a tingling of desire, wondering if I could touch him in the way that Fanny Hill described caresses from her lovers. Was it too terrible to feel such ardent curiosity, perhaps see what she had called 'the plenipotentiary instrument of the male machinery'?

Instead, I shuffled up against the bolster pillow. My arms were wrapped around the knees that I'd drawn against my breast. Meanwhile, Aleski made no comment, only smiled, but how that smile stirred more affection in my heart. So when he asked, as Captain had only the evening before, 'Are you happy here, Keziah, living with us in Linden House? Do you miss your other life?' – I didn't dither for a moment...

'I do sometimes miss my ma, but when she died—' I bit my tongue to stop the name of Betsy Jones spilling out onto the air. 'After that, everything changed.'

'What about the fairground? All the hustle and the bustle. The people and the noise?'

My cheeriness was somewhat forced. 'Doesn't the world come to our door, what with all the summer parties you and Captain hold downstairs. And I imagine there will be some hustle bustle later on at the pantomime tonight. But is that enough for *you*? You never talk about the life you might have had before we met.'

He looked up towards the ceiling. The long, straight profile of his nose was silhouetted through the finer strands of hair on his face. Had he ever shaved it off? What did he look like underneath? Not that I dared to ask the question for fear of causing him offence, and anyway, he'd started speaking:

'I was born in Russia. Only six years old when my mother sold her bastard to the owner of a circus.' He closed his eyes, and carried on. 'He kept me in a cage, just as he did the other creatures trained to entertain the crowds. I was fed on leaves and grass, or scraps of meat that were too rancid even to offer to the tigers. Children threw stones between the bars or prodded me with sticks. When I howled or whined in pain, they laughed to see the human bear. So many times, I fell asleep on the mounds of rotting straw provided as a bed, and I would pray to any god that might exist to let me die and never see another day.'

'Oh, Aleski!' I reached out and placed my hand upon his cheek. 'Did you escape? Of course, you did. You're lying here beside me now.'

'I would have been around fourteen. We were in America, touring from town to town, and in New York the circus owner sold me to another showman. Valentine Wilkins was his name, and he'd survived the Civil War only to find he had no heart to settle back to his old life. Being skilled with a gun, for some years he'd entertained as a sharpshooter in the shows that recreated the Wild West ... until his hands began to shake. Whatever his affliction, it turned out to be my blessing. He was considerate and kind, and wherever we might travel I had the comfort of a bed and decent food inside my belly. He also taught me how to read, and to play the violin he used to carry in his luggage. For the instrument it seemed that I possessed a natural talent, though where it came from, who can say?' Aleski frowned and heaved a sigh. 'The solace of the music offered me a sense of worth, as did

Valentine himself. Before each night's performance he would always say to me, 'Let's show them what you're worth. You are a beast superior to those jabbering bald monkeys. We'll see who ends up laughing when they've parted with their money and we become two wealthy men.'

Aleski's eyes took on a vagueness. 'I became The Dog-Faced Boy, introduced as the child whose mother had been ravaged by a bear while in a forest. The very spot where she then left her half-breed son alone to starve, or else to suffer from exposure in the bitter Russian winter. The story then described how a she-wolf heard my cries and dragged me deep into the cave where she had recently had cubs. I was nurtured on her milk and raised uncivilised and wild. Indeed, so wild, or so my trainer would inform his audience, that I had never learned to speak. But I could growl, and I could bark, and when the moon was full each month, I'd throw my head back to the skies and I would howl. As if a wolf.'

'How could you stand to do those things?'

'I met with others who had lives far less fortunate than mine. Once there was a woman who shared my own condition. Julia Pastrana was her name. She was displayed as The Baboon Girl, or sometimes The Nondescript. Her manager, a man called Lent, put out the fabrication that her mother had once mated with an orang utang. Julia was the result.' Aleski smiled bitterly. 'As you see, this can be a very common theme. But when she also mated, and many said it was with Lent, she sadly died while giving birth ... at which point Lent had the mother and her child preserved and stuffed, and then continued with his tour. I ask myself, who was the beast?

'We met him on his way to London, which is where Valentine decided he and I should travel next, planning to deal with theatre managers and organise some contracts. But Valentine collapsed and died, the second day of our arrival. Without his guidance I was lost, and as the money soon ran out and I no longer had the means to pay the bills for our hotel, I found myself thrown on the streets. It was a miserable existence, but I still had the violin, and I could play to earn some coins. Now and then to rent a bed. One night, by greatest luck, Captain walked past and heard my music. He stopped to ask if I was hungry and took me to a restaurant. We soon became the greatest friends, and in due course he asked if I would like to come and share this house. So, as you see, in many ways my life is charmed. I have a home. I have my friends. I have my music, and...'

'You're performing as a beast in the Christmas pantomime.' I bit my tongue, but much too late.

'This is true.' His voice was cold. 'Something I learned from Valentine was that my public personae – what I must do to earn my living – that is business. Only business. I think of this and do not mind when I am standing on a stage, for at such times I am admired. What is harder to accept is when I'm walking on the street, when strangers point and laugh at me, or children cry and run away. I know that Martha finds this too.'

At the mention of her name, Martha herself materialised. Standing in the bedroom doorway she held a tray, and on the tray rattled the cups that held the tea I had recently suggested going down to make myself. Over that, came the demand, 'Keziah Lovell! What in the name of all that's decent are you doing?'

Throwing off the sheets and quilts, flinging my feet down to the floor, I stood in nothing but my shift and watched her eyes rove round the room, before she gave a second gasp. 'Tilly! Not you as well!'

Only then, I realised Tilly was also in the bed, but on Aleski's other side. How long had she been there? Was it before, or after me? Did I really have to ask? I knew she would have been there first. Wherever Tilly Lovell went, didn't her sister always follow?

Whether or not she'd been asleep while I was talking with Aleski, she was now rising from her pillow and rubbing knuckles to her eyes as a tangled crown of ringlets fell in coils around her shoulders. Stretching her arms above her head, she enquired through a yawn, 'What's all this fuss? I've often slept here with Aleski on cold nights. I can assure you nothing more than snores and farts have stirred these sheets. And, as you can clearly see, the bed *is* big enough for—'

'Three,' I interrupted, before I fled from the room, pushing past Martha in the doorway, and almost knocking all the cups on her tray to the floor.

Rushing on towards my room, quite forgetting the dress I'd stripped off the night before and left beside Aleski's bed, I still heard Martha nattering as if she'd suddenly decided this was any normal day, telling my sister and Aleski that Captain had already made his way to Drury Lane and was expecting them by two...

'In light of which,' she carried on, 'you'll need to move yourselves, because it's near eleven now. I would have roused you earlier, but what with all the snow leaving us muffled in its silence, I didn't even hear the church bells ringing out on Turnham Green. Never before, in all the years that I have spent inside this house have I ever slept so late.'

Just like everybody else. But in the clear hard light of day when the whole house was wide awake, I realised I wasn't jealous of Aleski with my sister. Well, perhaps a little bit. But the essence of the sadness that engulfed me at that moment was the feeling of betrayal. To think that Tilly had decided she would rather share a bed with someone who wasn't me. And that I had done the same.

ELEVEN

A NIGHT IN DRURY LANE

'Theo, there you are. Surely, you've not forgotten? It's the pantomime tonight.'

The doctor's smiling face is poking through the workroom door, and Theo is surprised to see him looking so alert. Since Christmas Day, which they spent at the Cock and Herring pub – an ambiance as far removed from the Bosham vicarage as the day is to the night – Eugene Summerwell has suffered from a winter ague, only emerging from his rooms to apply more mustard plasters, or to deal with calls of nature.

Theo believes the lethargy is more likely to have stemmed from the empty whisky bottles piling up in the back alley. Truly, it is a wonder the doctor has not drowned in all the spirits he's imbibed over the course of these past weeks, and that excludes his constant sipping of Lovell's miracle elixir. Meanwhile, his appetite for food has all but disappeared. No pickled whelks. No Chelsea buns. Not even hot fried brandy balls have sufficed as a temptation, or prevented proclamations that his end is near at hand.

But lo! Tonight, Eugene appears to have risen from his death bed. Decked in his very best attire, his hair is newly coifed in little kiss curls round his brow. Any evidence remaining of the assault upon his liver has been artfully concealed by the industrial-strength cosmetics that would normally be used for touching up the model Venus. (The prodding fingers of the public can sometimes leave her surface soiled.) It gives Eugene a rather strange and somewhat plastic quality. Cracks form around the doctor's mouth when his questioning continues: 'Why are you working so late? You'll catch your death of cold back here!'

'I'm warm enough,' Theo replies. And yes, he is, wearing his muffler, a woollen hat and fleece-lined coat, also the heat of Pumblechook who is purring near his feet, both soaking up the fuggy heat emanating from the stove in one corner of the room.

The doctor coughs and blames the kerosene that's burning in the lamps. Even in the daytime hours the high barred window in this workroom lets in too little natural light. In these past weeks the London skies have been a mass of dense grey clouds. The streets are quiet, and trade's been scarce. For those who've braved the bitter weather, it's rarely been to make a trip to Dr Summerwell's museum. They have been busy buying gifts, or food to lay on festive tables. Things of jollity and life. Not morbid curiosities.

Theo enjoyed his Christmas shopping. In Samuels Emporium a china bowl cost six months' wages. But then, the handsome male assistant was delightfully persuasive and assured him that the gift would reach Miss Miller in one piece, packed up in sawdust, in a crate. Ever since, Theo's imagined it arriving at her door smashed into a thousand pieces, that's if it has arrived at all. She has not written for some weeks, and he fears she may be peeved that he declined the invitation to spend his Christmas Day in Bosham.

For Eugene, there was the present of a yellow silk cravat. It was chosen at the tailor's while Theo had a fitting for his own new winter jacket, a matching waistcoat and two pairs of rather splendid tartan trousers. All 'bang up to the elephant'. And now, he'll need to put them on if he's to look respectable for their trip to Drury Lane. Although, in truth he'd rather stay here in the workroom with the bones that are due to be delivered to St Barts this coming Monday.

The London teaching hospitals where Eugene still has connections will often purchase these exhibits as display aids for their students. As Theo is entrusted to oversee the transportation of the fragile specimens, he'll often try to time his visits so as to join the trainee medics crammed into the lecture theatres. These past few years he has observed many intricate procedures – and he has also been appalled at the brutal attitude of the so-called 'slasher' surgeons, in particular the one who boasted of being able to amputate a leg in less than seven seconds flat. From start to finish it was carnage. A major artery sprayed blood that turned the sawdust on the floor into a greasy slick of red, not to mention the effect on those observers who were seated on the benches at the front. But none of them were as unlucky as the patient who had struggled through his haze of chloroform to give an agonising groan, during which he bled to death. A little more than seven seconds.

From one lost limb, onto another. How *did* Eugene lose his leg? Could the claims about the old war injury really be true? Only the other day, Theo clearly heard the doctor telling a customer how he had once been savaged by a dog, after which the wound had festered and gangrene had set in. Whatever it had been, Theo hopes that the removal of the limb was less traumatic than the bloodbath he had witnessed. Perhaps, in this one matter, Theo's grandfather was right. There are some surgeons only fit for working in a slaughterhouse.

No gory butchery involved in Theo's present task, recreating plaster mouldings for finger phalanges and scaphoids that are missing from an otherwise intact small skeleton. The subterfuge is at times a necessary art, on this occasion being due to a group of half-drunk toffs in the museum recently, one of whom thought it a lark to take these bones in his arms, and then to dance around the aisles while he sang an Irish ballad. But then, the skeleton was labelled by Eugene as having been: *Remains discovered in 1600. A rare example of the Irish 'little people'. Now extinct.*

This was no leprechaun or pixie, but an infant who'd been born with achondroplasia. In other words, it was a dwarf. To add insult to injury, it also suffered from the rickets, the scourge of children of the poor when lack of sunlight and a dearth of decent food leads to a catastrophic warping of the bones. How did it die? Where did it die? Had its parents been ashamed and kept it hidden from the world?

Theo feels a grieving kinship for the remains of this child. He will make sure it is as comfortable as he would wish to be, warmly padded with a bed made up of tufts of woollen fleecing. He's also written instructions for the teaching hospital, with diagrams to show how every section must be linked at the time of reassembly. The limbs, the spine, the sternum, and the ribs are still connected by the finest metal wires. But the skull is separate, and when he wrapped it earlier he'd promised it would suffer from no more humiliation. In its new home it would be honoured, only observed by those physicians who'd be treating other children just as tragically afflicted. It had not lived and died in vain.

'Quite the osteologist.' Eugene comes closer and proclaims, 'What a talent you've developed for this aspect of the work. Such artistic, nimble fingers ... although I wonder you can feel them when it's as bitter as the Arctic? I don't know about brass monkeys, but I do fear for Cyril's plums.'

Eugene glances warily towards the small capuchin monkey sitting on a nearby shelf. 'He was my mother's. Did I tell you? I've never had the heart to sell him, although in truth the blasted creature was a perfect misery. Jealous of me! Can you believe? Always biting or delighting in tearing out my hair. If not that, then he'd be busy with the oiling of his whistle. I really should have had him stuffed in the act of masturbation. That might have made him happier.'

The hairless, all too human-looking face of the monkey does appear to hold a sneer of special malice for the doctor, who now continues with his nagging. 'This temperature can't do you good. Not when your hands must be as steady as...'

A surgeon's, Theo thinks, and Eugene heaves another sigh as if he's read the young man's mind. 'I understand your aspirations. If only I could offer more. In Harley Street I was considered the best of my profession. A list of patients from the gentry ... until one client set his mind upon my utter ruination. I was accused of negligence.' Eugene shudders at the thought. 'But there are cases that require the sparing of the knife and yet more pointless suffering, and sadly this was one of them. None of us are born immortal, and at times it is better to accept our destinies with quiet dignity and grace.' He shakes his head. A lengthy pause. 'I did, of course, walk free from court due to a lack of evidence. But the damage had been done. A dreadful whispering campaign. Enormous bills from my lawyers, much still owing to this day. So many scurrilous reports being published in the papers. My reputation was destroyed, I am afraid beyond all measure.'

One thing Eugene has never mentioned is the name of his accuser. Theo has never mentioned his acquaintance with the man who he believes had been behind the doctor's fall from grace. But Miss Miller clearly said that when she'd written to enquire if Dr Summerwell could help with finding Theo some employment, she'd explained his connection with Lord Seabrook's dead first wife – which means that Eugene Summerwell must be a most forgiving man. Theo's saviour, in a way.

Still, as Theo ties the dwarf's small finger phalanges in place, he waits to hear Eugene proclaim that all this talk of his past life is so distressing he will need a good half-hour to recover in a quiet, darkened room. Instead of which the doctor pats at his brilliantined black hair and cheerfully exclaims, 'Well, that's enough of such depressing grudge and gloom. And, yes, I know you'd rather stay and fester here among the bones. But I won't heed your protestations. Not for a second, not a minute. All work and little play makes Jack too dull a boy by far. Thinking of which, you do look wan. What about a stiffener to bring some colour to your cheeks? Perhaps you'd like' – the doctor reaches deep inside a jacket pocket – 'one of these pick-me-ups as well.'

Theo shakes his head, but he's relieved to see the legend *Dr*

Williams' Pink Pills for Pale People on the label of the box the
doctor holds. Not the Lovell offering.

❊

The orchestra begins to play. Music swells from the pit below the
stage to meet the red of the curtain still not raised. They are late.
But not too late to be allowed into the theatre, and now they
squeeze along the row, past other members of the audience
ensconced in their plush seats, whose tuts and grumbles can't be
missed. Nor can the yards of flowing skirts in which the doctor's
wooden leg is continually snagging. If not that hazard, it's the
children who point and giggle in delight while kicking out at
Theo's thighs, one of them sniggering aloud that they've been
joined by a clown. Perhaps the tartan trousers were not Theo's best
decision.

Eugene appears not to have noticed, only gushing with
excitement when they finally sit down. 'I do adore the smell of the
greasepaint. Isn't it thrilling to be here for the pantomime's last
night? And complimentary tickets too. Captain really is most
kind.'

Is Captain here tonight? Theo hopes he is, and that they'll see
him afterwards. He only met with disappointment the day he
walked to Drury Lane to deliver the swan's wings. A surly prop
man snatched the package from his arms then slammed the door,
sending Theo on his way. Meanwhile, he is distracted by the ice
cream the doctor's licking. Purchased in the entrance foyer, it has
the strangest shape and texture. Is there any cream involved, or is
it bear's grease, lard and water mixed with rotting strawberries?
Theo declines a taste, fixing his interest on the programme he has
opened on his lap, in which he sees – his heart is sinking – that
the pantomime will run for the duration of *four* hours.

He turns another page, but before he's had a chance to scan the
names of the cast, the lights are dimmed, the curtain's raised, the

music reaches a crescendo. There is a still and pregnant pause and then a great, communal gasp of expectation from the thousand other souls crushed close around him. Gazing behind and to the front, around a man in a top hat who is obstructing his view, Theo sees the glint of gold adorning balconies and boxes. He sees the gauze of dark-green smoke that floats among a silvered forest draped in the threads of giant cobwebs. He hears the sound of thumping feet. Not a troop of elephants, but a hundred little children who are dressed to look like fairies, all pirouetting on the stage in petalled skirts, with floral crowns and netted wings that catch the dazzle of the lights through coloured sequins.

Another scene, and people shriek at the sight of Little Titch, a midget clown who's wearing shoes that are as long as cricket bats, over which he twists and tumbles in some clumsy acrobatics. Theo does not laugh. He can appreciate the nimble choreography involved. But it fails to entertain – until the moment the comedian is dancing on his toes, like an *en-pointe* ballerina. With his shadow elongated on the backdrop hung behind, the clown's short legs and long feet merge and he's transformed into the vision of a looming, goat-legged satyr.

The old obsession is fermenting. Could Theo try attaching the lower body of a goat to the torso of an ape? Could visitors to the museum be persuaded that they'd seen the relic of an ancient Faunus? He wants to tell Eugene about this promising idea, but the return of the fairies leads to other flights of fancy. Pumblechook is often bringing fresh dead birds into the workroom. Could Theo take a pigeon's wings, skeletal or still intact, and then attach them to the spine of an even smaller monkey. He knows there is a species weighing barely more than ounces. He knows his work is good enough to be entirely convincing, and...

His memory is spinning back to the baby in the bottle he once saw in Dorney Hall, and inspiration is replaced by something heavy and depressing. Sinking back into his seat, his eyes refocus on the stage, where Little Titch is nothing more than a prancing buffoon. Beside him there's the dame, a man in drag who plays the cook in the Castle of the Beast. They barter tired jokes and then perform a tug of war with a string of sausages: a joke that everyone but Theo seems to find hilarious. And that is strange, because not all that long ago he would have relished the slapstick entertainment. But even when the drama heightens, when a wicked witch appears amid a roar of boos and hissing, even this cannot prevent the weary state of ennui in which he drifts into a doze, only jolted back to life by the sharp jab of Eugene's elbow, then Eugene's whisper in his ear. 'Won't you stop your snoring. Do wake up. It's Marie Lloyd!'

Theo blinks and shakes his head, trying to focus on the stage where a woman is kicking her legs high in the air with such vitality and flair, no one in the audience could have failed to get a sneak of the lace edges of her bloomers. There is a thunder of applause, whistles and shouts of 'what ho!' – and it comes as some surprise to hear Eugene among the loudest. But, at last, the cheering ends, and it is the interval. People are shuffling and stretching. Some are rising from their seats. But Eugene raises no more than one black brow as he exclaims, 'I'm glad there's *something* in the show to stir a little interest in those fancy tartan trousers. Now' – he reaches for his wallet – 'another strawberry ice cream?'

'My turn to buy,' Theo insists, wondering if there will be time to join the foyer queue and work his way back through the crowds before the second half resumes. A solution is at hand. From the aisle, down by the stage, he hears a shrill and cheerful voice: 'Lemony'ade to wet yer whistle. Bottle o' stout to oil the tickle in yer throats and stop the nuisance of yer coughing in the show.'

'That will do nicely,' says Eugene. 'I'll have a stout and lemonade.'

But a full five minutes later and Theo is still waiting in line for the refreshments. Growing bored, and glancing round at those still sitting in their seats, he does a sudden double-take at the sight of a young woman in the box above the stage.

It's her. It is Keziah! Theo is absolutely sure, although it must have been five years since they last met at Windsor Brocas. Is her sister here as well? And who's the woman in the veil sitting at Keziah's side? Or the weasel-faced young man slouching in the chair behind them, hurling insults at the boy selling the drinks in the aisle? The boy who winks back up at him...

Theo has no interest in the game these coves are playing, only in the girl who's been so magically transformed into this beautiful young woman. But the structure of the bones beneath the flesh remains the same. And the hair may have been curled and laced with ribbons made of silk, but it still gleams like ebony. The eyes are slanting, dark as coal. The full pink mouth is definitely the one that blessed him with a smile, when the two sisters waved goodbye and left him on the riverbank. And, now, this chance to meet again...

The grin on Theo's face could surely beat the Cheshire Cat's in *Alice in Wonderland* – until the reverie is broken by a tapping on his shoulder.

He looks around to see another face remembered from his past. Clements, Lord Seabrook's valet. A bland and fragile-looking man with mousey hair pomaded flat against the contours of his head, which is now turned towards the boxes on the stage's other side – from where a cold, malignant gaze chills the blood in Theo's veins.

Clements nudges at his arm, 'Would you care to step aside, into this corridor perhaps? Somewhere to talk more privately.'

Theo follows through a door, and then the curtains embroidered with: *ENTRANCE TO BOXES*. A single sputtering gas flame flickers across the passage wall to show a shadowed run of stairs. Near the top, the flitting movement of a mouse provides the only sign of life as Theo struggles to speak without emotion, 'Well, I'm here. What does he want?'

The valet wastes no time in his obsequious reply. 'I regret this interruption to your festive entertainment, but Lord Seabrook has observed you in the audience tonight. He wishes to remind you of the letter you were sent, when you were last at Dorney Hall. If you recall, it was made clear that you and he remain as strangers to each other in the future. On this particular occasion, when you are both in the same theatre, he is insistent that his wife and infant son should have no reason to suspect you might be present.'

What a spew of pompous bile. Theo's breathing comes too fast. His balling fists are trembling, but his voice is still controlled, each word precise and spoken low: 'Does he think I came along to sit and stare at him tonight, to spy on his new family? This is a public show and not some private entertainment solely for his own amusement. But if it makes him feel better, you can tell him there's no risk of being shamed by me tonight. You can tell him...' Theo feels as if his body is dissolving, the very substance of his flesh becoming nothing more than air. Only the Cheshire Cat's forced smile can still be seen when he goes on. '...That I would rather slit my throat than ever speak to him again.'

'He'll be so glad you understand.' The valet nods, but he avoids looking into Theo's eyes. 'It is regrettable, I know. But when Lord Seabrook takes a notion in his head...'

His words are interrupted by a squeaky, high-pitched chuckle coming from the stairs above. Theo mounts the lower treads, turning a bend before he sees the very weasel who was sitting with Keziah in her box. Resting his back against the wall, this fellow taps a gold-ringed finger to his nose while going on, 'Most amusing, gentleman. I shall not be in an 'urry to forget *this* entertainment. Better by far than anything I've sin on that flash stage tonight.'

A bell is clanging. An announcement. Only two minutes are remaining before the show will be resumed. Theo offers no reply, only descends the box's stairs and roughly brushes past the valet as he pushes back the drape to reach the auditorium. Once in the aisle, there is a moment when he's tempted to depart and find his way to Oxford Street. But what about Eugene, waiting alone for his refreshment? And then there is the other reason that compels him to stay. Keziah, in her box – though what on earth could she be doing with the low-life just encountered?

He doesn't care, instead decides that when the pantomime is over he'll make his way back down this aisle so as to capture her attention. She might remember him and smile. She might ignore him and look blank, but at least he will have tried to grab this chance that he's been given, to satisfy the curiosity he's felt across the years about the Lovell sisters' fates.

The next two hours are tortuous. Eugene is tetchy at the lack of the promised beverage, though he soon settles in his seat to view the dramas that unfold. Theo, who missed so much of the convoluted plot while he was sleeping earlier, is won over by the scene in which the two main characters – she The Beauty, he The Beast – throw off all pre-conceived conventions and begin to fall in love as they are dancing through the stillness of a gothic midnight castle. As the dreamy music swirls, it seems to Theo that the theatre starts to spin on some new axis. In this kaleidoscope of wonders, it's not Beauty who is drawing Theo's eyes, it is Keziah. If it's not her, it is the man who plays The Beast, who is compelling, his singing voice as smooth as honey. He has such mournful, large dark eyes that catch the glitter of the limes, reminding Theo of Lord Seabrook's lycanthrope at Dorney Hall.

Theo risks another glance at the boxes opposite. His grandfather is leaning forwards, teeth biting down upon a thumb as if to stifle his desire for what he sees upon the stage. But is he lusting after Beauty – or could it be The Beast? Does Theo even need to ask?

Is the new wife also aware of her husband's unique interests? She looks to be just as entranced. Her face is tilted to one side. Her mouth is slightly opened. Her eyes – can he be right, are they of different colours, or is that simply the effect of the lighting for the scene? –they are half closed, as if immersed in the glamour of the moment. By contrast, the small child who is sitting in her lap appears to be afraid. Or perhaps he's only fractious, needing to sleep because it's late. With a frown of irritation, he squirms and reaches up to try and touch his mother's hair. Hair so vivid in its redness, Theo doubts it can be natural. The mother slaps the infant's hands, then thrusts him back into the arms of a woman who is sitting close behind them in the box, and dressed so plainly he assumes she must be the child's nurse. In her embrace the boy grows calmer, his little face burrowing into the softness of her breast, so that Theo only sees the halo of his curls. The hair is golden, just like his. It is like looking in a mirror. A mirror into Theo's past.

He glances back towards Keziah, who is smiling at the stage. How he wishes she would drag her eyes away from what appears to be another forest setting, where fairies dance with giant insects, whose moulded papier-mâché costumes are a wonder to behold. Boggle eyes protrude from masks. Antennae look like horns as they wave from left to right. Butterflies with silken wings daubed in a myriad of colours flutter randomly about, only pausing as they smell the nectar of enormous flowers. There are caterpillars, centipedes and snails exuding slime in spooling nets of silver gauze – until the fanfare of a trumpet, and then the flares and booms of thunder which are all but deafening. Now, every being on the stage has stepped aside to form an aisle through which the tiny perfect creature hailed as The Queen of All the Fairies, appears to cast the spell with which to break the wicked curse, and so allow The Beast to be transformed and newly born as, 'the handsomest of princes, free to love and wed The Beauty who has seen beneath his skin to find the treasure of his heart'.

Having offered this pronouncement, The Fairy Queen begins to sing. She has the most exquisite voice, and as the final trilling note dissolves and melts into the air, she rises up on snow-white wings. Swan's wings, from Summerwell's. She is flying ever higher, and in ever-wider circles above the sea of all the faces staring upwards in amazement. She is gliding through the air and looks as if she is an angel. And from this angel comes the blessing of a single pure-white feather. It spirals downwards and it falls straight into Theo's outstretched hand.

TWELVE

OH NO, HE ISN'T ... OH YES, HE IS!

'Kezi, will you look?' Tilly's voice was overwhelmed by shrieks of laughter from the crowd standing around us in the bar. Her fingers grabbed my wrist, urging me to turn and see ... well, who? Who could she mean? Among the members of the cast, or their families and friends, nobody struck me as deserving such excitable behaviour.

Although we'd left the Theatre Royal, we were still in Drury Lane, only a hop, a skip and jump (and now and then an icy skid) along the snow-slushed pavement. And weren't we glad of Captain's arms to steer us safely through the crush milling around the backstage exit. On past the broughams and the cabs, and the hawkers with their barrows, until we reached some glass-etched doors, a quick ascent up marble stairs, and then the splendour and the warmth of this new palace of delights.

For a while, I stood there blinking, throat raw with cold, gasping for a breath. Goodness knows how Tilly managed keeping up with Captain's strides, but despite her shorter legs she didn't seem the least bit winded. So, perhaps it was just me, being less used to all the people in the busy London world, even though I'd come along to watch the panto several times since the Boxing Day delight.

The raising of the curtain never failed to send the tingle of shiver through my spine, as did the Doric columns of the theatre's entrance foyer, which seemed to me to be a temple with statues erected to the literary gods of Shakespeare, Garrick, Dean. What my sister must have felt to tread the stage on which their words had been orated in the past, to find herself smack bang and centred in that abracadabra magic! And when she'd soared into the air and flew above the audience, how proud I'd felt – and terrified. I swear, my heart was in my mouth, for if those wires should chance to snap ...

But Tilly never fell. She flew as if those wings were really growing from her back. Up she soared into the gods and looked as if, given the chance, she would have liked to carry on. On through the roof, to join the stars that lit the skies of London town.

That last night, when all the clapping and the cheering had subsided, Captain left his position at the piano in the pit and came to fetch us from the box – where we'd been joined by Ulysses. He'd trailed behind as Captain led us through the maze of passages, until we found ourselves backstage, where Martha and me went on alone into the dressing room where Tilly would be changing. Not a room of her own. She had to share it with the girls who played her troop of dancing fairies, and what a racket that entailed. All the giggling and screeching going on night after night would have driven me insane. But one look at Martha's veil, so dense and dark across her face and most of them were stunned to silence, as if she'd been a Christmas ghost materialising in their midst when we walked towards the screen erected at the room's far end.

My sister was behind it. The contraption of her wings, with straps and buckles still attached, was discarded on the floor, and looking somewhat worse for wear than when the panto's run began. Beyond the mounds of moulting feathers Tilly had stripped down to her bloomers so as to scrub the last few vestiges of grease paint from her face. When that was done, with cheeks rubbed red, she flung her arms around my waist and sobbed, 'Kezi, what shall I do without the panto every night? I'm going to miss it terribly.'

I did my best to ease her fears. 'I'm sure you'll soon be back on stage, especially with those reviews printed up in all the papers. Didn't every single one say Tilly Lovell was a wonder?'

Hoping to raise her spirits further, Martha handed her the parcel she'd been clutching in her lap for the entire night's performance. You'd almost think it was a bomb that might explode if she had dared to place it down for one split second. But what it actually contained was the new gown she'd made for Tilly to attend the last-night bash. Of course, I'd seen it in the making, and felt sure Tilly would love it. But I still held my breath in nervous trepidation as my sister's little fingers picked away the string and wrappings.

What a relief to see her smile as she drew out the fine silk gown. Cut to fit her to perfection, it was the palest oyster silver, and how it shimmered and bedazzled when reflected in the glass; as did a bracelet made of pearls that could be clasped as if a choker at my sister's tiny neck.

Another gift was to be found in the corridor outside. This time it came from Ulysses, and was a box containing – what? Was that a phial of Laudanum? No one noticed it but me. They only saw the rose corsage he also pressed into her hands, and how he crouched to try and slobber a wet kiss on Tilly's cheek – from which my sister flinched away. After that, amidst the pulling on of hats and shawls and coats, somehow the phial had been slipped into Tilly's reticule, but the flowers had been lost. Deliberate, or accidental I really couldn't say, though when I'd mentioned they were gone as we'd left the backstage door, Tilly only shrugged. 'Oh, never mind. Someone will find them. I'm sure they won't be wasted.'

Was that the moment when the worm of malice turned, once and for all, in the heart of Ulysses? Tilly's words were somewhat cruel, and loud enough for him to hear. And he had clearly made an effort to give a good impression, being spruced up to the nines in a fancy brown-tweed jacket with four rows of bright brass buttons, only to find his presence spurned.

No doubt that's why he'd disappeared into the darkness of the lanes as we continued on our way. But it wasn't only him. We'd

lost all sight of Martha too, though when I mentioned that to
Captain as we headed down the pavement, he said I had no need
to fret. 'She'll be waiting for Aleski. Most likely still inside the
theatre. They'll come and join us when they're ready.'

Once at the party, I confess I soon forgot the missing persons,
being immersed in the commotion of the greetings from all those
who gathered close around my sister. Oh, how she revelled in the
fussing, shining as brightly in the jets burning around the bar
room's walls as she'd done upon the stage. What a hubbub going
on, to the left and to the right, when Little Titch half walked, half
tumbled up the steps to come and join us. I felt quite giddy with
it all, when Tilly grabbed my arm again and insisted there was
someone in the room I had to meet.

'Is it Marie Lloyd?' I gazed around the crowd, for I was well
and truly star-struck with the cheeky Cockney singer.

'No!' Tilly's cheeks were blushing red. 'It's someone from our
past.'

'Pa?' I muttered low, fearing that mentioning his name would
somehow conjure up the devil.

'*No,* not Pa!' She grew impatient, stabbing a finger through the
crowds. 'There, beside the entrance doors. Surely you can see him
now?'

There was no face I recognised apart from those I'd seen on
stage. The only thing I could imagine was that my sister was
already halfway drunk on the glass thimblefuls of booze we'd both
received from aproned pot boys holding trays beside the doors on
our arrival. I'd sniffed at mine then set it down, not in the mood
for drinking gin. But there seemed no other option. All I could
see behind the counter were more caskets of the spirit, from which
the showy barmaids in paste diamonds served the customers with:
*Cream of the Valley. The Out and Out. The No Mistake, The Best
Butter. The Famous Medicated Cordial, most strongly recommended
by the landlord of this house.*

Pa *was* haunting me that night, for once again I was reminded of how he'd 'strongly recommended' his elixir to the gullibles who'd gathered at the fairs. But such a thought was interrupted by a voice close to my ear: 'Would you take a glass of port? A bit of sugar stirred inside? Something to warm the winter cockles.'

It was Ulysses again, puffing on a cigarette, resting an arm on the brass rail that ran below the polished counter, and quite as louche and confident as if he might have owned the place.

I said, 'Port is Martha's favourite, though I'm not sure where she has got to.'

'Dawdling in the street. Getting back to 'er old habits?'

'That's a wicked thing to say.' Did he know of Martha's past? Mortified on her behalf, my tongue continued with its lashing. 'Speaking of dawdling on the streets, what are *you* up to nowadays?'

He took the smoke out of his mouth, and held it up before his eyes, staring intently at the tip as he considered for a while. 'Procuring this, or selling that. Certain objects. Certain people. Certain useful information. Which reminds me...' Just as blatant as you like, he stubbed his cigarette out on the polished counter top. 'Do you want that glass of port? What else is tickling yer fancy?'

Before I had a chance to answer, Captain appeared to stand between us. Both of his arms were thrown out wide as he called, 'The best champagne. Nothing less will do for us to toast Miss Tilly Lovell.'

How could a glass of sugared port match the extravagance of bubbles? Not that Captain would have ever meant to cause yet more offence to the embittered Ulysses, or even known that he had been about to buy a drink for me. But all too clear to see was the expression on his face, where the flesh of sunken cheeks became a vivid blaze of red as, once again, Ulysses skulked away into the crowd.

No sooner had he gone than the flamboyant Mr Harris filled his place beside the bar. He was holding Tilly's hand and smiling down endearingly, although his words were meant for Captain. 'What a precious little butterfly you've landed in your net. A real star...' The man broke off to take the fizz that Captain offered. 'Did you hear the audience? They were in raptures, as was I!' He graced my sister with a bow as Tilly beamed back up at him, accepting yet more adulation like a duck dropped into water.

Of course, by then we'd both grown used to such gay theatre company, being familiar with the faces who attended Captain's soirees. Linden House was itself like the setting of a theatre with its gilded plaster roses, marble columns, and the glitter of the drops of chandeliers. The difference was that such a world contained Aleski Turgenev – who was still missing from this scene.

Could he be avoiding me? Since Christmas night when I'd audaciously crept into his bed, I'd hardly seen him in the house. But then he'd spent most waking hours working in London on the panto, arriving home well after midnight, then sleeping late until he rose to travel back to Drury Lane – which only made it even stranger that he wouldn't want to share this final night of celebration. Had he and Martha gone to Chiswick, slipping away as furtively as Ulysses had done? Despite the veil across her face, Martha was still extremely nervous about stepping out in public.

Looking around the room again, I saw a screened-off area signposted as *The Lounge*. Could they have gone in there? Nothing ventured, nothing gained, and with my champagne in my hand I wandered off to have a look – and found the cosiest of spaces quite devoid of other people. The lamps were burning low upon the claret-coloured walls. A fire crackled in a hearth, giving out such a warmth that I threw off the winter coat still draped around my shoulders. I even kicked away the shoes grown wet and muddy from the street. And how lovely it was to toast my toes before the flames as I sipped some more champagne and settled in a comfy chair, closing my eyes and very soon drifting off into a doze.

✳

Who was grabbing at my arm, shaking me back to consciousness? As my eyes began to focus I could see my sister's face. And someone else not far behind. Someone sitting on a chair behind a table by the fire. With my perspective oddly warped, at first I thought it must be Captain. But I saw no silver hair, only a mass of yellow curls, and...

That face! I knew that face. Struggling to sit up straight, I gasped aloud, 'Can it be you? God's Gift, from Windsor Brocas?'

'Yes, it is!' Tilly replied as she clasped my hands in hers, her face ecstatic with delight, whereas I think I must have looked as vacant as a missing tooth.

The fuggy air stretched thin around me, a heady elasticity that seemed to drag me back in time. How long could it have been? Five years. A little more? Greatly unnerved, and somewhat drunk, I grabbed the glass I'd placed nearby and swallowed down the final dregs. Newly fortified by that, I looked at Tilly and enquired, 'Have you told him we still have the purse belonging to his friend?'

'No, I haven't had the chance.' Tilly lost her natural poise, more like a silly love-struck girl as she gazed back into the blueness of the eyes that had been summoned like a phantom at a séance. My sister definitely simpered when she said, 'We were so sorry to have left you by the river. We'd really meant to see it through. We'd packed a bag. But then, our pa—'

'He stopped us leaving,' came my altogether brusquer interjection. 'And, well, here we are today.'

'And here am I!' He laughed his answer. Such an attractive, mellow timbre to his voice, I'd quite forgotten. Or had it deepened in the intervening years since we'd last met? I supposed it must have done, but it still took me by surprise, for it belied his boyish looks. The looks that, once again, reminded me of Captain. And someone else. Who could it be? Another face that would not come into the light but hid away in secret chambers of my mind.

'Do tell us more,' Tilly persisted. 'How do you come to be in London, and at this party here tonight? Are you involved in the production?'

'Perhaps, in some small way, for which my employer and myself were kindly sent a pair of complimentary tickets.' Here he paused and smiled at Tilly. 'The wings you wore as Fairy Queen, they were purchased from the shop in which I'm working nowadays.'

'A shop that sells swans' wings? You must tell us more about it.' Tilly wasn't wasting time, the questions running off her tongue.

'Where to start? I left my home not very long after we met. First, I lived in Sussex, and then I found some occupation...' There was a moment's hesitation. 'In an Oxford Street museum.'

'A shop, or a museum? Make your mind up,' Tilly laughed, before she grew more serious. 'Can we come along and visit?'

'Of course, you'd be most welcome, although it's only fair to warn you, some of the displays in the museum are quite gruesome.'

My turn to interrupt, senses at last fully restored, 'We don't mind gruesome, do we, Tilly? And now the pantomime is over we shall have lots of time to travel. But, what a serendipity, to meet you here like this tonight.'

It was a meeting much too short, for at that moment Mr Harris's bald head poked round the door, proclaiming in a stagey whisper, 'Ah, this is where you're hiding. I do apologise, dear Tilly, for the intrusion on your time, but' – the volume of his voice increased – 'there are some rather special guests who I'm about to go and dine with. Lord and Lady Seabrook. They were at the pantomime, and they've now expressed a wish that I should bring my Fairy Queen along to The Savoy. Lady Seabrook is a patron and investor in the opera, and tonight it's my intention to court more interest in your talents. Not that I'll have to work that hard. You'll only need to smile, and...'

'Really?' Tilly cried, as Mr Harris carried on.

'I'd understand if you would rather celebrate with Keziah.' He cast a gracious smile my way. 'But a few hours of your time would be worth the sacrifice.'

Tilly didn't hesitate. 'I'd love to come to dinner. I'm really not the least bit tired, and, as I never eat a thing for all the nerves before the shows, I am absolutely famished.'

As Tilly barely ate enough to keep a sparrow on its legs, I knew all that was just an act. But off she went with Mr Harris as if he was her favourite uncle, though at the door she did turn back to blow a kiss in my direction, the very picture of remorse when her eyes moved on to Theo and she said, 'I do apologise for leaving you like this. What is your name? I mean the last. I know the first is Theodore.'

'Miller. My name's Miller.' His voice was more subdued than it had been moments before.

'Well, Mr Miller,' Tilly said, 'we *will* come to your museum, and you must visit us in turn. Perhaps attend one of the soirees Captain holds from time to time.'

And that was that. She disappeared to spend the night with some rich toffs who she didn't know from Adam. Was Captain going too? And, if he was, then how on earth was I expected to get home?

I felt a fluttering of panic, but at least there was a chance to take a better look at Theo, what with his eyes still being fixed upon the door through which my sister had so recently departed. It also offered me the time to rearrange the wretched bustle that had slipped beneath my gown and was protruding to one side; although to anyone observing it must have looked as if I suffered from St Vitus' Dance, or had some ants stuck down my bloomers.

At last, I had the thing subdued and in its proper place again. Making a grab for my coat, I was about to say goodbye and go in search of the elusive Martha and Aleski when I noticed quite how anxious Theo's expression had become, which in turn led me to ask, 'Are you all right? You don't look well.'

'Quite well.' His smile was forced. 'But, it is getting rather late. I think it's best I head back home.'

'Oh, yes. I understand,' I said, while wondering if we should make some plan to meet again, for it would be such a shame to lose God's Gift a second time.

'You and your sister, Tilly.' His clear blue gaze grew more intense. 'You are acquaintances of Captain?'

'Yes. We live with him, in Chiswick. He's here tonight. At least he was.'

'Ah, so that is the connection,' Theo muttered to himself.

What did he mean by 'the connection'? I felt the rising of a blush and said, 'I hope you don't imagine our relationship is based on any immoralities. I know it might seem otherwise, but...' But hadn't Tilly just rushed off to spend the evening with some strangers, just because they might donate the funds to help her stage career?

As I took in the full extent of quite how bad that might appear, Theo gravely said, 'I am concerned about Tilly ... about her meeting with Lord Seabrook.'

'Don't say you know him, too? First, it's Captain, now some lord. You have been busy here in London.'

Theo frowned and turned away. 'Seabrook is not a pleasant man. Your sister should take care of the company she keeps.'

'But Mr Harris will be with her, and he is a proper gent.' I sounded confident enough, but then I glanced beyond the door and saw Augustus Harris with a paunchy-looking man who had a military air, a yellow-stained moustache and tufty sprouts of course white hair protruding from his flabby ears. I couldn't help but laugh. 'If that's your Lord Seabrook, then he looks more like an owl than any man I've ever known. I wonder if he hoots?'

Theo was not amused. 'That owl has claws as sharp as knives, and there is nothing it likes better than to prey on...' Here, he paused. 'On people who are different. People like your sister, Tilly. He will swallow them whole, and then he'll vomit out their bones.'

Well, that was brief and to the point. But no sooner had he spoken than we heard the sound of shouting. Was it coming from outside? A woman's voice, and then a scream. A dreadful cry that left me near to paralysed with fear – until I noticed Captain, rushing past the lounge's door and on towards the exit stairs. And, if Captain was reacting as dramatically as that...

Forgetting the shoes I'd kicked off beside the hearth, I held the hems of my skirts above my ankles as I left, pushing between the groups of guests who formed obstructions on the way.

Out in the street, I couldn't see. My view was blocked by yet more people thronging on the pavement. But, as a few of them moved off, so I caught a fleeting glimpse of the woman who was lying still and senseless on the ground. One dark-sleeved arm had been flung up to lie across the heavy veil that still obscured her face. A stockinged leg could be seen splayed to one side below her skirts, which were a sodden crumpled mess as they floated in the gutter. And yes, I know my thoughts were wicked, but in the panic of the moment I found myself reciting words inside my head as if a prayer: *It isn't Tilly. Tilly's safe. Tilly's safe. Tilly's safe.*

At the same time, I saw Aleski, a muffler wound around his face, and over that a wide-brimmed hat pulled very low across his eyes. Not that I would have failed to know him as he crouched at Martha's side, his voice appealing to the gawpers who were huddling around them, 'Is anybody here a doctor? This woman needs attention!'

Some of the people moved away, leaving space for me to see that Captain was there too. Also kneeling close to Martha, his mouth was lowered to her ear. His lips were moving, but what words they might have held, I couldn't tell; not with my own voice ringing out as I continued pushing forwards. 'Martha! What has happened?'

Someone offered me an answer. An old beggar man who took enormous glee in the pronouncement. 'Silly bint must 'ave bin blind. Screaming she was when she ran out. Got tangled underneath an 'orse. That man' – a finger wagged in the direction of Aleski – 'roared like a lion, so he did, when he leapt to 'er assistance. Dragged her back towards the pavement. But most probably too late. The situation don't look good.'

He shook his head and shuffled off. Several other people followed, clearly having had their fill of this impromptu entertainment. At the same time any shadow they had cast across the scene was suddenly removed and I saw the stain of blood that spread and puddled on the pavement. I feared the worst, but then my heart soared up with joy to see the flutter of the veil across her face. *Martha's alive!* I could have wept, just as I noticed Captain's eyes looking back towards the bar, and heard him calling urgently, 'Summerwell. Thank God, it's you! Come over here. We need your help.'

The gentleman Captain addressed – did he have a wooden leg, and was that rouge smeared on his cheeks? So odd, how the small details seemed so vivid in my mind, imagining he must have been another member of the cast still daubed in paint from the performance – he came limping fast towards us, leaning low over the victim before he straightened up again, and called for – Theo? Did he say Theo? – to make haste and hail a cab.

Amid the street's cacophony of rolling wheels, and horns, and hooves, a growler stopped, not that far off. The nearside door was opened wide, and I looked up to see that Theo had already leapt inside. How strange was his appearance, being so high above my head, just like the time when we'd first met, when he'd been kneeling in the grasses of the bank above the Thames. Back then, his handsome face had been silvered by the moon. Now it was gilded by coach lamps, his features taut with the strain as his arms were reaching down, helping Captain and Aleski lift Martha up, into the cab.

Meanwhile, the driver shouted, 'If that's another drunken whore then you can dump 'er straight back down onto that pavement again. This part of town is worse than Sodom during the hours of the night. I can't be doing with the bother.'

If only Martha *had* been drunk, but I suppose he'd failed to see the blood dissolving in the gutter. The blood now mixed with mud and excrement that flowed along the street, and in which I also stood. My shoeless feet were numb with cold. My entire body trembled. Even my teeth were chattering, quite unable to respond to the driver's cruel remark. But, as the horse threw back its head with a whinny, then a snort, the anger flashed through Captain's eyes. 'Does he want the job or not?'

Only the warning of the hand Aleski placed upon his arm seemed to restrain a violent outburst, during which the one-legged man called up towards the driver. 'Please, have some respect. Our friend here has been injured. We need to get her home ... to?'

'Chiswick. Chiswick High Road.' Aleski gave the address.

'That's off my route. Too far from town.' The driver hurled his answer back. 'You'll 'ave me nag walked off 'er legs.'

'Then we shall make it worth your trouble?' The so-called doctor pressed a banknote into the driver's hand as he climbed the carriage steps. Without waiting for an answer, his slender body then lurched forwards so as to sit at Theo's side, both of them facing the bench on which poor Martha lay sprawled, still unconscious of her fate.

How horrified she would have been to know the veil across her face had fallen back to show her mouth. I should have tried to pull it down. But Captain barred my way as he now stood upon the step, looking back towards Aleski when he said, 'Tilly's all right. She's gone for supper with Augustus and some of his investor friends. He'll make sure to get her home.'

These words were swiftly followed by a falling shelf of snow dislodged from rooftops high above us. A heavy thump, and several jagged clumps of ice scattered like knives. Finer particles exploded to form a misting cloud of white that spread across the open gutter in which Martha had been lying. It looked to me as if some remnant of her spirit still remained.

I suppose I must have jumped or cried out loud at what had seemed to me to be a dreadful omen. Captain's fingers reached for mine, and he made a shushing sound. His other hand caressed my cheek where it felt hot and slightly sticky, which I supposed was

Martha's blood. His voice came rough and somewhat breathless when he said, 'Stay with Aleski. He'll get you home. He'll keep you safe.'

THIRTEEN
FACES IN CARRIAGES

Theo is startled, jolts awake and feels a cramping in his arm. His neck is cricked. One of his cheeks is pressed against the window glass. He must have fallen asleep, looking across the night-time street. Waiting for Eugene to return.

Now he shivers in a draught. His bedroom door is standing open – which is strange because he's sure he closed it earlier. When did the fire die? It was still blazing when he heard the shop clock chime the hour of one.

Slumping back into the chair he hears a hissing of complaint. Pumblechook, curled on the cushion close behind is not best pleased to be so rudely disturbed. That's peculiar as well. Didn't Theo see the cat out in the street chasing a rat when he returned to Summerwell's? He feels a prickle of suspicion. Has someone been in the museum, or the shop? Inside his room?

A moment's dread, then common sense. It must have been Eugene. Eugene arriving home and letting Pumblechook back in. Eugene poking his nose around Theo's bedroom door, and then leaving it ajar when deciding not to wake him – which means whatever news the doctor has to tell must be good and can wait until the morning.

Feeling a sense of relief, Theo rubs at his arm. The aching numbness has become a tingling of pins and needles as his eyes look out to see the pink-and-orange glimmer of another winter morning rising over London rooftops. He's not the only one awake. He hears the cartmen yelling greetings. The muted clopping sound of hooves over the swooshing of the brushes as the road-sweeping machine is clearing debris from the gutters. The first small ripples of the living, before the tidal flow of traffic that will soon be following.

Closing his eyes, he reimagines last night in Drury Lane. The way the snow around the body of the woman in the gutter faded to pink as it dissolved. He thinks of how, inside the cab, the veil had fallen from her face. The interior was dark, but by the lamps of other vehicles on the road he'd clearly seen her facial abnormality.

The 'hare lip', or cleft palate, is a condition on display downstairs in the museum. The grotesquely formed wax head is something hideous to look at, but any interested observers might be lectured by Eugene on how those born with this affliction in the past – or present day in certain cultures of the world – would immediately be slain; mistakenly believed to be possessed by evil demons. Only in the 1500s was it eventually suggested that the disfigurement was caused by some late error of development in embryonic cells. And yet, throughout history there have been enlightened doctors who've attempted to repair such an unkind deformity. One record hails from ancient China, where a soldier underwent a cauterisation of the flesh, with a narrow piece of wood being inserted in the lip and then secured with twisted threads so as to hold the flesh in place. Today, some surgeons use a method whereby they take small flaps of flesh from other places on the body, employing them as bridges to join the sections of the lip. Such insertions will allow for a more natural appearance, with the degree of extra movement necessary for speech. With chloroform used as sedation, the entire operation can be endured with little trauma – although as Theo was staring at the woman in the carriage he'd wondered if she'd even live to see another day.

Despite the pity he'd been feeling, something more urgent had impelled him to shout for the cabman to stop and let him disembark.

'Whatever is it?' Eugene snapped. 'Calm yourself. Think of our patient!'

Captain, who'd been kneeling on the slatted floor between them as he cradled the injured woman's head between his hands, did not conceal his irritation.

Theo muttered his response, 'I ... I think I left my wallet in the bar at Drury Lane. I shall have to go and find it.'

He was lying through his teeth, but better that than waste more time in attempting to explain the overwhelming sense of dread at the thought of Tilly Lovell going off to meet Lord Seabrook. Meanwhile the carriage rumbled on before it slowed in a jam, which was his chance to grab the handle of the door and escape; an action not without some danger as he dodged slow-moving wheels and ducked below the harnesses of other horses in the road.

At last he reached the pavement, heading for Trafalgar Square, underneath the snow-capped Nelson standing tall upon his pillar, and from there along the Strand, where he was forced to stop a while so as to rest and catch his breath. Bending forwards, with both palms pressing down upon his knees, he closed his eyes until the sense of dizzy nausea had passed. But the spinning in his head only enhanced the dream-like atmosphere of all that had gone on since the evening first began. Seeing Keziah in her box. Seeing The Fairy on the stage. The strange elation he had felt to be conversing with the sisters at the party afterwards, only to have that precious moment snatched away so suddenly, when Tilly – little Tilly, all joy and life, lighter than air – was led off so willingly to meet Lord Seabrook and his wife.

He thought again about Keziah, trembling, as white as death when she'd been standing on the pavement, and then how Captain touched her cheek before he'd climbed into the cab. That demonstration of affection seemed to bode of more than friendship, though why should Theo be surprised? The handsome Captain did exude a certain aura of romance. And though Keziah had insisted on no impropriety, how could he know if she was honest? Even if she was lying, why should he make it his concern? After all, his own connection with the girls was based on nothing

but the briefest introduction. And yet his thoughts were
consumed, thinking of Tilly – Tilly – Tilly – as he reached the
narrow lane leading off to The Savoy.

Lurking near the hotel entrance, he watched the lines of cabs
pulling in from The Strand. The guests, arriving or departing, kept
the liveried young doormen occupied with toadying – giving Theo
the chance to slip on past and hide himself behind the foyer's
pillared doors.

What a welcome lay beyond them. The sparkling sheen of
chandeliers. The chequered marble of the floor, where Chinese pots
were filled with palms, reminding Theo of another in his mother's
stolen portrait. She would have lived in such a world, just as Theo
had himself when growing up at Dorney Hall. But, nowadays, that
memory is nothing but a faded backdrop strung across a theatre
stage. Once the curtains are closed, so the illusion disappears. What
is this grand hotel but another smoking pipedream, so far removed
from those who prowl the baser haunts of Covent Garden?

But perhaps he had that wrong. He felt a hand upon his arm.
Turning around, he expected a hotel uniform, instead of which it
was the weasel met so briefly in the theatre.

'Got a light?' the young man asked, a lazy drawl and then a
smile to show discoloured rotting teeth. At the same time, to make
his point, he waved an unlit cigarette below the tip of Theo's nose.
A distinctly herbal odour.

'No ... and would you mind?' Theo tried to pull away from the
grip of grubby hands, the fingernails filed to points, looking as
dangerous as weapons.

Everything about this stranger reeked of menace as he hissed,
'I'm minding *you*. I ask myself, why would the grandson of Lord
Seabrook be mooching round these doors like any other tawdry
beggar?'

'I've come to look for Tilly Lovell.' Theo decided it was best to
speak the truth and not waste time in the trading of riddles.
Meanwhile, inhaling the blasts of sour breath blown in his face,

the anatomist within him began to muse on the appearance of the features that loomed so near above his own: *The eyes are too close. The teeth appear too crowded. The jaw is asymmetrical. A break in childhood, perhaps?*

'Tilly is it, then?' The weasel's hold on him grew tighter. The leering grin that cracked his face appeared to freeze as he went on. 'Course, you'd 'ave sin her in the panto ... sin her flying through the air?' His hand was dropped and, stepping back, his eyes roved over Theo's body, from the head, down to the feet, settling around the groin, at which point the weasel winked. 'P'rhaps she'd deign to look your way from time to time. You never know. You do 'ave a pretty face and, oh, such lovely fairy curls.' His talons raked through Theo's hair. 'Seems a shame Lord Seabrook didn't invite you to the party. Why is that, I 'ave to wonder? What competition would you be for such a gnarly goat as 'im?'

Theo stepped away, and while deciding he must make another visit to his barber, to have his curls shorn off again – they always drew too much attention – he met the weasel's eyes and strained to keep his own voice level. 'I saw you sitting with Keziah in the theatre earlier, so I assumed you were acquainted. There's something Tilly needs to know. It's important. It's...'

The weasel clicked his fingers. *Snap. Snap. Snap.* And then the words, 'Cut out the dash-fire desperation. If it's something that important, spill the beans and I shall pass it on to Tilly soon enough, because' – his mouth drew close again, breath hot and damp in Theo's ear – 'let me inform you right and good, I'm as close as Tilly's brother, which is why I'm 'ere tonight. Looking after family interests.'

A strand of greasy hair fell across the weasel's eyes. He tossed it back, jerkily, looking almost like a puppet. 'Anyway, I would say you've shuffled up a little late. Over there's Lord Seabrook's carriage, already waiting by the doors. Seems the gent wasn't too 'appy with the service 'ere tonight. Him and all the other guests are 'eading back to 'is gaff. Knightsbridge way, I do believe.'

Theo gasped. 'But, she can't...'

'And why is that?'

'She'll be in danger.'

'Danger? Nah! If Tilly's wise she'll find 'erself set up for life. I knows MiLady Seabrook. We shares a certain business interest. In our Rina's company, all our Miss Tilly 'as to do is smile and sing, as sweet as sugar. Perhaps a bit of slap and tickle to amuse the wealthy gents who 'ave a liking for a freak. But if she's got 'er 'ead screwed on, she'll go 'ome a richer girl than when this evening first began.'

'You sound like her pimp.' Theo could not hide the revulsion in his voice.

'Don't knock the trade. It's lucrative, as many West End showgirls find. That's how our Rina started out, before she 'ad the guile to cast her nets and so employ what might be best described as specialities of nature ... appealing to gents predisposed to buy themselves a more unique experience. She discovered 'er first patrons after offering a bribe to the Holywell Street vendors of lewd printed publications, those with an intimate knowledge of their punters' inclinations. After that, well, word will spread, and she established her own club. Very select. Only twelve members permitted on the list. The Apostles they are called, and I imagine some of them would like to worship at *your* feet, if you don't mind the observation. Should you ever find yourself to be in need of extra tin, you just look out for Ulysses and I shall make the introductions. Might 'ave to rough you up a bit though. You've got a soapy look about you. But then, there's some who 'ave a liking for a virgin innocent.'

Theo bristled with disgust, about to turn and walk away, when his attention was distracted by the vision of his grandfather about to board his carriage. At closer range than in the theatre it was clear the old man had put on a deal of weight, and he was stiffer in his movements. Despite himself, Theo felt the stinging needle of compassion. He moved a little nearer, on the verge of calling out – but then Lord Seabrook disappeared. The door was slammed with a thud. The driver clicked his tongue and twitched his whip across the backs of a pair of pale-grey horses.

Theo's thoughts were all awhirl: *Is Tilly Lovell with Lord Seabrook, or has she gone with someone else? Has she gone home with Mr Harris?*

Waving his arms about like windmills, he chased the carriage down the lane, seeing it slow so as to turn and merge with traffic on The Strand. Although still some yards away, through a window he could see Tilly Lovell's perfect profile. Tilly Lovell's smiling mouth as she engaged in conversation with the other passengers.

'Stop! Get out!' He found his voice, but it was drowned by the commotion of the horns, the bells, the hooves that clattered on the busy road. What could he do but stand and stare, and then observe the other face that turned to glance out through the window? Did she know who Theo was? Her calculating expression suggested that she did. Theo froze as Lady Seabrook's mismatched eyes fused with his own.

⁂

Standing at his bedroom window, Theo hears a high-pitched whistle. Looking down across the street, there is a movement in the doorway of the tailor's opposite. A man steps out, looks up at him and Theo groans in misery. The weasel popping up again. Did he follow Theo home, only to lurk out there all night? He must be cold, the way he stoops, and wraps his arms across his chest, the brassy buttons of his jacket glinting in the cold dawn light. He spits a cigarette stub from his mouth down to the pavement. Grinding the butt beneath a boot, he digs a finger in one ear, peering intently at whatever has been mined upon its tip, before his eyes return to focus once again on Theo's window. A sneering smile is on his lips. He waves a hand as if in greeting. Or could it be goodbye?

The weasel wanders off and disappears into an alley, but Theo cannot move. He is trapped in the ghost of his reflection in the glass. Where the tangles of his curls have fallen to one side, somehow the broadness of his brow appears too pale and prominent, as do the angles of the cheekbones and the squareness of the jaw. Is his head quite so large, out of proportion with his body? And those bruised shadows round his eyes – is he unwell, or just exhausted?

He couldn't sleep if he tried. He leaves his room to find Eugene's and sees a bed that's not been slept in. He walks downstairs. The shop is silent. In the museum, the stuffed exhibits have no secrets to reveal. Meanwhile, he feels a bitter draught blowing towards him through the aisles and, as if his spirit guide, the cat is brushing past his legs before it slinks between the partly opened door into the workroom.

There, another door is open. The one that leads to the back yard. Whoever picked the lock has left small heaps of dusty ash scattered on the dwarf child's skull. A half-smoked cigarette has been pushed between the lips of the monkey on its stand.

Theo has no doubt, these are the weasel's calling cards. Staring at them in dismay, he takes the handle of a scalpel, wraps the blade in strips of linen and slips it in his jacket pocket. It would be wise to keep a weapon on his person from now on.

FOURTEEN

THE SMELL OF VIOLETS

Arriving home with Aleski, we found Captain and his doctor friend attending to the patient in the music room downstairs. The fire had been lit, filling the air with welcome warmth; which was really just as well. Martha's wet and bloodied clothes had been removed, and there she lay unconscious on the chaise in nothing but her shift.

Aleski gruffly asked. 'How bad is it? Will she live?'

'Hmm,' the doctor cogitated, pouring more whisky on the cloth with which he dabbed at Martha's head, having shaved away some hair to expose the gaping petals of torn flesh above one ear. 'The wound is very deep. I fear a fracture to the skull. We must hope there's been no rupture any deeper in the brain. But at least the bleeding's stopped, and now...' He shook his head. 'Rest is the only medicine. I suggest you find your beds. There's really nothing you can do here.'

Aleski left. I stayed downstairs, but being mortal tired I fell asleep in the chair I'd dragged up close beside the chaise so as to sit at Martha's side. Suddenly waking with a start, I found myself alone with her, but I could hear some male voices conversing in the hallway. Craning my neck to look around, I caught a glimpse of the doctor putting on his hat and his coat while giving Captain his instructions. 'Make sure to use a cloth to drip some water on her lips. Do you have opiates to hand? Something to sedate her, should she wake and be distressed? It is absolutely vital to keep the woman calm. It could be days before we come to know the full prognosis. Even then...'

As the doctor's voice trailed off, my heart dropped heavy as a stone to hear the caution in those words, also recalling what Aleski had informed me on our journey back to Chiswick from the theatre. How he and Martha had been walking down the lane towards the bar, when her attention had been drawn to the pavement opposite, where several private carriages were collecting passengers. Seeing them, she'd seemed upset, not that Aleski heard her words due to the screaming of a cabman ... when all at once, and with no warning, Martha ran into the road.

What on earth had Martha seen to make her act in such a way? I squeezed her hand. No sign of waking, and so I rose from my chair, going out to the hall to see the doctor in the porch, and Captain bidding him goodbye – before he noticed I was there and turned around to speak abruptly. 'We need some laudanum. Would you go upstairs, Keziah? Look for one of Tilly's bottles?'

He must have known then, of her habit, just the same as Ulysses. Ulysses who'd been supplying my sister with her tincture. How long had that been going on? I was too weary to care, only saw the doctor nod and heard him say, 'Yes, that should do. But, my dear Captain, I'd suggest you call in your own physician to visit Martha in the morning. I'd happily return, but in the present circumstances, the distance and delay would not be convenient.'

'Yes,' Captain said. 'Thank you, Eugene, for all you've done for us tonight, and so far from your own home.' He fondly clutched the doctor's hand. 'Always a friend to be relied on.'

What did that mean? Had Captain suffered some illness of his own? Something this man had helped to cure? And then, the doctor's name? Hadn't Theo also mentioned a Eugene as his employer in a shop? And a museum? What sort of doctor could he be?

I left the men to their goodbyes and walked upstairs towards the room in which I thought to find my sister sleeping soundly in her bed. I gently knocked upon the door, then crept inside, holding my breath, only to see the shutters open and a dreary morning light already slanting in between them. How it glimmered on the china figurines above the mantle. The shepherd and the shepherdess, with crooks festooned with leaves and flowers. The pretty lambs that frolicked round them. Tilly still loved to pick them up, moving the pieces here and there in a neatly structured dance of some impossible romance.

Moving on, my eyes now fell on the crumpled sheets and quilts strewn across her empty bed. Could she be sleeping with Aleski?

Returning to the passage, I walked towards his door, which I opened, first an inch, and then one more so as to push my nose on through and take a peek. Was he alone? I couldn't tell. I only heard the hush of breaths coming deep and regular, now and then a muffled snore. Oh, how I yearned to go and join him as I'd done some weeks before. But then, from lower in the house, there came a sudden thud and a rattling of chains as the front door was being closed. And, with those sounds I was reminded of the mission I'd been sent on.

Back in Tilly's room I opened the drawers in the chest beside her bed. There I found a little bottle that held a thick brown viscous liquid. The label on the side said *Burroughs Wellcome & Co. Tabloid Opium Tincture*. The cork was sealed and slightly dusty, as if during these past few months when Tilly came back to the house after performing on the stage, she no longer had the need of any drug's oblivion. But what about last night? The phial she took from Ulysses?

I felt another sting of dread when the bottle I'd picked up slipped through my fingers to the floor. Luckily, it didn't break, and when sufficiently composed I retrieved it and began to make my way downstairs – only to hear the fainter rattle of the door to the back yard, and then the vision of my sister emerging from the kitchen onto the chequered tiles below me.

For a while our four eyes locked in a tense, protracted silence – and it was odd, but in the dingy morning light the raised perspective of my gaze meant that Tilly looked like a woman fully grown. Her face looked older too. Without the glamour of the greasepaint and the limes, she was too pale. Her hair was limp and somewhat tousled. Long strands were falling from their pins.

Before I had the chance to speak, Tilly came walking up the stairs to stand beside me on the landing, words tumbling out in her excitement. 'Keziah, what a night! I visited the grandest house. But...' She paused to take a breath. 'What have you been getting up to? Look at your dress ... covered in mud.'

Ignoring that, I said, 'Whose house?' My voice was dull, a throaty droning that reflected my exhaustion, whereas her own was high and shrill. Perhaps she was a little drunk, for her smile was slightly crooked, a glassy shimmer in her eyes, and when she yawned I clearly saw how some of Tilly's large back teeth were showing signs of decay. Or was that the stain of black drop?

Unaware of my thoughts, Tilly continued with the dreamy recounting of her night. 'It was Lord and Lady Seabrook's. He's all right, but somewhat daunting. Rather cratchety and blunt. But she is very charming. She'd once aspired to be an actress. That's how Augustus comes to know her. But her husband disapproved, so she abandoned the profession. Mind you, Augustus did confide that anybody brave enough to wed that surly man must surely take the medal as the finest thespian ... if only for the great achievement of always keeping up a smile.'

Perhaps on any other day I would have found this tale amusing, but at the time I felt no more than acute exasperation. Placing my free hand on her shoulder, I insisted, 'Tilly, stop. You need to know. Not very long after you disappeared last night...'

'Oh, I guessed you'd be upset. But, don't you see, I *had* to go. If I can make the right connections, Augustus says...'

'Augustus says! Augustus says!' I shouted back in irritation. 'All of this flattery and fawning! Isn't it time you had some sense knocked into your head and realised your reputation will be ruined if you spend entire nights in the company of strangers?'

Tilly pouted back at me. 'They *are* respectable, and kind. Lady

Seabrook even said that I may use her Christian name, which is...'
She frowned with concentration: 'Zephyrina? Yes, that's it.'

'A gentle blowing wind?' I couldn't help but laugh.

'Yes! And every time she moved there was a lovely wafting
perfume.' Tilly stretched out both her arms and gently flapped
them in the air before becoming far more earnest. 'She took me
to her room and sprayed some on my wrist. What do you think?'
Her little hand was thrust beneath my nose. An overwhelming
scent of violets. Far too sickly for my taste, which I was just about
to say when Tilly started up again. 'She even let me see her jewels.
You've never dreamed so many diamonds. And her wardrobes. All
the clothes. Martha would have been in heaven. I only had to look
at this...' Tilly touched the shawl that was draped around her arms,
where golden threads were glistening among the green and
turquoise weave '...and she insisted I should take it as a token of
her friendship. Then, when we came to say goodbye, she asked if
I would go again, perhaps for tea one afternoon. She said that you
must come as well.'

'Tilly? Thank God, you're home.' Captain suddenly appeared
in the hallway down below us. His tired eyes moved on to mine.
'Keziah, have you found it? Martha's showing signs of waking.'

'Found what? What's going on?' Tilly stared back down at him,
looking even more confused when a moaning sound was heard
from the music room beyond.

Captain offered no reply, but headed back between the doors.
Tilly's gaze fell on the bottle I was holding in my hand. Seeing the
question in her eyes, I blurted out the explanation. 'That's what I
had to tell you. There's was an accident last night. Martha fell in
Drury Lane ... under the wheels of a cab.'

In her surprise Tilly stepped back, and just in time I grabbed
her arm to stop her tumbling down the stairs. As if we needed yet
another invalid with broken bones.

'How badly is she hurt? I need to see her,' Tilly cried as she
struggled from my grasp and then went rushing after Captain.

Very soon I was to follow, but not before I'd stooped to lift the shawl my sister dropped, when I caught another whiff of perfume oozing from the fabric. It made me feel a little dizzy. It took a while before I felt perfectly steady on my feet.

When I did, it was to find Tilly kneeling by the chaise, resting the pillow of her cheek against the flat of Martha's hand. Martha's eyes were partly opened, staring back into my sister's. But, from the hearth, before which Captain had been standing as he watched them, the fire reflected in his eyes indicated only anger.

When he spoke, his words were growled. 'So, Tilly, you've been out in the Seabrooks' company. If I'd known, I would have stopped you. You must never go again. You must forget you've ever met them. Do you understand?'

Tilly made her protest. 'But Augustus introduced me, so I thought you must have known. I thought...'

'Never for a moment did I imagine that Augustus...' Captain broke off, dragging one hand through his heavy silver hair, before he walked towards the chaise and roughly snatched at Tilly's arm. *'Semplicemente non ci credo.'*

Not knowing what he said, I responded anyway, thinking only of our pa and what he'd done so long ago when striking Tilly in a rage. 'Don't you dare hurt my sister, or I swear...'

I had to stop. Captain's eyes met mine with such defiance. But then, perhaps there was no need for me to say another word. His aggression fell away, and now he knelt at Tilly's side, taking her hands in both of his as his voice began to plead. 'You must listen. This Lord Seabrook. I know him well. The worst of men.'

Tilly's head was turned away, avoiding Captain's eyes, until his hand reached for her chin and gently drew it back again. 'I swear to you, I have good reason for this hatred in my heart. You must believe me. You must promise not to meet this man again.'

There was a pause before she spoke. 'If I must, then I shall promise. But...' Tilly started sobbing. 'Augustus told me the Seabrooks are investing in an opera, and there could be a part for me. Would you take away that hope, when you've encouraged me for years? What other life can I pursue? I can't be normal, like Keziah. I'd rather die than be like Martha, always hiding in this house, ashamed of my deformity. I only truly feel alive when I'm standing on a stage. I—'

Tilly broke off, breaths coming fast as Captain stood and carried on. 'Put your trust in me instead. You won't be giving up the stage, and neither do you need any investment from the Seabrooks. This pantomime has made your name, and there are other London theatres. Other places to perform in.'

'What if Augustus is offended? And what about your own position? Aleski's acting too?'

'The only thing I care about is that our family is safe.'

Tilly roughly wiped her eyes, at tears and snot on her face when she shouted back at him, 'You are *not* my family. My mother's dead. My father sold me to a stranger at a fair.'

Open-mouthed to hear such words, I watched my sister leave the room, her silk skirts hissing in her wake. Without a second glance at Captain, I followed her upstairs, and found her lying on her bed.

As I stood there in the doorway, I forced myself to ask the question, 'Did you mean what you said, about having no family? What about me? I am your sister.'

She struggled up, held out her arms. I sat beside her on the mattress and she showered me in kisses. Once again, I smelled the violets, mingled with the bitter odour of some spirit on her breath as she insisted, 'Oh Keziah, I do love you. I always will. Won't you forgive me? I was angry. I was frightened and I'm tired. So very tired. I need to sleep.'

I left the bed to close the shutters and block out the morning light. When I returned from the window Tilly's eyes were closed, and in her hand there was a bottle. The tincture's thick black liquid was smeared around her lips.

❈

Back downstairs I wasn't sure, was Martha sleeping or unconscious? Was she growing feverish? I touched my fingers to her brow. The dark-brown skin was smooth and cool, which did offer me some hope as I turned towards the door that led to Captain's room, and lightly called, 'Are you there?'

Standing at the passage end, he said, 'I'm sorry for that outburst. I have my reasons. You should know them. I've kept the secrets for too long.'

He beckoned me towards the spartan décor of the room that provided such a contrast to the rest of Linden House. With only whitewash on the walls it looked more like a prison cell. A single iron bed and a wardrobe for his clothes. The merest basics he required to sleep at night, and then to wash and dress each morning when he woke. But there was also the portrait, and the baby in the bottle. The things I'd seen when I'd looked in through this door five years before.

'Who is she?' I asked, staring intently at the painting.

'She is...' he began, then stopped to make the slight correction. 'She was Lord Seabrook's daughter.'

'Oh!' Impossible for me to try and hide the shock of that.

Captain nodded, looking pained. 'I met her not long after I first arrived in England, when I taught music at a school. She was sixteen. Me, ten years older. Understandably, her father raised the strongest of objections when we decided we would marry. Indeed, he made it more than clear that I could never be a match for his beloved Theodora.' Captain heaved a mournful sigh. *'Sogni persi.'*

'Sogni Persi?'

'Lost dreams,' he answered dully, reaching out to touch a finger to the portrait's smiling lips. 'I should have been more careful. We should have waited, but our passion, it was strong, and very soon Dora was carrying my child. At first, I thought it for the best. We were not rich, but we were happy, and by then I had the boat on which to make our home ... well away from prying eyes and the vicious gossips' tongues. But then, one day, she saw a newspaper reporting the story of her mother's tragic death. Ah, how my Dora wept at that. No chance to say goodbye, even to see her mother's grave. She was beyond my consolation. But I still thought, this child we made, it will heal the pain of grief and bring new joy to Dora's heart. Perhaps her father's, too. I thought, Lord Seabrook will repent and allow his Theodore to marry with his blessing. Surely, he would not wish to see his daughter ruined. But the only reply he made to any of her letters was to say he'd cast her off. From then on, she could find her own way in the world like any other common whore. She had deceived her parents' trust and now must bear her shame alone.'

Captain sighed. 'My Dora's sorrow, it began to consume her. Always too tired, too thin, too pale. She did not eat. She grew unwell. Soon, it was winter, damp and cold, and we had too little money. It seemed my every application for employment came to nothing. Rumours had spread. The scandal dogged me. I could not even find the fees for a physician to attend her. But then, one day, Dora spoke of a man her mother trusted. His name was Eugene Summerwell, and he had rooms in Harley Street. I went there with little hope to tell him of our plight, and was surprised when he said he would visit Theodora that very afternoon. No expectation of a payment.'

'Summerwell?' I interrupted. 'The doctor who's just left us?'

'Yes. And thanks to him Dora's health was much improved. He diagnosed chlorosis – a deficiency of iron, affecting the nerves and blood. A tonic was prescribed, and she did grow a little better – even singing again. Her voice was very beautiful. But then, one evening, I was out, having secured a part-time job playing in a music hall, only to come back home again and discover she was gone. She'd left a note to say she'd had a meeting with her father, and he'd persuaded her to spend the final months of her confinement in a house he owned in Knightsbridge. When the child was born, then more arrangements would be made with regard to Dora's future.'

'What arrangements?'

Captain shrugged. 'Perhaps to send the baby to an orphanage. These things happen all the time. But' – his voice contained such passion – '*not* to my child.'

'Did you go and see her?'

Captain shook his head. 'I tried. I found the house. But the servants had been told that Theodora was infected with a virulent disease. Only her father and the doctors were allowed into her room. Later, I came to learn she'd been moved to Dorney Hall, supposedly for the fresh air. I travelled there and made it clear that I would batter down the door if Seabrook wouldn't let me in. But...' Captain looked away, towards the portrait on the wall '... by then it was too late. Dora had given birth and was barely even conscious. They said she'd lost too much blood. There was no hope for her to live ... although they did at least allow me to visit the room where she'd spent her confinement. In the attics, well away from any servants in the house. No better than a prisoner. That's where I sat and held her hand, where she sank into her death as a child falls into sleep. At least, my Dora had that blessing.'

'And, what about the child?' Amid a sense of dawning horror, I turned around to stare at the baby in the jar.

'I was told he'd also died, and after several hours of waiting they finally agreed to let me hold him in my arms.' Captain paused and closed his eyes. 'I pulled the blanket from his face. He did not look newly born. His skin was grey and wrinkled, and he smelled peculiar. Something strongly chemical. But Seabrook's doctor explained that was the soap with which they'd washed him, and the withered appearance was because the child had perished in the womb some days before. He also told me something else. Taking the baby from my hands, he turned its body around and exposed the way the shoulder blades had ruptured through the flesh. He said the bones had been too brittle to sustain the slightest pressure. As a result, during the trauma of the birth...'

Captain opened his eyes, staring candidly at mine. 'I can't remember very much about what happened after that. Seabrook spread the news that Dora's death was the result of a severe pneumonia, after which she'd been buried in the family mausoleum. To that event, I was not welcome, just as Dora was excluded from the service for her mother. To tell the truth, I didn't care. What lies inside that sepulchre is not the woman I had loved, and...'

Captain broke off for a long moment. 'Since then, my life has changed. I have settled in this house and somehow found a sense of peace. But not so long before I met with you and Tilly on the Brocas, I was invited to a dinner where another of the guests was discussing Dora's father. He said he'd been to Dorney Hall. Some sort of party, I suppose. This man, he has an interest in natural history and science, and Seabrook had, so he was told, a fine collection of his own. But, while visiting the house, he also saw a private room with certain curiosities.'

'Curiosities?'

'What some might call human freaks.'

Another pause, during which my mind was whirling in distress. The air felt cloying, hard to breath. *The same Lord Seabrook Tilly met ... who Theo said was dangerous?*

Captain carried on. 'I'd assumed that my child had been buried with its mother. But, this man, he also told me of a baby in a bottle. A child with bones that had been broken, which were erupting through its flesh. I had no doubt this was my son, and how could I, in all good conscience, leave him there as one of Seabrook's macabre entertainments ... and inside the very house in which his mother also died? No.' His breathing grew more laboured. 'It could not be allowed. I travelled back to Dorney Hall, to find my child and bring him home.'

'Oh, I understand. That's why you were at the fair.'

'No, you do *not* understand! What you see inside that bottle is not what I believed it was. I only keep it to remind me that a man can be so blind that he will fail to see the truth when it is set before his eyes. Now, I know what *really* happened, and this truth demands revenge.'

Captain placed a hand against the vessel's clear glass side and then surprised me even further. 'Would it alarm you to be told that although I am still grieving for the woman stolen from me, I feel nothing whatsoever for this lump of cold dead meat.'

I clenched my hands against my sides, nails digging deep into the palms as I was thinking of my mother, and of the tiny baby brother who'd been buried in her arms. In grief and anger, I replied, 'You should not keep the child like this. It's a crime. He should be given a decent burial.'

'Ah, *mia caro*.' He touched my cheek. 'This is a complicated matter.'

As if looking in a mirror, I also raised a hand so as to brush away a tear that was spilling from his eye. We stood together for some time, only staring, motionless. Who can say what might have happened, if not for Martha, who'd revived and was now calling out my name – just as she'd done on Boxing Day when I'd been in Aleski's bed.

But as I startled to my senses, I felt less rattled at the thought of Martha seeing me with Captain. My only thoughts were for the milky vacant stare of the baby floating in its bottle. And for the brighter azure gaze of the young woman in the painting.

The same blue eyes as Theo Miller.

PART THREE

THE KINGDOM OF HEAVEN

'WHERE ARE YOU GOING, dear bear?' asked Snow-White.

Bear said, 'Into the forest to guard my treasures from the trolls. In the depths of the winter when the earth is cold and frozen, they stay hidden down below it. But when the sun has thawed the ice, they all come crawling out again. They search the world for precious things and keep them hidden in their caves, where they will never feel the warmth or see the light of day again.'

From Snow-White and Rose-Red

FIFTEEN
A DISAPPEARING ACT
IN THE EGYPTIAN HALL

Linden House
Chiswick High Road
June 17th, 1889

Dear God's Gift,

As Dr Summerwell is visiting with Martha here again, Tilly and me, we thought we'd take the opportunity of giving him the purse that was once stolen from your friend at Brocas Fair. In turn, he says he'll pass it on, and convey our deep regret for any grief she has been caused by our father's thieving ways, for which we still remain ashamed, even after all these years.

The other thing we want to send you is a personal invitation to Tilly's show this coming week at the Egyptian Hall in London. A ticket is enclosed, and should you find you have the time (and inclination) to attend, then afterwards we might take up where we left off in Drury Lane. We do so hope to see you there, and as they say it's third time lucky. On <u>this</u> occasion, we both swear to stick around more than an hour, and not to leave you in the lurch.

Sending you, dear Mr Miller, our very fond regards,
The Lovell Sisters. K & M.

There comes a moment in the show when Theo's eyes rise to the ceiling and he sees his face reflected in the circular glass dome above the auditorium. On the other side of that, the evening stars appear to blink in the dimming purple skies, while down below his earthbound self is in another Paradise – with Tilly Lovell on the stage barely ten feet away from him, and with Keziah in the chair immediately at his side.

He was late in his arrival, due to Eugene disappearing with the shop keys in his pocket. Where had he gone? Chiswick again? After searching high and low to find some spares, with no success, Theo feared his evening out was doomed to end even before it had a chance to begin. But, refusing to give in, he drew the bolts across the jambs and hoped their strength would be sufficient to dissuade any thieves or intruders from the street. One, in particular. One with a grinning weasel leer.

Theo left via the workroom, which he took care to double-lock before emerging through the dinge of the premises' side passage. He saw the windows in the street alight with fire from the last rays of the evening's setting sun. It was so dazzling a sight he felt a singing in his bones, spirits ascending to new heights after the drudgery and boredom of a winter that had seemed to drag forever and an age. Since *that* night in Drury Lane.

At least he'd heard from Eugene that Tilly Lovell had arrived safely home after her dinner at the Seabrooks' residence. On leaving Captain's Chiswick House, after attending to the woman who'd been hurt in Drury Lane, Eugene had seen 'the little fairy girl' descending from the cab that he'd then hailed for himself, sharing the journey back to London with Tilly's escort for the night, Mr Harris from the theatre.

Since then, Eugene has visited at frequent intervals to check the progress of his patient, although when Theo has suggested that he'd like to tag along, Eugene always requests that he stay and mind the shop. Trade has been picking up again.

That very afternoon it was filled with customers who Theo feared would never leave. He'd barely shaved and changed his clothes when the bells of nearby churches tolled the quarter before seven. It would be tight. Just fifteen minutes till the start of the performance. But if he dashed down Regent Street then took a left to Piccadilly, he'd soon arrive at the building with the stone Egyptian gods looming above the pillared porch, looking as if they'd been transported from a temple on the Nile.

Arriving breathless, very hot, he paused a while on the pavement, looking across the busy road to the grand arch that marked the entrance into Burlington House. The very place where, long ago, Miss Miller had suggested he might go to study art. Hadn't she always been inclined to view his skills through rose-hued glasses? Still, what talent he'd possessed had come in useful after all, designing labels for exhibits in Summerwell's Museum. Or for the sketches he still made in private notebooks, now and then.

He heard more chimes. Seven o'clock! Running through the entrance doors, he waved his ticket at the man seated behind a shuttered desk. Hurtling on through a vast room, he saw a blur of hanging frames displaying washed-out rural landscapes. And then the brighter square of gold that marked the auditorium, with the doors about to close just as he darted between them.

What an exotic fantasy. Above his head, a balcony was decorated in a sinuous design of palms and snakes. People, birds, and sacred beetles formed the painted plaster frescos running high around the walls. From the audience below, the insect hum of conversation and the rustling of programmes, listing the songs to be performed upon the stage where velvet curtains were, thankfully, still closed. And there before them was a stand holding the poster that announced –

**FOR ONE NIGHT ONLY
THE SENSATION OF**

THE
FAIRY QUEEN
MATILDA!

While reading this, he heard his name being called across the room – 'Theo! Mr Miller! I'm here. Down at the front.' Keziah waved a white-gloved hand, then pointed to an empty chair. First in the row. Right next to hers.

Sitting hastily upon it, he placed his hat between his feet, then wiped a hand across his brow. He hoped he didn't reek of sweat when Keziah leaned in close so as to whisper in his ear, 'You came. I hoped you would. I know that Tilly will be pleased.'

Keziah straightened up again, and through the corner of his eye he admired the lustrous ruching of red silk that draped in folds across the swelling of her breasts, but left her slender arms revealed. She, and all the other women in the audience that night had sensibly spurned the need for stifling attire, whereas Theo felt constricted in his newest summer jacket, a silk embroidered waistcoat and the garish paisley stock he'd knotted at his throat. Should he have dressed with more restraint? Most of the men wore evening suits.

Keziah tugged at his sleeve. 'Well, what do you think?'

'What do I think?'

'About my dress. I saw you looking. Do you like it? Martha made it just this week. And Tilly's costume too.'

'Martha ... is recovered?' Theo was surprised. 'I thought she must be convalescing. I mean, with Eugene visiting quite as often as he does.'

'Well, there was a little weakness in her left side for the first month, not that you'd ever notice now. The only thing that bothers her is that she still can't recall a single moment of what happened. Dr Summerwell explained that this can happen when a person has a bang on the head. The memories might return, or stay forever lost. There really is no way of telling. But, apart from that advice' – her voice dropped back into a whisper – 'I'd say his visits to the house are more romantically inclined. I think Martha might feel the same.'

Theo's mouth fell open. When had Eugene Summerwell

displayed the slightest inclination for the wooing of a woman? He felt disarmed of everything that, until that point in time, he had presumed to understand. Looking up towards the balcony and decorative frescos, he tried to change the conversation by exclaiming with some passion, 'This place is quite ... remarkable.'

'You can say that again. Mr Harris from the Drury, he has a friend who knows the gent who took the lease here recently. He said it was originally built as a museum. A Mr Bullock wished to show the natural specimens he'd found after joining Captain Cook on his Pacific expedition. He said this auditorium was such a wonder to behold, with lots of foreign trees and flowers, all sorts of birds and animals stuffed and transported from Hawaii. How I'd have loved to see it then, but these days it's mainly used for hosting magic shows. Sometimes the spiritualists as well. That did make Captain dubious, to think of Tilly singing here. But *she* was taken with the name.' Keziah smiled. 'Egyptian Hall ... with Egypt being the place our mother said her people hailed from. Anyway, it's just one night. Tilly's already had enquiries from Mr Moul at the Alhambra. He wants to nab her for the fairy in his pantomime next Christmas.' A white-gloved finger touched her lips to indicate this was a secret. 'Augustus Harris doesn't know, and I fear he'd be offended ... Oh!' she gasped and looked ahead. 'The show's about to start.'

A grand piano was revealed as the stage drapes were drawn aside. Captain was seated there before it, looking as elegant as ever in a long-tailed dinner coat, his hair restrained with a black ribbon. And then the beauty of the music as his fingers played the keys. If any melody could ever be described as having colour, this was blue and green and gold. It skimmed and danced in any light still shafting through the venue's windows. It flashed across the gilded snakes that garlanded the marble columns either side of the gauzy veils suspended high above the stage. And then the veils began to part, and Tilly Lovell was revealed in all her miniature perfection.

The fairy queen stood motionless, as if a statue made of stone. Dressed in a gown of fine white muslin tightly fitted at the bodice, several lengths then billowed out below her waist to reach her knees where the hems were cut away, resembling a flower's petals. White silk stockings. White silk shoes. And on her head white roses, too, with glints of gold and emerald ribbons setting off the gleaming darkness of her loosely waving hair. But her face could not be seen, being lowered at this point. And her hands were held in front – before they lifted either side, just as two giant netted wings extended from her back. A gorgeous butterfly effect, the fabric stitched with what appeared to be a thousand coloured beads.

When she danced, it was as if her feet were rising through the air. And in a less ambitious trick than that achieved in Drury Lane (here accompanied by creaks of all the hidden stage mechanics), she spread her wings as if to fly, one leg kicked back, the other bent as she went gliding past the images presented on the backdrops. First, a verdant summer meadow full of butterflies and daisies. And then, a midnight wood that Theo thought was very like a set in *Beauty and the Beast*, with starlight gleaming through the blackness of the trees, and...

※

We reach the point in the performance when Theo's eyes are glancing up to see his face reflected back in the dome of glass above. When they return to the stage, something peculiar occurs. With every lamp now being dimmed, and as the lingering last notes of the piano's arabesques fade and echo round the hall, the final words that Tilly sings are achingly familiar, though why that is he cannot say.

'*Come Unto Me. Come Unto Me.*'

The words are turning in his mind. Where has he heard the song before?

Meanwhile, Keziah looks his way and murmurs confidentially, 'Captain wrote that song, for a woman he once loved, when...' Her voice is all but drowned by the clapping and bravos as Tilly bows, then disappears back through the veils of fairyland, only then to re-emerge and sing the song a second time –

I sit beside the river. I watch the water flow,
As we watched it once together, but a little time ago.
How soft the rain fell on the leaves, how the grass was wet with dew.
Ah! 'Tis folly to remember, the day you first came unto to me.

The nightingales were singing. The month of June was lit with gold;
I still keep the rose I gave you. I see its blood-red heart unfold.
But breath of rose and lovely bird song are ever fraught with my regret.
'Tis my madness to remember, the day when you first came to me.

The river is now frozen. The nightingales have flown.
The leaves have fallen from the branches. There are thorns upon the rose.
I sit beside my lonely fire and pray for courage to forget,
That you'll no more come unto me. Come unto me. Come unto me.

During this reprise, Theo sees Captain glancing up through the piano's opened lid. To look his way? No, at Keziah. And she is staring back at him with such a fondness in her eyes, just as she did in Drury Lane – until the sudden new distraction of a pyrotechnic wonder.

As Tilly Lovell takes her bow, many flares begin to sizzle on the stage at her feet. The little fairy disappears in a great rainbow cloud of colour. One moment she is there, and the next—

'Where did she go?' He is astonished.

Keziah smiles. 'You must have guessed. There's a trap door built in the stage. By now, she'll be back in her changing room again, getting ready for our dinner at the Hotel Café Royal.' She stands and gives his hand a tug. 'Cheer up, God's Gift. You're coming too.'

A private door beside the stage is blocked by Captain's bulk as he fends off female admirers, and also the reporters keen to meet Miss Tilly Lovell. 'Not tonight.' Captain insists. 'There will be interviews next week. Announcements of some new events.'

One reporter turns around to see Keziah and calls out, 'What have we here? Has Tilly Lovell miraculously grown? The resemblance is uncanny.'

Keziah looks away, and her grip on Theo's hand is even tighter as she ducks around the group, then though the door to the passageway beyond. Here she is standing motionless, her back pressed hard against the wall. Her eyes are closed, breaths coming fast before she suddenly explains: 'I'll never know how Tilly stands it. All the fussing and attention. When people look at me like that, I only think about the time when we were slaving for our pa, deceiving all the punters in displays around the fairgrounds.'

Just as quickly she's recovered, moving on along the passage from where she throws a teasing smile. 'You stay put now, Mr Miller. You can come through when Tilly's decent. Not a moment earlier.'

A smell of lilies wafts towards him through the door Keziah opens. In next to no time, she is back, looking to the left and right, calling to a pair of workmen at the corridor's far end. 'Did Tilly come this way?'

One man, his shirt sleeves rolled, a flat tweed cap upon his head, shrugs his shoulders and suggests, 'Maybe she's still under the stage?'

Keziah turns to someone else who is emerging through the gloom. 'Aleski, could you look? You never know, she might have gone out front to meet with the reporters.'

Aleski? Theo's sure he's heard that name somewhere before. Was it in Drury Lane? The man who took Keziah home? Long-legged and broad of chest, he is refined and elegant in his formal dinner suit, which is where all convention ends. Without his hat and scarf, his appearance is hirsute. Heavy brows above his eyes spread across most of his forehead, merging with the lustrous mane that is growing from his head. The shorter down across his nose makes it look more like a muzzle. From his cheeks, long silky tresses blend with whiskers and a beard. The only places that appear to be devoid of any hair are his ears, and then the lids above and underneath his eyes. They are such mournful dark-brown eyes, and...

Suddenly, Theo is sure. This is the actor who performed as The Beast in Drury Lane. Which means he wasn't using make-up to affect any disguise.

Aleski turns and lopes away with an easy fluid grace. Keziah follows, leaving Theo with the workmen, who are busy stashing wires and fuses into metal boxes. Something to do with the explosion of smoke upon the stage?

The one who spoke before looks up and offers him a wink. 'I'd lay a bet our Tilly's only gone and fallen in a faint from the stink of all them lilies in 'er changing room tonight.'

Theo nods. The perfume's stifling, even in the corridor. And there's another scent as well. Could it be the smell of violets?

He feels a prickle in his belly. Something isn't right. Meanwhile, the man is going on: 'More lilies than you'd see for a funeral in church. They filled a gert big basket. Took two of them to carry it. Some chap and a posh toff. A friend of Tilly's, so she said. Come along to give assistance with the costume and—'

'No. That can't be right!' Keziah's voice is calling out as she returns, along with Captain. 'I helped with Tilly's costume and her make-up earlier. No-one else was in the room.'

'What did these other people look like?' Captain's voice is low and strained.

Meanwhile, Keziah's rushing back into the changing room again. There is a sound of rummaging, a hush of fabrics, metal chinking, and over this her voice is calling: 'Her clothes are all still here. The jewellery, and the dress she'd planned on wearing for the dinner.'

Keziah reappears, standing in the open doorway. A sheen of

pale-grey silk is draped across one of her arms. It is perhaps the very gown that Tilly wore some months before, after the Christmas pantomime. But now it's empty, looking ghostly. Looking as if the living body once inside it has been stolen by the magicians or the spiritualists who work inside this theatre.

Behind Keziah, Theo sees a mass of lilies strewn across a mirrored dressing table. Several more are on the floor, their pure white petals looking bruised, as if someone has trampled them.

The hirsute man is back again, and his voice – a Russian accent? – is slightly breathless when he says, 'The cellar's empty. She's not there.'

'Where could she possibly have gone?' Captain turns and spreads his arms in a show of his distress.

The prop man frowns as he replies. 'Woman's hair was brassy red. Too red to be quite natural. And so much slap I thought she might 've been about to take a turn with little Tilly on the stage. Very 'ard about the eyes ... and something else I couldn't help but cop about them peepers. One was blue and one was brown. Now...' he nods and carries on '...the bloke she was with, he'd be 'arder to describe. Nothing all that special. Bland sort of face and thin fair hair. Somewhat grey about the gills.'

'Did either of them give a name?' Captain abruptly asks.

'Not Madam High-and-Mighty. But I think I overheard 'er call the man something like Clements. Like the bells in the old song. Mentioned your Ulysses as well, though as far as I'm aware *he* never showed his face back 'ere.'

Keziah's eyes are fused with Captain's. 'Ulysses? Did you invite him?'

'No.' Captain shakes his head. 'I haven't met with him in months. But there were posters pasted up all over town. He might have seen them.'

Theo's voice is coming fast and somewhat garbled when he says, 'I know a man called Clements. He's the valet to Lord Seabrook. And the woman, with red hair, I think she is Lord Seabrook's wife.'

SIXTEEN

ULYSSES, THE MESSENGER

I was sitting with Aleski in the backstage changing room, where the sweetly cloying stench of all the lilies filled my nose. I clutched my sister's grey silk dress to my breast, closed my eyes and made the wish that she'd appear like a genie from a bottle – that she'd been playing hide and seek, and any moment she'd come leaping through some hidden cupboard door and shout, 'Ta da! I had you fooled!'

But we were only disturbed by the venue's janitor, when he came knocking to inform us that the hall must be locked up and we would have to leave.

He asked me, 'What about the flowers?'

I said, 'Perhaps you'll throw them out, or you might like to take them home.'

I really didn't care.

In something of a daze, out on the Piccadilly pavement I only vaguely registered the way pedestrians were staring so intently at Aleski. I hardly noticed how the temperature had dropped until I shivered, when Aleski removed the jacket from his back and draped its warmth around my shoulders. At least it wasn't very long until Theo and Captain returned from their excursion to the Seabrooks' Knightsbridge home, barely a mile or so away. Sadly, they had no news to tell. The maid who'd opened up the door had informed them that Lord Seabrook left the city just that morning. His wife had followed in the evening, having said they would be staying at their country residence for at least the next three days. Only their child and his nurse were still in the London house.

Theo suggested we all walk to Summerwell's in Oxford Street.
It wasn't far and we could privately decide a plan of action. So, off
we trudged through the crowds in glittering night avenues, until
he suddenly diverted through the dinge of a side alley. There was
a rattling of keys, and after that some kind of workroom, with a
narrow skylight window that allowed a near full moon to cast its
light across a bench. On that bench a wooden tray held rows of
butterflies and moths, the like of which I'd never seen. All so
enormous and exotic. All reminding me of Tilly and the costume
she had worn to perform that very night. That she might still be
wearing now.

Far less attractive were the amputated wings of tiny birds. Very
fresh they must have been. Muscle and sinew visible. Dragging my
eyes away from them, I saw instead a small, stuffed monkey looking
wizened and malicious. And there was worse, far worse, to come.

Theo lit some jets, and we were guided through the aisles of
Summerwell's Museum, which to my mind was more attuned to
the Screaming House of Horrors me and Tilly had once dared to
go and visit at a showground. How vividly that memory rushed
back into my mind, seeing again the awful image of a woman
wearing veils that billowed up to show a skull. And then the
swinging of a scythe covered in blood as it was cutting through
great swathes of dusty cobwebs.

In the museum was the model of a woman with her body
opened up, as if a bag. There were her entrails on display. Even a
baby in her womb. If it wasn't for Aleski standing near, holding
my hand, I might have fallen in a swoon, overcome as I was by
memories of Betsy Jones, and Betsy's hands splashed red with
blood, and in those hands the little bundle that contained a lifeless
child.

From there, we ducked below an arch, then through a thick
black drape to find ourselves inside a shop filled with macabre
merchandise. And had I really caught a glimpse of our father's
elixir on display behind the counter?

A clock began to chime the hour, the hammers striking twelve as our guide led the way up some steep and narrow stairs, where the carpet was so threadbare it must surely be a death trap. From there, the musty odour of a room where Theo lit the stubs of candles on a mantle, while on the other end of that, a large grey cat was sitting, staring. It was hissing viciously.

Avoiding the creature, I settled on a sofa where horsehair creaked and springs were twanging. Over that discordant music, I looked around and could not help but wonder at the nature of the kleptomaniacs who chose to live in such a place. Dried-out bats with leathered wings were hanging down from ceiling hooks – to make them feel more at home? Figurines of foreign gods stood next to taxidermied mice, rabbits, badgers, dogs and foxes, and several pairs of branching antlers. Fish were preserved in large glass cases. Birds with wondrous coloured plumaged perched on bars in metal cages. I'd never seen so many beetles, and of every size and colour. Human heads of porcelain were marked with rows of dotted lines and printed words to demonstrate the science of phrenology. Boxes were filled with spectacles, all different sizes and designs. I even saw a crystal ball nestled on a small brass stand.

The sphere itself looked black as lead, only the faintest threads of silver swirling in its solid depths. But it lured me like a siren, and I felt an overwhelming urge to hold it in my hands, to wipe it clean using the silk of Tilly's gown, still on my arm. As the glass began to warm, so its depths appeared to clear, until they looked almost transparent, which was a queer thing in itself. And then a picture started forming, rather hazy at the start, like the shadow of a leaf when it has fallen from a tree onto a patch of dewy ground, and even when it blows away a ghostly imprint remains. Next, albeit somewhat briefly, there loomed the figure of a … tiger? It stood erect upon hind legs with claws extending from its paws. It had fanged teeth and a forked tongue poking out between the gaps. More like something you would see on a heraldic coat of arms than any natural animal.

The crystal grew opaque again. I shook my head and felt as if I'd woken from the deepest sleep. Slowly returning to my senses, I raised my eyes to see that Captain stood before a cabinet, reaching out for a decanter from which he poured a pale-brown spirit into silvery etched glasses. Taking the one he offered me, I sipped the liquid's burn and felt its warmth spread through my veins, before I felt compelled to ask, 'What shall we do? What *can* we do, to try and bring my sister home?'

Theo was at the window, looking out as he replied: 'We have to go to Dorney Hall.'

'Yes,' Captain agreed. 'We'll rest a while, then head to Chiswick. If we take the boat, we can dock it at the Brocas. There is the lock at Boveney, but the ground there is more open. Better if we are concealed by the trees beside the river.'

Still with his back turned to the room, Theo's voice was hesitant. 'I ... I once lived at Dorney Hall, and so I know the house and grounds, if that might be of any use. Please understand, I am entirely estranged and independent from the Seabrooks, and have been for many years, but...' he paused, and turned to me '...Lord Seabrook is my grandfather. He took me in when I was orphaned, after my mother died in childbirth.'

Though I'd had my own suspicions about the similarity between Theo and the woman in the portrait back in Chiswick, I was still shocked by this admission. I also saw how Captain's eyes slid my way before he said, 'I know Lord Seabrook too. He once stole something dear to me, and I have waited half my life for that debt to be repaid. In Italy we have a saying: "*La vendetta 'e un piatto che ha un sapore migliore quando fa freddo.*" Revenge, it is a dish tasting best when it is cold.'

Captain eyes were fixed on Theo's, his lips compressed before he said: 'I confess I came to know of *your* connection with the Seabrooks when our mutual friend Eugene informed me of a letter from your old governess at Dorney. Miss Miller, is that right? The name you now take for your own?'

'Why would Eugene have told you that?'

Did I hear indignation, or alarm in Theo's voice?

Captain calmly answered, 'Eugene had his reasons. And, he and I, we have been friends for...' Captain walked across the room and placed a hand on Theo's shoulder with a steadying affection '...for more than twenty years. But we will speak of this again. Not here. Not on this night. Tonight, our thoughts must be on Tilly. Only Tilly.'

Only Tilly. Only Tilly. What hope could I still cling to? Had she gone off willingly to spend the evening with the Seabrooks? She'd done it once before, after the Christmas pantomime. But then, I knew she'd been excited about our meal with Theo Miller. And what about her clothes? She surely would have changed? No. She hadn't gone by choice.

A harsh, low sob caught in my throat. I felt a hand upon my arm and looked around to see Aleski on the sofa at my side. Until that point in the proceedings, he'd been lost in sombre brooding, but now he opened his mouth to give his full two pennies' worth: 'What if she's not at Dorney Hall? What if the maid at Seabrook's house had herself been misinformed? Should we go the police? We could report Tilly as missing.'

Captain's response was curt, 'After some days, perhaps a week, they might begin to show some interest. But, by then anything could happen, and...'

And he might have carried on, but for a rattling commotion coming from the shop below us. Nobody spoke. All ears were cocked, until Theo broke the spell and started heading for the door. 'That's probably Eugene. I drew the bolts across the shopfront when I left earlier this evening. Even with a key, he won't be able to get in.'

'I'll come as well,' Aleski said. 'In case it's not Eugene.'

Standing up, he snatched an iron candlestick from the muddle of the objects on the mantle. The cat, still sitting at one end, flattened its ears and flicked its tail.

❈

It *was* Doctor Summerwell, which proved to be a great relief. Even the cat changed from a feline Mr Hyde to Dr Jekyll, leaping down to the floor to wrap its purring body close around its master's legs. The one of flesh, the other wood.

'What a surprise to see you here.' The doctor beamed at me, then Captain.

We stared back to see a man looking worn-out and hollow-eyed as he cheerfully went on. 'I thought you'd still be dining. Drinking champagne, and—' He suddenly broke off, looking somewhat wary as he glanced about the room.

I thought, *He's noticed Tilly's absence*. But no, his eyes had come to fix on the glass ball in my lap, at which point he smiled anew. 'Perhaps I'll join you for a nightcap. Would anybody like a top-up, or are you waiting for the coffee I heard Theo mentioning when he let me in just now. I'm not sure if there's fresh milk, but...'

We heard the tinkling of china, which was Theo and Aleski making their way back up the stairs. As I gladly swapped my brandy for a muddy cup of coffee, hoping the brew would clear my head of the strange visions I'd just seen, the doctor produced a paper from his jacket pocket and announced, 'Theo, dear boy, when you were heading for the kitchen I found this lying by the door. Your name is written on the front. At least, some near ap-proximation.'

He passed the paper Theo's way. Theo opened it up, and then stared down in dumbstruck silence. But, at last, he bluntly said, 'He claims to know where Tilly is.'

'Who knows what? Is Tilly lost?' the doctor asked, looking bemused.

Captain muttered, 'Disappeared. Almost certainly abducted.' He snatched the note from Theo's hand, hurriedly scanning the words before he gasped: 'Ulysses!'

'So, the prop men had it right,' Aleski replied.

The doctor gave a ragged cry, and despite the dead of night, with only candlelight to see by, I could have sworn his features turned a sort of seasick shade of green. His hands were trembling so badly the contents of his glass went spilling to the floor. But he didn't seem to notice, only asked, 'What does it say?'

My turn to stand and take the paper, to see uneven lines of text scrawled across the crumpled page, the barely literate construction of the words that formed the message:

Deer Thio, Littal Lord,
Yor fary queen as got erself into sum trubbal with the Seebroks. I beeleev she has bin taykan to ther cuntree gaf wear ther will be sum kind of partee goin on tumorro nite. This is not gud. She cud end up beein in sum mortel daynjer. But yu must keep my secrit clos. If thay think the lor is on em then the seebroks are most likely to conseel Tilly away. Yu may not see the gurl agayn.
From yor frend yu can trust,
Ulysses the Wundurer.

After many stumbles, when I'd finished with the reading, Dr Summerwell responded, 'I wouldn't want to cause more worry, but before my fall from grace in the medical profession I came to know Lord Seabrook's wife. That is the first one, now deceased. There were times when she would speak about her worries with regard to her husband's choice of friends. Those intimates, who...' He looked flummoxed. 'Oh dear, should I go on, and break a patient's confidence?'

'*Lei e morta*,' Captain snapped. 'The dead don't listen to the living.'

'Very well,' the doctor sniffed. 'Lady Seabrook spoke about an acquaintance of her husband who held unnatural obsessions. There is a private club for those of similar perversions. She'd chanced to see the invitations, even some photographs her husband kept in his study desk. She spared me the details, and I can't vouch that he was actually involved in the events. After all there is a fertile trade in pornographic pictures touching on such proclivities.' Here, the doctor met my gaze, emotions rising as he said, 'It is imperative to know where your sister has been taken. Lord Seabrook *and* his present wife, a woman known for her loose morals – they think themselves above all law and, from my own experience' – his tone was filled with bitterness – 'believe that privilege and wealth give them the right to reign supreme.'

'Thinking of this second wife' – my thoughts came tumbling, unformed – 'when me and Tilly were first brought to live in Captain's house, Martha spoke about a woman who she'd known some years before, who...' Should I carry on and betray *that* confidence? 'Who had distinctive-looking eyes. There was nothing more specific. But then, the prop man just tonight, didn't he say the woman seen in Tilly's changing room had different-coloured eyes? He'd mentioned Ulysses as well. And now...' I turned to Theo. 'Ulysses is sending messages to *you* about my sister. Why not me? And why not Captain?'

'I barely know him,' Theo countered. 'I first saw him at the panto, when he was in a box with you, after which he came and eavesdropped on a private conversation between myself and Seabrook's valet. Perhaps he thinks this information of my family connection gives him some leverage of power. Later on, at The Savoy, where I had hoped to warn your sister to be wary of Lord Seabrook, Ulysses was there as well. Unlike me, he had a high regard for Tilly's newfound friends.'

'Is that why you left the cab, when we were taking Martha home?' Captain asked.

Theo nodded with the grimmest of expressions. 'For all the good that it did.'

Though Theo's protests seemed sincere, I had my doubts and demanded, 'If it's true, you've had no contact with the Seabrooks for some years, why were you meeting with the valet at the Christmas pantomime?'

'He was passing on reprisals. A warning from my grandfather that I should keep away from him and his new family.'

Theo turned, and raised both arms, hands grabbing at the mantel shelf, his fingers gripping so hard I saw his knuckles whitening as he carried on explaining. 'To this day he still despises me, for who and what I am. A bastard is the least of it. But even then, he'd always hoped I'd carry on the Seabrook line ... before he fathered his own son and I became disposable.'

Eugene burst out: 'My dearest boy, never give in to such despair. A man like that must be defied. He may have ruined my career, but I won't stand for the abuse and wicked way he's treated you. And now, this kidnapping of Tilly. It is too much. Simply too much.'

When these dramatics reached their end, Aleski spoke in measured tones. 'We must hope that Ulysses is telling us the truth. We know that blackmail is his business. His currency is information. We can be sure he keeps his ear close to the filth in every gutter. Even the ones that run outside the finest homes and private clubs.'

Captain stared back through weary eyes. 'We knew the Seabrooks were involved, and now this note confirms it. But why Ulysses should write to Theo, and not me...' He looked confused and heaved a sigh. 'Let's hope we find the answer soon.'

SEVENTEEN

RETURNING TO THE BROCAS

Theo looks back towards the shop, where the sign is turned to *CLOSED* and underneath there is the message Eugene's scribbled with a pencil: *Until further notice. Inconvenience regretted.*

Bleary-eyed, the small group huddles on the early-morning street. A growler's hailed. The cheerful driver agrees to take them all to Chiswick. Almost as soon as they are seated, Keziah's shoes have been kicked off and stockinged feet rest on the knees of Aleski, opposite. She yawns and quickly falls asleep, head lolling on the arm of Captain sitting close beside her. Such a natural easy bond there seems between the three of them. Or has exhaustion stripped away the need for any modesty? No, it is more than that. Here is a tender physicality that Theo's never known. It is friendship. It is trust. It is nothing to do with fucking.

Theo tries to sleep himself, having barely snatched as much as an hour the night before. But there is Eugene's monstrous snoring. And there is Eugene's booted foot, and Eugene's stump, and the clasp of Eugene's bag biting into Theo's ankles every time the older man shifts his position. *Why bring his work bag on this trip?*

Theo draws his legs in closer. Looking through the grimy windows, he sees the West End's grandeur fade to a grey suburban sprawl, and then the vibrant green expanses of the farms and market gardens leading to the Chiswick High Road.

When they arrive at Captain's house it is the middle of the morning. They enter through a back-yard door, straight into a large square room, which causes Theo to suffer from a yearning of nostalgia, being so vividly reminded of the kitchen back in

Dorney, and of the boy who used to sit at the enormous scrubbed pine table, nibbling warm currant biscuits, listening to all the chattering as Cook and her assistants bustled around him through the steam.

Here, in Linden House, the hare-lipped Martha is as busy. She helps Keziah and Aleski, dishing up bowls of creamy porridge, making pots of tea and coffee, buttering mounds of toasted bread. And then, the final contribution, scrambling two dozen eggs.

Only once they are all eating does Martha look around the table and enquire, 'Where's Tilly got to?'

Keziah is the one to tell the details of last night. But when she fails to make a mention of the woman with red hair and her oddly mismatched eyes, Theo interrupts and the picture is completed.

Martha's reaction is extreme. She pushes back her chair and, as she stands, she's crying out: 'That's who it was! Now, I remember. She was there, in Drury Lane. Standing across the street with Tilly, about to get into a carriage. I tried to warn Tilly. I did. I...'

'Don't upset yourself, dear Martha.' Eugene is reaching for her arm and gently urging her to sit.

'Are you sure?' Martha persists, looking anxiously at Theo. 'Our Tilly's with that woman now?'

Aleski nods, and then begins, 'Ulysses. He—'

'Ulysses!' Martha exclaims as yet another splash of oil stirs the fires of her passion. The ill-formed flesh around her mouth is twisted in a wild grimace. Saliva dribbles down her chin as she gasps and slurs the words. 'If he has harmed that precious child, I'll murder him with my own hands.'

Her breaths are coming fast as Captain tries to reassure her. 'There may be goodness in his heart. I believe he wants to help.'

'Pah!' she all but spits. 'He is a devil in disguise.'

After that, there's little talk. Nobody wants to eat. Martha starts to clear the table, and Eugene offers his assistance, also rising from his seat to carry plates to the sink. Theo sits and stares in wonder. What *has* come over his employer, with this unprecedented show

of willing domesticity, even taking off his coat and rolling sleeves
to scrub at pans? The world has turned upon its head. Theo's own
head is slightly fuzzy, as if it's full of cotton wool, and such a sense
of disconnection when his eyelids start to droop...

'Theo, are you all right?' He wakes to see the table empty and
Keziah at his side, looking down through shadowed eyes. 'Captain
and Aleski are checking on the boat. I'm about to go upstairs. I
must get changed out this dress. But first, I thought I'd show you
somewhere more comfortable to rest.' She glances back towards
the sink, where a cacophony of clattering and banging carries on.
'Somewhere more peaceful than in here.'

✣

He wakes again, but can't remember where he is. He feels drunk.
His head is swimming with the music of the song Tilly was singing
yesterday in Piccadilly: *Come unto me. Come unto me.*

But it's not Tilly's voice he hears. This tone is altogether deeper.
And now, it's getting clearer. Is someone singing in this room?
Shaking his head, he sits up straighter, squinting his eyes against
the sunlight slanting through some tall French doors. Beyond the
glass, the flaking paint of an ironwork veranda is swathed in
summer foliage. Dripping wisteria racemes. A pink clematis.
Rambling roses. More floral echoes in the room's decorative
plaster covings, or faded silk that lines the walls – in which a door
is camouflaged.

He only notices it's there because he hears the faintest creak,
then sees it swaying on its hinges. No more than an inch, but
enough to sense the coolness of a draught blowing through. The
air outside is still. The leaves and flowers at the windows have not
so much as trembled. And yet, this door continues moving,
opening a little wider to reveal a narrow passage, and at its end...

Theo could swear that he has seen his mother's smiling face.
Almost as soon, she disappears. The door has thudded to a close.

He stands and stumbles towards it. But it's locked. It can't be budged. He tries to think. Is this a dream? One of those lucid, waking visions induced by lack of sleep? Is it the coffee he's been drinking through the night, again at breakfast? He does feel twitchy and uneasy. His bladder aches. He needs to piss.

Heading out into the hall he sees Keziah high above him, making her way down the stairs. No longer in her evening gown, she wears a shirt and large tweed jacket over a pair of plain grey trousers, all of which have clearly come from the wardrobe of a man. There's a belt around her waist to help draw in the extra cloth, and her hair, which earlier had been a mass of heavy waves, has been knotted at her nape. On her head there is a cap.

'I hope Aleski doesn't mind me stealing clothes from his room.' She pauses on the small half-landing, holding Theo once again in her intense black gaze. 'I know they don't exactly fit, but ... good enough to be convincing?'

What can he say? If she presumes any strangers will be fooled into thinking she's a man – well, the deceit *might* just succeed during the hours of the night. But, in the clearer light of day, Keziah's figure is too full, and her features are too fine, her cheeks and lips a bloom of pink even without cosmetic paints. There's something else that doesn't fit. Despite the masculine attire, on one hand she wears an ostentatious-looking opal ring. She didn't have it on before. He would have noticed. Couldn't miss it!

'You make a very pretty boy,' Aleski's voice breaks through the silence.

How long has he been standing in the doorway to the kitchen? His jacket's been discarded, but otherwise he is still dressed in what he wore for last night's show. A plain white shirt that is now streaked with the stains of engine grease. The same with Captain just behind him. But whatever they've been doing on the boat, it seems the tasks have been completed and they're ready. Captain speaks with urgency, '*Pronto?* It is time. We must leave without delay.'

✳

It is already nine at night when the engine of the boat stops its hypnotic, rhythmic thrumming. Theo, who's been dozing, sprawled across a narrow bunk, peers around through the half-light to find he is alone, except for Captain's big grey hound lying on the floor nearby, her muzzle resting on her paws. He swings his legs across the bunk, she mirrors him and also rises, clawed feet scritch-scratching on the floor before she stops and rests the softness of her chin upon his knee. After some murmured pleasantries, Theo notices the mug of lukewarm tea left on a shelf fixed to the bottom of the bunk. He takes a sip. Too sweet for him, but it doesn't go to waste. The dog is lapping greedily – until they're both disturbed by sounds of thudding on the deck.

Standing himself, yawning and stretching, Theo heads towards some steps, emerging through a door to see Aleski and the Captain using ropes to moor the boat to the trunks of nearby willows. The branches form an arch, leaves trailing down into the water – just as they'd done some years before on another balmy night, when Theo had been hiding as he'd spied upon the sisters.

He barely notices the swans. Two of them rising from the waters, their spread wings snapping sharp as drums as they soar above the trees. Underneath, and on the tow path, Keziah's staring at the Brocas, and such a sadness in her voice when she suddenly announces, 'I thought the fair might still be here.'

'It is too late now, *mio caro*,' Captain softly says as he offers her a hand. 'The summer show has been and gone.'

In some communion of silence, her fingers twist through his. Her eyes are glittering with tears before she suddenly exclaims, 'Tilly's somewhere near. I can feel it in my bones.'

'We are not far from Dorney Hall.' Captain nods back along the path, and as he speaks the dog is barking, scrabbling across the deck, where it stands with hackles raised, a low vibration in its throat. As if to mirror this concern, Captain's shoulders also stiffen. He sniffs the air. His eyes are slits, following the little orb of fiery red that dips and hovers through the dense green foliage – from which a figure is emerging.

'Ulysses!' Keziah shouts.

'Evening … you took your time. I'd very nearly given up.' The weasel ambles on towards them, stopping about ten feet away. With a flourish he removes his brown felt hat and makes a bow. 'At your service, my old friends.'

'I hope you won't be causing trouble.' Aleski is not smiling.

Ulysses ignores him. 'Is Martha here as well?' He twists his lips to imitate the expression on her face.

Martha stayed in Linden House, along with Eugene Summerwell. Captain wanted someone there in case this search for Tilly Lovell proved to be a wild-goose chase. If she came home, at least she wouldn't find the house to be deserted. But there's no doubt in Theo's mind that Captain's rationale has more to do with Eugene's stump, which often makes him slow and clumsy, and Martha's lack of self-restraint with regard to her dislike of the young man who's come to meet them.

Ulysses stubs out his smoke on the bark of a tree. He spits. A gob of phlegm finds its target on the tow path, missing Aleski by an inch. Meanwhile, his eyes are raised to Captain's, for a moment looking plaintive before the chirpiness returns. 'And so, we rendezvous where the chapter in the story of the sisters first began. And here I am, the bent brown penny spinning back to your assistance.'

'I guessed you would be here.' Captain's response is cool, revealing no emotion when he asks, 'What's going on?'

'I've come to bring you this. An invitation for tonight.'

From a pocket in the lining of his brass-buttoned jacket, Ulysses extracts a card. It is made of laid white paper, gilded edges, very heavy, and there's the faintest smell of violets when he waves it in the air.

'Where did you get this?' Captain asks above the dog's new bout of growling, its fanged teeth bared at Ulysses.

'A member of the Seabrooks' club. The Bacchanalians, they're called. There's one particular old cove who has a fancy for my boys. He'll dandle them upon his knee. They'll slip their fingers in his pockets. Sometimes, burrowing for coins. Sometimes, for other sorts of treasure.' He taps a finger to his nose. 'That's what I trains my mice to do. I only ever 'as to offer them the smallest crumb of cheese as the promise of reward, and back they scurry with the needful.'

'How do we know it's genuine?' Aleski sternly asks. 'Are *you* expecting some reward?'

'Well, now you comes to mention it, there might be a *little* one. But that is something to discuss when this adventure's put behind us.' Ulysses arches a brow below his lank and greasy fringe. 'Much like you, it's my desire to see our Tilly free again, to save her wings from being clipped. Or am I wasting precious time, hobnobbing by the Thames as if we're on a pleasure trip? I 'ave to say I don't exactly sense the heartiest of welcomes, so if you'd rather I fucked off and disappeared, and left you to it...'

'No!' Keziah's voice is urgent. 'I believe you, Ulysses. We need your help. *She* needs your help.'

EIGHTEEN

THE COVEN OF THE BACCHANALIANS
INVITES ITS TWELVE APOSTLES TO

A MIDSUMMER NIGHT'S DREAM

NYMPHS & SHEPHERDS COME AWAY
TAKE YOUR PLEASURE AS YOU DALLY WITH
THE FAIRIES & THE FREAKS

While I was still in Linden House, the china shepherdess and shepherd gleamed with a fragile innocence on my sister's bedroom's mantle. The living versions we would see later that night proved to be nowhere near as virtuous, though I'd already feared the worst before our journey even started – when I'd asked the tarot cards if they might offer me some clue regarding Tilly's whereabouts.

Holding my breath in concentration, I shuffled through the deck, telling myself, *I'll turn one card, only one card...*

It was The Tower, struck by lightning, flames bursting out through the windows and the tiles of the roof, while the ground on which it stood had been engulfed in raging seas. Between the natural elements of water, earth, and air, and fire, two human figures could be seen as they plunged down ... towards their deaths?

I had no skill in the interpreting of messages back then, but an image depicting such chaos and destruction, it did give me the queerest turn, and I confess it didn't fill me with the hope that I'd been seeking. Neither did the sound of music rising upwards through the house. A woman's voice, and very faint, and afterwards I wasn't sure if I'd imagined the whole thing, being so desperate to believe it was Tilly home again – that she was in the music room, singing Captain's composition: *Come unto me. Come unto me.* But it wasn't Tilly's voice, being more of a contralto. Which in turn had begged the question – all those times when I'd believed Tilly was lost in black-drop dreams, had she been hearing something real?

I told myself I was exhausted, fraught with anguish for my sister. Perhaps a guilty conscience too, having deliberately taken Theo Miller to the music room to sleep an hour before. But I'd made sure the passage door leading on to Captain's room had been securely closed, so it was really most unlikely that he'd chance to see the portrait of the woman he resembled. Or had I secretly been hoping that his curiosity might lead him to her anyway? *Stupid. Stupid. Stupid!* Whatever madness had consumed me? This was a puzzle that had waited many years for the pieces to be set in their right places. They were never in my hands. And as Captain said last night, for the present we must concentrate on Tilly. Only Tilly.

※

Once Captain's boat had docked at Windsor, when Ulysses turned up to meet us with his pilfered invitation, he'd smiled at me with something rare. A hint of kindness. Or regret? But the old cockiness returned when he said, 'I must confess I've often fancied an invite to the Seabrooks' private parties. But, alas, my dear friend Rina 'as become somewhat selective since she's netted her old Lord. Prefers them toffs she calls Apostles to the devils from 'er past.'

'How do you know her?' asked Aleski.

Ulysses gave a smirk, puffing out his pigeon chest, 'Oh, I've known her many years, for as long as I remember. Before I ever came to Chiswick, I'd often 'ang about 'er 'ouse, where I'd be fed and made a fuss of. Any number of the whores who used to work for Zephyrina could perhaps 'ave bin my mother, even Rina 'erself. Course *she* denies it viciously, and since she's spawned the Seabrook 'eir she's upped and moved 'erself to Knightsbridge, from where she's taken to parading round the town like royalty. However, there was a time when Rina's scope was somewhat lower … when you might say she developed the foundations that 'ave led to 'er meteoric rise … when Lord Seabrook started visiting her Bloomsbury brothel and she set her cap at him, and also took to warning me to make me presence scarce. Course, she's changed her tune since then. Now she's got what she wants. And I do 'ave my unique uses. But, back then, I spent so many days and nights lurking about in the basement area, in the 'ope she might relent and take me in again … and that was how I came to witness Martha's own evacuation. Very curious I was. Intrigued by such an ugly dial, which I'd not seen until that point … not with 'er 'aving bin imprisoned, well away from prying eyes. But where could she be going, I wondered to myself? If it was anywhere near decent, could I tap 'er up for tin?'

Here Captain butted in, looking entirely mystified. 'You never mentioned this before. I had no idea…'

Ulysses batted back: 'Neither was Martha aware that I'd followed 'er that day, not then knowing me from Adam. But what a blessing that I did, for that was 'ow I also came to be acquainted with yerself. I spied you with 'er on that bridge, when I thought it more than likely she would jump and top 'erself. I saw you save 'er and I thought, well 'ere's an 'andsome, kindly gent whose pockets might be worth a pick. I saw you waving down a cab. I heard you give a destination. Took me an age, but I followed. Walked all the way out there from London. Ulysses the Wanderer. That's what you called me, isn't it, that day when we first met outside your fancy Chiswick gaff? When I begged you for a coin and you asked me where I'd come from. And the rest ...is 'istory. Course I told you some old bumph. I always like to keep my different lives entirely separate. I likes to keep my secrets close.'

Ulysses' smile held affection. 'You were good to me back then, and I shall always 'ave a fondness for the Captain of my ship ... which is why I'm 'ere tonight. My loyalty to Lady Rina goes so far, but...'

'The woman is a witch,' I interrupted angrily.

'A witch indeed,' Ulysses nodded. 'And now she's even more audacious ... which is exactly where the older, bolder Ulysses comes in. I confess, in the past I've 'elped procure the willing flesh for the amusements of 'er guests, whether in London, or the country. The country 'aving the advantage of its hidden mausoleum.'

'The mausoleum?' Theo said, at the same time looking perplexed.

Ulysses gave him a wink. 'All lit up with candelabras and decorated with the Seabrook's own collection of exhibits.'

'And is this where they have Tilly?' Aleski calmly asked.

Ulysses answered with a nod, thrusting an arm towards a path worn through the grass between the trees. 'Shall I lead the way?'

�

Off we trudged, a good half-hour across the misted night-time meadows, and for some time we could still hear the whining of the dog Captain left chained beside the boat. I found the sound to be distressing, but Captain said he couldn't take the risk of Dolce running off, or maybe barking to alert the party-goers of our presence. In which case, I had to wonder, why did he bring her in the first place? I believe his plans were changed the moment Ulysses appeared and Dolce snarled and bared her teeth.

I also felt my hackles rising when I saw the house ahead, with rows of silhouetted gargoyles looming on the parapets. But more alarming was the tower rising high above a chapel where slits of windows glinted gold, just like the tarot card I'd drawn. How the resemblance made me shiver, my eyes transfixed on such a vision, until Captain grabbed my arm and pulled me down behind some brambles, so as to hide when a barouche went rolling past towards the gates that marked the drive of Dorney Hall.

Taking advantage of the chatter going on between the gateman and the guests, who had been asked to show the proof of invitations, we slipped on past to make our way around the hall's perimeters. Wasn't I glad not to be wearing yards of petticoats and skirts as we pushed on through thorns and nettles that were seeking to entrap us. Gladder still when Ulysses stopped to stroke his hand across an ivy-covered wall, before he turned to look at Captain. 'If I remember rightly, 'ere's the place through which we made our entrance once before?'

Could he be right? There was no gate or garden door that I could see. Were we all to be propelled across the wall like acrobats? Thankfully, before I'd steeled myself to take that course of action, Captain was kneeling on the grass, murmuring to himself, 'Yes, this is the place.'

His fingers nimbly pulled away the barricade of foliage, after which he prized them deeper into gaps where the mortar of the brickwork had eroded to nothing more than dust. First, one brick was pulled away, and then another, and another, all being piled upon the ground until a space had been revealed, quite large enough for anyone to crawl on through into the garden.

'Bravo, Captain,' said Aleski. I heard the smile in his voice.

Theo's came much harder. 'This must be where Miss Miller once saw a stranger in the garden. The evening of the Brocas Fair, when someone broke into the house.'

'Most likely me,' said Ulysses. 'I squeezed through first to take a gander, being the smallest at the time.' He nudged at Theo's arm, 'Not the case anymore.'

Theo turned to look at Captain. 'You broke into Dorney Hall and took the painting of my mother? The painting I felt sure I saw today in Linden House. I thought I'd dreamed it at the time. But, now—'

'I did not come here for the painting,' Captain interrupted. 'But when I saw my Dora's face, how could I bear to leave her here, with the brute of a man who'd lied to me, who was so evil as to—'

'Steal a child from its father?' Theo's eyes were wide as saucers, staring at Captain through a silence hanging so thick upon the air I could have touched it with my fingers. But, at last, he carried on. 'The child he raised as if his heir, until another came along.'

'He has no heart. He never did. If my Dora had survived, what different lives would have been had by...' Captain's voice faltered with emotion, during which we were disturbed by some rustlings and grunts from the garden's shrubberies.

Everybody froze. Every ear was listening. It seemed a small eternity until I found the nerve to whisper, 'Are there dogs guarding the house?'

Theo's voice was also hushed. 'There were never dogs before. Lord Seabrook doesn't like them, not unless they're dead and stuffed. He will tolerate the hounds that run with the hunts, but none of them are kennelled here.'

Captain, who'd been peering intently through the wall, now smiled back up at me. '*Il porcospino*. Just a hedgehog roaming about in the bushes. It is all more overgrown since the last time I visited. And that is good. Better to hide.'

Ulysses chipped in again. 'Theo and me should make a move. Our little lord will know the best way to find the house's kitchens. We'll stick our lug 'oles to the door and see what gossip's going down. Staff is always in the know, and might divulge more information of our Tilly's whereabouts.'

Aleski looked at Theo, 'Are you sure? There is no need for you to place yourself in danger.'

Ulysses sighed and clicked his tongue. 'Danger! What's this

danger? It's a fucking country party, not the Crimean War. The only blood likely to spill is little Till's virginity.'

Horrified to hear those words, I could do nothing more than watch as Ulysses crawled through the wall. Still crouching on the other side, he turned his head to grin at Captain. 'Can't teach your granny to suck eggs. I knows the game of loyalty. You taught me well, and I assure you *everything* will go to plan. Me and Theo, we will meet you at the mausoleum doors. If Tilly isn't at the house' – he tapped a finger to his nose – 'that's where she'll be. Mark Ulysses.'

Without another word, Theo clambered after him. Once on the other side, framed by rough bricks and foliage, he offered me the briefest flicker of a smile before the two of them moved off into the shadows.

That's when I had the sudden urge to call his name, to shout for Theo to come back and stay with Captain – stay with Aleski – stay with me. Not to go with Ulysses. I drew a breath to do just that, but Captain turned to give a warning. 'Less noise now, *mia caro*. If you are nervous, would you rather stay and wait for our return?'

Stay! Was he insane? I muttered back, 'I'll be more careful. I...' The sentence didn't end, and any brooding premonition I had felt faded away, this time diverted by the sounds of distant shrieks and splashing water.

'What's going on?' Aleski asked, before he climbed through the wall so as to get a better look.

I followed swiftly in his wake, pushing through the shrubberies where I caught the fragrant drifts of nutmeg from some nearby flowers. And something else that seemed familiar, something cloying and astringent. But my thoughts went tugging on, suddenly getting a good view of the house that lay ahead, and the glitter of the moonlight on an ornamental pond.

Rising from the water's centre was a statue of Poseidon. A fountain spouted from his mouth, raining down on the small group of naked people underneath it. What a racket they were making as they splashed and crawled about over reclining marble sea nymphs, their antics only silenced by the tolling of a bell from some far corner of the gardens.

As the chiming carried on, so the bathers left the water and were joined on the terrace by another group of people. Hard to see them very well, but could they be in fancy dress?

As they descended some steps, walking across the lawns towards us, Captain touched me on the shoulder and whispered urgently, 'They're heading for the mausoleum. Quickly. Follow me.'

✖

The tolling led us to a chapel, where the doors were firmly locked. Raising my eyes towards the glinting threads of light that were escaping through the tower's slitted windows, I suggested, 'I could climb. Look through a window. See inside.'

Captain nodded, '*Buona*. Aleski, can you help her? I'll head around the back to see if there's another exit. If we go in, we must be sure of also getting out again.'

My good idea was somewhat easier to speak of than perform. But having used the iron brackets of a drainpipe as a ladder, and with a good hard push or two from Aleski down below, I was soon crouching and then crawling through a leaded rooftop gulley, moving on towards the tower at the entrance to the chapel.

Steeped in the darkness of its shadows, I waited for Aleski to also climb and reach my side. Without a word, he clasped his hands around my waist to hoist me up. My teeth were gritted with the effort. My fingers grasped at the stone ledge of the window that was nearest, through which I looked, just as I heard the sounds of movements in the garden. I held my breath. My body stiffened. Aleski's grip became much tighter. Afterwards, I'd find the bruises of his fingers on my skin. But at the time I barely noticed, straining instead to hear a husky woman's voice some way below:

'My dearest friends, we reach the moment you've been eagerly awaiting. An exclusive viewing of our latest acquisitions. But of course, the promised highlight of the night will be no other than our precious fairy queen.'

I missed the rest. Her words were drowned by jeering calls and lewd suggestions, too obscene to be repeated. Why, you only need to conjure up the basest of the terms alluding to a female's sex, or else the act of copulation, and you will have the gist of it. None of those words were new to me. I'd read the whole of *Fanny Hill*, and cruder terms too often issued from my father's drunken lips. But to think of them connected with my sister – I was frightened, even more so than before. I only wished my hands were free so as clap them to my ears, to try and block the clamour out. Such a cacophony it was. Less a gathering of toffs more like a zoo of animals who were all lusting to be fed. And over that, a heavy knocking, followed by the lower tones of a man who gruffly called, 'Clements? Are you there? For God's sake man, do let us in.'

Now, more faintly – from inside? – came the chink and scrape of metal, which left me yet more sick with dread, for those sounds put me in mind of all the musty gothic novels I'd devoured in Linden House. The tales of evil monks, or ruined maidens trapped in chains, confined to dungeons dank as tombs. Truly, my panic knew no bounds. My mind was spiralling with fear, only anchored back to earth when I heard Aleski murmur, 'They must be opening the doors.'

Craning my neck and looking down, I muttered back, 'Push me higher.'

I heard him groaning with the effort, and I was raised an inch at best. But an inch was good enough for me to spy through the glass, to see the bell rope that still swayed as it dangled over murals painted on the grey stone walls. The paint looked fresh. The colours gaudy. There were stars, and suns, and moons, but also lions, crabs, and bulls, and fish and goats, and other creatures – to represent a zodiac? And, in the centre of it all was the figure of a tiger. The tiger wore a golden crown.

My head was swimming with the vision seen inside the crystal ball back at Summerwell's Museum. And though my fingers were now numb, I forced myself to grasp the ledge even more tightly than before. I *had* to see what lay below.

Candles burned in iron sconces. Wax dripped across a flag-stone floor to form an intricate white lace. Within this web, beyond some pews and before a small stone altar, a slender man in a dark suit looked as serious and solemn as a funeral director. He gave a deferential bow as two others stepped towards him. A man and a woman, who I supposed must be the hosts.

She wore a wreath of golden leaves on her abundant scarlet tresses. Barely covering her breasts was a white, transparent shift. Was she supposed to be some raddled high priestess from ancient Egypt?

The gent I recognised from that brief glimpse in the bar after the Christmas pantomime. He wore a formal dinner suit and seemed considerably older than the woman at his side. Maybe he'd reached the dizzy age, for he did not appear to be all that steady on his feet. He had a humpty-dumpty paunch, looking even more pronounced due to the angle of my vision. His shoulders stooped. His head was bald, but for the tufts of thick grey hair sprouting above a starched white collar. And his voice, the very one I'd heard some moments earlier, was slightly cracked and thick with phlegm, but held a military brusqueness when he addressed the 'undertaker': 'Is everything prepared?'

The servant bowed and turned away so as to walk behind the altar. The Seabrooks seemed about to follow – but not before the old lord raised his head and, for a moment, I believed my cover blown. I know I should have ducked and tried to hide myself away, but I was oddly mesmerised by the suspicious, flinty hardness in his animal pale eyes, and at the way the tower's darkness and the glimmer of the candles caused such a chiaroscuro contrast as it fell across the warts and reddened folds of pitted flesh around the tusks of his moustache.

But perhaps he was dim-sighted and hadn't noticed me at all. His head was lowered again, now looking back towards the doors through which he'd entered from the garden, slowly lifting a hand so as to beckon to his guests.

By then the muscles in my arms were all but screaming with the pain. I lost my grip and slumped back down to feel warm breath against my cheek, when Aleski hissed the question, 'Well, what did you see?'

'Tilly didn't seem to be there, but...' I stopped, because I heard more muffled voices from the chapel. A sort of humming expectation.

'Quick, help me up again.'

I pressed my nose against the glass, and what a turn I had to see the freak show gathering below. It was as if all of the creatures in the painting on the ceiling had been conjured into life. But below the beastly masks that all those whooper-uppers wore were the bodies of grown men. Some were lean, appearing youthful. Others more aged, like Lord Seabrook, were hunched and stiff, or corpulent. Most were dressed in dinner suits, but some had stripped to all-in-ones for their dipping in the fountain, with the damp linen of their drawers clinging to bags-o-mystery. Not quite mysterious enough! It was the same with two women, only wearing sodden bloomers, each of them brandishing a shepherdess's crook in her hand. The diamonds clasped at one bare neck captured the glimmer of the candles, throwing out a rainbow light that, for a moment, left me dazzled. And by the time I looked again, every soul had disappeared. Not another sound to hear, until, from somewhere in the garden, came two hoots, and then a whistle. Captain's sign for us to find him.

He was at the chapel's doors, pressing a finger to his lips before he whispered cautiously, 'I had no time to search inside. We shall have to take our chance.'

'Or stay put?' Aleski murmured. 'Wait for Ulysses and Theo?'

Captain did not respond to that, only asked me, 'What did you see?'

'The red-haired woman and Lord Seabrook. And several others wearing masks, like the stuffed heads of animals. All different sorts of animals.'

'And the basket?' Captain asked.

I shook my head. 'I saw no basket.'

'Some of them carried one inside. Large enough to hold a person.'

'Tilly?' Aleski muttered. 'At the Egyptian Hall, didn't the prop man speak about a basket being used to carry in the lilies. Was she carried out in that?'

Captain frowned, then asked Aleski, 'Did you bring the gun?'

Aleski opened his jacket to show a narrow leather belt that he'd strapped around one shoulder. Attached to that was a holster, holding a gun with a bone handle, and the handle was inscribed with the initials V.W. Valentine Wilkins, I supposed, to whom Aleski was once sold. Well, I hoped that Mr Wilkins had taught him how to use it, though Captain seemed to have no qualms, only nodded his approval before, as silent as the night, he slipped between the chapel's doors.

Following behind, as my body hugged the curve of the tower's cold stone walls, I was perplexed and couldn't think where the zoo had vanished to. But then I saw a glint of light shining faintly through a door a little way behind the altar; and that's where Captain was now heading, only briefly looking back so as to nod in our direction.

Entering a narrow passage, the ground sloped down. The air was damp. Lamps on the walls flared and dipped. As the tunnel opened out, a vault held coffins on stone ledges. Some were the normal adult size, but others were small and must have held remains of children. Further off, more rotting caskets were too horrible to think of, with splintered wood and fraying shrouds through which the grey of bones protruded. Less a sepulchre of grandeur, more a charnel house of horror. But there were also sealed vaults, and before them marble statues, such as the angel

on a plinth where a name had been inscribed: *Theodora Seabrook.*
Beloved Daughter. Gone too soon.

When Captain paused before that angel, I feared he'd also
turned to stone. It seemed an age that he was lost in some private
reverie, before he snapped out of his daze and walked towards an
open arch, over which – when the candles flickered in a sudden
draught – I saw some letters glitter dimly through the murk to
form the words: *Midnight Garden of Delights.*

They might as well have said: *Welcome to Hell, and All It Holds,*
such was the panic they instilled. But also anger when I thought,
Tilly Lovell, what sort of trouble have you got yourself mixed up in
... and dragged your sister into too?

I was on the verge of turning, running back towards the
gardens. But Aleski grabbed my arm, and on we pressed, below
the arch into a muddy, greenish glow. What sort of garden grew
in darkness, and in that foul illumination? Soon enough we would
find out, for as we shuffled round a bend and descended three
wide steps, we entered something like a dream. A dream imagined
by a mind steeped in the sickest of perversions.

Between stone pillars holding up the vaulting brickwork of the
ceilings the walls had all been muralled to resemble a forest.
Among exotic trees and flowers, birds and butterflies were flying.
Woodland animals peeked out to watch horned satyrs who
cavorted with a group of naked nymphs. Caught in the flicker of
more candles, the paintings seemed to judder, almost as if they
were alive – despite the ingress of the damp causing the pigment
of the paints to bubble up and flake away.

The same corruption permeated what looked to me like
curtained fair booths. Holding my breath in trepidation, I pulled
one drape aside and saw a box of tempered glass fitted within a
metal frame. At first, I thought that what it held must have been
modelled out of wax, or was it papier-mâché? But by the texture
of the skin, the hair, the fingernails, the teeth, I was left in little
doubt that this mutilated hybrid had once existed as two separate

and independent living beings. What artist's hand possessed the skill to meld the torso of a youth to the hindquarters of a goat? To tell the truth, the memory is one that haunts me to this day. The way it stood on cloven feet, as if a living incarnation of the devils depicted in the paintings on the walls.

Within the second tank I saw the body of a man, but with the head of a horned stag. A third contained a woman with two extra pairs of limbs protruding from her hips like an Indian deity. She wore a crown with coloured gemstones, and her eyes were rimmed with kohl. *So beautiful, and yet grotesque*, I was thinking to myself as I heard Aleski groan – turning around to see the palms of both his hands being pressed against another wall of glass.

He was staring at a head that had been severed from its body. It could well have been his own, with such dense coverings of hair. On a plaque fixed underneath, a single word had been engraved...

'Lycanthrope,' I whispered, before another voice startled us both back to our senses.

'A fancy name for such an ugly-looking bastard, don't you think?'

How long had Ulysses been there, creeping silently behind us? And he was joined by echoed shouts from somewhere deeper in the tombs. Not that he seemed the least concerned, only smiled casually. 'Deary me. Sounds like there's trouble.'

'Why are you alone? Where's Theo? Where's Captain?' Aleski asked with suspicion.

In reply Ulysses pointed to another open arch. 'Gone on ahead, and from that racket I don't reckon we should stand around 'ere chatting for much longer. Sounds like they've found the party, and their presence isn't welcome.'

Aleski's voice was filled scorn: 'You're telling me Theo walked past us, and we didn't even notice? You're a liar, Ulysses. I don't trust you for a moment.'

That was when we heard the music. The tinkling and jerky notes. The sort of melody you'd hear when a music box is playing.

It took me back in such a rush to a box our ma once owned in the cottage in the lane. When the lid was lifted up, it showed a dancer spinning round, and in the mirrors either side were more reflections just the same. An infinity of dancers who turned in endless circles as the music mesmerised. And meanwhile, Ma used to sing...

Was that Tilly, singing now? Tilly's voice coming too frail as it floated to our ears?

Ulysses raised a hand and cupped it to his ear. 'Ah, there she is, our little songbird. Hark how she trills 'er blessed 'eart out. I think it's best we gets a move on before she's finished 'er recital. For 'owever entertaining it may be to dilly dally with the other special guests invited down 'ere in the past, the problem is, as you can see, none 'ave yet lived to tell the tale.'

NINETEEN

A BACCHANALIA OF BEASTS

Creeping after Ulysses, Theo looks back towards the grove in which Miss Miller once believed her baby had been buried. But the memory is lost when Ulysses prods at his arm, and by the volume of his voice it seems this weasel has no fear of being heard by any others wandering the night-time gardens.

'Fancy a stiffener?' he asks, waving a miniature extracted from the pocket of his jacket, though he appears to have some trouble pulling out the bottle's stopper.

Theo shakes his head. Surely, they need to keep their wits. But there's a pop. The stopper's free, and he notices a smell that all but stops him in his tracks. The odour of formaldehyde. He would know it anywhere, being a common disinfectant used at Summerwell's Museum. But despite this recognition, he is too slow to guess the danger when, as agile as a snake, Ulysses launches his attack.

Caught entirely off guard, and with an arm locked at his throat, Theo is wrestled to the ground. A cloth is pressed against his face. It isn't quick. Several minutes of a suffocating struggle, during which he hears the urgent tones of other male voices. Also, the clanging of a bell vibrating loud inside his head. And then he's numb, become so light he seems to rise into the air. Shadowy figures mass around him. Above his head the sky is full of tiny stars that slowly fade, till nothing but the black remains. Like being swallowed in a grave.

When he comes to, his head is throbbing. Thoughts are slow to comprehend the zigzag weave of pale light dancing across his vision. Arms and legs are oddly cramped. His hands brush over – is it wicker? Is he trapped inside a basket? It starts to move, and now it's tipped. A lid flies open, and he's sprawled across a cold stone floor.

Gradually rising all fours, he inhales the stink of rot, of damp, and dust, and ... is that honey? Honeyed perfume from the candles placed in niches in brick walls. Before each recess is a gate of rusted iron draped in cobwebs. In his state of fugged confusion they remind him of the entrance to Tilly's theatre fairyland in the Egyptian Hall last night. But there's no magic to be found in the coffins that contain the ancient bones of long-dead Seabrooks.

The cobweb veils begin to flutter, caught in a sudden draught of air. Where is it coming from? The candles flare, releasing plumes of thick black smoke that make him cough. Rubbing his eyes against the sting, Theo sees the blurring shapes of monsters moving through the gloom, and for a moment he's thrown back into the horrors of the nightmares that tormented his childhood, that sometimes still torment him now. He wants to wake. He *has* to wake and escape the memories. But then, his vision clears, and he wants to laugh out loud. There are no monsters, only people masked to look like animals. A fat-cheeked pig in a top hat is snuffling and snorting. A fox is barking, 'Tally ho!' A black-beaked crow is crouching down, fingers pointing, as if pecking at the figure of a man lying prone on the ground about ten feet or so away.

The man attempts to rise, but other hands restrain him. 'Theo!' he shouts, before a fist is slammed into his mouth.

'Captain!' Theo gasps, just as he becomes aware of someone standing close behind him. Is it Ulysses again? Straining to look around, he sees instead Lord Seabrook's valet. Less composed than usual, Clements drags him to his feet, before he forces his captive to face a pair of chairs. Chairs like thrones, with arms resembling the figures of four sphinxes.

The red-haired woman Theo saw with Lord Seabrook in the theatre reclines in one of them. What is she wearing? A white shroud? She is very far from dead, though even softened by the darkness and the shimmer of the candles it's clear she's past the bloom of youth. The lurid spots of rouge dabbed on her cheeks imitate the brothel bawds in Georgian pamphlets. Much like the ones Theo once saw in his grandfather's study. Cartoons of whores whose destiny was to be shown with pox-scarred faces, with toothless gums, and staring eyes as hollow as a skull's.

This woman's face is fleshy, and it has a robust beauty, much enhanced when she smiles and lifts a silver goblet from the table at her side. She drinks deeply of its contents and then leans her body forwards, as if to look at him more closely. In a seductive, gravelled voice, she says, 'Well, well, what have we here? Jack tumbling out from his box. It would be fun to see more tricks, but time is short and we should talk about the business of the night.'

'Business?' Theo asks. His mouth is sore and dry. His tongue is stiff. It feels too big.

She sets her goblet down, and her face is serious, 'It is time to pay the debt, for all those years of care and comfort that your grandfather provided. Ulysses, my clever spy – hmm, I wonder where he's got to? – he has told me you are skilled in matters of anatomy. Which is really just as well, what with your mentor now declining to continue with our work.'

'My mentor?'

'Your employer.'

As she says this, Theo registers the husband at her side. The man who, long ago, sought to destroy the reputation of Doctor Eugene Summerwell.

Lord Seabrook sits in silence. His legs are splayed like a frog below the belly that is straining at the buttons of a waistcoat worn below a black frock coat. It is ridiculously old-fashioned. The same tufts of bristled white sprout from his nostrils and his ears, but the tusks of his moustache are much sparser than before. This loss emasculates the man, as do the sores on his face that all too strongly suggest a later stage of syphilis. He's rendered yet more pitiful by the stuffed tiger's head he's wearing, like a crown on his head. Is it the tiger that once lay on Lord Seabrook's study floor? The pelt is caped around his shoulders. The clawed paws drape across his arms? It is the cruellest conjunction of the power of a once-beautiful wild animal with the body of a man in a state of aged decay.

Lord Seabrook meets his grandson's gaze, and where his arrogance once reigned there is misery and shame in the rheum of bloodshot eyes. 'Didn't I warn you?' he is saying. 'Didn't I tell you years ago to keep your distance from this house?'

Theo doesn't answer. Instead, he asks the woman, 'Is it true? You have some dealings with Eugene Summerwell?'

She nods and explains. 'After the death of his first wife, Lord Seabrook was determined that Summerwell should hang, or die inside a prison cell. Not enough for him to see the man struck off the register, and then be further debased in that slum in Oxford Street. It was I who suggested some arrangement that might prove beneficial to both parties. That is, the court case could be dropped if Summerwell only agreed to help in the creation of our Garden of Delights. For all his faults, he is a man of unique artistic talents ... which makes it even more galling that he's chosen to lie low instead of joining us tonight. But all's not lost. Here you are. All hail, the new creator!'

Theo's voice betrays his fear, 'I don't understand. Why have you brought me to this place?'

'You brought yourself. Didn't you come hoping to rescue Tilly Lovell?' She pouts to imitate remorse. 'But that will be impossible. A man of science, such as you are ... or at least aspire to be ... must surely understand the value in so rare a human specimen. Shouldn't her beauty be preserved? Shouldn't Tilly be enshrined, a natural wonder to be worshipped and adored, as if a goddess?'

Lord Seabrook clears his throat. His hooded eyes are fixed on

Theo's when he says, 'I'd no idea you were employed by Summerwell. Not until I saw you with him at the pantomime last Christmas. Did he take you on to spite me? It would be just the sort of thing the crippled wretch would find amusing.'

'Spite you? You didn't want me. You threw me out of my own home. Eugene kindly took me in, after Miss Miller wrote to him, and—'

'Ah! So, *she's* the connection. But then of course, she never knew about her doctor friend's involvements in creating our displays.' Lord Seabrook's laugh becomes a cough, thick and rattling with phlegm.

'Such as the baby in the bottle? Your own flesh and blood!' Theo can barely stifle the rising of his anger.

His grandfather shows no remorse. 'That travesty could not have lived. It's in the Seabrook blood. Sons born deformed and doomed to die before their infancy is out. You've seen the coffins. All my children ... Whereas *you*, my daughter's bastard – *you* survived. And here you are, still taunting me today.'

'Theo would not have been a bastard,' Captain struggles up to shout, his voice reverberating loud around the dampness of stone walls. 'I would have married Theodora, instead of which you stole her from me. You—'

Captain is silenced again. A hand is clasped across his mouth.

Meanwhile, Lady Seabrook is rising from her chair, pointing a finger Captain's way. '*His* birth was never registered. It is as if he never lived. You may have hoped to gain by some connection with the Seabrooks, but they are not your family. When my husband comes to die, this whole estate will fall to me. To me, and to *my* child.' Her demon mask is calcified, as cold as marble when she glances down at Seabrook again. The inference in her expression is all too plain to understand: *When he is dead and in this grave.*

To think Lord Seabrook's fascination for the freakish and macabre has led him to this harridan – whose cloying violet perfume is much too strong in Theo's nose when she takes a step towards him and inclines her painted face so as to sniff at his hair, around his ears and down his neck. It is as if she is the tiger and he the prey who she will tease, until deciding to bite.

At last, she straightens up and continues her tormenting. 'I should have had a costume made for you to wear on this occasion. Cupid, perhaps? You've the physique. Why you would only need to strip, to hold a tiny bow and arrow, and...' She breaks off. A better thought: 'A medieval jester. Wouldn't that be quite the thing? A tabard, hat and bell would suit you down to the ground, although those garish tartan trousers already mark you as a clown. Any circus would employ you, should Eugene have failed to do so. However, I forget...' She strikes a thoughtful pose, one finger pressed against her cheek, leaving a pause to allow for the sycophantic laughter from her carnival of beasts. But then, she raises an arm as if to chide the audience. 'Our little lord must not be mocked. He deserves our full respect and praise for his abilities.'

Little lord! It makes him fume. Isn't that the very term the weasel used at The Savoy, and in his letter afterwards? The weasel who has lured him here to Dorney Hall tonight. Not just him, but Captain too. Captain, who is ... his father?

How can Theo think of that in the midst of all this madness? Instead, he looks for Ulysses. Is he here, in the crypt? Perhaps he wears another mask. But then, the second Lady Seabrook speaks again. The devil's name.

'Ulysses has been our spy, stalking you on your excursions to the teaching hospitals. Creeping into the museum to observe you as you work ... on the most intricate endeavours. Ah,' she laughs. 'Perhaps you were aware of him from time to time. Did you sense him in your room after the Christmas pantomime? While you lay dreaming, he discovered your most secret fantasies. He tore some pictures from your sketchbooks, and he brought them back to me.'

'I don't believe you,' Theo says, still attempting to escape the iron vice of Clements' arms. The valet is much stronger than he could ever have imagined.

'Oh, but you must. Indeed, you will. We have the proof of the endeavour.' Now she is glancing at her husband as she prompts, 'Go on then. Show him. You did bring them, didn't you?'

Lord Seabrook looks reluctant, but he does as she commands. Reaching a hand into his jacket he fetches out some crumpled papers. She snatches them impatiently, smiling at Theo when she says, 'I have been thinking you might classify a species in my name. Tilly the butterfly could be *Lycaenidae Zephyrina*? Or would a swan be as fitting? Yes, I think a swan is perfect, and I've acquired the very wings Tilly wore in Drury Lane. Augustus Harris packed them up and sent them to the Knightsbridge house when I said I'd treasure them as a memento of the panto. Of course, the man has no idea of why I really wanted them, and they are a little grubby. But you could dye them if you wish. Why not black, to match her hair? This is only a suggestion. You are the artist, with carte blanche to do whatever you think best. We have a fine laboratory, converted from the disused stables. All the equipment is first class. No expenses have been spared.'

Theo can hardly form the words, 'You cannot possibly believe that I would ever do such things? Those illustrations, they are drawn from nothing but imagination, never intended to be real.'

'Imagination is enough. I would say it's *everything*. And we offer you the chance to make your dreams realities. Not in some grubby little shop selling tricks and tat to tourists. You will have Dorney to yourself. I much prefer the Knightsbridge house. It is too dreary here by far, except of course for the occasions of our bacchanalias. But, for the most part you'll be left entirely to your own devices, and you can visit the mausoleum freaks in privacy, at any time you desire. Think of that. Your own museum. No distractions from the public.'

Theo's head begins to pound. *What freaks does she mean? She is mad if she believes that I could share her vile obsessions. But is it true, about Eugene? And, if it is, does Eugene know about what's happening right now?*

A man in the disguise of a cockerel is crowing, 'Oh do get on! This is too dull. Does this midget fairy queen you've been dangling on a hook even actually exist? Where are the whores and mollies promised? Where is the food? By God, I'm famished!'

Lady Seabrook's voice is cold. 'All good things come to those who wait. Afterwards we will dine on the finest breast of Venus. Apollo's loin if you prefer. And all swilled down with devil's punch, made to the very recipes used at the Hell Fire Club at Wycombe. Those blasphemous occasions we now strive to emulate.' She twirls a languid hand. '*Fais ce que voudras*. In other words, do what you will. Fuck the laws of church and state! And, afterwards,' she smiles slyly, 'the grand finale of the night will leave each one of you replete, *whatever* your appetites.'

Theo is filled with yet more dread. What does she mean to do with Tilly?

He doesn't have to wait much longer. The woman strides towards a recess in the chamber's farthest corner. There is a click, a whine of hinges, and a barred door is being opened. Tilly Lovell is pulled out.

How tired she looks, as if she hasn't slept a wink since her performance in the Egyptian Hall last night. Her once-white dress is creased and stained. The fragile netting of her wings has been torn in many places. Her hair is knotted and the flowers on her head are withering. Has she been scratching at her face? The mole is scabbed, crusted with blood. Her eyes are oddly vacant, as if she is affected by some intoxicating substance.

Unsteady on her feet, she is led towards the chairs amid excited exclamations rising from the audience: 'What a minimus she is!' 'Exquisite. Quite unique.' 'She is everything you promised. How could we ever think to doubt you?' '*Brava*, dear Lady Seabrook.'

Above all this, Lord Seabrook wheezes, reaching out towards a lacquered oriental-looking box placed on a table at his side. Is it a music box? Does he intend to wind it up? But if this act has been rehearsed, it fails to go as planned. The old man's hands are trembling. He's slumping back into his chair, as if the weight of the striped pelt around his shoulders is too much. The tiger's head is also slipping, falling down across his face. Only the wisps of his moustache and flabby lips are visible. He is gasping like a trout when it's been hooked out of the water. Lord Seabrook looks ridiculous. More than that, he looks defeated. But he still struggles with the winding of the box, and an erratic jingling melody is heard.

The battered fairy queen seems mesmerised by the music. Does she even realise there's a new audience before her as she looks up at Lady Seabrook with a slow and sleepy smile?

The beasts set up a chant: 'Dance. Dance.' And Tilly tries. She lifts a slender arm to show the hollow of one armpit. Such a pretty, perfect armpit, and not a single hair to mar it. But she is clumsy in her movements, and she cannot help but stumble. When the music box runs down, she also seems to need rewinding, which, in a way is what occurs – when Lady Seabrook claps her hands and calls. 'Enough! Now you must sing.'

The woman laughs and claps again. This captures Tilly's full attention. Looking up towards her captor, her voice is feeble and despairing. 'And after that, you'll let me sleep?'

'For a hundred years and more,' comes the sinister reply as Lady Seabrook reaches down to caress the bleeding cheek, before she stoops to place her lips directly over Tilly's mouth. A kiss that lingers for too long.

The men are groaning, pressing forwards in the heat of their desire. Lady Seabrook's mismatched eyes are gleaming and triumphant when her pet begins to sing – although at first the words are stammered and the notes all come off-key. But soon enough the volume rises and the voice is confident, reverberating off stone walls that echo in accompaniment. The sound is eerie and discordant, and even more so after Tilly has collapsed to her knees, when her mouth is firmly closed and yet the echoes carry on, almost as if a second singer has now joined her in the ronde that is repeating and repeating – *Come unto me. Come unto me...*

The reaction of the men beneath the masks cannot be seen, but every one of them stands rigid as they listen to this deeper voice now circling around them. Only Tilly seems delighted and entirely unafraid when she looks up and speaks again. 'She has come. She's come to *me*! The woman singing in my dreams.'

It is the voice Theo heard in Linden House some hours before. And Captain seems to know it too, grunting and struggling anew against the hands that gag his mouth. Meanwhile, the singing carries on, still echoing around the chamber, and only ending when Lord Seabrook howls like a dog in his distress. 'Theodora. Leave me be!'

His wife snaps back, 'What do you mean?'

Is she losing her control of pandemonium tonight? She watches open-mouthed as the old man rocks back and forth in his chair as one demented. But he does stop, eventually, throwing off the tiger's head, flinging the pelt down to the ground. The tiger's dead glass eyes catch the flicker of the candles. They look as if they are alive.

His wife is clearly shocked. Her bravado cannot hide the colour draining from her cheeks, where the rouge that remains looks more like hectic spots of fever. 'It's an echo! You're a fool. A sick, old fool who is too mad to know what's real and what's not.'

Her husband doesn't seem to hear her. He is weeping openly, showing emotion that his grandson never dreamed was possible. Theo has to look away rather than face such desperate grief, and, when he does, he sees the witch dragging Tilly to her feet.

She strokes a hand across the curve of the small breasts below the bodice while reciting what appears to be a speech that she has practised, and is determined to perform regardless of the interruptions: 'My exquisite Queen Matilda, I know how weary you must be.'

Tilly is wincing at the touch, and silent tears run from her eyes when Lady Seabrook turns around to lift a phial from her chair, saying, 'Drink, and you will dream. You have my word. There'll be no pain.'

Tilly's lips are forced apart, and Lady Seabrook tips the contents of the bottle in her mouth as she excitedly proclaims, 'Don't be afraid, my fairy queen. Death is but a little sleep.'

Theo thinks back to the night of the fair at Windsor Brocas. The man who stood on a stage and boasted of the time he'd forced his miracle elixir into the mouth of a sick child. Professor Lovell might have claimed that Tilly spat his potion out, but now she swallows willingly, and Theo's powerless to stop her, still restrained as he is by the hands of Seabrook's valet. But he can speak, and with the voice that holds a deepness many people often seem to find surprising, and which now resonates like thunder in the confines of the crypt – 'How low Lord Seabrook falls, to find his pleasures wallowing in such a den of vice as this. I always knew he was a monster, but...' Theo breaks off, because he's seen two shadowed figures creeping underneath an arch in one far corner. A dull green light is seeping through it to illuminate their features.

Theo knows he has to act, and cause some new distraction before the others in the room notice Keziah and Aleski. He draws more air into his lungs, gathers every ounce of strength and kicks his heels at Clements' shins, then even higher to the groin. He meets the target. Clements groans, and is impotent to stop the jabbing of the elbows striking hard against his ribs. Theo is free to turn around and throw a punch at Clements' chin. He hears the cracking of bone. He sees the butler's stunned expression, the way his darkly suited body gently sways, then hits the ground.

The victory is too short-lived. Theo's surrounded on three sides. Here is a fox. And here a horse. And here, a unicorn. But the masks the men are wearing are large and cumbersome, and surely hinder any vision. Or are those who hide behind them only cautious of the scalpel now produced from Theo's pocket, when they step back and leave him free to look around again for Tilly, only to see her being grasped in Lady Seabrook's greedy hands?

Lady Seabrook's eyes are wild. She has sensed something amiss. Something more than Theo's sudden violent bid for liberty. But she does not see two figures creep around the chamber's walls into the gloom behind the thrones. She is looking at the person now emerging through the archway, and she is smiling when she cries, 'Ah, here he is. My prince of pimps has come to join the revelries.'

The hand not holding onto Tilly reaches back to lift her goblet, to consume another draught of whatever it might hold before her welcome carries on. 'Tell us, Ulysses, what of the other tender morsels you promised us tonight? I do hope you haven't lost them. My guests are hungry for amusement.'

Before Ulysses responds, Keziah's voice is calling out, almost sounding like a joker in a pantomime production. 'We're here already. Look behind you!'

Lady Seabrook spins around, and without a second thought Theo drops the knife he's holding and kicks it hard towards Keziah. As she stoops to pick it up, Aleski also joins the stage. Silent and lithe as any wolf, he moves towards Lord Seabrook's chair – just as Ulysses is shouting, 'What the fuck d'you think yer doing?'

What Aleski does is to calmly hold the barrel of a gun to Seabrook's head. Seabrook doesn't react, but the knuckles of his hands are clenched across the chair's sphinx arms. At the same time Theo hears the phlegmy whistle in his throat. A sound that's only drowned by his wife's low muffled, 'Oh!'

Dragging Tilly even closer, Lady Seabrook shuffles back and almost falls across the valet still unconscious on the floor. Curses are flying from her mouth. Most are aimed at Ulysses, before she yells the final threat: 'You promised much, and you have failed. What a fiasco you have caused. I will see you pay for this.'

'What?' Ulysses looks mortified. 'It ain't my fault. They got suspicious. I was jumped. See this wound...' He tips his head to the one side, and the candle flames expose the red that dribbles down his face. He wipes it off, and, for a moment, stares at what is on his palm. 'At least they left me alive, me veins still running 'ot with blood. Not the stinking chilly fluids that are used for your embalming. Speaking of which' – Ulysses nods, motioning towards Aleski – 'I would say this living werewolf puts the dead one 'ere to shame. I'd say you owes me quite a lot.' Ulysses turns to grin at Theo. 'As her ladyship's anatomist you'd 'ave 'ad *that* stuffing pleasure. But now I fear you'll end up standing on a plinth with Little Tilly. Won't that make a pretty scene? The marriage of the midget.'

His flinty gaze moves on to Captain. 'Dear, dear, it does appear as if there's bin a mutiny. Ulysses is not so loyal. But 'e would rather see his Captain sailing free than leave 'im buried in this dump of mouldered bones. P'rhaps MiLady over there could be enticed to let you go. The dashing Dago to be traded in return for 'er old codger, although...' he winks at Lady Seabrook ... 'from our private tête-à-têtes I know she wouldn't be averse to play the merry widow, and our Captain is most 'andsome.'

The redhead glares at Ulysses. 'You are a liar and a menace, which is why you'll never rise above the trading of your mollies. I saw the promise in you once, a boy so feral, yet so cunning, who was always keen to learn...'

'For which you promised me first bite at Tilly's cherry 'ere tonight. For me to wear the mask of the *Midsummer Night's Dream* donkey.'

She laughs contemptuously. 'You really thought I'd place such treasure in *your* hands. Tilly is not some penny fuck. She commands a higher price than *you* could ever think to pay.'

Refusing to be chastened, Ulysses keeps up his banter. 'And what's the price of your old man? I sense Aleski grows impatient.'

'Do you think he'll dare to do it?' Her eyes return to the gun being held at Seabrook's head.

'Personally,' Ulysses muses, 'I doubt the weapon's even loaded, or if Aleski Turgenev 'as squeezed a trigger in 'is life. Under all that fur is nothing but the softest puppy. There is no bite to match 'is growl.'

'There you would be wrong.' Keziah steps into the light, and she is brandishing the knife. 'Would you prefer Aleski's bite, or for me to demonstrate how deep this blade can cut?'

What is it called, when a magician draws the audience's attention away from what his hands are doing? An act of misdirection. That's what Keziah's planning now, spitting her threats at Ulysses, while all along her feet are inching closer to her true objective – when there's a sudden flash of metal and the steel is being pressed at Lady Seabrook's powdered throat.

The older woman looks astonished, but then reclaims her self-composure as the bartering begins. Only the slightest tremble can be heard beneath her words. 'Kill my husband if you will. He is a bully and tormenter. I lay myself upon your mercy. I have a child, a little boy who would be lost without his mother. Here ... take Tilly back! This is a game. Only a game. A drama for our guests. I never meant to do her harm.'

Keziah scorns the woman who's been spouting desperate falsehoods: '*You*, bullied by a husband? Claiming to be a loving mother? I pity any child spawned from the cesspit of your womb. Give my sister back to me!'

Tilly is pushed away, and so roughly that the garland on her head falls to the floor. She stumbles over scattered petals, and the pages Ulysses must have torn from Theo's sketchbooks. The scenes drawn from his darkest dreams. Vampiric men with wings of bats, black and spiked and rubbery. Incisors sharp as any tiger. Centaurs with penises erect. A Medusa with her hair a writhing mass of hissing snakes. Every one of them depicting the very basest human instincts.

Feeling ashamed, but fast returning to his senses again, Theo throws out both his arms to catch the girl who falls towards him. She feels clammy, much too cold, and the pupils of her eyes are nothing more than pinpoints. Whatever drug she has been given, he needs to get her out of here, to let her breathe some fresher air.

With Tilly cradled in his arms, he makes his way towards the arch below which Ulysses is standing. What if he will not move, or tries to wrestle Tilly from him? But the Weasel takes a bow and steps aside for them to pass, though not before the chilling comment, '*This* time you win, little lord. But watch your back in future. I'll always 'ave you in my sights, which is a shame, is it not? When we first met I 'ad the notion that you might 'ave made a pal for Ulysses to dally with.'

With that the weasel grins, and lifts both arms high in the air, almost as if about to dance. But then, he's gone. He's disappeared into the shadows of the passage, along which Theo must now follow, for there is no other exit.

But not before Keziah joins him. Keziah, with the knife still pressed at Lady Seabrook's throat, using the woman as a shield against the tomb's menagerie as she heads towards the arch. Aleski does the same, his gun held close to Seabrook's head as the old man is forced to stand and shuffle through the crowd. But seeing Captain, still constrained and lying on the floor, Theo panics and calls out, 'Grandfather, will you do just one good thing? One thing to please me? Call off your dogs. Set Captain free.'

'Do as he says!' the redhead cries, though her words are oddly slurred. Her limbs are twitching, which in turn makes the blade Keziah holds break the surface of her skin. A bead of blood, red as ruby, oozes out over her flesh.

Whatever may have caused the wife's erratic, jerking movements, her husband doesn't seem to notice. He does not answer Theo's plea – not until Aleski drives him to the arch, where at last the old man gazes at his grandson.

His voice is barely audible: 'You always had your mother's eyes. Her mouth. Her golden hair.' A trembling hand cups Theo's chin. 'Because of her, I kept you close. I raised you here in my own home. But where was the consolation? Every time I looked at you...'

He is searching for the words. Releasing Theo's chin, his fingers jab his grandson's breast, and his voice is growing louder. 'You may have thought me cruel, but I did my best to save you. I told you, keep away – from this house, and from my wife. If she could, she'd have your soul. She'd suck you dry and throw your husk to the devils down in Hell. In which case...' Lord Seabrook pauses '... you'd spend eternity with me.'

Theo steps back. He is unnerved to see his grandfather's distress. But any pity dissipates in the split second it takes for the old man to spin around and make a grab for the gun still being held against his head. Aleski is disarmed, and all too easily. Now, only calloused, hairless fingers wrap around the white bone handle to seek the trigger underneath. It is squeezed, but just enough to cause the metal to give out the softest warning of a click. There is no shot, at least not yet, only Lord Seabrook's brusque command. 'Get out of here. Every last wretch. Go, and don't come back. I'm sick and tired of these games. I only want my Theodora. To see her face. To make my peace.'

There it is, a second time, the ghost of something almost tender gleaming in the old man's eyes, when he murmurs, 'Theo Seabrook. This will be our last goodbye.'

Theo's reply holds no affection. 'I no longer use that name. As you once told me in a letter, it was never mine to take.'

'We learn from our mistakes. In the end, blood will out. My people have been issued with instructions where to find you. I shouldn't try to hide from them.'

Having made this cryptic threat, Lord Seabrook starts to nod, head angled forwards, looking hawk-like as he stares at his wife: 'All she ever had to do was hold a mirror to my soul. What you see before you now, this is the monster that was always lurking underneath the skin. But it was she who lured it out, until it could not be restrained. And now, the flesh on which the parasite has fed becomes this wreck.'

Theo is speechless as he hears this confession of self-hatred. Meanwhile, some way behind, Captain is on his feet again and walking swiftly to the arch. Without a glance at the old man, he motions for Theo to follow him into the passage – though hard for Theo to keep up when Captain's legs are so much longer, when Theo's arms are holding Tilly, when he's afraid that Ulysses might still be lurking in the shadows.

Entering another chamber, Theo feels a little safer, slowing his pace sufficiently to look around and see the details of the paintings on the walls, and then the specimens that stand behind glass walls in velvet booths. The things unnoticed earlier, when he was doped and barely conscious, caged inside a wicker basket. Now he stares at them and wonders, what is this sickness in his blood, the dark inheritance that's urging him to stop and look more closely, to appreciate the skill and the artistry involved in deconstructing then remaking the commonplace into the most exotic of creations.

The fascination is intense. But the revulsion is much stronger. When Captain calls, 'Come with me!' Theo instinctively obeys. But he does pause at the statue set above his mother's tomb. He thinks if only she could spread her angel wings and fly away. But her wings are made of marble, forever cold and motionless – whereas Captain's hand is warm, and it is urging Theo on as they walk into the chapel, through the doorway to the garden.

They take the final step as one. They lift their faces to the moon and all the stars that shine above. It is serene and wondrous, this cloudless summer's night – until the deafening retort of the pistol going off.

TWENTY

AS THE TWO SISTERS crossed the heath, they came upon a troll burying a bag of precious stones. 'Why are you gaping?' he cried, his face a copper red with rage. He was so angry they were fearful he might try to do them harm. But then they heard a dreadful growling from the edges of the forest, and a bear came rushing out.

The troll sprang up and cried: 'Dear Bear, please spare my life. Look at these jewels! Look at these girls! The loveliest you've ever seen. You can take them to your lair, for they will make a tender meal, their flesh as plump and sweet as quail.'

The bear struck out with his great paw and knocked the villain to the ground. After this the troll lay still, and he never moved again.

From *Snow-White and Rose-Red*

I often think how right Ma was – how the tale of those two sisters, Rose-Red and Rose-White, was to echo through our lives. Well, to some extent. But, the troll, who could that be? You're no doubt thinking Ulysses. But why not make it Lady Seabrook, gloating as she did over her trove of stolen lives? *She* is not dead, at least not yet, though such a fate might well be kinder than the lingering effects of the strychnine in her blood. The very stuff Mr Wainewright used to kill his relatives.

Theo knew what I had done. He'd watched me spill the powder from the ring that I'd been wearing into Lady Seabrook's goblet. The powder taken from a box Martha kept underneath the sink, and which she used to kill the rats that sometimes ventured from the river. It had been nothing but a gamble. A wild surmise that I had never really thought to carry out. More to the point, who could have known that Lady Seabrook would so greedily accept the poisoned chalice?

But she had, and some weeks later, on a day when we were sitting quite alone in Linden House, Theo told me he had heard she was still suffering convulsions. He said these symptoms might improve, depending on the dose ingested. But, for now, she would most likely be confined to darkened rooms, kept well away from any stimulus of normal human life, or extremes of light and sound. To all effects, she was imprisoned.

It was as much as she deserved, and at least she was alive, which meant that I could face the mirror in my bedroom every morning and not be ridden with the guilt of seeing Murder staring back.

Did Bohemia feel such shame, after the farmer she had cursed ended up paralysed for life? I feared that she had not. I also feared what I'd become if I allowed that darker side of my own blood to take control. Might I try and seek revenge on every guest who had attended the Seabrook's *Midsummer Night's Dream*? But what would that achieve, even *if* I had the wherewithal to try and track them down? The guilty had already covered up the truth, and how could I be sure of that? Well, take a gander at this cutting that was printed in *The Times* a few days after the event ...

THE MYSTERIOUS SUICIDE OF LORD SEABROOK

An extraordinary suicide has caused a sensation in London's aristocratic circles.

The night before the tragedy occurred at Dorney Hall, Lord Seabrook's butler had reported hearing a loud explosion coming from the house's study. There he found his master dead, with a pistol in his hand.

Lady Seabrook's personal maid insists her mistress had been sleeping when the suicide occurred, having felt unwell and then retiring to bed after dining with her husband. The doctor who attended her next morning has suggested she is now gravely ill, possibly due to the ingestion of some unknown toxic substance.

Before his death Lord Seabrook gave the household staff at Dorney Hall three days of leave from the house. This suggests premeditation. Firstly, for the attempted murder of his wife, and secondly, his suicide. He may also be connected to the discovery of a second body in the grounds. This has not been identified and police are appealing for any witnesses who may have information to approach them.

I imagine any guests still inside the mausoleum after the pistol had been fired must have contrived to move the body of Lord Seabrook to the house. Any doctors or detectives called in to make investigations were then informed that he had shot himself while sitting in his study.

But did he kill himself? I've often pondered over that. Or had his wife taken the gun to point the barrel at his head? Could she have acted so directly with the poison in her blood? It is a truth we'll never know, unless her cronies spill the beans. But as that would then result in their involvement being known ... No, it really isn't likely.

And what about the second body found in the gardens of the house? Did they keep that secret too? If asked, then I could tell ...

✳

After the gunshot blasted out, when the buzzing and the ringing in our ears began to fade, that's when we heard the panicked shouts: 'Seabrook's shot.' 'My God, he's dead.' 'We need to leave. Get out of here.'

Captain and Theo rushed away into the darkness of the gardens, taking Tilly on ahead to the safety of the boat. Meanwhile, Aleski and me lingered by the mausoleum, to distract anyone who might have tried to follow them. But in the end, there was need. We might have been invisible, the way those cowards scattered past us, heading back towards the house like rats fleeing a sinking ship. And when they'd gone, we carried on, almost at the broken wall when I heard a long, low whistle, then a whisper of my name.

Even though the voice was hushed, I knew exactly who it was. I looked around. He must be near, so very near that I could smell the stench of nicotine on his breath and on his clothes. Had Aleski noticed too? Where was Aleski, anyway? I should have thought to call his name, but my reactions were too slow. As fast as lightning, Ulysses crept up and took me by surprise. He dragged me off, behind some bushes. He pressed one hand against my mouth, the other squeezing like a vice to break my hold on Theo's knife. My knuckles cracked. I gasped with pain. The blade was dropped and hit the ground, before he snatched it for himself. By which point it's fair to say he had me done up like a kipper.

Just as I'd done with Lady Seabrook, he pressed the blade against my neck, and was not dainty in his actions. I felt the searing of the pain as metal penetrated flesh. I heard his words, hot in my ear. 'Sshh now. No fuss and bother, or it will go the worse for you. My dander's up and needs a brushing. A little tenderness and kindness to soothe the evening's disappointments. I may be labelled as the snake cast from the garden of delights, but my tail still 'as its sting. If denied the fairy queen, I'll take the sister in 'er place. Should recompense for all the black drop I've supplied to Tilly Lovell on my visits down to Chiswick.'

How my hatred seethed when I hissed back, 'What if she's dead? What if you've killed my sister? You have no soul. You are a monster.'

He laughed. 'What do I care? And a bird in the hand...'

I retched at the graze of his teeth against my ears, his hot dry lips seeking my mouth. His breath was noxious, made me gag. I would have screamed but had no voice due to the pressure his fingers were exerting on my windpipe. My ears were filled with rushing sounds, and my vision started blurring as the knife was pointed lower to slice the buttons from my shirt, and then the ribbons of the shift I'd been wearing underneath it. As I trembled with fear – how I despised myself for that – there was a moment's hesitation when he froze and cocked his head. What had he heard? I listened too. Above the racing of my heart there came the thud of running feet, the fast approach of panting breaths. And then, the growling, fierce command, 'Drop the knife and let her go.'

'Or what?' Ulysses drawled, as bold and breezy as you like.

'Or you'll be sorry. Please don't test me,' Aleski gave his answer.

Ulysses began to laugh. His horrible hyena laugh. But that brazen confidence turned out to be a big mistake. He hadn't noticed other movements in the bushes close around us, from where Hell's furies were released. One fury anyway. The attacker leapt towards us, jaws opened wide, lips curling back to show the fangs that barely missed me by an inch as they were plunged into the throat of Ulysses. I heard the sound of tearing flesh. I saw the wildly flailing arms, hands reaching out to try and clamber up the ivy on the wall. But the pursuer only followed, dragging Ulysses back down with such brute force that when one trouser leg had snagged upon a branch, he was suspended upside down, his head but inches from the ground. In that position, how could Ulysses have hoped to fend away such a brutal mass of muscle, or avoid the dark-brown eyes lit with the lusting for his blood? It was the most horrific sight, the way the moonlight caught the gleam of the terror in his own. And then to hear the gurgled whimpers as he tried to beg for mercy.

When it was done, and Ulysses no longer struggled for his life, Captain appeared between the bushes. 'Dolce, off!' He called the dog, still busy lapping at the gore puddled below the dead man's head. As she reluctantly obeyed, only then did I observe the chewed remains of fraying rope that had previously been used to keep her tethered to the boat. She must have gnawed till she was free, then traced our scent to Dorney Hall. And now, still trembling but calm, she pressed her flank to Captain's leg, as if to ask him for forgiveness.

He ignored her, walking closer towards the scene of carnage. Only the quiver of the tendons either side of Captain's mouth betrayed emotion when he knelt, bowing his head as if to pray. His voice was low. I heard some words: '*Addio*. I tried my best. You never wanted to be saved.'

Did I faint? I may have done, coming to while being lifted up into Aleski's arms. Looking back across his shoulder, I relived the awful moment when Dolce sprang through the air. How she had shaken, snarled and savaged with delirious abandon, like the dogs that used to skulk around the vardos at the shows when hunting down and killing rats. Nature red in tooth and claw.

TWENTY-ONE

A RETURN TO LINDEN HOUSE

While Captain searches on the tow path for the dog that has escaped after biting through its leash, Theo bars the cabin door and contemplates lighting the lamp that hangs beside the iron stove. But his hands are trembling too violently to strike a match and, anyway, there is no need. The moonlight's glow is creeping in around the canvas at the windows.

He draws a chair close to the bunk on which the sleeping Tilly lies. His eyes are fixed on her one hand. How small it is, the fingers splayed across the mattress's bare ticking to form the pattern of starfish. A starfish, pale as death.

'Don't die.' He almost sobs, even though she doesn't hear him. She is as limp as a cloth doll. Her long hair falls across her face when Theo lifts her body and then removes the leather straps and ragged netting of her wings. Once her arms are free again, he lays her back across the bed, where she rolls over on her front. Above the bodice of her gown her shoulder blades are visible. His fingers trace the shell-like contours of the bones beneath the skin. He whispers in her ear, 'You do not need a pair of wings. You are quite perfect as you are.'

There is no answer to his words. Only the shallow rise and falling of her breaths below the blanket that he draws across her body. Only the gentle lap and lullabying rocking of the Thames.

His own thoughts also ebb and flow, but in a whirlpool of confusion. To know what his grandfather and that devil of his wife had planned for Tilly tonight. To have been told about Eugene – Eugene, his teacher and his friend, who he had trusted and relied on – it is too terrible to think of. He cannot help but recall all of those times when Eugene went on 'East End holidays', returning home again grey-faced and complaining of exhaustion. Instead of smoking opium in the dens around the docks, had he travelled further west and come to visit Dorney Hall? The thought is like a knife, as cold as steel in Theo's heart. Will there be a final twist?

He thinks of Martha, all alone with Eugene in Linden House. He tries, but can't dispel the image forming in his mind. A severed head. Another freak displayed in Summerwell's Museum. He tells himself he's being foolish, and that Eugene is a good man. Even so, Theo is forced to swallow down the rise of bile as he recalls what has he has seen in the Seabrook mausoleum.

And what of Captain, who was told his son had died at birth? Is it not the greatest marvel to have found each other now? Theo smiles. He cannot help it. But then, there is the guilt, because it was his birth that caused his mother's death. That's why his grandfather despised him. Well, it's one reason, and the other—

These bitter thoughts are interrupted by some movements on the deck. Captain's voice is calling out for him to open the door. He's found the dog, and now he's joined by Aleski and Keziah.

As they descend the cabin steps, Keziah looks deflated, as if the life and bravery she demonstrated in the tombs has been sucked out of her veins. One of her hands hangs at her side with the knuckles red and bruised. She has a cut across her neck which will surely need attention. But, for the present, Captain binds it with a cotton handkerchief, and as he knots the cloth in place, he stoops to kiss her on the brow. His voice is breaking when he says, 'The wound is shallow, *mia caro*. There is no need for you to worry. He cannot hurt you anymore.'

Theo wonders what he means. *He cannot hurt you anymore.* But the riddle goes untold. Captain leaves to take the wheel, clicking his tongue to give the signal that Dolce is to follow. Keziah doesn't speak, and neither does Aleski. A long time they sit like that, through all the hours that seem to last for a small eternity as they are sailing down the Thames. But finally, there comes a moment when Keziah rises up and walks towards her sister's bed. She makes the gentlest cooing sounds as she enfolds her larger body close around the sleeping Tilly. Theo can hear the muffled whispers as Keziah tells a story. He can make out the odd snatched word. 'Widow ... Cottage ... Snow-White ... Rose-Red ... The Angel Boy ... The Troll ... The Bear...'

❈

By the time they dock at Chiswick, the dawn is blooming red and gold, reflected back across the Thames like an impressionistic painting. A group of coots call rusty squeakings, but there's no other human soul out on the tow path to observe this motley crew leaving their ship.

Keziah carries Tilly, like a mother with her child. Tilly moans. Her cheeks are tinged with a hectic flush of pink, but when her eyes are briefly opened, the pupils look more natural.

Captain strides on ahead and unlocks the wooden gate set in the orchard's high brick wall. They follow under branches from which ripened pears and apples droop heavy on the branches, on past a ramshackle old glasshouse, and the raised parterres around it. And then, at last, through the door into the kitchen of the house. But there's no Martha or Eugene chattering beside the sink. The air is steeped in heavy silence. The sort of stillness that exists when a house has been abandoned.

'Hello!' Aleski calls. There is no answer to be heard.

Keziah says, 'It's very early. Martha's probably still sleeping.'

'I'll go and see,' Aleski says, and is already on his way; heading through the hall and then ascending the stairs.

Keziah is about to follow, to carry Tilly to her bed. But, before she leaves the kitchen, one of her hands goes drifting out and her fingers gently stroke the blooming bruise on Captain's cheek.

When only Theo and Captain remain in the room, Captain asks the simple question, 'Would you like some coffee?'

Theo can only nod when his father – how is *that* even a possibility? – suggests that when it's made they will talk more privately.

What will Captain say to him? Theo is dizzy with emotion, and the hazy, disembodied sense of somehow floating up to leave his body on the ground. But he hears the splash of brandy Captain adds to two large cups. The rawness held in Captain's voice when he forces a smile, 'I think we're both in need of this.'

Theo agrees. Before he knows it, he's following his father to the room with silk-lined walls in which he dozed the day before, where Captain sets the cups of coffee on a table by the chaise, then turns around and bluntly asks, 'Would you like to see the painting ... of your mother, Theodora?'

Without waiting for an answer Captain is opening the door that leads into a narrow passage. And then, another that reveals Theo's mother's smiling face on the wall above a bed.

Dora is forever young, whereas the man she once loved has aged ten years in just one night. But his charm is still apparent when he says, 'You are so like her. I suppose that's why your grandfather called you Theodore. He must have cared, in his own way.'

Theo's response is less composed and there is anger in his voice. 'Perhaps he did, when he first saw me. The newborn child that inherited its mother's hair and eyes. But a baby is one thing. A growing boy is another. Much harder to conceal from any staff or visitors. And then, the gossip sure to follow. The embarrassment. The shame...'

'You do not embarrass me.' Captain's voice is low and steady. 'I would be proud to call you son, to show you off to all the world. And, despite what he has done, I still have to thank Eugene for bringing us together. It was Eugene who wrote to tell me when he had a new assistant with a connection to the Seabrooks. Do you know, those first few years, I'd often come to Oxford Street? I'd stand outside the shop and look in through the window to see you there behind the counter, but I never found the courage to come and introduce myself. And then, one day...'

'You came inside to buy the wings for Tilly Lovell.'

'That gave me the excuse, and ... ah, *mio figlio*. I wasn't sure, but when we spoke, and when I looked into your eyes, how could I ever think to doubt that you were my Dora's son?'

'What name would I have had, *if* you'd been married to my mother. Everybody calls you Captain, but...'

His father laughs. 'That is my name! Alessandro Capitano.'

'Alessandro Capitano.' Theo smiles, rolling his tongue around the vowels and consonants.

But then, his father speaks again, breaking the air of levity. 'To think I believed you were the baby in the bottle that I stole from Dorney Hall.'

Theo frowns as he replies, 'I know the mother of that baby. My old governess, Miss Miller, who so kindly took me in when my grandfather remarried, she was once his lover. She had a child. It didn't live. She believed it had been buried in the gardens of the house.' Theo pauses for a moment, wondering how he could ever tell the story of the night when he had tried to help Miss Miller resurrect her baby's grave, only to find that it was empty? No. He will skirt around those facts, and say instead, 'I know it grieved her to discover she'd been lied to. But to this day she doesn't know the awful truth of what was done.'

Theo carries on with passion. 'She should have her baby back, but...' All at once he's filled with doubt, speaking as if he's on his own. 'How would this news affect her? Could the horror of the past also ruin any future?'

Captain suggests, 'You could write? But would she cope with such a truth?'

Theo hesitates. 'No, I should visit her in person. It's been too long, and...'

He breaks off, conscious that Captain's eyes are searching round the room. Suddenly, his father mutters, '*Dov'é il bambino?*'

'What is it?' Theo asks.

'The baby. It was here. But now it's gone. Where has it gone?'

Captain has barely finished speaking when they both hear the sound of footsteps fast approaching in the passage.

It is Aleski, and he's breathless as he stops in Captain's doorway, 'Thank God you're here. I thought you must have gone back down to the boat. Something terrible has happened. I think Martha may be dead.'

✻

There are many flights of stairs and Theo's legs, already tired from the previous night's exertions, are aching badly by the time he's reached the door on the top floor. Entering a large, square room he sees a breeze catching the panel of some lace hung at a window. Outside a blackbird's singing. The most exquisite, piping music. But the fresher summer air that blows inside cannot disguise the heavy taint of chloroform. Something else. Cloying. Metallic. On the floor he sees a bucket holding crumpled balls of linen. They are stained the rusty red of blood when dried and oxidised. A fly begins to buzz, hovering above the debris.

Otherwise, there are no sounds but the breaths of the two men standing close beside a bed. Both of them are as immobile as the headless tailor's dummies posed at the attic's other end. Aleski's lips are tightly closed. He's staring fiercely at the body underneath the mounds of sheeting. Captain's hands cover his face, and when he speaks his words are muffled: 'Butcher! *Assassino. Uomo malvagio.*'

Theo grabs the bed's brass ends, steeling himself to look through gaps between the bars and so ensure that Martha's head and neck remain upon her shoulders. They do, and that is something. But the skin of her face is now a lurid shade of purple around the squares of clean white gauze entirely covering her mouth. There is no fluttering of air, sucking in or blowing out to give a sign of life below, leading Theo to presume that, yes, she must be dead. But then, her eyelids start to flicker and Martha draws a breath. As she continues to revive, the gasps come stronger, and much faster. Her hands are raised above the sheets, trying to pull away the dressing.

Theo calls for her to stop: 'Martha, no. You must be careful. Let me help and do that for you.'

His eyes cast round the room again. He needs to wash his hands. He sees the stand with the machine Martha must use for her sewing. Shelves are filled to overflowing with buttons, lace and other notions. Several bolts of coloured cloth rest against the sloping walls and, finally, there is a washstand. And the same carbolic soap they always use at Summerwell's.

He scrubs his hands and shakes them dry before he walks back to the bed, where he sees a piece of paper placed below the bedside lamp. It is a memo and relates to the medical procedure Dr Eugene Summerwell has only recently performed. The words of his instructions are formal and precise:

Martha has been sedated. Anaesthesia was inhaled through the means of a small nose cap. Sensation was abolished, but not the reflex of the cough to prevent the patient choking. The operation was not complex, taking less than fifteen minutes. Luckily, only the smallest area of the soft palate had been affected by the cleft. The lips were scarified, compressed and stitched to form a whole. Any blood she has ingested will naturally coagulate before elimination through the process of digestion. The swelling to her face should subside in a few days. If there is no sign of rupture, the removal of the stitches should take place after one week. Ensure the wound is sanitised to minimise risk of infection.

Martha is aware that there will be initial pain, and it will take a little time to grow accustomed to the newly altered contours of her mouth, in turn affecting speech. But with patience and endurance she will adapt, and she will thrive.

The business matters now concluded, there is a different tone to the remainder of the message ...

Theo, my dearest boy,

I pray you are safely returned from Dorney Hall, where you'll no doubt have been informed of shameful aspects of my past. You will have seen the blasphemies created in the name of art.

Another such abomination I have more recently discovered within the walls of Linden House. I know its origin too well, and I believe that it is time for me to take it to Miss Miller, whose address I still retain from the occasion when she wrote enquiring after your future in the medical profession.

As to your present occupation, I'm sure you'll understand that the doors of Summerwell's must now be permanently closed. Perhaps it is too much to hope that you might think of our acquaintance there with fondness in your heart. But please believe me when I say that I consider myself blessed to have shared your company over these past three years.

You have great talent, my dear Theo. Use it wisely. Use it well, and for the good of fellow men.

Theo swallows down the anguish threatening to overwhelm him. Meanwhile, the patient's eyes have opened wide in shock and panic. But only for a fleeting moment, before she gives the slightest nod as if to say: *So, here you are, and doing this, which is exactly as Eugene told me you would.*

He smiles to reassure her, before he stretches out his arms to reach across the bed's white sheets, where his fingers start to ease away the dressings of her face, and hardly noticing the soreness of the knuckles that last night were used to knock a man unconscious.

Meanwhile, Aleski is demanding, 'What has the madman done to Martha?'

Captain is more restrained. Having taken Theo's place behind the bedstead's barred brass ends, he says, 'I trusted him completely. Never would I have believed...'

'Trust!' Aleski snaps. 'You trusted Ulysses as well, and look where that has led us.'

Theo hears this frank exchange born of frustration and fatigue as if he's in a different room. He must focus on the linen being lifting from the wound, which takes much longer than expected due to the scabbing of the blood that has congealed on Martha's lip – the upper lip that, once he's eased the final barrier away leaves him staring in amazement.

How meticulous the work, with any stitches concealed almost entirely in the mouth. Yes, there are ugly threads of gut knotted underneath the nose, but very soon they'll be extracted. And despite the swollen skin, the outer line of the repair resembles nothing but the natural dipping groove that marks the point of symmetry in any lip.

'Mon Dieu!' Aleski cries.

Captain gasps and makes the sign of the cross at his breast.

Seeing this, poor Martha whimpers in distress and tries to speak. 'Ith it bad? I wan oo ee. Pleeth ... let me ee.'

'Ssh!' Theo warns. 'You'll risk re-opening the wound.' But he has understood her meaning and appeals to the others, 'Is there a mirror? Bring a mirror.'

The looking glass upon a stand is very heavy, hard to move. But Captain and Aleski have soon dragged it near enough so that, when Martha struggles up and is supported on her elbow, she can look without obstruction at the face reflected back. She cannot smile. At least not yet. That flexibility will come. But there is joy in Martha's eyes, and joy is followed by her tears, through which she blinks and turns her head to see the latest visitor arriving at her attic door.

For a moment Theo thinks, *Is it Eugene? Eugene come back?* But no, it is Keziah, and Keziah also gasps before she laughs and then pronounces what the rest of them are thinking – 'It's a blooming miracle!'

And yes, it is a miracle.

Unlike the mausoleum freaks that were created from the dead, Martha is very much alive. Eugene has given her this gift for a chance of happiness, free from prejudice and spite. But can it ever be enough to balance or atone for all the sins that the doctor has committed in his past?

TWENTY-TWO

THE BEAR CALLED after the two sisters. 'Wait! Let me come with you.'

They turned around and saw his coat of thick black fur fall to the ground. In its place there was a man clothed all in gold, who did not growl, but addressed them in a voice that was gentle and refined: 'Years ago, the wicked troll stole all the treasure from my castle. He also laid a curse on me, that I should turn into a bear and live forever in the forest. But now he's dead and I am free. Now, I am a prince again.

From *Snow-White and Rose-Red*

When I stood at Martha's door and saw her lying on the bed, with Captain, Theo, and Aleski smiling down at her like loons ... well, I was gobsmacked, I can tell you. It was as if she had been sprinkled with a box of magic dust, and there she was, swollen and bruised, but otherwise as good as new.

Within a week her wound had healed, and the stitches were removed. Within a month her speech was clear, and barely blighted by a lisp. And how she smiled when she went walking in the street to show her brand new, spanking self to all the world. And how that smiling was infectious as if – *Yes,* Martha was saying, *Look at me! Am I not fine? Something in hiding for too long.*

Her happiness did help dispel the mood of gloom for those of us who had experienced the horrors in the Seabrook mausoleum. The things we'd seen. The things we'd done – and how we'd feared for Tilly's life when we'd come back to Linden House, still then unsure of what that witch, Lady Seabrook dosed her with. But Tilly's old addiction proved a blessing in disguise, with her system more than able to endure the opiates that might have felled a full-grown horse, and in her case did little more than leave her sleeping for three days.

Three. Isn't that always the number of enchantment to be found in fairy tales? Mind you, on that third morning, it was the last thing I'd expected to see my sister's waking face looking as fresh as any daisy but for the scabbing of her mole, though even that was nearly healed. And what a joy to hear her say, 'Hello, Keziah! Darling sister.'

Her arms reached out, hands stroked my cheeks, until she suddenly exclaimed, 'Oh, what's this – here on your neck?'

It was the mark of Ulysses. But, as Captain had assured me on the boat the night it happened, it wasn't deep, had almost healed, and so I smiled and blithely said, 'Oh, I caught it on a thorn, out in the dark the other night. I'll be more careful in the future.'

My looking glass in miniature seemed unconvinced by this bravado. But she let the matter rest, and with a sigh allowed her head to settle back against the pillow. From there she solemnly pronounced, 'I have come to a decision. To throw my laudanum away and never touch another drop for as long as I shall live. This time I mean it. *Really* mean it. But I can't do it on my own. Will you stay with me at night, in case I fall into temptation?'

I cupped my hands around her face and kissed her nose, and in my mind I thought I'd heard it all before. Promises were made in earnest, but very soon enough another bottle would be slipped under her pillow and I would smell the tell-tale sweetness on her breath, or see her eyes take on the vague and glassy look of the elixir's influence. But, with no Ulysses to keep replenishing my sister's stocks, perhaps there was a chance; though to be honest what concerned me even more at that one moment was what Tilly next announced.

'And I'll give up my singing too.'

'But Tilly, you don't mean that?'

'Yes, I do!' She was insistent. 'I wouldn't change my mind, not even if the Queen of England came knocking on the door to beg me. How vain and frivolous I was, always too willingly seduced by the false flattery of people I believed to be my friends. They never cared about the music. Only my size. The way I look. Matilda Lovell. Pygmy freak!'

'Please, Tilly, stop. Don't talk like this.' Tears were welling in my eyes to hear my sister's bitterness, to think her glittering ambitions had been smashed like so much glass.

'Kezi,' she sighed, looking despondent. 'It's time for me to face the truth, to see myself for what I am, and to admit that I was wrong to turn away from those who love me ... who risked their lives to come and save me. You, and Captain, and Aleski. And ... Theo Miller too.'

Tilly paused and closed her eyes, and I presumed she was brooding on the ordeal of her abduction. But perhaps it wasn't that, for after saying Theo's name how her cheeks flushed up with red. She looked at me below her lashes and coyly asked, 'Will you come with me, if I make a trip to London? I want to thank Theo in person. My memories are somewhat vague, but he was with me on the boat. And when he thought I was asleep I heard him say the sweetest things.'

'He is kind,' I agreed. 'The care he gives to Martha is...'

'Martha? What do you mean?'

Tilly didn't know what we'd found on our return, and how Martha's twisted face had been transformed by the same man who'd created the monsters in the Seabrook mausoleum. Had Tilly seen them too, all the taxidermied freaks in the tombs below the chapel? Or did she keep such secrets hidden? Just as I now kept my own when it came to Ulysses? Of course, she'd learn about his death, and soon enough. How could she not? But it would not be from my lips.

Pushing the memory away, I left the bed, opened the shutters at the windows and allowed the room to fill with moted gold. Meanwhile, my sister swung her legs across the mattress and announced, 'I still feel a little woozy, but I really should get up ... get washed and dressed and leave this room. I need to go and visit Martha, and then...'

'And then?' I asked.

'Well, *will* you come to London too?'

'Tilly,' I smiled, 'there is no need for gallivanting into town. Theo's been here in Linden House since the day we brought you home.'

✳

I hoped he'd stay forever. I know that Tilly felt the same. And, best of all, Captain had found his long-lost son, and Theo Miller had been given back his father. A father *anyone* would wish for.

The two of them spent many hours in each other's company, which I supposed must be important in renewing the acquaintance denied since Theo's birth. Still, I was curious to know where they both went for days on end. Back to Summerwell's Museum? Perhaps to fetch Theo's possessions from his room above the shop? But if that was the case, then why did Theo sometimes have to borrow Captain's clothes when his were being laundered? With Captain being so much taller, the rolled-up hems produced a somewhat swashbuckling appearance. I rather liked it, was reminded of when I'd worn Aleski's trousers.

I still kept them in my room, and now and then I'd hold the fabric to my nose to smell his fragrance. Tilly caught me at it once. She sat beside me on the mattress and smiled, too knowingly. 'Do you recall Christmas night, when we both crept into his bed? I thought you might have got ideas ... from reading *Fanny Hill*.'

'You knew about that book?'

'Fanny's antics helped no end to stem the boredom of the hours spent at the pantomime rehearsals. And, when I'd finished ...

when I came home one night and found you were asleep, I pushed it underneath your pillow.' Tilly's words went rushing on. 'I can't imagine Fanny Hill being satisfied with cuddling an empty pair of trousers. And what if Martha finds them here? She'll have them bundled in the wash before you say Jack Robinson.'

It was true, Martha was back to her busy domestic ways. In due course she had begun to sew new clothes for Theo, too. More of his favoured tartan checks, paisley cravats and linen shirts. Meanwhile, Captain and Aleski had returned to their composing. The house was filled with music – but always with the one omission. My sister kept her word and did not sing another note, and no one pressed her in this matter. She was clearly very frail and, for once, appeared content to do no more than sit and listen; sometimes outside on the veranda below the trailing summer roses, so abundant I would pick and place the blooms around the house. Their drowsy fragrance made me think about our mother in the cottage, and of the story she'd once read to entertain her infant daughters. But if Tilly felt the same, she never said or seemed to notice. Her main concern was Theo Miller, and as she grew a little stronger she liked to coax him from the house to go on walks beside the river, or challenge him to games of cards in the music room at night. Darby and Joan, I used to think as I observed them together. Her laughter, like a bell. The warm affection in his eyes.

I often wished that spell of summer happiness could last forever. But at least it endured until the day the outside world came to knock upon our door.

✳

We'd barely finished with our breakfast, still sitting round the kitchen table when Dolce's snarling frenzy set my nerves on edge with fear. Could it be Ulysses, a goblin risen from the dead to try and seek jealous revenge? I knew that was impossible. But still, I couldn't quite relax until Aleski went to look and very soon was calling back, 'A cartman's left some boxes underneath the front-door porch. Theo's name is on the labels. There's a basket, and it seems to have an animal inside it.'

Captain and Aleski dragged the luggage to the hall, last of all the wicker basket rocking violently about on the chequered marble tiles. From this there came the sound of hissing, and then a most discordant yowl, which in turn left Theo flushed and sounding flustered when he said, 'Pumblechook! From Summerwell's. Why would Eugene send him here?'

'Oh, it's a cat,' Tilly announced, kneeling on the floor and peering through the wire door.

'Do you dare to let it out?' I glanced back warily at Dolce. Dolce growling. Dolce's hackles standing on her back like bristles.

'I shouldn't worry,' Theo said. 'Any dogs around the shop always turned tail and ran away if Pumblechook was in the street.'

Martha asked. 'Is it a mouser? Better a cat than any poison. And when it comes to Dolce, her bark is far worse than her bite. That dog would never hurt a fly. She is so old and slow these days, I do believe the river rats could try to climb up on her back and take themselves off for a ride. She'd sit and let them plait her whiskers, if such a thing were possible.'

Hmm, I thought, but mentioned nothing. Nor did anybody else who'd witnessed what the dog could do. Theo did briefly glance my way when Martha spoke of 'poison'. But the ring still on my finger no longer held a trace of it. I'd scrubbed it clean, inside and out, since when I'd taken quite a liking to the lustre of the opal. I liked its weight and how it offered me a feeling of empowerment – and more empowerment to come when Theo opened a big trunk, and nesting there among the folds of all the clothes I saw the crystal. The very ball in which I'd scried a fleeting vision on the night we went to Summerwell's Museum. There was a note tied to the metal of the stand packed at its side. It said, *For Miss Keziah Lovell, who I believe may have an interest.*

Dr Eugene Summerwell had sent this as a gift for me? How did he know I'd wanted it? How the strange magic had entranced me? And though at first I was reluctant when Theo set it in my hands, how could I help but be immersed, staring down into the depths of the swirling, misty grey – and then to hear the sound of chimes. Were they coming from the church not that far off, on Turnham Green?

'Can you hear them ... the bells?' I looked up and asked the others, although no sooner had I spoken than the carillon was fading.

'Bells? What do you mean?' Tilly piped her reply.

A deeper voice said, 'Get some water. Grab the ball, before she drops it.'

I was feeling very queer, with no idea how long it was before my senses returned, when it was obvious that no one else but me had heard the music. That left me somewhat mortified – until Theo, who'd been reading a letter from the trunk, held up a large white card embossed with flowers, bells and ribbons. It was a wedding invitation.

❈

August arrived and off we went, taking the dog, leaving the cat, every one of us invited to join Theo for the marriage of his childhood governess. It proved to be a great excitement. New dresses, hats and shoes. A cab to London, and that followed by a train to Chichester. And from there we were collected in the flies that Agnes Miller sent to carry us to Bosham.

Tilly and me sat on the bench fitted in the back of one, while Aleski perched up front beside the driver, who kept giving him a sheepish kind of look. Eventually, the man gathered the nerve to ask outright, 'Are you a freak-show entertainer, travelling with your wife and daughter? Not that I mean to cause offence. But with your physical appearance, and all the fairs this time of year. Big one at Chichester last week.'

Had Tilly heard the driver's words, how he'd thought she was a child? I suppose her face was shadowed by the brim of her straw hat, with the flutter of the ribbons blowing round her like a maypole. And then of course there was the fact that underneath her summer shawl no one would notice any curves that might betray maturity.

Aleski held his tongue, but I saw his body stiffen.

Meanwhile, Tilly turned to me, her voice a yearning of nostalgia. 'Oh Keziah, do you think we'll ever see another fair?'

Since we'd been sharing a bed, we'd often spent the night-time hours musing back over our childhoods and our travels in the vardo. We'd both agreed we sometimes missed the vibrant showground atmospheres. The noise. The smell of grease. The lights. The barrel organ music. Had our pa ever felt the slightest glimmer of remorse, or even wondered where we were?

As the fly continued rolling on its way, I was distracted from the sorrow of such notions. The air took on a salty taste. The road sloped down into a village. A small stone church. A pointed steeple, looking like a witch's hat. And then a bridge over a stream, before a lane that ran along a wall that marked a stretch of harbour. On the other side of that we saw a steepish run of steps leading to a row of cottages behind some long front gardens. One of them was Agnes Miller's – which she'd generously said we could lodge in for the week, having gone to spend the eve of her wedding with a friend. And after that she'd be residing at the Bosham vicarage.

The driver helped Aleski take the luggage to the door and was already on his way when Theo suddenly appeared behind the garden's wooden gate. 'Ah, my missing bags. What a relief!' He smiled at us. 'And while I'm here, I must remember – Miss Miller sent this key.'

As he walked up the garden path, Tilly called, 'I wonder, Theo, would you take my bag with yours. I really need to be with Martha, staying in the vicarage. Only she can dress my hair the way I want it for the wedding.'

Despite all Tilly's protestations about avoiding public places, my sister was determined to deck herself out like a princess for this country-village wedding. What a palaver it had been, looking through the endless plates in Martha's fashion magazines to choose the styles she liked the best. The sort of vanity and fuss for which I'd rarely had the patience, and even less so nowadays.

'Well, I'm happy staying here,' I replied. And it was true, very glad to spend a night with a whole mattress to myself. How a person Tilly's size managed to fill a bed, and even push me off the edge, was yet another ceaseless wonder. And then there was the fact that this cottage made me think of our old home, back in the lane. Although, instead of looking out to see the green of tunnelled trees, there was the blueness of the quay. I raised a hand to shield my eyes against the glaring of the sun that lit the water molten gold as it was sinking in the sky. I saw some swans among the reeds. They looked like cut-out silhouettes. The scene imbued me with a sense of such serenity and peace that, only then, I realised I had not felt for several months.

'You won't be left alone.' There was my sister's voice again, breaking through the reverie. 'Aleski will be here.'

'If you won't feel compromised,' Theo cast me an anxious look.

'Oh, Theo!' Tilly laughed, as she replied on my behalf. 'Don't they already live and sleep under one roof in Linden House?'

Who could deny that was true?

Over the rattle of the key Theo turned in the door. He looked back at us and said, 'I'll have to rush, or I'll be late for my rehearsal with Miss Miller. Captain's already in the church, practising what he'll be playing at the wedding in the morning.'

'Your rehearsal?' Tilly asked, looking somewhat perplexed. In all the weeks at Linden House, Theo had never shown the slightest inclination to join in with any singing or performing.

'Of a kind,' Theo replied. 'I hadn't realised before, but Miss Miller is expecting me to walk her down the aisle.'

'Go on then. Better hurry,' Aleski smiled as he walked through the house's open door.

Meanwhile, I lingered by the porch, watching Theo and my sister head towards the harbour road – he with a case in either hand, she with her hat box in her arms – before she dropped it to the ground, running back to me again.

With her long hair and bonnet ribbons streaming in the air behind, and such a sparkle in her eyes, she called, 'Theo forgot to tell you – Miss Miller's left you bread and cheese. There's some fruitcake in a tin ... and other things as well. I can't remember all of it. But you are free to help yourself to whatever you might fancy. And' – having reached my side, Tilly's voice grew more subdued – 'you don't mind me disappearing, to go and spend the night with Martha?'

Crouching down to reassure her, my face held level with her own, I took my sister's hands in mine and said, 'You won't be far away. I'll be with you in the morning at the church, so—'

'Sshh!' she interrupted, her mouth now pressed against my ear. 'What I really came to say was, remember Fanny Hill. Imagine what she would have done, if *she'd* been left on her own with Aleski for the night.'

'Tilly!' I exclaimed, shocked to hear the bold suggestion. But in a trice the little Cupid flew away to leave me flustered, only realising then the implication of our sleeping arrangements for the night. Yes, I *had* lived under one roof with Aleski Turgenev since I was fifteen years of age. But, even on the night when Fanny Hill had fired me up and I'd gone creeping to his bed, we had never been alone. Tilly Lovell was there too.

With my nerves all of a jangle, I also entered the cottage – and felt immediately at home. How welcoming it was, with little china figurines scattered about on every shelf. Even a row of courting shepherds with their pretty shepherdesses, which were very like the ones displayed on Tilly's bedroom mantle. Bible proverbs stitched in silks hung next to watercolour landscapes. There was a clock that would have fitted very well in Linden House, its antique dial framed in a nest of golden leaves and flowers.

Tick tock. Tick tock. How many seconds had gone by before I dragged my eyes away and looked instead towards a bowl that held green apples? I picked one up, then put it back. I had no appetite for food.

Where was Aleski at that moment? I heard some movements from a room that was most probably the kitchen. But, instead of going there, I climbed the stairs to the small landing and saw a door on either side. Despite the dimming light, it was obvious to see which one Miss Miller must have slept in, with its chintzy floral walls, tapestry cushions, and lace bedspread, and a little oval portrait of Charles Dickens on a table. I supposed the other room, being altogether plainer, must be where Theo had once stayed, and around the very time when me and Tilly had gone off to make a life in Captain's house. What adventures we'd all had since that first meeting on the Brocas...

Stepping through that door, I settled down upon the bed and stroked its cotton patchwork cover. I was confused, I won't deny it, noticing the felt-stuffed rabbit and the pile of children's clothes so neatly folded on the dresser. Also, a wooden Noah's ark with pairs of animals inside.

Hadn't Theo been too old for children's toys when he had stayed here? My eyes moved on towards some books stacked on a shelf above the bed. Reaching up, I took one down. *Gulliver's Travels* was new to me, and very soon I was immersed in flicking through the illustrations and the fancy chapter headings that named the hero's voyages to Laputa, Balnibarbi, Glubbduddrib – and Japan! In the pages that referred to the land of Lilliput, I discovered hand-drawn pictures inked across some of the borders that almost took my breath away. There was me, and there was Tilly, two skinny, dark-haired girls, and every detail so precise. Even the mole on Tilly's cheek.

'What are you looking at, Keziah, to make your face so serious?'

I glanced up to see Aleski standing in the open door, holding our luggage in his hands.

'I found a portrait of my sister and myself in this book.' I held it up so as to show him. 'A picture Theo must have made. It's from about five years ago, but Tilly hasn't changed a jot. It is as if my sister's cursed to have the heart and the mind of a woman fully grown, but to be thought of as a child. That driver today – he'd been entirely convinced.'

Aleski set the luggage down and joined me on the bed. 'Life for Tilly must be hard, although at least she has the blessing of her beauty and her charm. But I've been thinking too. About that driver – what he said about my own appearance. I think it's best if I don't go to the wedding tomorrow. I *am* a freak-show entertainment. I don't want the other guests to look at me, and not the bride, to turn the day into a circus.'

'Oh, but that would be a shame.' Letting the book drop to my lap, I sat there staring straight ahead. One of my hands reached out for his, to touch the growth of soft dark hair that spread so thickly on its back. Meanwhile, a silence fell between us, only broken by our breaths, the distant ticking of the clock – until, at last, I found the courage to voice what whirled inside my mind. 'You are a man who has been blessed with your acting and your music, to hold an audience transfixed. These are rare and precious things, to be envied and admired. But, if it means so much to you to mingle with a crowd and have your freedom for a day, then I wonder have you never thought to shave those areas that are not hidden by your clothes?'

'I would need to rise at dawn, and...'

'I can help you, if you like.' I was so taken with the notion, all but itching to get started.

'And do you have about your person the tools required for this profession?'

'Ah!' I answered with a smile. 'I don't, but I imagine there are razors to be found at the Bosham vicarage. I've no idea about the vicar, but doesn't Captain always shave? So does Theo, come to that. Why don't you go and ask?'

❈

Tick tock, tick tock counted the seconds and the minutes that elapsed before Aleski returned, during which time I prepared for the task that lay ahead. Pushing up my sleeves, tying an apron at my waist, I boiled some water in the kettle that was standing on the range, which was then poured into a bowl, and the large enamelled tub I'd found hanging in a storeroom just beside the kitchen larder. How vividly it conjured up another memory of mine from the cottage in the lane. Me and Tilly in the tinnie. Ma's fingers soaping up our hair. But soon the present called me back, and in a voice a great deal deeper than our mother's ever was: 'So, you're expecting me to strip off all my clothes, to get in that?'

Aleski's question made me jump, turning around to see him holding a box of polished wood, and on the front there was a label with the legend: *Star Safe Razor.*

Aleski's smile was tentative. 'I met the Reverend Price, about to leave the vicarage, looking for Martha and Tilly who'd gone walking round the village. He very kindly gave me this. Apparently, it was a gift that he has never used.'

He placed the box down on the table and raised the lid to show the contents. The blades were all still wrapped in folded sheets of tissue paper. There were also other things needed for the act of shaving. A pair of scissors. A badger brush, A tub of soap and oil pomade.

'We'll need more light. It's getting dark.' At least I sounded in control as I was scraping at a match to light the candles on the table, and all the while my eyes kept flicking back to where Aleski stood – Aleski dragging off his jacket, and then his shirt, before he raised his summer vest above his head, which is where I thought he'd stop. But, no, his trousers were unbuttoned, dropped to his knees and then his ankles. Next, he was the sitting on a chair, bending forwards to remove his shoes and then his socks. Wearing nothing but his drawers, Aleski Turgenev stood up, *almost* as nature had intended – and what a work of art she'd made, with his pelt of glossy hair, and the subtle musky odour of his animal attraction. I breathed him in. I closed my eyes. I had to struggle to contain the fervent aching of my longing.

I soaped the brush, and wondered where on earth it might be best to start; especially when he was teasing – at least I think he was teasing, 'Keziah, you will promise not to cut my face to ribbons?'

If only Martha had been with us to give a helping hand, for with her calm authority she'd know exactly what to do. *Slow. Slow, with this Keziah. There is no need for you to rush.*

Well, I supposed I had all night, and stepping back I took a while to assess the task in hand. Aleski's mane, so sleek and dark, had already been tied back, so I would start there at the forehead, just below the natural growth of the hair upon his head. Next would come the brows, which I would leave and so create two arching frames above his eyes. Oh, his eyes. His lovely eyes, the dark-brown irises reflecting glints of yellow from the candles, in which I also saw myself as I implored, 'Will you sit down, and close your eyes. You make me nervous. All this staring as I'm working.'

Aleski did as I suggested – after which I found it easier to concentrate my mind, before my fingers closed around the razor's handle yet again, and – *Take a breath. Hold tight, Keziah. Make sure your fingers do not tremble* – I stroked, and stroked, and stroked in the direction of the growth. The meticulous attention to the process was exhausting. But, thankfully, Aleski's ears and the lids across his eyes were already free of hair, for I doubt I should have dared to risk the slipping of my fingers in areas so delicate. Moving on across his cheeks, around his mouth and then the nose, I became more confident, although the caution did return when I asked if he would sit a little lower in the chair, when I tilted back his head to work around his Adam's apple.

Why *did* men have those growths, whereas most women never did? I should ask Theo. He would know. Didn't he always have his head stuck in his medical books, having a yearning to attend some form of university so as to train to be a doctor?

What was my ambition? It was *not* to be a barber! For the hundredth time that night I'd had to stop and change the water in the bowl that I was using, to wash away the clumps of hair and lather from Aleski's face. Meanwhile, his eyes were kept tight closed against the stinging of the soap, leaving me entirely free to stare without the least restraint at the beauty I'd revealed. His skin was still a little red from the scraping of the blade. Apart from that, it was as creamy and as soft as buttermilk. Not marred by sunlight, I supposed. The nose was long and straight and loaned the noblest of airs. His mouth, his lovely mouth, was very generous and pink. To tell the truth, I don't know how I stopped myself from kissing it. Instead of which I simply asked, 'Do you think I've done enough? Your clothes should cover all the rest.'

'Why not go on? A little further?'

I saw the laughter in the eyes that were now staring back at mine. Did Miss Keziah Lovell have the nerve to take the bait? But there was something so erotic, so near hypnotic in the magic of the shedding of the hair, to see Aleski born anew. First, his back, and then his arms, although what grew across his fingers was a trial and a half, as were the nipples of his breasts which grew erect below my touch, at which I heard Aleski sigh, and...

Where *did* I stop? Where did *he* stop, when my own hands no longer moved over the contours of his body? I'll only say that if the famous Mr Ruskin had walked in and found me sitting in the tub, my legs splayed out across the sides, and with Aleski crouched between them with the razor in his hands, well, he may not have been as shocked by what he saw as you'd imagine. No, I believe that Mr Ruskin might admire *my* transformation. The mound of flesh between my thighs become as naked, pure and white as any woman carved of marble.

Beyond such brazen information, no matter what my sister hinted, I am not a Fanny Hill keen to describe my every exploit in the most explicit manner. Instead, I offer you these lines that the poet Shelley wrote, which I once found inside a book upon the shelves in Linden House:

> 'The Satyr loved with wasting madness wild
> The bright nymph Lyda...'

TWENTY-THREE
COME LIVE WITH ME AND BE MY LOVE

'Miss Miller – I mean Agnes – I have something to give you. I meant to wait until the wedding, when the twins were here as well. But, somehow, now seems more apt.'

Theo is speaking as the two of them emerge from the church into the dusky evening light. He is pleased that the rehearsal of the walking up the aisle has been deemed a success. What does it matter if his arm is aching from the strain of being held in an unnatural position for so long, with Miss Miller clinging on to him as if she was a limpet? But perhaps when she receives the stolen purse that he produces from his inside jacket pocket, the treasured objects it contains may go some way to calm her nerves.

'Oh, Theo! What to say?' She wipes her sleeve across her eyes and holds the sprig of lucky heather. 'I shall have the gypsy's token woven into my bouquet. And this...' The double portrait is pressed against her lips. 'I almost feel as if my parents will be here to share the wedding.'

Without the harsher glare of sunlight falling unsparing on her face, Miss Miller quite belies her age of sixty years, though anxious wrinkles do appear when Theo says, 'I'm glad Eugene sent the purse to Linden House, along with all my other things. I should have brought it here before, when the sisters first returned it, but...'

'It's with me now.' She smiles through tears. 'And so are you. That's all that matters. It means so much to see you. Your father, too. Who would have thought it?'

From deeper in the church the organ pipes can still be heard as Captain plays Miss Miller's choice of 'Jesu, Joy of Man's Desiring'.

She smiles and reaches out to touch the velvety red petals of a rose that is growing close beside the church's doors. While still staring down at that she says, 'He visited, you know. Dr Eugene Summerwell. He travelled here to Bosham, and he also brought a gift. Something else that had been stolen.'

Theo is struggling for words, but there's no need. She carries on, her voice now barely audible. 'This rose is called Arthur De Sansal. Arthur ... that was his name. My baby boy. At least, the one he would have had if ... if he'd been strong enough to live. Dear Reverend Price, he found this bush, and we planted it together.'

'In hallowed ground,' Theo says, remembering a wish she'd expressed some years ago, before he asks with some surprise, 'The Reverend knows?'

'We have no secrets from each other. Truly, he is the best of men.'

There is a silence during which they both reflect on what a monster Theo's grandfather had been. And, also on Eugene.

'I read the news, of Summerwell's.' Miss Miller speaks with sympathy. 'It didn't come as a surprise. The man was in a dreadful state the day he came to see me here, even collapsing on his knees and begging for forgiveness when...' She stops to draw a breath. 'He told me how Lord Seabrook once asked him to preserve the body of a newborn child. A child with' – her eyes are closed – 'certain peculiarities.'

'I'm glad Arthur's with you now.'

Theo can only hope she knows nothing of the freaks in Lord Seabrook's mausoleum. All those blasphemies far worse than anything on display at Summerwell's Museum.

Things that *were* on display. Theo has learned that the night before the boxes and the cat were sent to him in Linden House, the museum was destroyed. Arson was suspected. The reports in the papers mentioned cans of kerosene being found among the debris. The fire was described by all who'd chanced to witness it as a furious inferno that went tearing through the building. Everything completely razed.

Theo thinks again of the exhibits he'd been making in the workrooms at the back. The gossamer of the moths' wings. The minute skulls and skeletons, and imitation plaster mouldings. All elements to be combined for a special exhibition called *The Discoverie of Fairies*. How Eugene Summerwell had gushed when told of the idea, insisting Theo's work was on a par with the great artists. One more example of the man's optimistic bluff and bluster. But now, those dreams, they have all melted. Also gone is the place Theo had come to call his home. What would be left? Puddles of wax. The charred white feather from a swan that once fell into Theo's hand during a Christmas pantomime. Heaps of dust, and bricks and rubble. And the bones. There would be bones. Human skeletons among them. Perhaps one of them, a male, lacked a tibia and fibula, all the tarsals, metatarsals, and the phalanges of toes of an amputated limb? Theo does not know, and now he never will, unless Eugene emerges as a phoenix from the ashes. But, no, Eugene has surely burned with the rest of his collection. And that acknowledgement still leaves a stone of grief in Theo's heart, despite the crimes his friend committed. Because Eugene *had* been a friend.

※

There is one enemy remaining. The spider in black weeds who squats amid the darkened corners of the rooms of Dorney Hall. Theo and Captain visited the house only last month, after a series of meetings held with Lord Seabrook's London's lawyers; the company being instructed to oversee the final wishes of the will the old man changed only days before his death.

Perhaps his grandfather had found a shred of conscience after all. One chink of light among the darkness through which he'd hoped to seek redemption. Redemption visited by Theo when he was lost once again among the pall and dinge and dust that furred the trays containing butterflies and beetles still displayed in the gloom of Seabrook's study.

Among this clutter came the voice that softly croaked, 'Ah, here he is. The little lord pops up again.'

Draped in black nets of lace and shadow, she didn't look herself at all, more like a photographic negative of Dickens' Havisham. To see her there, so thin and frail, Theo felt a wave of pity. But just as soon the thought returned of what she'd meant to do to Tilly, and the murders carried out on other innocents before. Pity was the last thing such a woman deserved.

Thin rays of sunshine slanted through the gaps around the shutters closed across the study's windows. It glistened in the eyes of the stuffed deer heads on the walls. But not the eyes of the tiger, no longer lying on the floor. Even so, the sense of malice once exuding from its stare had never truly been diluted. Theo had to pause, to take a breath, to tell himself that he was now a man, not a child to be tormented. And he had not arrived alone. Captain was standing close behind him, as was the lawyer who had joined them for the train journey to Windsor, before the three then shared a cab for the drive to Dorney Hall.

Theo's feet began to move, across the ladder of light that shone across the study floor until his eyes acclimatised to see in even greater detail the uncombed nest of greying hair that before had been concealed by the lustre of a wig, and under that the frozen features of the woman who was sitting in a leather fireside chair. Perhaps the very chair in which her husband was 'discovered' after his so-called suicide? The chair still reeking of tobacco from the pipe Grandfather smoked, only now that stench was mingled with the sickly violet perfume emanating from his widow.

The leather creaked as she hunched forwards, her voice as clear and sharp as steel. 'I can't imagine why you're here. Surely you haven't come to offer your condolences?'

Theo stumbled on his words. 'I'm here to let you know in

person, I've arranged for some revisions to the documents the lawyers will have sent to you last week, to—'

'Spit it out!' She cut across him in a hiss of irritation, breath foetid with decay. 'You are here to give me notice. To throw me out onto the streets. Unless...' Her staccato rhythm slowed, and held the seed of desperate hope. 'Am I to keep the Knightsbridge house?'

'That is no longer possible. You'll be aware the property had been heavily re-mortgaged. Those debts were left unpaid, which means the only option was to sell before the interest could become further compounded. But Dorney Hall has been secured, and Mr Threlfall' – Theo turned to indicate the legal man – 'will be employed to oversee the estate and house accounts.'

'I see.' Her black-gloved hands began to tremble in her lap. 'When will you and your small coterie of freaks be moving in?'

'Not straight away.' Theo struggled to keep an even temper, blinking his eyes as thoughts were gathered. 'For the next five years or so, the hall will be leased out. The money raised from that, and any profits from the farms, will be collected in my name. It will be used to pay the fees while I study medicine.'

The woman's laugh was filled with scorn. 'Are you fit for such a role?'

'Eugene taught me well, as you observed not long ago, which means exceptions have been made. I've been allowed to sit exams, and—'

Her voice cut through his again. 'You'll be another heartless quack who has no remedy to offer for my endless sufferings. And now you cast me from my home! Where is the pity and compassion? Where is this invalid to live?'

'You will return to Bloomsbury. It is my understanding that the brothel you once ran is still open for business. But should you choose to close it down and raise your son there decently, Lord Seabrook did arrange for a small annuity. I'm afraid it won't permit the lavish lifestyle you've grown used to, and I'm sure you'll be restricted in your choice of entertainments.'

Another pause for her to fully comprehend what he was saying. During this, one shaking hand plucked at the shawl around her shoulders. The fine black lace began to slip, and Theo noticed that the flesh remembered for its milky weight had now grown creped, riven with wrinkles through which the clavicles were jutting.

But she still possessed some pride, tilting her chin as she addressed him through the spite in narrowed eyes. 'You contradict my understanding, which is that a lawful husband has denied his wife and child what should have been their rightful home – taking the notion that I'd tried to place a cuckoo in his nest. A cuckoo!' she screeched, startling her visitors.

Now, her hand reached down into the shadows by her chair – where the globe had stood before. Had it been sold with other treasures, siphoned off to auction houses? Theo had heard the rumours of the woman's pilfering, and for the most part didn't care. But still, the wonder of the globe in all its swimming greens and blues – he *would* have liked to see it spin, if only just the once.

The thought was fleeting, interrupted by the sight of the small boy the mother thrust in his direction. The child from the pantomime, but in a much-neglected state, frightened eyes looking too large in an emaciated face.

As Theo stared at him in shock, he heard the mother ask, 'Do you deny the resemblance? The hair alone should leave no doubt. But then, his father only ever longed to stroke the golden curls of his beloved Theodora. He was obsessed with her, you know. How he despised the man who stole her, and the child whose birth had killed her. The past twelve months were such a trial. He claimed to see her all the time, even though she'd long been buried in her mausoleum coffin. Sometimes, I'd find him in this chair, conversing with the empty air. And there were nights when he would wake and claim to hear his daughter singing. Of course, his mind had gone. It was the blight of syphilis. Everything unravelling.' The smile that flickered on her lips was calculated to produce the deepest wound in Theo's side. 'What carnal appetites

can lead to! Decay and madness and delusion. Deformities in any
offspring spawned from the loins of the afflicted. Which only
makes me more convinced that the sainted Theodora may have
also been infected. At least inherited the same untethered passions
as her father.'

'Hold the venom of your tongue!' Standing close at Theo's side,
Captain's voice came thick with threat. 'Lest *my* son's charitable
offer of allowing you your freedom be rescinded just as soon. If
the choice was in my hands, you would already have been dumped
outside the doors of Newgate Gaol. If there was any hope of justice
for my darling Theodora, then...' Captain could not go on.

Theo continued in his place. 'I'm sure that Lady Seabrook will
keep her insults to herself. If she does not, and if she wishes to
contest her husband's will, she must be made to understand that
her own depraved obsessions will be set before the public when
the case is brought to court. No detail will be spared. With that
in mind...' Theo paused '...I must insist on one condition.' He
motioned back to Mr Threlfall, standing near the study door.
'Would you mind leaving us a moment? Perhaps you'd also take
the boy.'

'No!' the mother snapped, just as the child flinched away,
clearly expecting to be struck. '*I* and I alone say when the brat can
leave the room.'

Next came the thudding beat of Threlfall's fast-retreating
footsteps, and then the rattle of the handle when the door was
closed behind him to plunge the study even deeper in the miasma
of its gloom, in which the only sounds to hear were the child's
frightened whimpers.

Pained to hear such misery, Theo reached into a pocket and
removed a handkerchief wrapped round the piece of cherry cake
he'd been eating on the train. 'Are you hungry? Would you like
this?' He'd barely had the chance to ask before the child snatched
it from him, cramming the cake into his mouth.

'Well?' the mother said, oblivious of the disgrace of a son so ravenous. 'What is this mystery condition your legal people have concocted?

Wary that the lawyer might have an ear pressed to the door, Theo's response was somewhat cryptic. 'Last time we met at Dorney Hall, you and your husband arranged some rather unique entertainments. Since then, I've often wondered, are they still in residence?'

What Theo hoped to hear was that the mausoleum freaks had been disposed of with respect, given a decent burial. If not, such a commitment would be required of Lady Seabrook as a condition of her crimes not being publicly exposed. He did not care to save her name. But her child – he was so young. Why should he bear his parents' guilt? The awful scandals that would dog him for the rest of his life?

The woman smiled in reply. 'You're much too late for such concerns. But please don't waste another moment worrying about *their* welfare. Every one of them has travelled to another country house. You don't need to know the name, and for the moment I forget it, but the family are titled. Our guests reside in pomp and splendour, and are *very* much admired by all who go to visit them.'

'You forget the name? You are a liar!' Captain cried, which caused the child to hide his face behind his hands and cry again.

The mother snapped, 'Oh do shut up! I cannot bear your snivelling. It's enough to drive me mad, or bring on another fit. You were supposed to guarantee my future wealth and social status, not to see me so reduced, all but crawling in the gutter!'

She looked at Theo and implored. 'If only there were funds to employ some decent staff, I'd find the boy another nurse. The last one left me stranded. She, and that ingrate butler, Clements. Both of them fled from this house and stole the finest of my jewels. What price loyalty? There's none!'

A spear of light was glistening across her snake-like, mismatched eyes as her appeal became a simper. 'Or, would your charity extend to the donation I would need to send the boy away to school? If not, he could be fostered with a gentleman acquaintance. One of Ulysses' best clients. I know he has a fondness for small boys with pretty faces.'

She *is* the devil in disguise, Theo thought, and also wondered if the woman was aware of the death of Ulysses. As he concluded that she must be, Captain urgently demanded, 'How old is he, your child?'

Theo heard the number: 'Five'. But then he knew that already. Five years ago, hadn't he stood inside this very room and read the letter to inform him of the news of a birth?

The boy looked younger, also older, being so thin, with features wizened. What future horrors would befall him if his mother had her way, with another Seabrook child condemned to taunts and bullying, or to a fate yet more distressing? He only hoped the widow's words were empty threats for bargaining, which she now started up again: 'I am sure that I should feel more maternally disposed without the endless trial of...' She glared at her son. 'The reminder of a husband's cruel betrayal of his wife.'

She shrugged her shoulders, smiled again, but with spite in her eyes. 'I want the brat out of my sight. Out of sight and out of mind. The problem is...' a twitching started at the corner of her mouth, twisting her features horribly '...he reminds me so of you. The *real* cuckoo in this nest. The pathetic *little* lord, who I despise with all my heart.'

※

Pathetic little lord. Weeks have passed, and yet those words still have the power to torment as Theo stands beside Miss Miller at the doors of Bosham church. He's been so lost in his thoughts he's failed to notice that the music from the organ has stopped. Instead, he hears the songs of birds roosting in branches of the trees, or under eaves of nearby houses. Over that sound is the chattering of people who are heading through the churchyard gates towards them.

Martha and Tilly walk beside the bulky man with yellow hair and a froth of greying whiskers. He is calling, 'Hello Agnes! We've been touring the village. Hadn't thought to find you here. Shouldn't the bride be in her bed, dreaming of the day to come?'

The Reverend Price is teasing. His intended smiles back. 'I should. But that would be a waste of such a lovely evening.'

'Red sky at night, shepherd's delight.' The Reverend's eyes lift to the heavens. 'Which means a fine, dry day ahead for our picnic in the garden, and...'

And such pleasures will come later. For now, there is the interruption of some pretty piping music. It is Captain and his flute, the notes rebounding off the stone of the walls inside the church. As he emerges from the porch, so the silver-haired pied piper is pursued by a small boy.

'Who is this raggle-taggle gypsy?' Martha is the first to ask, seeing the cherub of a child whose golden halo of bright curls is identical to Theo's, although his eyes are not the same, being a darker shade of hazel.

The boy is patting the dog sitting at her master's feet. While doing this he looks at Martha with a frown, as if he's thinking: *And who are you? And ... who is this?* His eyes move on to Tilly Lovell in a state of slack-jawed wonder, blinking in just the way that Theo does when lost for words. He doesn't ask if she's a fairy or an angel, or perhaps another child of his own age who has been brought along to play, though all these things may very well be in his mind as he speaks, in the most serious of tones: 'My name is Bertram. But the Reverend Mr Price, he calls me Bert, which I think I like much better. I've been on holiday in Bosham with Miss Miller, and tonight we've been practising our walking up the aisle – to get it right, for when I have to hold her veil for the wedding in the morning. After that, there will be cake.'

'With strawberries, I hope,' Theo softly interjects.

'Oh yes,' Bert replies. 'That's my very special favourite. Which is because Miss Miller told me that *you* always liked it too.'

TWENTY-FOUR

SNOW-WHITE married the prince. Rose-Red became his brother's bride. The treasure stolen by the troll was shared between them all. Their happy lives were made complete when the mother of the sisters came to live inside the castle, where the rose trees that she loved were placed in pots below her window. There, with every passing year, they bore the loveliest of blooms.

From Snow-White and Rose-Red

We woke up late, me and Aleski, both being thoroughly worn out after a night of little sleep. We had ourselves a slapdash wash, flinging on our clothes and hats, and only in the nick of time clattered through the church's doors. Every guest there turned to stare as we searched for the pew containing Martha and my sister. And then, the boggled-eyed expressions on *their* faces – what a picture! Until it hit them, and they realised they knew Aleski's eyes. Aleski's strangely hairless smile.

My own surprise came not much later, when I saw the little boy holding the train behind the bride. I whispered close in Tilly's ear, 'Whoever can that be? The very miniature of Theo.'

Tilly's answer wasn't heard because the organ started blasting, and we all stood to sing a hymn. Indeed, there would be hours before the mystery was solved – what with the photographs to pose for outside the church's doors, and then the picnic celebration in the vicarage's garden. There were speeches. There were toasts, and even one made for the queen, what with that summer also being her own Golden Jubilee. And after that, there was the music, with Captain playing on his flute, and Aleski being handed a battered violin. The bride announced it had belonged to her father, long ago. However, now it was so cracked and out of tune it sounded worse than Pumblechook when he was yowling after rats down by river. I would have used the wood for kindling and thrown it on a fire, but Aleski's nimble fingers had the knack to tune the strings, on which he played a lively jig.

Oh, what joy that dancing was. Martha, Theo and myself laughed and whirled about for hours, only stopping when we found ourselves too breathless to go on. By then, most other guests had disappeared to find their homes, but still the music carried on, only with slower melodies to suit the languor of the mood, when even the flowers growing around us in the garden began to wilt in the heat.

Feeling much the same, I grabbed a glass and sought some shade underneath one of the trees. With my back pressed to the trunk, I took a glug of warm champagne, although it really didn't do so very much to quench my thirst. Still, I was pleasantly relaxed until my sister interrupted: 'Keziah! Stop your boozing! I declare, your face is turning even redder than a beetroot.'

Poking out my tongue, I watched her settle on the grass, lying down to rest her head across the pillow of my lap. My sister's cheeks were also flushed, hair falling loose from its restraints. I used a fingertip to brush away the strands across her brow, on which I planted a kiss.

'What's that for?' She laughed out loud. The bell-like tinkle of her laugh.

'Oh, I don't know. Because I'm happy. Happy to see you happy, too. Could that be because of Theo?'

Tilly squinted up at me, before she sighed. 'You are a dunce. Theo will always be my friend, and as beloved as a brother. But I'm afraid that when it comes to any notions of romance, he is not for me. Or should I say, I'm not for him. Come to that, no woman is. Not big, or little, fat or thin. Seems I shall have to be content with following your own adventures.'

She shifted up onto her knees. 'Well, what about last night? You haven't told me anything.'

'There really hasn't been a chance.'

'Well, here it is!'

I smiled coyly. 'What do you think about Aleski's transformation?'

As I spoke, I raised my head and threw a glance across the lawns. Already I could see a blueish shadow of the hair newly sprouting on his face. But being heaviest by far about his mouth and round his chin, it didn't look unnatural.

Tilly hummed and ha'ed before she finally announced, 'He does look striking. Younger, too. But, vulnerable without his armour. On the whole, I think I'd say I prefer him as our bear.'

I supposed I did as well, which I was just about to say when she took on a bitter tone. 'At least it means there's one less freak to draw attention from the crowds. With Aleski's face all shaved, and Martha's mouth so pretty now, there's only two of us today.'

'Two?' Who could she mean, apart from her own tiny self? For a moment I'd forgotten. And anyway, the talk was stopped when Martha came to sit beside us.

Holding up a hand to shield her eyes from the low sun, she didn't look at the musicians, but at the area of garden where the groom lay out spread-eagled, snoring soundly on a rug. His wife was sitting at his side, cucumber cool as she was sipping from a glass of lemonade. The little boy with golden curls was lying on the ground between them, head hanging low over the illustrated pages of a book. Zebras, lions, elephants. *The Animals of Africa*.

Once again, I was amazed at his resemblance to Theo. Despite what Tilly had inferred, could our friend have sown wild oats while he'd been living here in Bosham? If that was so, who was the mother? Had she been at the wedding too? But Martha and my sister soon informed me otherwise, after which Tilly sighed. 'Poor little Bertram, doomed be another homeless waif and stray.'

I considered for some time before I said, 'He doesn't look much like a waif and stray to me. Dressed up in all that lace and velvet, he's a Lilliput Beau Brummel. And, why's he living here in Bosham, not with us in Linden House?'

I may have sounded prickly, but in truth I was confused. A little guilty at the thought that my own actions had affected this boy's life and might continue doing so for years to come. I did not dare to voice the fear, but what if Bertram should inherit the worst of the traits of one or both his natural parents? What had he seen? What had he heard during the span of his short life? Had he been damaged in some way?

It was wrong of me to judge a child so young and innocent. After all, me and Tilly were nothing like our father. Oh yes, she shared his craving for intoxicating spirits. But, true to her word, she hadn't touched a drop for weeks.

And what of Theo, dearest Theo, the grandson of Lord Seabrook, which meant the family connection between himself and this small boy must be – it set my head into a spin when I tried to work it out. Was Bertram Theo's uncle?

Martha broke my reverie. She still had the slightest lisp, but otherwise her voice was clear, and as talkative as ever. 'He's safer here. At least for now. In case his mother has a sudden change of heart and wants him back. By all accounts he's settled well, and though the newly-weds have passed the age for children of their own, they are young enough in spirit. They will take good care of him until he makes his own decisions, whether to live in Bosham, or to come to Linden House, or...'

Tilly hissed dramatically. 'Nowhere near his mother's clutches. I'd murder her with my own hands if it ever came to that.'

She didn't know I almost had.

'Anyway,' Martha continued, 'he's very young and needs attention, not to mention being schooled. Life in Linden House won't be as quiet as it was. I have new clients for my gowns, and there's a shop put up for lease in a lane off Chiswick High Road.

I've a mind to go and see if I can come to some arrangement. It
has always been my dream to have a premises to trade from.'

Why should I have been surprised to hear this new
announcement? Thanks to Eugene Summerwell, Martha had
found such confidence. Not that his name was ever mentioned.
But did that silence bode of things almost too dangerous to voice?
All I can say is that when Martha heard the news about the fire in
his Oxford Street museum, she'd locked herself up in her room,
and there she'd stayed for two whole days.

'A shop?' Tilly enquired, beaming with excitement. 'Keziah and
myself could help to serve the customers. We might get lonely in
the house, with Captain and Aleski soon to be going out more
often, working on the pantomime. And...' Tilly's downcast mood
returned '...when Theo's studying begins.'

'Well, I'm sure he'll come and see us when he can,' Martha said
kindly. 'And *you*, Miss Tilly Lovell, might find yourself in London
too. If you should stumble on your senses and decide to make
another stab at working in the theatre. You're older now, and wiser.
I doubt that any ne'er-do-wells will take you for a fool again. Will
you sit back and let the Seabrooks ruin your entire future, hiding
your light under a bushel?'

That's when Tilly upped and left us, as she very often did if ever
pressed upon the subject of her retirement from performing.

Martha turned to me instead. 'What is the pantomime this
year?'

'I believe it's *Cinderella*.'

In truth there was no 'thinking' to be done upon the matter.
Only last week, Augustus Harris sent a basket full of flowers, still
hoping to persuade Tilly to join his new production.

'She'll do it,' Martha nodded. 'You mark my words. She's
coming round. But what about yourself? I've seen you in the
music room, peering into your crystal ball, or staring down at all
those cards with the fancy-looking pictures. It is balderdash to me,
but I'm curious to know, do you believe in it, Keziah?'

That's when it all came gushing out, when I told Martha of my longing to go travelling again, to have a vardo of my own in which to visit country fairs. I said, 'Perhaps, only perhaps, this is the path that I must follow ... having inherited the talent from an ancestor of mine. She was called Bohemia.'

To speak the name, it was like the raising of a ghost. I felt quite shivery inside.

Meanwhile, Martha softly said, 'Well, there you are. It's in your blood. But more than that, there is the fact that Captain has his boat, and I know he's missed the fairs held at the towns along the Thames. He mentioned just the other day that come next year he might go back to play the roaming minstrel. You could join him, couldn't you? Call *yourself* Bohemia. I can see you in a tent, telling fortunes, casting spells. I could make one if you like. Green velvet lined with red damask. A fringe of gilded tassels. Turkish rugs and cushioned chairs around a Chinese lacquered table. I'm sure we've got all that we need somewhere to hand in Linden House.'

'You've been planning this already!' My turn to smile as I imagined that my dream was possible.

'Well, Captain surely has. Although...' She paused, and looked concerned. 'It seems to me you've already made your choice. And it's Aleski.'

'You mean that Captain—'

'Yes, I do. Though he would never let it show.'

But he had. Of course, he had! My mind ran back towards the night of Martha's accident, when I'd gone into his room and we had very nearly kissed. And after that, there had been moments of brief touches, lingered glances – though not so much since the time of our trip to Dorney Hall.

'Martha...' I began. I didn't know how best to phrase what was stirring in my mind, or even if I should. 'Do you think it's possible to love two people at one time? My mother used to say that Bohemia once travelled with two husbands in her vardo.'

The words came flying out before I'd had a chance to think. In the silence following I could have kicked myself ten times. How I wished I'd never spoken, fearing the ground would open up and I'd be swallowed down to Hell for such blasphemy and sin.

But Martha only said, 'Linden House has never been the most conventional of homes, which is why we all belong there. You must listen to your heart, follow its yearnings, if you will. But understand it could be broken by a man who loves a ghost, and I believe he always will.'

As she spoke the music stopped. A breeze was gusting up around us. The evening's cooler air soughed through the leaves above our heads. It rippled through the purple beads of lavender along the paths. Confetti petals that we'd thrown across the couple at the church now floated over the wall to the vicarage's lawn. Little Bert was laughing gaily, clambering on Theo's shoulders, reaching out with both his arms to try and catch them as they dropped. Me and Martha went to join them. So did Aleski Turgenev.

As the new bride observed the scene, I saw the glisten of a tear behind the spectacles she wore, but then it could have been the rain, with a shower starting up just as the church's bells were tolling out the hour of eight o'clock. When the last began to fade, I wondered where my sister was. And, where was Captain, come to that? But they hadn't gone so far, only beyond the French glass windows leading to the house's parlour where Captain sat at a piano to play a melody I knew, although the lyrics he was singing had been changed. Were happier.

> 'The evening nightingales are singing.
> The month of August lit with gold;
> I still keep the rose you gave me,
> I watch its red silk heart unfold.
>
> The breath of rose, the sound of bird's song
> Are ever tangled with romance.

Tis my pleasure to remember;
The day when you first came to me...'

That's when Tilly started singing: *'Come unto me. Come unto me.'* Which is what everybody did, running inside, out of the rain. Except for me. I stayed and listened from the garden, getting drenched, just as I'd done that dismal morning when I'd stood outside Pa's vardo on the grass of Windsor Brocas.

To this day, I still don't know what Captain had intended with this new message in his song – whether or not it was for me. But for then it was enough to be a member of his crew. Only one thing could make it better. And that would be to turn around and find my mother at my side. I closed my eyes, and I could smell her fragrance on the air. Rose, and amber, and patchouli.

※

When we were girls, not long before we'd travelled to the Brocas Fair, Alfred Lovell drove his daughters to the nearby town of Leominster for a photographic portrait. His intention had been to place our likeness on a poster printed up so as to advertise his wondrous elixir. I'm not sure he ever did. And having seen that portrait once, I never wished to again, for the difference in appearance between my sister and myself was then quite indisputable. There I towered over Tilly, who was barely half my height, glassy-eyed, all skin and bone. Neither one of us was smiling.

What a difference it was to see the happiest memento from the wedding day in Bosham, when a photograph arrived in the post from Agnes Price.

It seemed that only yesterday we had arrived back home in Chiswick after our week of holiday, with me and Tilly having turned a somewhat darker shade of brown than Martha ever was, after stripping to our petticoats and soaking up the sun on the beach at Wittering.

Only a few miles on from Bosham, it was a heaven of a place, the sea so blue and glittering, waves crashing down above my head as I swam out against the tide, feeling as if I'd been baptised in all the glory of the world. I'd stood there dripping in the foam as I emerged back on the shore, blinking the salt out my eyes to see the swathes of yellow sand, surely as empty as the island on which Crusoe had been shipwrecked. But I wasn't there alone. Martha was reclining underneath a parasol, with Dolce lying at her side. Theo, Bert and Tilly were paddling in rock pools, holding nets for catching crabs. Captain was still swimming in the sea some way behind me. But Aleski was much nearer, also rising from the waves, skin glistening and briny wet as I splashed my way towards him, reaching out to touch the hair already growing on his cheek.

When the photograph arrived, Theo had gone to live in London. He'd taken lodgings in a house very near Lincoln's Inn Fields as he embarked upon his dream as an undergraduate at the Royal College of Surgeons. He had great hopes to one day open up a hospital or commune in the grounds of Dorney Hall. A place where those who'd been born 'different' could be helped, as Martha had, or simply find themselves a haven.

Despite her previous protestations, Tilly's haven was more public. To be precise, back in the theatre where she'd gone that very day, along with Captain and Aleski, for a meeting that concerned the pantomime in Drury Lane – in which my sister *would* be starring as the fairy after all. And Martha, she was visiting the shop that she had rented, where the carpenters she'd hired were fitting mirrors on the walls.

All on my own in Linden House, there was another sort of mirror in the picture revealed below the wrappings of brown paper, the sheets of card, and fine white tissue. How I smiled to see the group who posed before the church's doors where, in the middle of us all, the married couple looked resplendent. Aleski and myself had been placed beside the groom. My hat was definitely crooked, but I clearly wasn't bothered, for on my face there was the grin of the cat who'd licked the cream. Beside the bride, Captain and Martha could have been another couple, which did give me some pause for thought. Perhaps I'd ask the cards, or look into my crystal ball. Or, better still, open my eyes.

But, for then, I only saw the trio who were standing in the forefront of the picture. Theo in his tartan suit and extravagant cravat. Little Bert, pressed close beside him, staring sideways at my sister, as if transfixed by some enchantment. Or could it be her heart-shaped mole? Was she smiling back at him, or had Theo drawn her gaze? Theo, with his golden curls and pale-blue eyes that caught the light in such a way they shone like diamonds through the picture's monochrome, just as they did in real life.

If he'd been standing at my side in Linden House at that one moment, I'd only look into those eyes and seldom notice that his height was little more than four foot ten – because Theo is a dwarf, what some refer to as a freak. But then, those people only stare into the abyss of black souls. Their eyes are blind. They do not see his charisma and his light. And, to put the matter bluntly, they are not fit to lick the mud from the bottom of his shoes. His dandy patent-leather shoes.

AFTERWORD

This story of this novel is entirely fictional. But there are references to actual historical settings, and to Victorian characters who have inspired my own creations, or who appear in cameos as minor players in the plot.

The lanes of rural Herefordshire have many ancient timbered houses, such as the one in which my twins, Tilly and Keziah, are born and spend their youth. I was raised there myself, and can remember being told of the old folk-lore superstitions, such as the slime of a snail making a mole disappear. I can also recall once having warts on my hand, and an old man coming to visit with a bag containing something like fine slices of white radish. He rubbed one over my fingers and, no word of a lie, when I woke up the next morning every wart had disappeared.

The details of the country fairs were greatly inspired by the autobiography of the famous Lord George Sanger. As a Victorian circus manager, his adult profession was influenced by escapades with his roguish showman father. The young Sanger also trained his own performing troop of mice, and this aspect of his story is briefly echoed in my novel's character of Ulysses. And then there is the tale told by Keziah and Tilly, of having seen a dead man's face outside the window of their vardo, which was another memory recalled from Sanger's youth – when grave robbers hitched a ride on his father's fairground wagon, and the corpse they had stolen and stored up on the roof started slipping from its wrappings.

Another real character is Thomas Griffiths Wainewright, who really deserves a whole novel of his own. But for the purposes of this one, he once resided in Chiswick, in the grand house where my sisters live with Captain and his crew, after escaping from their father at the Windsor Brocas fair. In Linden House they learn how Wainewright murdered some of his relatives, using poison that he kept concealed inside a ring. This is mirrored in the book when Keziah finds a ring with a hidden compartment lying underneath her bed. Also drawn from Wainewright's life is the fact that other relatives of his were the publishers of the best-selling, pornographic *Memoirs of Fanny Hill*. Still available today, the book is highly entertaining and extraordinarily explicit. Quite the sexual education for Keziah and Tilly Lovell.

The real Linden House no longer exists, and in this book I take some liberties with its geography, with the land at the back stretching down towards the Thames. In reality, the river is somewhat more distant from the mansion that once stood along the Chiswick High Road.

Although I've seen some etchings made of the house when it survived, it has long been demolished and replaced with a development of late-Victorian terraced houses. I lived in Linden Gardens myself for fifteen years, since when the story of Wainewright has always been nagging to find its way into a novel.

Another house in the novel is that of Dorney Hall, loosely based on Dorney Court situated near to Windsor. There is no mausoleum, at least not one I know of. But the scenes I describe are influenced by real stories of eighteenth-century Hellfire Clubs. At these 'satanic' gatherings, 'persons of quality' engaged in squalid entertainments and mock religious ceremonies, some taking place in a network of caves near to High Wycombe. There was undoubtedly a lot of drinking, eating and wenching, with many rumours of much worse.

Near to Dorney Court are the swathes of common land and meadows leading to the Thames, through which Theo and Miss Miller walk to reach the Brocas Fair. The location of the fair can be visited today, just across the Windsor Bridge and down a narrow Eton lane. There you will see swans on the river, and houseboats moored in the shelter of willows growing on the banks.

Having sailed to London in the houseboat Captain owns, Tilly and Keziah discover the glamour of the London West End theatres in the Christmas pantomimes. Augustus Harris did once manage The Royal in Drury Lane, and he produced the most remarkable spectaculars on stage, often with casts of hundreds, and with the era's biggest stars – such as the clown, Little Titch, and the singer Marie Lloyd. The panto runs would last for weeks to recoup enormous budgets. Nowadays, the sums invested would amount to millions.

No longer in existence is the Egyptian Hall that once stood on Piccadilly. Built in 1812, and replicating the architecture of temples on the Nile, it was first used as a museum to show the curiosities brought back by Captain Cook from his South Sea expeditions. (To get a flavour of this, an exhibition of Cook's voyage, along with flora and fauna collected by Joseph Banks, is on display in Eton College's natural-history museum. This is open to the public on certain occasions and is well worth a visit.) As time went by, the Egyptian Hall held painting exhibitions, hosted lectures, and put on other more general entertainments. By the later 1800s when Tilly goes there to perform it was best known for magic shows and spiritualist acts. Sadly, it was demolished in 1905.

The Oxford Street museum where Theo is employed by Dr Eugene Summerwell was another real venue run by a Doctor Joseph Kahn. Known at the time as a gloomy sepulchre of horror, it claimed to educate the masses on reproduction and good health, for which it also sold medicinal pamphlets and quack cures. It provided titillation, with wax models that showed the ravages of venereal disease. There were also displays of so-called freaks of nature, while the Anatomical Venus represented a woman whose torso was exposed to reveal the inner workings of the organs of the body, even a baby in the womb. The museum was closed down

and its exhibits were destroyed after complaints from the Society
for the Suppression of Vice. However, such collections were
popular at the time, and today for those inclined to see a similar
display, Viktor Wynd's Museum of Curiosities, Fine Art, and
UnNatural History is situated in East London. For less bizarre
but equally macabre displays, there are specimens on show in the
Hunterian Museum, which is currently owned by the Royal
College of Surgeons.

Surgeons working at the time when this novel takes place were
often known as butchers. Many operations were performed with no
sedation before an audience of students. The gruesome scene of
carnage in which Theo views one surgeon claiming he'll amputate
a leg in less than seven seconds is based on a true story. One of the
places where such acts would have been regularly performed can
still be visited today. The Old Operating Theatre, once connected
to the site of St Thomas's hospital, is located in Southwark.

Somewhat less bloody, but perhaps equally cruel entertainments were to be found in the freakshows of anatomical 'wonders'.
Living human exhibits such as the Elephant Man would be toured
around the showgrounds, where their appearances resulted in pity,
shock, and disgust. My own imaginary Aleski with his dense
growth of body hair is partly based on the real Fedor Jeftichew.
Fedor was called the 'Dog-Faced Boy' and was displayed all over
Europe. He was then hired by P.T. Barnum who took him to
America, claiming the boy was raised by wolves and so wild he
only ever barked or growled in conversation. (In fact, he was well
educated, and was fluent in the languages of Russian, German and
English.) My Aleski also speaks about a Julia Pastrana, another
real and unnaturally hirsute young woman who was born in
Mexico. It was claimed that Julia had an ape for a father, and that
when she died in childbirth the showman who had 'owned' her
(most probably the baby's father) had Julia and her child
embalmed so as to carry on the business of his touring. The greed
for money and fame was what produced the real monsters.

My imagined Alfred Lovell, father of Tilly and Keziah, is another callous man, preying on the gullible as he tours the country showgrounds with his miracle elixir. But despite the exploitation of his daughters' differences, or the menace in the fairy-tale allusions that imbue the story of the sisters' lives, this is essentially a novel about acceptance of the 'other'.

The final Bosham wedding scenes, and then the beach at Wittering, celebrate the redemption and the hope that is found by the family of 'freaks' who form *The Fascination*'s cast. Tilly, Keziah and Theo, Captain, Martha and Aleski may only live and breathe within the pages of this book, but for me they all exist as vividly as anyone I've ever met in real life. I'm sad to say goodbye to them.

E. F.

For more detailed information about the themes and real stories discovered in The Fascination, *please visit Essie Fox's website, www.essiefox.com, or The Virtual Victorian, a historical blog based on 'facts, fancies, and fabrications' relating to the era: www.virtualvictorian.blogspot.com*

BIBLIOGRAPHY

Strange Victoriana – Jan Bondeson, Amberley Publishing, 2016

Gypsy Witchcraft and Magic – Raymond Buckland, Llewellyn Publications, 1998

Gypsy Magic – Patrinella Cooper, Rider, 2001

Victorian Sensation – Michael Diamond, Anthem Press, 2004

Morbid Curiosities – Paul Gambino, Laurence King Publishing, 2016

The folk-lore of Herefordshire – Ella Mary Leather, Logaston Press, 2018

Quack Doctor: Historical Remedies for All Your Ills – Caroline Rance, History Press, 2013

Seventy Years a Showman – Lord George Sanger, Seton Press, 2008

Terror and Wonder: The Gothic Imagination – Dale Townsend, The British Library, 2014

The Wonders – John Woolf, Michael O'Mara Books, 2019

The Unnatural History Museum – Viktor Wynd, Prestel, 2020

ACKNOWLEDGEMENTS

I began writing *The Fascination* during the first Covid lockdown. But despite the darker themes this is a book filled with joy, ending in gratitude and hope.

My personal gratitude goes to my agent, David Headley, whose support for my writing means so much to me – and to Karen Sullivan of Orenda Books for believing in this story.

Special thanks to my 'amigos', Wendy Wallace and Denise Meredith, for always being there. Also, my much-admired fellow writing friends – M. L. Stedman, Susannah Rickards, Linda Buckley Archer, Julie Ann Corrigan, Kate Griffin, Anna Mazzola, Catriona Ward, and all in Facebook's 'Lounge'. Your company, kindness, and sage advice over these past few years means more than I can say.

The essence of this book is about love and acceptance for people who are 'different', and it's no coincidence that I've dedicated the story to Millie Ann Prelogar. Millie, who I'm honoured to know as a friend, is a tireless campaigner for all those born with Down Syndrome. She is a beautiful young woman, and a talented actor. The perfect pantomime princess.

Last, and by no means least, my heartfelt thanks goes to my husband, who is enduringly patient with my writing obsession ... and who makes a damn fine coffee.